THE
WAY
OF AN
EAGLE

For J.D.—who I wish had lived long enough to read this book.

THE
WAY
OF AN
EAGLE

Joe Bergeron

Endurian Press

The Way of an Eagle is a work of fiction. Names, places, and incidents either are products of the author's imagination or are used fictitiously.

First Edition, 2015

ISBN: 978-0-9914005-3-9

Cover illustration by Joe Bergeron.

Published by The Endurian Press

www.joebergeron.com

Part One
A Pilgrim of the Air

Chapter One

1977

The peace native to Rocky Mountain National Park
deepened with the coming of autumn. There came a hush, a
pause to take stock of the fruits of summer and to take heed
of the winter which lay only weeks ahead. Park visitation
thinned to the point where it wasn't worthwhile to man the
entry stations, allowing stragglers to enter freely. Seasonal
rangers, who in summertime collected fees, led campfire
sing-a-longs, told stories, and herded visitors on nature
walks, returned to their off-season work as teachers or students.

As the summer ended, these rangers smiled as they
packed their belongings and loaded their pickups, thinking
of the new story that added a touch of mystery to the shadows beyond the firelight—the tale of the pilgrim who wandered in these mountains, shy as Bigfoot, more elusive than
the bighorn. He was said to be a light-haired young man,
but that was about all anyone could say about him. He kept
to the back country, avoiding human contact, seen only
when caught unawares. Once a ranger had spied him running across a meadow and making a series of spasmodic
leaps. The few who had gotten close enough to trade a
word or two with him variously reported him as peaceful,

1

agitated, distraught, sullen, or serene. On a few occasions he had been heard in the distance, usually at night, sometimes laughing madly, or sobbing, or howling like a wolf.

Or at least the rangers attributed these cries to the mystery man, there being no better explanation. Almost every ranger who patrolled the back country had come across some trace of his presence — usually a campsite, with a cold circle of ashes (small, but still against park regulations). Yet there was never any litter, vandalism, or theft.

That was all the contact any ranger ever reported.

Next year the rangers would tell these campfire tales again, and smile as visitors looked over their shoulders into the surrounding darkness, wondering if this strange creature might be peering back at them.

At least, they would tell these stories until their supervisors ordered them to stop. It wouldn't do for visitors to learn it was possible to flout Park regulations in this manner. It wouldn't do to frighten visitors with tales of this wildman.

The wanderer was an embarrassment to the Park administration. His extended, un-permitted back country presence was illegal and set a very bad example. But the rangers carried a spark of anarchy in their hearts, and would not readily let his legend die.

The park's permanent staff savored the few peaceful weeks between the waning of the summer crowds and the onset of the winter skiing season. Already the Alpine Visitors Center was boarded up for the winter. The upper regions of Trail Ridge Road were barricaded; snowfall had already made it impassible. Meeker Mountain, Isolation Peak, and the blunt-topped wedge of mighty Longs Peak were capped in white. Snow had also visited the grim dome of Terah Tomah and its angular neighbors Cracktop and Mount Julian. The deep forests at their feet had yet to feel their first dusting, but it couldn't be far off. The aspens had shed their papery yellow leaves, while the conifers, disdaining to overreact to the coming cold, huddled silently in their green-shadowed depths. In the open valleys the grass remained green. On grey days of scudding cloud the moraines seemed haunted and gloomy. On crisp days of clear white sunlight they glowed like banks of emerald. From the Never Summer Range to Wild Basin, from the sapphire of Sky Pond to the rocky bed of the Big Thompson River, Autumn was at the height of its calm yet melancholy reign.

The Sun crept farther south day by day. Those who were aware of the world's rhythms took note of this southward drift, rapid at first, then slowing as the Sun neared its solstice. By then its daily path was but a brief sweep along the southern horizon. The Rockies were tilting into the season of twilight and night.

And still that elusive pilgrim walked among the heights, unseen until the final day of Fall.

This is how John Avril came to die.

He had come to these mountains to try madness when reason offered no path he wished to walk. Greyness had stolen over his soul, robbing the world of the magic that had once filled it. He was not as young as he looked. Experience had opened his eyes to the evils of the world, while veiling the beauties that lived beyond them. Disappointment and disillusionment had overtaken him.

Worst was his disillusionment about himself. He was not the man he'd imagined he could become when he was a boy. Far from it—his life had become cramped and bitter, his thoughts veering onto paths that brought him to despair.

The mountains, he believed, offered a final chance: a chance to see clearly for just a moment, and then, with that vision still bright in his eyes, to die before they could be darkened again.

He had stared into high mountain lakes while the Sun wheeled across the sky, leaving a glittering path across his vision. He had walked though deep woods where owls followed him with their yellow gazes. He had stood on narrow ridges blasted by buffeting winds, trying to reconcile himself to their wildness, to understand their force. He had heard glacial meltwater tinkling beneath boulder fields on high Alpine meadows near Snowdrift Peak. And he had looked down, down, down, upon a world suffused with light or concealed by clouds and rain.

At last the quiet of the world had laid to rest all his cares and doubts, all confusions and woes. This world, the real world, did not shame him, did not berate him, did not assault him with horrors. His flaws and failures, defeats and sorrows, finally lay at peace. The newfound simplicities of life and his imminent death had stripped away all ambiguities. The world held nothing more that he either desired or feared.

Therefore John Jacob Avril sat down in a high meadow with his back resting against a pine. He had chosen this mountainside with care. Far from any trail, it was too rough and remote for skiers, and should remain unvisited over the winter. He had been here often without once finding any trace of human visitation. He doubted that most of the park rangers so much as knew its name.

He was already shivering. The sun was strong on his back, but it couldn't replace the heat being drawn from his body by the chill autumn air. Autumn was fleeting at these heights, and a mass of wintry air was rolling in from Wyoming. He was in for a nippy evening.

He laughed at the understatement of this thought, which started a liquid cough deep in his chest. Pneumonia, he suspected. He hoped that would help speed his passing, if not make it any easier.

He lay back in the grass to better see the sky. Reefs of mid-altitude cloud tumbled down from the north, sometimes hiding the Sun, his most frequent companion during these past six months, though not quite the best. Sometimes the clouds fractured the sunlight into iridescence, throwing it back as crimson, blistering green, and violet. To John Avril, it was a final gift from the world of light, sky, and mountains, whose peace and grace he had sought and at last attained.

It was easy to stay warm while hiking, but now that he was inactive the chill flowed into him avidly. Far above, wispy cirrus clouds drifted imperceptibly, crystalline and serene, blue frost against a background of deepest sapphire. Their coldness, their silence, made them seem part of another world, a world he could only desire from afar, pristine, remote, and unreachable.

All his life he had longed to explore those heights, to know the spirits of the upper air. Perhaps with death he could ascend and roam among them.

He hugged himself and huddled against the tree, his instincts urging him to preserve his warmth as long as possible. Soon the Sun, heading toward the horizon behind him, passed behind the peak, depriving him of its rays. Shadows climbed the range across the valley.

Tears sprang from his eyes. He looked skyward, beseeching something he could not name, but received no reply from those cold, immense spaces of light and air. The enormity of what he was doing did not escape him. He felt as though something in that great vastness was watching him, judging him.

After a while the tears gave way to quiet laughter. He stared at the horizon as the sky deepened to purple. The temperature plunged. His shivering increased nearly to convulsions, and then abruptly ceased. The cold had invaded him completely. Now he could relax. The pain was gone; indeed all feeling had departed his limbs and face. The stars traced their paths across the sky, rising before him. The glowering face of Taurus the Bull emerged from the twilight. With the sky fully black, it was met and driven back by Orion, the celestial warrior who never wavered in his battle to push back the forces of the dark.

Somehow John lasted through the long night until morning. The sole remaining urgency of his life was to survive for one final glimpse of the Sun. To herald it came a panoply of planets: first Venus, illuminating his face with pale beauty; then Jupiter, its majesty undisguised by distance; and finally Mercury, a golden point leaping into the heavens to announce an imminent coming.

The eastern sky took on a sheen of grey, then shifted through a series of pastel colors. Warm greys, lavenders, pearly greens, all raised themselves to make room for the grand presence beneath.

Just as John Avril could wait no longer, a notch across the valley began to blaze with golden light, casting luminous shafts which crept down the slope to pick him out as he sat straight-backed against the tree.

It was at that moment that Avril had the one great inspiration of this strange pilgrimage of his. With the sunlight came a dazzling realization: he had a choice. He did not have to die; nor must he fall back into his old ways of weakness and corruption. It was all up to him, and had always been. He did not have to die. *He could live.*

And indeed, he could live as he wished to live, and do the things he wished to do.

John Jacob Avril gazed full into the face of the rising Sun. He faced it alertly, with clear eyes, as though it had imparted some great secret.

"Thank you," he whispered.

And yet, he lay mortally weakened by the cold, and could not rise, though he would have done so.

When winter gained a foothold in the alpine country it was not easily pried loose. The Sun did not banish the freeze that day, nor did it for months thereafter. Avril was well and solidly frozen by that first evening, and so he remained.

Marmots and picas lapsed into winter sleep in their burrows. Mule deer and elk made their way to the warmer pastures of the valley floors. Only a few hung on at this more rigorous altitude. The deer who wandered into John Avril's meadow at first regarded him with alarm, and later suspicion. Frozen he might be, but his human scent lingered, and these mountain deer had not been tamed and diminished by campground handouts. Soon his harmlessness became apparent, and the deer ignored him, browsing nearby, treating him as part of the landscape. Bull elk stood next to him and brayed out challenges to their rivals.

A coyote came upon him once, its breath puffing out quick shots of vapor as it anxiously sniffed the body, but it was easier to dig up unwary rodents than to gnaw into this hard-frozen corpse.

Presently the hard blue autumn sky gave way to the dense, ragged grey of winter. Snow covered the landscape and John Avril as well, reducing him to a softly rounded form. He could hardly have been less conspicuous. His meadow was abandoned; the snows had conspired to drive away even the hardiest beasts.

The Sun, now heading slowly northward, no longer appeared in the notch in the mountains when it rose. It barely climbed high enough to shine upon Avril's meadow for a brief hour.

By that time the mountains had seemingly given up all memory of summer and all hope of spring. The snow piled ever higher, smothering the sculptural curves that marked John Avril's resting place. Even their smoothness was lost when a blast of wind brought down the load of snow carried by the lodge pole pine at his back.

The Sun's hesitant northward trek grew bolder. By March the air was perceptibly warmer—not yet above freezing, but warm and dry enough to begin to reduce the snow cover by sublimation. The breezes carried away a little more snow every day, exposing the tips of brown grasses and twigs.

In April the temperatures did climb above freezing, and the snows began to melt in a process both slow and grudging. The rays of the strengthening Sun were reflected by the vast snowfields, and every night brought a return to hard winter, with the water that had been set free once more stopped in its tracks.

But the process, once started, was inexorable. Elk returned to the heights as the snow depth decreased enough to allow their sharp hooves to paw through to the dry grasses below. One young cow elk took to visiting Avril's meadow regularly, foraging beneath the snow as she awaited her calving.

Presently John Avril lay revealed, unchanged, well-treated by the winter. Often the cow elk rested sphinx-like beside him in the morning, her dark eyes catching the sun's fiery glint as it rose.

Spring mornings marched by in perfect succession, each one aspiring to new beauty.

One particular morning outdid all the others. The color of new foliage passed from misty grey to brilliant green-gold as the Sun rolled up over the wall of crags across the valley. Tender grass sparkled with sunlight focused by a billion drops of dew. Those renewing rays sent up streamers of vapor which fled into the forest.

Their flight, or something even less tangible, seemed to disturb the cow elk who rested at her usual place beside Avril's pale form. Nervously she snorted, sniffed, then heaved herself up and trotted into the forest, leaving behind a profound silence and stillness.

Still more weeks passed as the Sun surged northward, gaining strength and authority by the day. Now daytime clearly dominated the night, and High Summer was in its ascendancy. The cow elk soon returned to the meadow, now accompanied by a gangling, bright-eyed calf. She gradually resumed her post beside Avril's silent form, on whose chill brow the final flakes of nighttime snow flurries still lingered.

There came a morning when the sun again made an early appearance in the deep crack in the mountain wall across the valley. Once again something intangible seemed to puzzle and disturb the elk, and she heaved herself upright, interrupting the nursing of her calf. With a snort she urged it to follow her into the forest.

And yet, despite their absence, liquid, living eyes still caught the Sun's rising light.

John Jacob Avril gazed into the flood of golden light. He lay there relaxed and happy, a small smile on his lips. The morning was timeless. The Sun seemed to hang motionless, regarding him as a father might watch his newborn son.

At length he got up and stretched. His clothing had been reduced by weather and hard use to little more than rags—it fell into shreds as he plucked it from his body. Naked, he absorbed the Sun's warmth and savored the stillness that pervaded the morning. He raised his arms, reaching towards the sky, looking into the high cold realm of sunlight and air. He reached up. A wind ruffled his hair, strengthening and rushing past his face. He looked down, and was neither surprised nor afraid to see the meadow falling away, the mountains receding beneath him.

He saw thunderclouds looming over the plains to the east, massive purplish towers half-hidden by mists of bronze. Bending his flight in that direction, with the wind roaring around him, he looked far below as the peaks of the Front Range crept by one by one, their summits crowned with snow and ice, their middles encased in pillars of grey rock, their feet wrapped in forests of deep green. He had no idea how fast he was flying, but it took a while for the Front Range to fall away to the high plain of eastern Colorado, a timeless, joyful interval which he did not begrudge. The thunderstorms looked no closer, but he kept up his pursuit nevertheless. As he overtook them he noticed a change in the air, a cooling, an added turbulence, a sense of power. Lightning flickered to the ground far below, and passed from cloud to cloud before him. He chose the most magnificent of the great storms and approached it in awe. It swelled into a turbulent giant, a grey world of wind and towering fury that blotted out all else. He reached the wall and let himself drop, past huge thrusting masses of dark cloud, down and down. He darted into great yawning caves of ever-shifting cloud, some gloomy and dark, others weirdly lit by shafts of sunlight that pierced them at odd angles, creating a tangled chaos of golden gleams and cold wet shadows. Winds seized him and knocked him around, lifted and spun him. He penetrated a chilly mist of cloud, and suddenly found himself in a great unexpected open area within the storm, with cloud walls surging and towering on all sides of a dizzying clear upended corridor that stretched for miles above and below. An updraft took him, and he let it loft him many thousands of feet, until he topped the inner cloud wall and found himself on the brink of a vast cloud canyon, seething and roiling. Into this clear space he plunged, and then he dove into the core of the storm, a wild darkness of wind and rain and great cracks of thunder almost simultaneous with the flashes that created them. Here the wind pulled him down, but he resisted it, penetrating the storm more deeply until the downdraft abruptly reversed, pulling him upwards again. Soon the rain turned to sleet, a storm of icy pearls frozen motionless with every lightning flash. The updraft sucked them up, and Avril followed them, watching as they grew, gaining layer after layer of ice. He climbed higher, feeling the cold but not distressed by it, following the ascending ice grains, until finally he reached a place of wonder, and let himself hover there. Floating all around him were millions of icy spheres the size of oranges, each a tiny white planet slowly bobbing and rotating, until finally each grew too heavy to be borne up by the updraft, and sank down. He floated in this secret birthplace of hail for a while, then climbed even further, leaving it behind. Presently the sound of thunder faded and the glare of lightning was veiled. Yet these upper regions of the storm had their own lights: hovering green orbs that darted and fleeted into being and then out again, and red swords of fire stabbing upward, bidding him to follow. He did so, and abruptly broke out of the storm, into a realm where the Sun reigned in an unsullied dome of deep sapphire blue. Below was the great elliptical plane of the thunderstorm's anvil top, sheared off by the lordly winds of these heights, winds that took no notice of the unruly tumults that afflicted the wet, murky lower regions of the air. Here Avril breathed hard and fast, but whether it was because of his bliss and exhilaration or because the air was thin, he did not know. He flew toward the trailing edge of the storm, gasping and feeling a moment of vertigo as he finally looked over its edge. The ground was so very far below that it was almost lost in the skirts of the storm. Nothing lay between himself and that hard ground but miles of air. Through that greenish mist of falling rain he dimly saw some farm town of the high plains. Down there people were scrambling to escape the rain. And yet, here he was. Somehow he had brought himself to this height, and here he could stay. He twisted in the air, laughing loudly. Far below, the people heard nothing but thunder.

Chapter Two

Elise Boutin ambled along a road in a valley covered with fresh green grass. The silent peaks on either side were still snow-clad halfway down to the level of the valley, glimmering in the purple twilight enveloping the sky. Today summer had begun by the reckoning of the Sun, though the heights would remain unaware of this for some weeks yet.

Her time here in the Park was nearing an end. She had arranged an unusual extension of last year's seasonal duties to survey the elk population of the back country as part of her graduate studies in wildlife biology. The survey was complete; now she would resume her ranger uniform and her duties as an interpreter until fall.

It had been Elise's first winter in the Park. The early nightfalls of winter had changed its character in ways that still haunted her. During the winter sun's brief swings across the southern sky a thought-provoking hush had settled over everything. At times the wind had howled through the pines. The mountains, usually seen in darkness, had loomed over everything like unfriendly giants.

Elise shuddered, wrenching her mind back to the present, glad of an evening which was soft and sweet. She'd been thinking of John Avril all day. It was now eight months since she'd last seen him. There was no sign of him at his usual haunts. She found it hard to imagine what he could be eating, or how he could have survived the winter. She'd left food for him in the usual places, but it was always still there when she checked later, if it hadn't been eaten by bears or buried by snow.

Elise had done her best to understand the man and his strange quest. She had provided him with what little company he would accept. She had told him that his sins seemed less grievous to her than they apparently did to him, and that it might be appropriate for him to have some mercy on himself.

Now she had to admit he had probably found his final release, the death he had been preparing himself to accept. His body might well be lying frozen on some mountainside, perhaps never to be discovered.

Either that, or he had recovered his senses and left the Park. But that she doubted. She had never glimpsed this thought in John's too-bright eyes. She had never been able to decide if his commitment to his cause was more frightening or inspiring.

Elise turned onto a smaller road that curved around a stand of newly-leafed aspens. It led to a cluster of ranger residences: a few tidy little cabins, plus the women's dorm, a rustic two-story log building. She started up the walkway to the dorm without raising her thoughtful gaze from the flagstones. The flat brim of her ranger hat blocked her view of the sky.

As she approached the stoop, the sound of her name came down softly from above.

She looked up, glimpsed a shape on the roof, and backed up to get a better view. The twilight was not yet so deep that her surroundings were concealed, yet still she blinked and squinted. The scene was simply hard to interpret, for one does not expect to find naked men perched on rooftops. She stared for an unconscionably long time. Finally her mouth dropped open and she said, "John Avril—? Is that you? What are you doing up there?"

"Feeling a little lost at the moment."

"You aren't wearing any clothes," she stated.

"That's true. They fell off. Please don't make me explain while I'm freezing up here. Will you help me get inside?"

"But how did you get up there?"

"Please let me in and I'll tell you all about it."

Elise dashed inside and ran up the stairs to her room. At the moment her main concern was to get John inside before he was seen. The thought of trying to explain this to anyone left her flushed with embarrassment. She heaved open her window—a noisy operation, as it hadn't been opened in months—and stuck her head out. "John?" she called.

"You're over there? I'm coming."

She heard him scrambling across the roof. A moment later his feet dangled in front of the window, toes in.

"Let your legs down and I'll guide you down to the sill," she said.

"Ow... these shingles are rough!" John gave a wry laugh which Elise considered quite inappropriate under the circumstances. "Do you see my feet?"

"Yes," she said tensely. "You're not lined up quite right. Squinch over about six inches to your right."

John complied. Suddenly he slipped a few inches. Elise flung her shoulders out the window and wrapped her arms around his knees.

"*Mmph!* I've got you." Elise was far from comfortable with this peculiar and unexpected intimacy. At least John smelled clean, for once.

John's feet finally made contact with the windowsill. He bent down, grabbed the window frame, and fell into the room. Picking himself up, he perched on the edge of Elise's bed, sitting primly with his hands in his lap, and a far-off look in his eye. After a while a small smile stole over his face.

"Oh yes, Mister John *Avril*, this is all very funny. But don't think you're going to sit around in here naked. Here!" She flung him a pair of jeans and an Earthwarden T-shirt. He stood up and pulled them on.

He looked at her innocently. "We can wear the same size T-shirt, but your jeans are a little too full in the hips and short in the leg for me, Elise."

She gave him an annoyed glance. "I suppose you were naked because you're so hard to fit?"

John sat down again and grew thoughtful. "No," he said, "I was naked because all I had left were rags. Rags weren't appropriate for what I did today. My skin was a more fitting costume for a venture into the heavens."

Elise sat down in a wooden chair and looked at John more carefully. Seeing him at all, here in her little room, in the habitat of the very people he had avoided all summer, was strange enough, even without having him turn up on the roof. He looked out of place. In her mind, John Avril was a creature of the wild. He was the phantom of the ridge crests, the gloomy, sunny, bright-eyed anomaly whose secret life she had concealed from others only with reluctance.

She leaned toward the bed and took his hand. "I was so worried about you. I haven't been able to find you in months. How long have you been back in the Park?"

"I never left."

"You must be kidding. You were up there all winter? How did you survive?"

"I—didn't really try to." He gave her a haunted smile. "I'm not sure what happened. You know what I was trying to do out there. I was leaving behind all the garbage I'd accumulated in my life. I was trying to forget fear and desire, and give my spirit a chance to heal. I learned how to talk and how to listen. I reached a point where I knew I wasn't going to get any closer to what I was after. There was no more point in hanging on. It got cold, I got sick, and I— I froze to death on the side of a mountain. Or I should have, anyway.

"So what happened then? Something in the universe—figured I wasn't done yet, I guess. I don't know. This morning I woke up, and you know what? *I knew how to fly.* Elise, it's so easy. I should have known it long before. As long as someone knows who he is in the world, he should be able to fly, or do anything else he might want to. But there was just too much debris in my mind for me to see the way. You could do it too. I could help you."

Elise sat very still, soberly regarding John Avril with his shining eyes, this emaciated, battered figure with his matted hair, still shivering from the cold, sitting there while madly offering to teach her how to fly. Her heart ached, and speech was difficult. Finally she swallowed and forced out some words, immediately regretting their tone.

"Okay, John. So you're Peter Pan and I'm Wendy. How did you end up stuck on the roof?"

Now John looked bewildered. "I don't know. I landed on the roof, meaning to swoop down and surprise you. But as it was getting dark, everything changed. I just lost it all of a sudden. I don't know how to fly anymore. But—I don't even care. I flew. I did it. And I'm alive. And I don't know any more lies."

Elise nodded and sat in pensive silence for a while. The utter sincerity of John's words made her afraid. He had come here naked, scaled the building, and now sat before her believing he could fly. Clearly his spiritual quest had broken him in the end. It was very sad to see such an act of hope and faith fail so completely. Elise herself sometimes found it difficult to cling to hope and faith in a world so dominated by ignorance and malice. To see those virtues betray someone as pure as John Avril was a serious blow. She wanted to cry.

"John, I'm going downstairs to fix some dinner. You stay here. I'll bring something up to you."

"Oh, thank you. I'm starving."

Elise knew he was not exaggerating.

John sat waiting for her to continue.

She swallowed and said, "I want you to stay here tonight. You'd better keep quiet, because I don't want to try to explain why you're here and wearing my clothes. In the morning I'm going to take you into town to get help."

"I don't need any more help, Elise," John said softly.

Elise looked away, nodding, not knowing what else to do. "Will you stay?" she whispered.

"Of course I will. For human beings there's no such thing as a purely random event. You would never have found me out there if I weren't meant to trust you. You helped save me."

Elise tried to smile, but failed and fled the room. Luckily the kitchen was deserted, sparing her from questions as she shed tears into a pot of leftover stew she heated on the stove. She ate alone at the table to avoid facing John's trusting eyes again quite so soon, then carried up a bowl and a bottle of green tea. John ate deliberately, studying each spoonful as though whole worlds were being delivered into his mouth.

After that, John, unable to remain awake, requested a pillow and her sleeping bag so he could curl up on the floor. Elise was inclined to give him the bed, but he laughed, assuring her he was used to sleeping in places far less comfortable than her floor. And so, a few minutes later he lay asleep, his face innocent in its dreaming, and somehow wise.

Elise looked down at him, bewildered by this erratic, inexplicable man. She studied him closely. He had always been thin, but now his body was positively ascetic, burnt brown. He should have looked like a starving war refugee, but somehow this leanness suited him. His body had been minimized and simplified, just as his life had been.

Elise sighed. Her own body was in no danger of emaciation. She considered her thighs too thick and her butt too prominent. "Pear-shaped" was the term she used. But her neck was long and graceful and her black hair tumbled into favorable arrangements ninety percent of the time.

John had often told her she was beautiful. She smiled slightly. She did not see it herself. John's solitude had left him prone to many spurious visions.

She lay on her bed and opened a book. As she read, her eyes kept straying to John's sleeping form.

A breeze in the pine boughs outside the window seemed to give voice to the night. At some point she fell asleep with the book open on her breast.

The sun is rising.

Elise woke abruptly, hearing those words as though the wind itself had called them out. The fine hairs on the nape of her neck stood erect as a tingle ran up her spine.

She looked again at John Avril, still fast asleep in the shadows. The room was still dark; the sky showed just the first uncertain hint of dawn. She shivered, not knowing if it was just some forgotten dream that had awakened her so suddenly. She lay afraid in the darkness. Something uncanny was happening. John was not merely lost and pathetic. He was something else. The night itself, so watchful, was something else, and it was speaking words she did not understand.

She awoke again in the brighter glimmer of dawn. John stood at the window, perfectly still, gazing out with a look of calm expectation. The strengthening light glowed on his face, revealing a purity and grace she had never noticed there before. As the light rose from lavender through hot orange, she was amazed at the change it brought about.

The rays of the rising sun poured into the room, transforming John into a figure of pristine fire who stared into the solar blaze with no sign of discomfort. Before her eyes he seemed to straighten and expand, to fill the room with hope and wonder. And yet objectively he looked no different than before.

He turned to Elise with a gentle smile as she lay looking at him in bewilderment. He reached down and effortlessly lifted her to her feet.

"So maybe you've started to believe. I now understand a bit more than I did myself." He laughed, his eyes dancing. "I'm going to fly around some more! I'll be back by sunset.

Can I borrow these clothes? I'll get something more appropriate later."

Elise's breath caught as she tried to speak. She tried again. "What's happened to you, John?"

John Avril radiated love at her. She felt it flowing through her like a tropical current, strong and sweet, without the undercurrents of pain and need she'd felt from him before.

"I figured it out, Elise. I finally figured out how to live. I didn't think I ever would, and I almost didn't, but somehow it happened. It's so damn simple. Keep being my friend. I'll help you find your own path."

"I am your friend," said Elise. "I always have been. I was hurt and scared when you vanished. I'm not about to lose track of you now. But I sure don't know what learning how to live has to do with learning how to fly."

John studied her for a moment, then stepped forward and gently took her in his arms. Elise began to tremble.

"Don't be afraid, Elise. Good things are going to happen from now on. Come outside with me. I want you to see."

They left the room. John flung himself down the stairs in a way not physically possible. No one else was yet awake as they stepped out onto the porch.

"I want you to see me leave. I've learned how to make the kind of dramatic exits I always wanted to." He bent and kissed her forehead. "I'll see you later!"

He ran down the walk, sprang into the air with an appearance of utter natural ease, and swept out of sight into a broken deck of golden morning clouds.

Elise snapped out of her daze. She jumped up and down, yelling and crying, having seen with waking eyes that dream which tantalizes the sleeping minds of all those who long for freedom.

She decided to take the morning off, as she felt too unsettled to face anyone. At lunchtime she succumbed to a panic attack. She could not explain her distress to her housemates as she sat on the porch, shaking and staring up at the sky. In truth she could not explain it even to herself.

Chapter Three

John spent the day among the peaks of the Rockies, soaring from summit to summit, exploring remote crags that had never known a human footfall. Whenever some proud lord of the Front Range caught his eye, he would circle and come to rest on any convenient ledge or slope. Seated upon one, he gazed out across immense gulfs of air to the High Plains in the east, where storm clouds beckoned him to come and play. He smiled, lazy in the sunshine. There was nothing he need do, nowhere he must go, save as the spirit suggested.

His vision had become preternaturally sharp, or rather, he had learned to see beyond the limits of sight. The mountains around him were inscribed with exquisite detail.

Something on a distant ridge caught his attention: a bit of angular whiteness, a small building of some kind. Idly curious, John floated over the intervening ranges until he recognized the structure as a fire tower. Was that smoke rising from its chimney? Intrigued, he plumped down into deep snow just out of sight. It occurred to him that he ought not to be seen. He had no way of explaining his presence on this snowbound peak, not in this wholly inadequate clothing. And yet he didn't feel the least bit cold.

He peeked around an outcropping of rock. The "tower" was actually a squat wooden structure with windows on all four sides. A figure was visible within. A radio squawked from speakers mounted under the eaves, making various terse announcements.

The door swung open. The lookout, a woman dressed in a heavy parka, emerged carrying binoculars. She raised them, peering around the horizon.

The hut's loudspeakers crackled with a fresh announcement.

"Mayday received from light plane November Whisky Zero One Niner, VFR pilot, disoriented and running low on fuel in storm system under IFR conditions. Last known position twenty miles east of Fort Collins, course southeast. Any stations within range report sightings of this aircraft."

The announcer sounded bored, as though this was a distraction to be perfunctorily mentioned and then forgotten.

John Avril, on the other hand, had a different view of the matter. If he understood correctly, that lost pilot was rated to fly only in conditions of good visibility.

John stared across the miles at the streams of cloud that concealed a man in danger.

"Hey!"

This high-pitched cry startled John out of his concentration. He looked toward the lookout tower, whose occupant had her glasses trained on him.

"Are you all right?" she called.

"I'm fine! Bye now."

John smiled foolishly and gave her a wave. Suddenly he no longer felt even slightly lazy. He ducked out of sight behind the rock, leaned forward, and leaped off the side of the mountain.

He had to cover at least fifty miles; surely he could not take an hour to do it and still arrive in time. He flew as fast as he could, accelerating until the blast of air resistance overcame his ability to speed up. It seemed to take about fifteen seconds to reach this maximum speed. He had no idea what his speed really was, but the wind in his face was considerable. He had to clamp his lips shut to keep his cheeks from inflating. He squinted, climbing; the thinner air would present less resistance. His clothing flapped, then it vibrated and whined, then it was shredded and torn from his body.

Sorry, Elise!

The ground moved beneath him at a gratifying pace. He passed over the foothills of the Front Range and over the beginning of the High Plains, nearing Fort Collins and the boundary of the storm front. He forced his arms, palms flat, forward into the blast of the wind.

In minutes he reached the western fringe of the storm that had trapped the unwary pilot. His task now was to locate an aluminum gnat buzzing somewhere in the thick cloud deck below. He dropped through the clouds, flashing over the landscape at about a thousand feet, right below the cloud ceiling. He heard nothing but the turbulent wind in his ears. He couldn't hope to pick out the mutter of a small airplane engine at any distance. Somehow he'd have to spot the plane by eye, despite the clouds and the mix of snow and rain that made it feel like he was flying though thousands of cold taut wires.

Bill Waters fought to keep his hand steady on the yoke, resisting the urge to make some drastic maneuver that could easily kill him. The view from the cockpit of his Cessna was frightening. Beyond the heavy rain and snow streaking his windshield was nothing but featureless greyness. Something was wrong with his instruments. The artificial horizon and rate-of-climb indicator showed he was climbing, but his inner ear told him with far greater urgency that he was in fact descending steeply. His wings weren't level either; he was tempted to apply some aileron to correct the bank he could feel so plainly, despite the spurious reading of the turn-and-bank indicator. And what was wrong with the engine? He was losing airspeed as he pulled back to cut his descent. He gave it full throttle, but still the plane lurched with an impending stall as he tried to resume level flight. He eased the yoke forward again—stalling was the last thing he needed. He must have wing icing, or maybe the engine was about to cut out.

He picked up the microphone to report his situation. His voice was shaky, breathless; he was afraid he was less than fully coherent. The instructions Air Traffic Control kept giving him didn't make any sense—they didn't understand that his instruments had all malfunctioned. Cold sweat soaked his clothes. Nothing made much sense to him since he'd foolishly continued into the weather despite his VFR rating, thinking he could make it to his intended airfield before the clouds closed in. But he'd become disoriented almost immediately. He couldn't even be certain which way was down. He began to face the knowledge that his impatience and overconfidence were about to cost him his life.

To be more honest, nothing had made much sense to him in a long time. His life in general wasn't much different than this flight—turbulent, cloudy, and aimless. His behavior in recent years had been poor. His career in insurance seemed a wasteland, his wife befuddled and clingy, his children remote. Bill's flailing response to his dissatisfaction had led him to this present situation. The women... the drugs...self-indulgences like the flying lessons...all had combined to ruin his finances and alienate his family. And now here he sat, about to be smashed in a tiny airplane he didn't even own, all because he'd been stupid enough to fly when he was too emotionally impaired to make good judgments. His hands on the yoke were weak and slick with sweat.

Flying, he realized, was not something one should do with a heart that was less than calm.

The engine sputtered and cut out—out of gas. His heart pounded wildly as he heard the dismal moan of the wind rushing by his wings and struts. The world was cold, grey, and devoid of guidance. Calmness found him belatedly, brought out by the certain knowledge of his imminent death. He wished he knew how to pray.

"God," he said at last, "please take care of my family, and please have mercy on a fool."

There was a thump, a shudder. Bill looked around. A naked man was clinging to the strut of the left wing. Bill Waters yelped, then stared at this apparition. The man looked sinister in the poor lighting. Clumps of his rain-soaked hair flapped in the wind. He squinted into the plane at Bill, then turned to look forward and downward, his gaze intense as that of an eagle. Rain flew off his body in a spray. He turned back to Bill, giving him a quick thumbs up. Waters numbly returned the gesture. The man dropped off the plane and vanished.

Something bumped the plane again. Waters looked out, down; a figure was partially visible, one arm wrapped around a wheel strut. The plane continued its gliding descent. Presently it fell clear of the clouds. Visibility was still poor due to the snow and rain, but at least Waters could glimpse the ground. Now the plane surged forward as though under power, rose slightly, and entered a banking turn. In an uncanny silence it lined up on a small rural landing strip and descended. The wheels touched down on the turf. Waters heard something dragging beneath the plane, which rolled to a halt.

Waters banged open his door and tumbled out just in time to see his savior climbing to his feet from beneath the plane, his body streaked with grass and mud. He shot Bill a quick sharp grin over his shoulder, then inexplicably hurtled into the air, vanishing in a turbulent swirl of cloud.

Waters stared after him for minutes, oblivious to the freezing rain. Some wholly unexpected part of the world, of reality, had just reached out to him, saving him, dissolving the limits of his life and destroying his sense of what was real and what was not.

His problems had not gone anywhere. They remained obstacles yet to be faced. Yet Waters regarded them with a peculiar calm. Somehow they seemed less formidable than they had before.

John Avril felt a burning light even before he emerged from the clouds back into the sun. He felt it in his hands, in his heart, and behind his eyes. He had saved someone's life. This was the outcome of all his years of struggle, confusion, and pain, and it had all been worth it. The power that propelled him through the sky, whatever its source, flowed through him with a special vigor in this moment of elation and joy. His thoughts and his vision seemed to be suffused with light.

But...what was that buzzing sound? John snapped out of his reverie. He turned his head, which so compromised his stability that he nearly entered a flat spin. Flying beside him, only a hundred feet away, was another light plane. Seated within it were a middle-aged man and a young girl, both of whom goggled at him with such astonishment that he would have laughed, except he didn't want to open his mouth and let a blast of cold air force its way into his lungs.

Their faces showed something else as well: confusion, maybe fear? In any event, they appeared fretful.

John's joy abated a little. Obviously, he couldn't let himself be followed all the way back to the Park, but he doubted he could outfly even this little plane. Still, he was able do things no airplane could match.

John stopped flying. Wind resistance instantly slowed him; his trajectory began to curve down towards a deck of low clouds. The plane buzzed on ahead as he fell into the cloud deck.

Vast shapes loomed around him in the mist. He was among the foothills! He caught himself and slowed his fall just in time to thump down on a wild rocky slope. Wind-blown clouds flowed by around him.

He leaped downhill over frosted granite boulders, finally reaching a cliff which offered a view of a valley thick with evergreens. On the far side was another looming mountain wall, barely visible.

Suddenly he no longer felt so clever about eluding that plane. Sunset was only a few hours off. He was not cold now, but once the sun went down that might change.

Another thought came to him with a start. How fast had he been flying up there to keep pace with even that little plane? He would have guessed he'd been doing maybe fifty miles per hour, based purely on the buffet of the wind on his body. He must be wrong by a factor of two or three at least. And yet such speed had not been difficult, or even very uncomfortable.

Come to think of it…during his dreamlike first flight, he had ventured all the way to the top of a thunderhead. How high was that, fifty thousand feet? More? And yet he had not felt any distress from cold or lack of oxygen or pressure.

It began to dawn on John that the rebirth which had transformed his relationship to the world was not limited in its effect to flight alone. He looked into the sky as though it were new to him, aware that the forces of wind and gravity and light could be more liberal in their gifts than even he could have guessed. A stillness settled over his mind.

After a thoughtful half hour or so he lifted off into a peaceful sky.

Soon the Front Range loomed ahead in the fog and mist. He followed Highway 34 through wild, twisting valleys to the park. The local time was 3:30—Elise was probably still working, either at Visitor Center or leading a hike in the rain. He made a quick tour of the usual nature walk routes, scrutinizing with his eagle's vision the few people braving the weather. He was fortunate to spot Elise leading a small group around Dream Lake. Alighting on the adjacent Hallett Peak, he kept watch between the clots of billowing scud until presently the hike finished and broke up. Elise, her flat hat wrapped in plastic and her shoulders draped with a green Park Service raincoat, sauntered down the trail toward her Park Service car.

Avril leaped from his perch to soar gracefully down through the Tyndall Gorge into the small, mountain-ringed valley that sheltered Dream Lake and its sister lakes Bear, Nymph, and Emerald. He brought himself up short and dropped a few feet to land beside Elise.

She gave a fleeting smile and flashed him a sidelong glance as she kept on walking. "I hope you didn't expect me to be scared. I've been expecting you to arrive this way."

"Scare you? Farthest thing from my mind. So what have you been up to today?"

"Oh, I spent some time this afternoon putting my new "Fish and Streams" show together, then I had some project time so I sat in the library and tried to look busy, then I had this nice rainy hike. What have you been doing? I see you're naked again. We're really going to have to do something about that. Put on this raincoat before you get arrested."

"I saved someone's life!" said John, shrugging on the raincoat.

Elise blinked and said, "Really? How?"

John described everything he'd done, outlandish as it all sounded, even to him.

"So," said Elise thoughtfully. "You were seen by at least four people."

John laughed, saying, "What of it? Who will believe them? And even if someone does, how can it be traced to me? It's not like I have wings on my back. Sorry about the clothes. I'll pay you…"

"Oh, forget it."

They reached her car. "Do you want a ride?" asked Elise.

John shook his head. "It would be silly for me to crawl along in that contraption when I can fly."

"Do you want to meet me for dinner? In Estes Park? I think it would be good to get you some clothes, too."

"Okay, but I'm buying. I owe you for the clothes I ruined. The cafe?"

"That'll be nice. I'll be there in about an hour and a half."

John grinned dangerously. "I think I could fly you there."

"No! I'm not ready for that."

"All right then. Meet you there." He looked around to be sure they were alone, then looked straight up. The world seemed to turn upside down, and he fell into the sky.

"Don't ruin my raincoat!" cried Elise.

"I won't!"

He burst through the cloud deck to emerge in the perpetual kingdom of clear skies which reigned above the mists and fogs of the lower world. He made a leisurely climb to a layer of thin cirrus that drifted over the world in Olympian splendor. Carelessly he drifted among them, floating through trailing streamers of ice crystals, sailing lazily above the rippled surfaces of the clouds that inhabited this pristine realm of crystal cold.

The cirrus glowed a delicate gold as the Sun began to decline. It was time to get down—he didn't care to see what would happen to him if the Sun were to set while he loitered at 40,000 feet.

Chapter Four

A pensive Elise sat at a table in the glassed-in terrace of the Roaring Fork Cafe, waiting for John. The rain had stopped, and the cloud cover was breaking up as a cold front churned by on its way east. The sky was a collage of dull grey, luminous indigo, and brilliant gold as the evening came on.

Elise regretted her decision to wear a dress, much less her coral red one that revealed her shoulders and a bit of cleavage. This was not the time to be sending mixed signals. In fact, she regretted suggesting this public meeting at all. What if Pablo or Chris should see her here with John? Too many questions could be asked.

And now here came John, striding in on his long legs, looking quite ridiculous in her raincoat and nothing else, yet also very straight and tall. He sat down across from her and smiled.

"I'm flattered that you got dressed up for me," said John.

Elise winced internally. "We might not see each other again for a while. See this bag? It's clothing for you. Please go change now so people will quit looking at your bare legs beneath my raincoat."

"Yes Ma'am." John took the bag into the men's room, returning to the table wearing jeans, a t-shirt, a sweatshirt, and sneakers. He handed Elise her neatly-folded raincoat and said, "Thank you very much. I do like your dress, by the way."

He slumped slightly as the sun set, returning him to the world of flightless humanity. "I'm grounded."

"John, why does that happen to you?"

"I'm not really sure. Maybe being able to fly is just too draining for me to do it all the time."

"So you're solar powered? Is that it?"

"Oh no. I don't think so. The Sun is more like a switch for me, I think. If anything, I think the power, the actual energy, comes somehow from the Earth. I guess this is just my down time."

"I have something else for you." Elise produced John's weather-stained wallet from her purse and placed it on the table. "I found it where you left it months ago, in your usual cache. I figured it was better for me to hold onto it than to let it rot away in that jar. I'm not sure how you expected to pay for this dinner without it."

John picked it up and flipped through it. "Wow, you're right. I'd forgotten all about this. Thanks. This is like a relic from a previous life. Which it is."

"One more thing." Elise handed John a Denver newspaper.

The headline read:

Weird "Sky Man" Sighted

Below the headline was a photograph, surprisingly clear, of John in flight.

John groaned. "I never even noticed they had a camera."

Elise watched as John read the story. Fortunately, the wind had distorted his face enough to make him unrecognizable. The story contained the account of the pilot of the second small plane and his daughter, who referred to John as a "flying naked hobgoblin." There was no mention of the man he'd rescued, or of the fire lookout.

"The story is all over TV, too," said Elise quietly. "One station is calling you the 'Missile Man'. They're making you sound like a dangerous weapon. Another one calls you 'The Streaker' for obvious reasons. Luckily most people think the photo is a fake."

John nodded. "Sky Man. Missile Man," he said reflectively. "I like those better than 'hobgoblin'. But I don't want to be a Sky Man. I want to be a Sky Ranger."

"John, does anyone know that we know each other, do you think?"

He shook his head. "I'm pretty sure not. Not unless you've talked about it."

"No, I haven't. What are you going to do?"

"Hmm. That's quite a question. It's not the easiest one in the world to answer," He sat in silence as a fresh patter of rain ran down the cafe's glass enclosure. "You have to remember I've only been—back—since yesterday morning. Since then I've had so many new things to take in—I can hardly look beyond the revelations of the moment to look to the future. But I know I've been granted an incomparable gift—a second chance at life. I'm going to live it. Enjoy myself, explore. And help people when I get the chance."

"How much can you really do for them?"

"What do you mean?"

"I mean, you can fly, but once you get there, what next? You're just another person. Unless you're saying you can also bend steel, bounce bullets, and all that."

"No, I don't think so. But I think I can still do a lot. I can go anywhere. I can do search and rescue. That seems like plenty right there."

He looked so happy. Even sitting there dressed in cheap clothing, with his sandy hair still wild, he glowed with happiness.

Elise heaved a big sigh. "That's wonderful. But John, I'm sorry, you have to leave. You can stay with me tonight if you need to, but you have to go in the morning."

John's expression barely changed, but she knew him well enough to have some idea of what her words meant to him. He looked at her gently and steadily. "Why, Elise?"

There was no point in holding anything back. "I'm just so scared after reading this paper. Everybody in the world will be screaming to know if you're real and who you are. They'll find out someday. I don't want the FBI and the police and everybody else pounding on my door to take me away to find out what I know about you. I'll be fired, and I might even wind up in jail. I need my job, and I just want to be a happy little person and get on with my life. John, you don't need me, I'm nothing. You can just go live on a mountaintop and be happy and save the world or whatever." She looked away, lip trembling, tears staining her cheeks.

John raised a finger, touched her cheek, and turned her face back toward his. "Please don't ever tell me again that I'm better or more important than you. You're not the one who wound up living in the mountains wanting to die. If you think I'm special, ask yourself why you were the first person in the world I came to after I woke up on that mountainside. But I understand why you're worried. I'll leave. I never planned to move in with you or anything. I just wanted you to know I'm alive. It's kind of late in the day for me to go now, so if you don't mind I'll wait till morning. I don't think anything will happen before then. Okay?"

Trembling and sniffling, Elise nodded her head. "I hope you don't think I'm a terrible person because of this."

John laughed. "Hardly. If some flying fool showed up naked on my roof I'd probably do the same thing."

They shared a dinner of spaghetti with pesto sauce followed by ice cream and fruit. Elise said little, preferring to listen as John described his experiences in a hushed voice, as though he couldn't quite believe them himself. Throughout their dinner he kept a bright smile on his face, though it was mostly there for Elise's benefit.

As they prepared to leave, John said "You know what? It's such a nice evening, and the moon is out. I think I'll spend the night in one of my old haunts. You can just drop me off at the trailhead if you don't mind."

Elise bit her lip. "It'll take you at least three hours to get up there."

"Yeah, it'll be a nice hike. It's really been quite a while since I've gotten any exercise." He gave an unconvincing laugh.

Elise made no further objection. They were quiet as they drove into the park. John gave her a wave as he left the car and disappeared into the darkness of the trees. Elise sat there looking after him for a while, then she drove home, went upstairs, stripped off her dress, which she suddenly hated, and wept until she fell asleep.

John walked until he was out of Elise's sight, then stopped. He heard her car moving off, its sound dwindling into silence.

It would not be an easy walk to the place where, months before, he had stashed an old sleeping bag and a little food. He was already tired. Yet he could not bear the thought of spending another night in Elise's room, when he knew he was unwanted. He could not stand the look in her eyes. He had frightened her.

John had imagined his return would be for Elise a source of unalloyed joy. He had thought her eyes would light up, her spirit soar, when she learned what he had done, what he had become. Instead, she had rarely looked him in the eyes. She'd been uneasy, haunted. If she, a close friend and a woman of spirit and imagination, found him threatening, how might the rest of humanity react to his rude intrusion into the normal order of things?

He still had a bit of twilight to work with as he began his hike. He passed a few other hikers on their way out, usually happy couples, it seemed. Suddenly he felt conspicuously alone, and conspicuously out of place. As he climbed away from the lakes he left them all behind. The trail entered a series of switchbacks, climbing through the forests on the side of a mountain. The sad wail of a screech owl sounded somewhere in the distance.

John huffed his way up the mountain. He really wasn't in very good condition after lying dead on another mountainside for six months. The sweat grew chill on his body as he trudged along, looking for roots and rocks in the trail by the moon's fugitive light.

The trees grew stunted and sparse as he approached the timberline. Thankfully, the cairn he'd erected to mark the turnoff was still recognizable. He left the trail and blundered off into the scant woods, seeking one of his old campsites, a spot he'd never thought to visit again, and which he was not eager to see. It was part of a past full of mixed memories.

But there it was, a U-shaped outcropping of boulders overlooking the valley. A few lights twinkled out there: cars moving on the roads, mostly.

The old ice chest where John had stored his things was still there, but the cover had been knocked off. John drew out its contents. Mice fell squeaking about his feet and scattered. They'd discovered the sleeping bag and pad, chewing them up and removing much of their insulation for nesting material. The remnants were not especially inviting, mice being what they were. At the bottom of the cooler was a can of tuna, the only food they'd been unable to open. The can bulged from being repeatedly frozen. John ignored it, sighed, and unrolled the befouled mat. He stretched out on it, using the bag as a blanket. Both were disgusting, but he must sleep.

John laughed, reflecting on his present situation versus the glamour and joy he'd known just hours before.

From the moment he'd first seen Elise he had felt they possessed a shared destiny. In her huge dark eyes he had seen his ideal, and his love for her was an inner ache, one that was especially poignant at the moment. He had kept these feelings to himself while his only ambition was to find a peaceful death in these mountains. But now he was more alive than anyone had ever been. He had miraculously escaped his own death, and that must mean something. He must keep and nurture his faith that he and she were bound together. To abandon that faith now would be to open too large a hole in himself, just as he felt all such holes were filled.

He fell asleep with difficulty. He dreamed he was walking along a crowded city street, hemmed in by masses of people, unable to make much progress. Everyone around him seemed listless, lifeless, and dull. Belatedly remembering that he could fly, he leaped upward, soaring and swooping over the streets and from building to building.

To his bafflement, no one below noticed him or saw what he was doing. Among them was Elise. Even she did not lift her eyes skyward. Even she.

John woke up beneath a quiet sky. The stars were calm overhead, yet John's heart was troubled. So much for his conquest of uncertainty and fear. He hoped he'd still remember how to fly when the Sun rose, then was shocked by that thought.

At some point he fell asleep again without noticing.

Elise dreamed she was aboard a big military cargo plane during a turbulent flight through troubled skies. She kept trying to grab onto things to keep from plunging around during the plane's unpredictable twists and dips. Finally she caught herself against a man-sized cylinder of warm blue metal and clung to it for dear life. She sensed a deadly quiet power within the cylinder and pried her eyes open to examine it more closely. The legend CAUTION: THERMONUCLEAR DEVICE was printed on it in white letters.

With a start she snapped awake. She stared into the glowing face of the newly risen sun as it shone through her window. She rolled out of bed, slid open the window, and stuck out her head.

What was that passing overhead? It was moving very straight and fast, not at all like any bird, and there was no sound of any engine.

Chapter 5

The clarity of daylight did much to settle John's mind. He flew southwest, searching for Vail, or Aspen, or indeed any ski town. In order to keep his clothes from ripping off his body he had to fly slowly. For some reason this was more difficult than flying at his full speed, requiring constant concentration. After today he hoped to have a solution to this problem.

He flew low, skimming over range after range, bemused by the realization that he could alight anywhere at will, visit any summit, dip his feet in any lake.

After an hour's flight he spied a town surrounded by ski slopes. Dropping onto a meadow just outside its boundaries, he ambled into town, pleased to discover it was in fact Vail. He walked into a big downtown ski shop, its stock a little sparse at this time of the year. Nevertheless, he was able to select three speed skating suits in various shades of blue and white, plus a daypack. He had a scary moment when he presented his credit card: would it still work after so many months of disuse? It did.

With his new goodies packed away, John bought lunch in an outdoor cafe. The day was warm and beautiful. He felt quite pleased with himself, all the more so because Elise was not weighing on his mind. He had confronted her with too much, too soon. She would surely come around after she'd had time to process the novelty of having a friend who had flown off a mountainside after coming back from the dead.

With the day still young he walked out of town, climbed into a stand of pines, and changed into one of the tight-fitting ski suits. With the pack's straps cinched up tightly, he moved into the open.

A group of young people came walking and laughing along the nearest road, only a hundred yards away. John smiled, looked upward, and fell away from the ground.

The teenagers did not notice his departure.

John's plan for the rest of the day was simple. He would soar east over the mountains, and then, near sunset, he would land in some small town on the plains and treat himself to a cheap motel room. There he would experience such luxuries as a shower and a warm bed. After that, he'd have to make plans for more permanent lodging of some kind, something that would accommodate his unique new lifestyle.

With a shattering sound, two blurs passed close by on either side. He recognized them as fighter jets, but he was no student of warplanes and could say no more. Noses high, they popped out their speed brakes, rolled into steep banks, and flew horizontal loops, returning to pace him on either side. John turned his head to look at one of the planes, even though it was difficult to fly straight with his head cocked like that. He stared into the astonished face of the pilot. The planes, whatever model they were, were howling angular beasts. They were not comfortable flying companions. He was far more afraid of their brutal physicality than he was of the tens of thousands of feet of air beneath hum. What did they want with him? Well, that was a stupid question. The American government was not known for its easy tolerance of anything that might be outside its control.

John let himself drop, intending once again to lose himself in the mountains. Quiet returned as the jets shot ahead.

They were just beginning to double back when he fell into the cloud deck. He heard them pass overhead, then all was silent.

He made a neat landing on a nondescript slope which overlooked a minor road, then sat down on a log to collect his thoughts.

The sound of helicopters reached him from a distance, making his hair stand on end. He was amazed at all the fuss he seemed to be causing. Though he was not conspicuous in this great shrouded land, he did not know what resources his seekers could bring to bear.

A military helicopter moved into view at the end of the valley, flying low over the trees. A tentacle of grey cloud hid it from view, but the sullen mutter of its rotor remained.

John's options were simple enough. He could try to hide here on the slopes, or in the woods, and then risk hypothermia after sundown. Or...he could fly away. If pursued, he would test the limits of his ability.

A tingle moved up and down his spine. *Why should there be any limits?* To fly at all was already impossible in terms of any known science. How much less plausible was it that he might also outfly a helicopter, or even a jet, and survive the rigors of such flight?

With a shrug and a smile of sheer audacity he leaned off the steep slope, reversed his fall, and flung himself up through the clouds, into the supernal world of sunlight and space that glowed above them.

By now John realized that his metal packframe must have made him highly visible to radar. He'd paid good money for the pack and its contents (or would, once he figured out how to pay off the credit card), and would not abandon them.

Almost at once John spied two distant specks. Even as he watched, they made wide turns and headed his way.

He twisted in the air, leaving his feet pointing at the ground and his face aimed at the stars. He climbed, straight up, in a conspiracy of wind and energy and gravity itself. The color of the sky deepened, losing its watery veil of white, passing through pure cerulean on its way to ultramarine. He approached a layer of cirrus which resolved into ever greater icy detail as he neared it, until it expanded before him and he was through it in a moment's cold tingle. The clouds then dwindled below him. John laughed, but the sound was small and remote, for even the wind had faded to a thin cold flow over his face. Now the sky was indigo, and the horizon was curved, and far across the continent he could see the Great Salt Lake beyond the ranges to the west, the Grand Canyon to the south, while far to the east, cities glimmered in the shadows which lay in that direction.

John laughed again, in near silence, lost in dreamlike wonder at where he was and what he had done. The sky overhead was deepest blue. His breathing was rapid, yet he felt no distress.

He cast his gaze far below, to the hazy boundary between the plains and the mountains. Milling around thousands of feet beneath him were the fighters, looking like two tiny silver moths.

John slipped into an awestruck reverie as he eased his way west. Here was his private realm...this place he had to himself.

His complacence was abruptly ended as his peripheral vision revealed on ominous black shape beside him. He twisted his head in the slipstream to behold an awesome black plane paralleling him with utmost ease. He tried to shout an exclamation, but the wind forced its way into his throat and rattled his vocal cords uselessly. The plane was a sleek curvaceous bat of a type he did not recognize. A very serious-looking pilot peered at him from the cockpit; another man looked out from the port behind. John gave them a wave and a grin. The rear-seat man replied by snapping off a few shots with a hand-held camera.

Feeling curious, John drifted closer to the plane's canopy. The pilot made a decisive hand-gesture ordering him down to the ground. John tried to convey regret as he shook his head in negation. The pilot spoke into his microphone. To John's surprise and amusement, the back-seat man then held up a little white card which appeared to contain writing. At this distance it was too small to read even with John's sharpened vision. He slipped closer to the plane, very cautiously, aware of the jet intake not very far behind. He was surprised at the reaction of the rear-seat man as he approached. He flinched; his face revealed fear, even horror. John frowned. These men were riding in a large airplane, probably armed, yet both were spooked by a man flying in a ski suit.

The card had been scribbled by hand. It read:

We are authorized by the govt. of the United States of America to conduct you to a nearby base for questioning. You must accompany us without deviation. Failure to comply may result in your actions being interpreted (sic) *as hostile.*

It was a lot of copy for such a small card. John responded by shaking his head. Obviously he had to elude these men, but how? Speed was out—this superplane was no doubt hypersonic. That left altitude. Even a plane such as this was an aerodynamic, air-breathing jet, while he was a flying man operating beyond the limits of science.

The pilot, his face without humor, again made his peremptory landing gesture. John responded with the opposite gesture—an index finger pointing straight up. He bent his course to a forty-five degree climb and began to pull away. Even in this scanty air he could hear afterburners erupt behind him as the mystery plane struggled to match his ascent.

It struggled, and it failed.

John kept his eyes locked on his pursuer as it dwindled to a black wedge-shape directly below. As the air thinned further, the low-speed climb became impossible for the jet, which went back on afterburner to pull ahead and attempt a rapid climb. It banked in a wide circle below him, spiraling up in a valiant attempt to match him. John wondered who would give out first. He still felt no ill effect from his enormous altitude, but how long could that last?

He took his eyes off the plane long enough to note the sky, and gasped in the near-vacuum. The sky had faded from ultramarine to deep indigo along the horizon, and almost black overhead. A few stars shone in the darkness like steel points. As far as he was concerned, he was flying in space. His diaphragm continued to move up and down, drawing only a few molecules of thin gas into his lungs. Yet he felt no distress. The ultimate reaches of Earth's atmosphere seemed enough to sustain him in this exalted state of being. His skin felt tight and cold, but otherwise fine. What were the limits of his durability?

And where was that darn plane? He scanned the sky with his eagle's vision, finally spotting it as a black speck far below, its ceiling reached. He had no doubt that he was still the primary target on the jet's radar. As long as that plane tagged along he couldn't touch down anywhere without compromising his privacy. He doubted he could outlast it—the plane could probably cruise at this low speed until long after sunset—and he'd better be down by then.

John abruptly realized he'd used exactly the wrong tactic to elude this plane. Though it was clearly a king of the heights, it was a soaring bird, not some tiny wren to dip and twist over the treetops.

He glanced once more at the stars at the edge of space, pointed his toes at the ground, relaxed, and let himself fall.

Somehow, dropping through the sky the way anyone else would made the pursuing airplane seem far off, impotent, and unimportant. Cold air slipped past his face like ghost water, its wispy resistance steadily building as he descended and gained speed, until he felt like he was standing on a wobbly padded floor. He gave a quick salute as he shot by the plane's knifelike nose and kept right on going. The rapid buildup of air pressure had him swallowing madly to clear his ears. The hands of an altimeter would've spun like helicopter rotors as he rushed downward. Then he slowed, buoyed by the thickening air, until he fell at only the sedate pace of a skydiver.

Switching to level flight, he whipped low over the sagebrush somewhere over the Great Plains. The plane was doubtless still overhead, but he was too small a target to be tracked optically, and now too low for radar, or so he hoped. He'd given the Air Force the slip. He made a few random evasive turns, then settled down on a western course, hugging the ground at a few tens of feet, keeping an eye peeled for transmitters, power lines, and other obstacles. Fortunately, he was a seasoned traveler and a good student of geography. With a map of the United States clear in his mind, he was able to orient himself adequately by an occasional glimpse of a familiar road or town. The sky clouded over. Speeding through rain showers, the drops stung his face like fine sleet.

His motel plan still seemed like a good one. In any case, he'd soon be obliged to stop somewhere. He passed over a small farming town; on its outskirts was a little motel. John dropped into a nearby copse of trees, where he changed out of his ski suit and into his street clothes. He then shouldered the pack (which was already substantially weathered, for all of being new) and sauntered over to the motel.

He had no difficulty renting a room, though the clerk looked at him strangely. Entering his room, John glanced in a mirror, dropped his pack in shock, and understood why he had stood out.

The skin of his face had turned a deep bronze. Well, what did he expect? He had flown in space, fully exposed to the Sun's ultraviolet light. His skin could react either by blistering off, or by adapting itself to the radiation in a manner which should not be possible. Happily, it had chosen the latter.

John slowly sat down on the bed. How far had he flown today, how high, and how fast? Many hundreds of miles, leading here to this little Kansas town.

John wandered out the door in a daze. The sky had cleared and was now a fading dome of clear amethyst. The Sun had set without his noticing. The world around him seemed to glow with wonder. He tilted his head and looked up into the sky. He had *been* there. *Way* up there. Way, way

The Way of an Eagle

the heck up there. He began to wander along the road. He had flown at nearly the speed of sound. How? Why? It hadn't felt any different than his usual speed at low altitude. It had been no more difficult.

He drifted into a little diner where he spent a few dollars on a meal he couldn't remember an hour later.

That night John dreamed he was walking around on some Kansas wheat field as tractors and combines roared and growled in the distance. They disturbed his peace, and though he attempted to walk away from them, somehow they, or others like them, were always not far ahead.

The engine noises persisted when the Sun abruptly woke him. With a feeling of apprehension John leaped from his bed and peeked through the blinds. The town should have been quiet at such an hour, but instead it was swarming with military vehicles: troop carriers, armored vehicles, radar trucks, and more. So far they were milling about the town's modest central district, but their area of interest was expanding, and they would soon reach this isolated little motel.

John frowned as he climbed into one of his ski suits. Unless Kansas was being invaded by the Soviets, he had to assume this was about him. Evidently, he was easier to track then he had imagined or hoped, or at least, it was easier to deduce where he might be found.

With a sigh he glanced at his pack. Something told him to leave it behind. He stepped out into the golden sunlight of early morning. Before anyone could notice him, he looked up, inverted his frame of reference, and fell into the sky.

The town dwindled below and behind him. John headed
west, flying low and slow, cautious and alert. He passed
another farm town to its south, and was relieved to see it
too was infested with Army vehicles, as well as helicopters.
Maybe this was just a general sweep, and he had not been
tracked and located as accurately as he had feared.

ROAR! ROAR! Two grey fighters flashed by from behind, one on either side. They flared away from each other
and then peeled back his way. Confused, John looked up to
find two more planes diving on him. No time to think! He
lit out in a random direction, zipping around in wild maneuvers that no aerodynamic plane could match. But he
couldn't long evade four fast jets like that. His only hope
was to exceed their ceiling as he had before. He heard afterburners roar as the jets stood on their tails in pursuit. He
looked down at them between his feet as he shot upward. A
fountain of fire burst from the nose of the lead plane. With
his enhanced reflexes he could see the shells heading his
way. A line of tracers snaked by and drifted closer as the
pilot corrected his aim. John veered aside. He was beginning to get angry. At the same time he didn't want to find
out what that machine gun, or whatever it was called, could
do to him.

Two narrow cylinders dropped from the wings of his
foremost antagonist. Missiles! With more than a little panic
John poured on speed, although he knew he couldn't hope
to outpace the missiles, which must fly much faster than
sound. As he approached the "wall" at Mach 1 he felt a buffeting shock wave building up as he smashed his way
through the air with his knobby, hopelessly un-aerodynamic
human form. He kept pushing harder, hoping to keep far
enough ahead of the missiles to outlast their fuel supplies.

Suddenly the air flow smoothed out dramatically and he continued to pick up speed. His eyes grew wide, although the air blast felt like it was drying them into hard boiled eggs. He must be supersonic! He'd assumed he was limited to subsonic speeds—what an idiot! With everything else he could do, why assume that the discredited old bogeyman of the "sound barrier" could hold him back?

He blinked, squinted, and looked down again. The missiles were close enough that he could read warnings against touching the transparent windows on their noses—but they were losing ground. The jets themselves were mere twinkles in the distance below. Nothing in the sky could catch him.

The missiles detonated harmlessly as they reached the end of their endurance. Bursting with exhilaration, John Avril flattened his climb. Who could say what his limits were? He kept pushing, and his body responded by moving faster and faster. He had no built-in Mach meter, but by the speed with which the distant earth was sliding by he knew he must be approaching hypersonic velocity.

The knowledge was reinforced a moment later when he felt a warm liquid sliding over his body. He looked down to see his skating suit melting and flowing away in fat blue drops and spatters. He slowed down and the cooling liquid nylon began to trail as threads and streamers of solidifying plastic. He tore the ruined suit completely from his body. So much for another suit of clothes.

He scowled at the planes still circling in futility far below. He must do something to put an end to this harassment, or else he must flee all inhabited lands and become an airborne hermit. Perhaps he ought to have accepted yesterday's peremptory invitation after all. Maybe it wasn't too late.

John dropped down, shaping the direction of his fall, but not really flying actively. He had his eye on one of the planes, and apparently its pilot was aware of him as well, because the plane entered a swooping, evasive turn as John approached it. But it couldn't approach John's aerial agility or reflexes. John slowed at the last instant, reached out and grabbed the leading edge of the wing.

The pilot decided he didn't want some crazy aerial remora latching onto his plane. He flung his craft into a series of maneuvers that must have greyed out his vision several times—high-G loops, rolls, and spins. John hung on desperately, fearing that if he was dislodged he might end up in one of those big squared-off engine intakes. Eventually the pilot seemed to give up, or maybe he wore himself out. John turned him a stern look. With his options exhausted, the pilot could only stare back. John took one hand from the wing and made a peremptory gesture—an order for the pilot to land his plane at once. The other planes paralleled them in futile formation. John could see their pilots conferring with each other, and probably with their base as well. Finally the pilot of John's plane signaled assent. The jets made a synchronized turn to a new heading.

A few minutes later they broke through the clouds. Spread out before them was an Air Force base near Wichita. It was a wide expanse of hangars, radomes, and many other structures, with warplanes parked in neat rows here and there. John eyed this with some apprehension. He had no experience with the military, and suddenly he felt that challenging it was perhaps more foolish and arrogant that his first flush of exhilaration had led him to believe. He decided his best option was to put on the best mask of confidence he could manage.

John relaxed on the wing as his plane touched down and taxied to the flight line. The engines began to spool down and John jumped to the ground. He shook his head—his ears felt cottony from the scream of the engines. He hoped his hearing was resilient as the rest of him.

They were met by several jeeps full of MPs armed with automatic rifles. The troops piled out and aimed their weapons at John, who was very uncomfortable about being the target of a group of armed and frightened men.

It took all the composure he could muster to maintain his air of confidence. He singled out their officer and said "If you men turn around and leave right now, I'll stay and explain myself. If you continue to threaten me, I'll flit away and you won't see me again. Ask these pilots if I can't do it."

The fighter pilots had climbed down from their cockpits and were standing off to the side. The MP lieutenant looked them over. "Can he do what he says, Colonel?"

The Colonel looked dazed. He stood with his flight helmet dangling from one hand as he stared blank-faced at John.

"Sir?"

The Colonel started and blinked. "Huh? Yes. Yes, he can. I don't know how, but this man flies better bare-assed than we do in our Eagles. You might as well back off."

The lieutenant lowered his weapon slowly and ordered his men to withdraw.

"You damaged my wing," said the Colonel, turning cautiously to John.

"What?" John looked at the plane. The leading edge of one wing was indeed crimped where he had gripped it. Had he really done that? "Well, sorry, but next time mind your own business and leave me alone, and maybe I won't have to hurt your plane," he blustered.

"How do you want to proceed?"

"Take me to your leader?"

"Um. You don't have any grudge against Air Force flag officers, do you?"

"Not yet."

"All right. Lieutenant, contact your commander and have him check with the CO's office about this. I don't want to just march this man in there without permission."

That left a long, awkward interval while they waited. No one seemed to know what to say. John manfully did his best to maintain his feigned air of confidence in the midst of his uncertainty and embarrassment. In his previous life he had not escaped the common dream of finding himself naked in a public place. Living out that dream in waking life was not comfortable.

Airmen approached driving tractors, ready to tow the planes to their hangars. In uncertain astonishment they stared at the spectacle of a naked man standing with a crowd of officers and MPs. John turned to them. "Excuse me. You, the tall one? Would you mind lending me your coverall? I'm not exactly dressed to meet your general."

The Colonel nodded. "Go ahead, give the man your garment."

The airman stripped down to his underwear and handed over the coverall. John felt far less conspicuous once he was wearing it.

"Sir? Permission to withdraw to quarters for new clothes?" said the airman. This was granted.

At length the lieutenant returned and spoke softly to the Colonel, who acknowledged the man and turned to John.

"All right, I've been authorized to take you to our commanding officer. Someone bring a car around."

"No, thanks. I try to avoid riding in cars. Where's the general's office?"

The Colonel rolled his eyes. "Oh man. Look, if you don't want to ride we'll just walk you over to him, all right? Please don't, uh, fly ahead."

John shrugged. "Good enough."

They strolled to the base HQ, accompanied by a growing retinue. No one wanted to miss the chance to glimpse the Skyman.

The procession entered a nondescript two-story building and filed through corridors, past an anteroom, and to an office with a heavy oaken door. Being cooped up in that building made John feel trapped and vulnerable.

A moment later John found himself confronting a lean, balding man at work behind a cluttered desk. He had about five rows of ribbons on his blue uniform jacket.

The general looked up at the intruder impassively.

"Airman? Don't you know enough to salute a general when you barge in on him?"

"This is the Skyman, sir," said the Colonel.

"General, I'm not an airman, or even a Skyman," said John. "I'm a Sky Ranger."

The general appeared taken aback for a moment. "Well, Sky Ranger, I wasn't aware we'd signed you up already."

"If those were recruiting tactics your pilots tried on me, I'd say they're a little too aggressive."

"Colonel, you and your men can leave us alone. I'll be interested to read your reports."

"Are you sure, sir?"

"Yes, I think our young guest here looks harmless enough."

The others filed out with many a backwards glance.

The general stood up and offered his hand. "I'm Eric Hunter, the base commander. The pilots who took those potshots at you weren't under orders to fire. One of them just got a little hot under the collar. I apologize for his rudeness. He will be disciplined. But give the man a break. He was never trained to deal with a man who can fly without using some noisy old airplane. None of us really know what to do when faced with the impossible or the ridiculous."

"Apology accepted." John took the proffered hand.

"Now, would you mind telling me who you are and what your purpose is?"

"I don't think I'm ready to give out my real name. I'd like to protect the privacy of my family for as long as I can."

"We can probably find out your name. You're not exactly in disguise."

John shrugged. "True. I'm just not going to make it any easier for you. As for my purpose, I intend to make myself generally useful, if I can."

"Useful to who?"

"To anyone with legitimate problems that I can correct."

"I see. The government would no doubt find it useful to learn how you are able to perform your remarkable feats."

John laughed loudly, but without malice. "General, I'm happy to tell you here and now how I perform those feats, and it won't do you a bit of good. I learned how to fly as a side-effect of thinking clean thoughts. Do you think the Air Force can teach that?"

"Are you serious?"

John fixed the general with a look most unequivocal. "I am indeed."

"So—you're not an alien?"

John was startled by this question. "An alien? No…I'm pretty sure I'm not. And now that I think about it, that question seems preposterous. I don't know anything about aliens, or even if any exist, but I think the chances of an alien looking so exactly human that you couldn't tell the difference are very slight. In fact I'd call the idea a lot of vain and childish nonsense."

Hunter, at a loss, stared into space for a moment and drummed his fingers.

"Then you are an anomaly. One-of-a-kind."

"Not necessarily," said John quietly. "But as far as I know, I am the only one. Mine is a—condition not casually or easily attained."

"That I can well believe. Still, the airspace of the United States is regulated by federal law. Your flying may be in violation of those laws."

John smiled and glanced around at the memorabilia scattered in Hunter's office. Pictures and models of pioneering high-performance aircraft brought something to mind.

"Eric Hunter. You were one of the top test pilots at Edwards, weren't you? First man to exceed Mach 3 in a rocket plane, right?"

"That's correct."

"Well, I'm the first man to exceed Mach 3 unassisted. I'm no lawyer, but I doubt that FAA regulations extend to a man in self-powered flight."

"I'm sure that's true at the present time."

"General, let me make myself clear. I don't want or intend to antagonize the U.S. military or anyone else. I want my contribution to the world to be wholly positive. But I will ignore attempts made by this government or any other to control or regulate me. I am a free agent with ready access to the world, and I'll stay that way."

Hunter reddened. "Are you a U.S. citizen?"

"I'm not sure. It depends on what statutes of limitation apply."

"Please don't be cryptic."

"To protect my privacy, I must be."

"How would you react to government interference in your activities?"

"Let's stick to your area of authority for now. In the air, I'd rip the canopies off your planes, reach into the cockpits and pull the ejection rings, then guide the empty planes to crash in an uninhabited area. I sincerely hope it will never come to that."

Hunter blinked. He was now facing audacity beyond reason.

"You can do that?" he said lamely.

"I can outfly anything in the air. I can hardly believe it myself, but it's true. Your men taught me that. Are you going to report all this to your superiors?"

Hunter sat with his palms flat on his desk, studying John.

"Yup. I'm pretty sure we have a carrier pigeon on the runway warming up for a flight to the Pentagon right now."

John laughed. "You don't seem like a bad guy, General."

"Thanks. That's the impression I try to convey to the naive and the uninitiated."

"And is that how you see me?"

Hunter thought for another few moments. "Just to look at you and talk to you, yes. But, considering the way you got here...I don't know what to think. Are you willing to meet with higher government officials if asked?"

"I'll talk to the President if he wants."

"How may we contact you?"

John frowned. "How did you track me today? I didn't think there was a radar capable of detecting a man at any distance."

Hunter smiled weakly. "It's reassuring that we at least have one secret you cannot divine."

"Touché. You may contact me by putting a message out over the air. We can agree on a frequency."

"You can hear radio waves?" asked Hunter half-seriously.

"No. I can get a radio."

"Very well. And what are we to call you?"

"Haven't we settled on Sky Ranger?"

John was in the air a few minutes later. Although he felt he had handled this encounter fairly well, any cockiness ebbed swiftly as he pondered the apparent fact that the government could track him by some unknown means.

He returned to the town where he'd spent the night, relieved to see it back to its normal peaceful self. His motel room was locked, and he'd lost the key. With some trepidation he entered the motel office. The clerk blinked at his USAF coverall and said, "Well, hello there. I wasn't sure if we'd see you again. It's past checkout time, you know."

"Yes, I suppose it is. Do you happen to have my things?"

The clerk reached behind the counter and produced John's pack. "Here you go. Did you boys find whatever it was you were looking for?"

"Uh, no, we didn't. Thanks for looking after my stuff."

"No problem, Mister Smith. Come back again."

John eyed this man with curiosity. He had stupidly rented his room under his own name, using his own credit card.

"Right. Thanks again." John departed, feeling cautiously hopeful that his carelessness might not have given away his identity, this time.

Hugging the ground, seeking overcast skies where possible, he took a circuitous route back to Rocky Mountain. As he spied Elise's dorm he considered flying on to some other destination. He had no reason to believe Elise expected or would welcome his return, and why risk her privacy? He then considered flying into her open window, but it was too dark inside to see well, and Elise might be standing right in his path for all he knew. Besides, his sudden arrival might frighten her. What if she wasn't even dressed?

In the end he landed in front of the building, approached the door, and knocked like a normal person. It opened to reveal one of the other rangers...Holly, was it? who looked at him askance, with his wild hair and unusual clothing.

"Er, hello. Is Elise here?"

"She might be. Who are you?"

"I'm her friend, John."

"Ah, the notorious John. Hold on and I'll see if she wants to deal with you right now."

Feeling like an intruder, and wondering how much Holly and the others knew about him, John waited. The longer he waited, the more uncomfortable and out of place he felt. A faint alarm was sounding in his mind. He was not only endangering Elise, he was also risking his own peace of mind, on which depended his anomalous status in the world, and his ability to bend its very nature to his will.

When Elise finally, and reluctantly, emerged, she found the doorstep unoccupied. She searched the sky, frowned, and retreated back into the house with a shrug.

While Elise prepared her lunch, John Avril sat on the summit of Storm King Peak, hundreds of miles away. Its north face fell thousands of feet to an alpine lake that glimmered at its foot. It was part of a remote range, rarely visited, and a very wild place. Turbulent clouds flowed by in a thick layer not far overhead, parting only occasionally to permit a searching beam of sunlight to sweep over the land.

In the midst of this solitude, John Avril sat and carefully stilled his mind, seeking to leave his past behind him, once again.

It was time to get down to the business of being Sky Ranger.

Chapter Six

John hurtled north along the spine of the Rockies. When he crossed the Canadian border he felt a little safer from interference—the American Air Force couldn't cross that line with all the freedom they might like, he hoped, and the Canadians probably didn't have the resources to dog him as thoroughly as the Americans could.

Living in Canada might ease some of his problems. Other than that, his plans were vague. He intended to stay in the Rockies—they had nurtured him, been the site of his second birth—he could hardly imagine living anywhere else. His options were limited by his financial resources. Unless he chose to waste his uniquely valuable time with a job of some kind, his wallet wasn't likely to get any fatter. That is, unless he found a way to profit from his new abilities—but that was contrary to his purpose and would surely erode the peace of mind he'd found so difficult to attain.

Of course, his powers in themselves constituted a great resource he could use in lieu of money to construct or obtain some sort of permanent dwelling. But that was a project better suited to spare moments over a lengthy period. If he was to transform himself in the eyes of the world from a freak of nature to a dependable and trusted force for good, he'd best get going. He needed a temporary dwelling in the meantime, and as he soared over the peaks and lakes north of Banff, his eagle's vision found one.

Far from any road, a tiny cabin stood in a clearing in a dense evergreen forest high on a mountain flank. The setting was superb—a cobalt-blue tarn nestled in a rocky bowl a short distance upslope, while the face of the mountain itself reared up like a guardian wall behind it. John made a slow, quiet overflight, but saw no sign of habitation or use. He turned back and alighted beside it.

The door swung open with a rusty protest. Inside, daylight leaked in through windows filmy with cobwebs. But the door was solid, and the windowpanes were intact. Squirrels and wood rats scurried from their nests as he entered. Empty tin cans littered the floor, and cold grey ashes filled the fireplace. There was no sign that anyone had been here in years.

A quick look around the grounds revealed why the cabin was hidden so well. In the back was a pile of bones and scraps of skin, plus a few broken horns—the horns of bighorn sheep. The cabin had probably been used by poachers who'd plundered nearby Banff National Park for trophy heads meant for the walls of people with money but neither ethics nor a steady aim. He kicked at the bones with contempt. If the poachers or their like happened to return while he occupied the cabin, they'd find themselves facing something wholly unanticipated.

Though filthy in more ways than one, the cabin was sound and most certainly secluded. John changed into normal clothes, lifted off, and soon returned with a broom, an ax, some cleansers, a few tools, and some food. His energetic sweeping and scrubbing sent billows of dust shooting out of the door and windows. In short order the cabin was habitable. He took another fifteen minutes to cut a large pile of firewood.

Food, water, warmth—he had everything he needed, with one exception—electricity. He'd need a small but dependable supply to power a radio, for without it or some other contact with the wider world, his contributions to its welfare could be only haphazard and sporadic. Commercial power was out, and a generator would be noisy, smelly, and troublesome. The ideal would be photovoltaics—solar electric cells—but they were very expensive, beyond what he could afford with his savings. In fact, they were so expensive that the only agency he knew that had them in any quantity was NASA, which used them to power spacecraft—like the abandoned Skylab space station...

He dropped his ax and stared up into the blank blue sky. Skylab was abandoned—he'd followed the space program closely and knew there were no plans to reoccupy it. With the extended Apollo lunar exploration going on, and work on the Space Shuttle proceeding at a painfully slow pace, Skylab had been forgotten. In time it would reenter the atmosphere and burn up uselessly. Attached to it were large arrays of silicon solar cells.

Of course, abandoned or not, Skylab didn't belong to him. He doubted that NASA had given up any claim to its ownership.

A short time later a thoughtful Sky Ranger sauntered into the law library at the University of Calgary. He'd already been to the science library to check on Skylab's current status and to ascertain that NASA truly had no further use for it. Finding his way around the law books was considerably more difficult, but he finally located an outline of international salvage law that he could puzzle out. As far as he could make out, it seemed that any craft or vessel which was abandoned by the original owners, with no intention of recovery on their part, became legal salvage for anyone who was able to claim it.

Well, of all men on Earth he was surely the only one personally able to take charge of Skylab! Or could he? He'd already flown at very high altitudes without ill effect—but venturing beyond even the last discernible wisps of the atmosphere might present him with challenges he hadn't foreseen. Only one way to find out!

His next stop was a hardware store, where he purchased a big hacksaw, wire cutters, some pliers and screwdrivers, and a tool belt. He lifted off, puttered back to his cabin, and changed into one of his remaining skating suits.

He had developed an internal sun clock, or more accurately a sun computer. Though without a watch, he knew perfectly well that the sun was some three hours from the horizon at this site. He was far from certain that was enough time for the mission he'd set himself, but he'd give it a try.

With his gaze turned skyward once again, he laughed with the excitement and sheer unlikeliness of what he was about to attempt. He fell into the sky, soared some miles through canyons and valleys to put distance between himself and his refuge, then shot straight up with a sense of abandon. Let the military track him! No airplane could follow where he proposed to go. Slowly at first he passed through the cool spectrum of darkening sky colors that led into space. He put on more speed as the air grew thin. Noise and turbulence died around him, and the tools hung heavy at his waist as he continued to accelerate. He could feel his eardrums bulging, and he swallowed constantly to relieve the pressure. His lungs felt cold and constricted as their contents escaped into the near-emptiness around him.

The Pacific Ocean was easily visible in the west as the edge of the world began to show its curvature. In the opposite direction he could glimpse the Great Lakes just coming into view. The atmosphere was confined to a diffuse blue band that blended the rim of the world with the awful blackness of the sky above it. He was in space!

Overwhelmed by the view, stunned by the scope of his abilities, John relaxed his flight impulse and went into free fall. The tools on his belt began to float on their hooks. The Sun glared fiercely; even he couldn't bear to look at it for more than an instant. It was a harsh white in color, an unfamiliar orb to one used to the gentler aspect of a sun tamed and filtered by the atmosphere. Only by shading his eyes and turning away from it and the bright bluish-tan surface below could John glimpse even a few stars.

His speed was only about a thousand miles per hour, far short of that needed to enter an orbit or escape the Earth. Thus Earth's omnipresent gravity slowed him as he floated and gaped, and soon began to pull him down again.

And it was just as well. His heart was pounding with excitement, making impossible demands on lungs empty of all but a few useless atoms of gas. John abruptly realized he was in pain, with an urgent need to breathe and lungs that felt like they were full of ground glass.

He turned nose down and added his impulse to the force of gravity. He bored down through the upper atmosphere and in a few minutes was cruising at 10,000 feet, gratefully ventilating his lungs in air that felt thick and warm as soup.

A valuable lesson learned—he needed some trace of air to function for more than a few minutes. Lacking the space equivalent of a scuba outfit, how much time would he gain by simply holding his breath rather than letting his lungs empty into the vacuum?

He hyperventilated for a minute, filled his lungs, and again soared into the nearest reaches of space. After a few minutes in another suborbital trajectory he felt fine.

Now he confronted the problem of how to find Skylab in the vast volume of low Earth orbit space it inhabited. Skylab was the biggest thing in orbit, so it ought to be easy to see if he could get close enough. However, if it was currently on the night side of its orbit he might have to wait 45 minutes or so for it to enter his general vicinity.

Shading his eyes from the sun's arc-light fire, John began to search the sky for satellites. It took only a moment to see that he was dealing with an embarrassment of riches. Tiny starlike dots swept across the sky almost everywhere. How was he to guess which one of this multitude was Skylab? He spotted an unusually bright object approaching from the east. As it got nearer he could make out its cylindrical shape—this could be Skylab. It was about a hundred miles higher than he was. He let it sweep nearer and then began to pour on speed to match its orbital velocity of some 17,500 miles per hour. Achieving this kind of astonishing speed was actually easier than flying at Mach 3 in the lower atmosphere, thanks to the lack of air resistance.

He began to make out details as he closed to within 30 miles of the satellite. It had a large rocket motor mounted on one end and a big paraboloidal antenna on the other. Not Skylab—but then what was it? He decided to investigate and closed to within a few yards. The satellite was surprisingly big, about a hundred feet from end to end. Large attitude-control thrusters bristled from the hull—between them and the big main engine, it looked like this thing was designed to go somewhere in a hurry. It was unmarked, but had an awkward look that he'd come to associate with Soviet space hardware. Could it be a Russian space station? No—it had no windows, and no docking port for visiting spacecraft.

John made a slow tour of the inert, enigmatic object. The main dish antenna was not pointed Earthward, which seemed to rule out it being some kind of radar spy satellite. He caught a flash of movement—a mirror pivoting beneath a sun-shade cowling. The moving mirror brought into view a lens system, now pointed straight at him.

This was a highly mobile satellite designed to detect, rendezvous with, and observe other orbiting objects. This sudden deduction caused him to zoom away. The satellite exploded behind him...

In Cheyenne Mountain, an alarm horn sounded and characters flashed in red on a large CRT display. The sergeant at the console called to the major at the far end of the control room, who was already on his way after hearing the alarm. The sergeant pointed to his radar screen, where an expanding spherical nebula had joined a constellation of orbiting points.

General Eric Hunter stood looking over the sergeant's shoulder.

"General, Subject AHE-01 achieved a rendezvous with the big Soviet satellite that was launched last week. The satellite now appears to have exploded."

"What the hell is an AHE-01?" demanded Hunter.

"Anomalous Humanoid Entity Number One, sir."

"Okay, I don't know who got paid to think up that bullshit, but we're scrapping it right now. He has a name. He calls himself the Sky Ranger. Where is he now?"

"Don't see him yet, sir. His signal is still confused with the debris cloud."

"Did Sky Ranger ram the satellite?"

"Negative, sir. He was leaving the Russian bird when it blew."

The gaunt-faced general rubbed his chin. "So our young friend can fly into orbit anytime he pleases." Hunter shook his head in appreciative wonder.

"What kind of a bird do you think he flushed out there, General?" asked the major.

"You mean the satellite? It's an ASAT. Anti-satellite hunter-killer. We already knew that much." Hunter gave a hard, wicked grin. "The Russians must have picked up Sky Ranger's baby-faced smile on their sensors and blown their bird to keep him from capturing it, or maybe out of sheer panic. They must be going ape over in Moscow. I'm sure they didn't plan on testing this thing over the state of Washington."

Hunter picked up the phone to the NORAD commander. He set it down and chuckled. "Your CO is on the phone to Washington with this interesting tidbit about the peaceful Russian space effort. Ought to open a few eyes out there."

The sergeant, his eyes still glued to his screen, spoke up. "Picking up a target separating from the cloud. Leaving the area and accelerating rapidly. Looks like the Sky Ranger, sir."

"Good boy!" said Hunter.

The major turned a wry look of puzzlement on his superior. "General, this is certainly a tricky situation. Won't the Russians protest our interference with their satellite?"

"And admit to having a functioning ASAT capability? Not hardly. They might complain that we've blown up a peaceful weather satellite, but after we get through with them no one will believe it. Besides, Sky Ranger's not exactly under our control, is he?"

"He sure isn't. What are we going to do about him, sir?"

"Major, as of today, that's what I'm being paid to find out."

The exploded satellite looked like a twinkling star cluster in the distance. At this moment John was willing to bet that the Russians, or whoever had owned that satellite, were angry with him. But considering the obvious purpose of their satellite, he felt no guilt. He reached down and rubbed the bruises he'd collected from shrapnel from the explosion. They stung a bit, but there was no blood. It seemed that being able to fly at orbital speeds brought with it a certain level of durability. He was more rueful about the holes in this, his second skating suit of only three. The suit was still usable if he took it easy and repaired the rips as soon as possible, but he began to wonder if he shouldn't just give up on the idea of wearing clothes and start referring to himself as Nakedman.

He glanced up as movement again caught his eye. A very bright object was drifting by, not 100 miles away. His eagle's vision revealed its characteristic windmill shape. There was Skylab! He quickly caught up with the big station and slowed to fly in formation with it. It looked magnificent in the intense sunlight—gold sunshields, erected in the aftermath of the launch accident that had torn off the original shield, glittered blindingly. The five solar arrays, four that radiated like windmill blades from the Apollo Telescope Mount, and the blunter panel that remained on the workshop, gleamed with reflections of deep purple and royal blue. They looked like they were coated with a lacquer made from amethyst and sapphire. John suddenly coveted them as much for their beauty as for their utility. The panels, and the station as a whole, appeared in to be good condition, as it had not been abandoned long. Pausing along the flank of the cylindrical workshop, he peered into the 18-inch porthole. The interior looked sad and haunted in the light that leaked in over the lattice flooring, casting strange shadows.

He pulled away, entered the shade of the docking module, and felt an urge to enter and explore this lonely outpost. But he knew nothing about operating the station—even if he could get in, he might be unable to use the airlock, or even turn on the lights. Best to limit his vandalism as much as possible.

He drifted around to the Apollo Telescope Mount with its radial solar panels. He'd already decided to take one of them— they were smaller than the array remaining on the workshop, and could be more easily spared if NASA did ever decide to revisit the station. The optics of the numerous solar telescopes of the ATM were protected by oddly shaped white covers. He slid one aside and looked admiringly into the precision mirror system that had once imaged the sun with unprecedented clarity from this lofty vantage.

Feeling some misgivings, he unlatched his hacksaw from his belt. Each of the four long panels was attached to the central body of the ATM by five main spars. He selected a panel, grabbed a spar, and quickly sawed through it in a strange silence. Aluminum sawdust drifted away. He was a very energetic hacksawyer—in minutes he'd severed every spar and cable and had the big array floating free.

Guilt flared up again as he saw the results of his handi-work on the already injured station. He kept telling himself that the station was doomed in any event, but he hated to contribute to its destruction. What could he do to repay NASA for what he'd taken? He knew the Skylab would fall into the atmosphere in a few years if not boosted to a higher orbit. But that boost would require a visit from the Space Shuttle, a troubled vehicle still years from its first flight. Certainly NASA didn't want to divert valuable Apollo hardware from its extended moon program to save the station. The only "booster" John could think of for the job was—himself.

John wished he had air to spare for laughter—it was a fitting response for a thought so outrageous. Yet instead of dismissing it, he found himself reviewing his knowledge of orbital mechanics. To raise the orbit he'd have to start by adding energy to the station—to give Skylab a push, in other words. But he'd have to push along the long axis of the station, and it was flying in a "nose down" attitude. First step—he grabbed the docking ring at the end of the docking module and carefully rotated the 100-ton station to line it up with its orbital motion. He moved slowly to keep from overshooting the desired attitude and perhaps stressing the station by trying to stop it too quickly. Then he put his shoulder to the docking ring and started pushing. He had no real way to gauge what he was doing, but he put about as much effort into it as would have been required to accelerate himself to Mach 2 at sea level. He hoped that would be enough, but not too much! To boost Skylab entirely out of Earth orbit would be a mishap both embarrassing and hard to explain.

He relaxed, let go and sailed back to where his panel glittered in the sun. He watched as the Station slowly retreated. By adding the extra energy he had de-circularized the station's orbit. It was now climbing toward a new apogee height, which it would attain half way around its orbit. Then it would drop back to the same perigee at which it had started. To circularize the orbit at the higher level, he'd have to catch it at its apogee and give it another push. But that was a project for another day. Today it would reach that highpoint while over the planet's night side. Besides, the shadows were getting long down in Alberta, and it was time to be heading down to the ground.

In Cheyenne Mountain, high-ranking military officers crowded around the consoles while the President called periodically to get the latest information. General Hunter, the new Sky Ranger Information Project Commander, was on the line with him right now.

"That's right, Mr. President, after triggering the detonation of the Russian ASAT, Sky Ranger rendezvoused with our Skylab. Our ground-based optics reveal that he has detached one of the solar cell panels from the station. Hold on, sir, I'm getting a new report..."

The console sergeant announced, "Change in Skylab velocity. It is accelerating along its orbital path."

"Mr. President, it appears that Sky Ranger is giving the station a push. No, he's speeding it up. If he meant to crash it he'd slow it down. Yes sir, it is NASA property. But as I recall, it was your science advisor who recommended that no further missions to the station be funded. Hold on please..."

"Skylab no longer accelerating. Sky Ranger is separating and returning to the detached panel."

Another phone rang. CINC NORAD himself picked it up.

"Yes?" He listened, hung up, and looked at Hunter. "Skylab has entered a new orbit which will bring it to an apogee of about eight hundred nautical miles."

"Mr. President, Sky Ranger seems to be engaged in putting the Skylab into a new orbit that will be stable for about a thousand years. A little hard to reach, but stable. Sir, I'm having the time of my life with this assignment. Yes sir, we'll look forward to your call."

Hunter hung up and looked at his colleagues.

CINC NORAD shook his head in bewilderment. "What do you make of this Sky Ranger, Eric?"

Hunter grinned. "The kid's got style. I like him. My first impression was that he's a naive kid who has a fairly simple-minded view of the world. That much may be true. But he's sure on to something that none of us men of the world can match, isn't he? I wonder what he'll do next."

The question now was how to get the fragile solar array down on the ground intact, and without wasting too much time. He had some distance to cover to get home—following Skylab in its orbit had taken him halfway across the Pacific. He'd have to slow the panel down to almost zero speed before he'd dare enter the atmosphere with it, but he couldn't slow it too fast or it would break up.

He grabbed the panel and twisted it to put it face on to its direction of motion. Then he plastered himself spread-eagled to the middle of its leading face. He wanted to apply force through the maximum amount of surface area he could cover to minimize the stress on the delicate structure. He began to slow down, vectoring his flight impulse from his front to his back, rather than from his nose to his feet—a difference that required some concentration. Too much force! The long, narrow array began to flex and vibrate. This was wrong—he was pushing the panel along its weakest direction. He'd either wreck it or take too long to make the large velocity changes he needed. He flipped it again—this time he lined it up lengthwise with its orbital path, and pushed as if he were shoving a sheet of plywood over a table. He wished he knew how to fold the panel to its original compact configuration, but he didn't, and couldn't afford the time to experiment.

He pushed as hard as he dared. The sun was behind him—he looked over his shoulder and saw it was already getting down toward the horizon, and he was still far west of his destination. He had little time. He debated leaving the panel in orbit and trying to relocate it tomorrow. But he'd already changed its speed quite a bit—certainly enough to cause it to reenter the atmosphere in a short time if he left it now. He could re-boost it, but he had no real way to know what kind of an orbit he'd put it into—he might never see it again. He resumed pushing steadily, eyes down to the blue and white vastness of the Pacific. The Hawaiian Islands were in the clear; he used them to judge his progress. Finally they stopped their apparent slide to the east, stood still, and slowly seemed to creep to the west. He'd have to return to Alberta, stop again, then slowly guide the panel down through the atmosphere.

He glanced back at the sun. It was only a few degrees over the rim of the world; it must already be down in Alberta. Now what? He grew hot with embarrassment as he considered the possibility that he might be forced to abandon the panel and let it burn up. Well, he obviously wasn't going to spend tonight in the cabin. He'd have to settle for the nearest landfall—the islands below.

He began to pull the panel westward to kill its slight eastward speed. With close to zero velocity relative to the ground, gravity dragged them down. John didn't resist at first, but then he began to apply power to keep the panel from falling in at a dangerous speed. The islands grew larger, and a trace of violet returned to the sky. John grabbed onto the center of the array and dangled beneath it. As the air thickened it began to flutter like a falling leaf. John hung on and kept it under control.

Wind, sound, and skylight returned. John belatedly realized he could breathe again. He expelled his hoarded lungful and gladly sucked in fresh stratospheric air. He'd held his breath for over half an hour without discomfort.

The islands assumed a look of depth and mass as he closed in on them. He was over the western end of the chain—below was Kauai, with a smaller island just to the west and a still smaller one west of that. He decided to hide the panel on that islet, which he hoped was uninhabited. By now the air was so thick that he stopped bothering to fly— he just let himself fall with the big, springy panel acting like a parachute. A few minutes later he eased down to a soft landing near the center of the tiny island, a rather barren outcrop of rock and scrub.

He must hurry. He couldn't have been a more blatant radar target on his long, fluttering descent, and the sun was about to touch the horizon. If he didn't want any possible pursuers to catch him here in his de-powered state, he'd better get out soon. Using his full speed he ripped up some sparse, arid growth and tried to conceal the panel. It might easily still be found, but it couldn't be helped. That done, he ripped into the air, glad to be free of the encumbrance of the panel, and sped east, flying just above the waves. He touched down on a beach on Kauai just as the sun dipped down, leaving him slow, weak-sighted, and flightless—normal, in other words.

John sighed and relaxed. He began to stroll down the beach, with no destination in mind. Just inland he saw occasional car headlights through the trees as darkness came on. He walked a couple of miles in the tropical dusk and came to the town of Waimea. He'd never been to Hawaii before—to come here unexpectedly under these circumstances seemed incredibly exotic and romantic. He peeled off his hood and continued into town, ignoring the smiles and odd looks he got from the tourists and townsfolk. Would they figure out who he was? Probably they would tomorrow when they learned he'd been detected in their area. For now they seemed to view him only as a young man with a curious wardrobe—perhaps a scuba diver with a moth problem.

He had a twenty dollar bill rolled up in his damaged skating suit. He took a table at an outdoor restaurant built on a terrace on the beach. He smiled tiredly at the plump Polynesian waitress and ordered fruit, rice, and stir-fried vegetables. The night was extravagantly lush, with warm breezes carrying fragrances from both sea and forest. A crescent moon kept company with Venus and Saturn in the west. John caught his first glimpse of the Southern Cross as it hovered near the southern horizon. Glittering fiercely just over the horizon was Alpha Centauri, nearest star system to the Sun, another first sighting for him.

All in all, he was satisfied with his day, long as it had been. But he wished for a moment that Elise could be here to share this beauty with him.

When he finished eating he strolled back up the beach, found a soft spot under some palms, and slept soundly until the voice of Aurora bid him awake again.

A phone rang in Cheyenne Mountain; Hunter's personal aide picked it up. "Radars at Pearl and Midway show the panel down on the islet of Kaula," he reported.

A console operator spoke up. "Red Eye 2 picking up a weak signal—he's heading east at about Mach 1, altitude very low."

CINC NORAD looked at Eric Hunter. "Any idea why Sky Ranger would want to transport a Skylab solar panel to the Hawaiian Islands?"

Hunter looked at the big map display on the wall. The shading that marked the sunset line was just west of Kauai.

"It looks to me like he wanted to get down before dark. If he navigates mainly by sight, he may not be too confident about night flying. My guess is he'll pop up in the morning and head back to Alberta with the panel. What's the story on the Russians, General?"

"We're providing them with a desensitized version of our data on the Sky Ranger. The President wants to convince them that Sky Ranger is neither known to us nor is a weapon under our control. Their claim that we blew up a 'peaceful weather satellite' is almost mild—they're so embarrassed they're practically inventing excuses for us."

Hunter chuckled.

"Sirs, Red Eye 2 has lost signal near the island of Kauai."

"Ha! If I were Sky Ranger I'd rather spend the night on Kauai than on some rock too," said Hunter.

"Without Sky Ranger on guard, it looks like we can get that panel back if we want to," said CINC NORAD.

"Yes sir, I guess that's true. But I don't recommend it. We got a real bargain in exchange for that panel. Even if we never visit Skylab again, we won't have to worry about the political fallout if it should reenter and fall on somebody. In fact…" Hunter drummed his fingers for a moment, then turned to his aide. "Jim, I need to talk to somebody high up in NASA. And find a helicopter somewhere in the Islands that will reach this Kaula."

In the morning John woke up and charged back over the water to Kaula.

The solar array was not as he'd left it. To begin with, it was neatly folded to occupy about a fifth of its former area. Even so, he was struck by its size. He must not have been thinking too clearly yesterday. A single section of this array would have been more than sufficient for his modest needs. Well, maybe he'd someday find a use for the surplus power.

Second, nearby was an aluminum box the size of a large suitcase. Its matte-silver surface had both NASA and USAF markings. Rather guilelessly, he walked over, flipped the latches, and opened it up. It contained an electronic "black box", a spool of electrical cable, and some sealed battery cells.

Third was an envelope taped to the box. He opened it and removed a document. It read:

The National Aeronautics and Space Administration and the United States Air Force donate this surplus power equipment for the personal use of Sky Ranger, with the compliments of the President of the United States.

There was also a letter typed on USAF stationery:

Dear Sky Ranger,

NASA and the Air Force really appreciate the service you've done us by boosting Skylab into a higher orbit. However, NASA requests that you confer with them before taking any similar actions with their other vehicles. NASA wants you to have the panel. And to make up for those pot-shots we took at you a couple days ago, we're throwing in some other equipment you might need. Use it all in good health and don't worry. You're a good boy. Drop in for a visit anytime you please.

(signed)
Eric Hunter
Commander, Sky Ranger
Information Project

John dropped the letter to his side and threw his head back in laughter. He wondered if it wouldn't save time if he just filed a flight plan with the Air Force every time he went anywhere. He wished he knew how they managed to track him with such apparent ease.

A third item in the envelope was an instruction manual for wiring up the panels. They were to be connected to the battery, which in turn was to feed the "black box", an inverter to produce standard AC house current. The booklet also gave suggestions for weatherproofing the space-rated panels. They'd thought of everything.

The final sheet described the times and coordinates where Skylab could be found at its apogee over the next few days, to aid him in circularizing its orbit.

Once he'd absorbed all this, John ferried the case and panel to Alberta, where the day was already hours old. He entered the mountains, skimming through wild valleys, hoping to baffle whatever surveillance was being used against him.

He was relieved to find the cabin undisturbed—he'd half expected to find it ransacked by government agents. He assembled his tools and got to work, mounting two of the five panels on the roof—they more than covered the cabin. He'd store the other three nearby as replacements.

At the proper time he made a direct ascent into orbit, neatly rendezvousing with Skylab as it reached the peak of its orbit. He pushed the station gently until he had no sense that it was losing altitude. That should give it a roughly circular orbit—he was sure he'd hear about it if he'd goofed and sent it plunging on some wild loop.

He returned to the cabin and plugged his radio into an outlet mounted right on the inverter. These past few days he'd spent far too much time messing around, trying to get himself in order, while accomplishing little. He had to get busy if the people of the world were to come to view him as a force for good and not merely some mysterious mischief maker. The sooner he got started the more trust he could earn.

The first thing the radio picked up was an interview with Bill Waters that came crackling over the AM band.

"Yeah, that Sky Ranger guy helped get me down. I'm grateful for that, but I think I could've wrestled my bird down myself. The air was fairly calm and the ground was level. All I had to do was drop out of the clouds and touch down on some nice flat pasture."

True, but he'd have to be in control of the plane and himself before he could do that! John laughed ruefully. He settled down for a serious radio vigil.

Forty-five minutes later a blue bolt erupted from the cabin, rushed through a few random valleys, then drilled into the heights faster than any bullet made by man. The thunder of its sonic boom was the first hint to many of the locals that something beyond the ordinary had taken roost among the peaks of their mountain home.

Twenty minutes later, in Bakersfield, California, the universe threw a wild card into the chaotic game of human life. From beyond hope came an anomaly, a singular violation of all known physical law, to frustrate madness and thwart death for a time. A crack of thunder sounded, and a blinding golden blur interposed itself between a sputtering automatic weapon and a bus full of young school children. The blur focused into the form of a young man as the projectiles slammed into him, their momentum knocking him off his feet and kicking him back. But then he gathered himself, rose to his feet and appeared to lean into the stream of bullets, advancing against it, ignoring the impacts, as though he could negate them simply by an act of will. The gunman appeared oblivious to this wonder—his face remained set and his eyes glazed—and if he saw before him the implacable advance of Nemesis, perhaps it was no more than he'd expected to find as the price of his deeds.

The rifle clip ran out. Before the gunman could fit another, the rifle was ripped from his hands, breaking his wrist in the process. He found himself slammed to the ground hard enough to skew his vision and knock the breath out of him.

Sky Ranger, who had left his second skating suit behind as a hot vapor in the ionosphere, stood over the killer and stared down with fierce eyes at his tousled head and pseudo-military clothing. Paramedics rushed forward to attend to those who'd already been shot—several children, the bus driver, and a policeman. Other policemen ran forward, holding their revolvers stiff-armed on the killer, while their glances and an occasional gun barrel strayed toward Sky Ranger.

Assured that his prey was down, John turned and walked unsteadily toward the bus. The uninjured children were being led off. They barely noticed him—even the sight of a man naked in public was insufficient to penetrate the fog of shock and fear that muffled their minds. John climbed up into the bus, its windows shattered and its side peppered with bullet holes. The paramedics huddled over several wounded children.

"This boy needs blood within a few minutes or he'll die," said one.

John said nothing. He stepped forward, and without anyone's leave, lifted the boy carefully, left the bus, and made a gentle takeoff. He departed the scene of the massacre in full few of spectators, the police, and a local TV news camera crew. The onlookers weren't quite sure what to feel, weren't quite sure just what they'd seen. The younger children thought they saw an angel, which was something that grownups had always assured them really existed, so it seemed reasonable to finally see one. The older kids saw something that both tested and confirmed their parent's professed belief in the inevitable triumph of order and goodness. The adults saw something most unexpected — that whatever despair their lives might have driven them to, however cynical they had become in the face of futility, evil, and madness — miracles *were* possible.

Two minutes later, Sky Ranger delivered the boy to an emergency room, where he was saved.

Television networks later aired the video without any attempt to conceal Sky Ranger's nudity, nor any reference to it. So compelling was the image of murder being stopped by a factor beyond all expectation that even the breaking of this taboo seemed insignificant.

And that was only the beginning.

Chapter Seven

A few days later, General Hunter entered the White House for a meeting with the President and his chosen aides and appointees. He sat exchanging polite greetings with the men, mostly civilians, who arrived to take their places at the meeting table. Hunter soon concluded he'd be, in effect, the lowest-ranking person at the meeting, and also the target of most of the questions, which would make this more of an interrogation than an interview for him. Luck might have made him head of the Sky Ranger Information Project rather than CO of an airbase whose main mission was to reelect a congressman, but Sky Ranger-related policy decisions would be made by figures far over his head. The President, accompanied by the Canadian ambassador, arrived last. Everyone rose in greeting. The President waved them back down. Introductions were made, and the President turned directly to Hunter.

"Well, General, we're here to make some preliminary decisions on how to deal with this unprecedented, uh, unless you read comic books, person, whom we're calling Sky Ranger. First of all, do we have a less, uh, colorful name to apply to this man?"

"Mr. President, I'd like to refer that question to Director Horton. He's been conducting this investigation at my request, since we assume Sky Ranger is a civilian."

FBI Director Horton frowned in clear dislike of what he had to say. "Sir, we have not determined the Sky Ranger's identity as yet. We have fingerprints, but no match in our files. We have agents showing our best photographs in the areas he's known to have visited, but so far nothing has turned up. The best pictures are none too good. The only potentially recognizable ones were taken with long lenses while Sky Ranger was in action on the ground. He moves very fast. Pictures of him in flight are useless as his features are distorted by the airblast."

Horton passed out glossy prints of a few photographs showing a rather distant, blurred figure.

"We've interviewed people who've sighted him in Colorado, but no one has recognized him. So far he's not known to have done anything there except rescue that pilot and make an inquiry at a sporting goods shop."

"What kind of an inquiry?" asked the President.

"He asked where he could buy speed-skater's uniforms."

Remo Cosimano, one of the President's security advisors, spoke up. "You believe Sky Ranger has some prior connection with that area."

"That is correct," said Horton.

"I suggest you check the local banks for large withdrawals or recent account closeouts. Also check all recent sales of skating suits anywhere in Colorado. You wouldn't expect them to sell well at this time of year."

Horton blinked. "Good idea."

"Anything else?" asked the President.

Horton continued. "Mr. President, the pictures are also widely distributed over the media. We've received many identifications from members of the public, including some of people who are known or believed dead. Most such claims are easily dismissed. We plan to turn our attention to the Estes Park-Rocky Mountain National Park area in Colorado, as the first detections of Sky Ranger took place in that area. The staff of the Park are Federal employees, so we should be able to question them more closely than we can other civilians."

"We'll take that up later. General Hunter, what are your capabilities for locating the Sky Ranger?"

"Sir, he's invisible on the ground, and not too easy to spot in the air. He has a poor radar signature unless he's carrying a metallic object, and as we know, he has trouble even keeping a shirt on his back. The Red Eye series of infrared surveillance satellites can detect him under good conditions, especially if he's above the cloud deck and making enough speed to generate some friction heat. That's it for NORAD-related sensors. His sonic boom can be heard when he's supersonic at relatively low altitudes. And we have a surprising number of ground-based visual sightings—if he's flying over low clouds, he often pops down for a look at the ground. If he's not in a hurry he sometimes even lands, apparently just to smell the flowers."

The FBI director turned to him in irritation. "You could easily have put a radio beacon in that box of electrical equipment you gave him. At least then we'd know where he spends the night."

"My plan was to gain his confidence, not antagonize him."

The President broke in. "And that is the plan we will follow unless we find a definite reason against it."

"Thank you, Sir." Hunter nodded toward the Canadian. "As the Ambassador knows, we've already determined that Sky Ranger has taken to spending his nights somewhere in the Banff area of Alberta."

"And we'd like to thank your government for its cooperation, and for tolerating the unconventional activities and presence of our mysterious citizen in your country."

"Thank you, Mr. President. We are really quite intrigued by him. Our view is that he is, or will soon become, a matter of concern beyond the borders of the U.S.A. alone."

"Are we convinced that he is in fact a United States citizen?" asked Horton.

Hunter answered. "No, he could be a flying Russian for all we know. But I spoke to him, and he had no trace of an accent, either foreign or regional. I suppose he might be a Canadian."

"Draft evader," snapped Cosimano.

"What?" said Hunter.

"I've read the transcript of your conversation with him. The bit about his being unsure whether he's still a citizen. Could be he's in Canada now because that's where he ran to stay out of Vietnam."

"That's an interesting guess, but nothing else," said Hunter.

The President broke in. "Mr. Ambassador, I believe your government has plans to locate Sky Ranger's hideout?"

"Yes, sir. Our air force will soon begin a photographic reconnaissance of the whole Banff area. We reason that the solar panels you gave him, if in use, will be fairly easy to spot from the air. Of course, we're dealing with an area of over ten thousand square miles, so it could take some time."

"I suggest you limit your searches to times when Sky Ranger is known to be out of the area," said Hunter. "Otherwise your pilots could find themselves being forcibly ejected from their planes. The boy is touchy about his privacy."

"Your warning is well taken."

"All right," said the President, "I'd like your specific recommendations on how to deal with Sky Ranger over the short term. Glen?"

Horton said, "Sir, Sky Ranger is a complete unknown and a potential danger. I recommend that we make every effort to learn everything we can about him, monitor him, and prepare to take him down if he becomes a threat or an embarrassment to this country."

"I would amplify what Mr. Horton has said," said Cosimano. The Sky Ranger is not only a chaotic, uncontrollable element in the world, but I believe he represents a danger to order and to respect for law in this country. His stunts and antics hold the public enthralled. By flouting certain laws and regulations, and in effect superseding authority in the situations in which he's intervened, he is breeding a lack of respect for our institutions. His pillage of Skylab is a perfect example."

Hunter fixed him with a fighter-jock's stare. "His 'pillage' was more accurately the salvage of a derelict vehicle."

"Fine. We can be grateful he didn't elect to 'salvage' the panels from one of our surveillance satellites."

"Gentlemen," said the President. "Remo, it seems clear that his choice of Skylab was deliberate and well-considered. I agree that it would have been far preferable, though, if he'd asked our permission before taking that action."

"Sir, in my opinion it would have been preferable if he'd asked our permission merely to come into existence. I would have withheld it."

Hunter's reply was icy. "That would have been unfortunate for the fifty-some Americans and Canadians whose lives he's saved so far."

Cosimano replied in kind. "General, no man should be able to fly without having one of your airplanes wrapped around him. If I were in a situation whose natural outcome should be that I lose my life, I would rather lose it than see order and sanity discarded to preserve it. He may be thwarting the will of God."

"That is an extreme view. I'll try to see that Sky Ranger learns of it."

The President cut off what promised to be a caustic rejoinder. "That's enough. General... "

"Pardon me, sir, but I haven't yet given my specific recommendation," said Cosimano with some asperity.

The President blinked. "Proceed," he said cooly.

"First, I advise that we investigate all employees of Rocky Mountain National Park and also interrogate them for reasons of national security. Once we learn Sky Ranger's identity, we should locate his family, or anyone close to him, who could be used to exert control over him. Also, we should attempt to describe and quantify his abilities and devise a means to destroy him, if the need should arise, as I believe it will."

"Did you wake up on the wrong side of the Berlin Wall this morning?" muttered Hunter. This brought an annoyed glance from the Chief Executive.

"Your views, General?"

"Sir—" he paused, regaining his balance and deciding how far he wanted to commit himself. "I believe that Sky Ranger is a fine young man of untold promise and value to our country. I say this on the basis of the good he's done already, and also from my personal experience. He said he was prepared to meet with you. I request that you do so, in order to form your own opinion of his character. Beyond that, I say study him, yes, but don't harass or alienate him. Let's keep him on our side."

"Mr. President, I'm sure the Secret Service would object strenuously to your meeting with an anonymous individual who may have the power to kill you at will, regardless of any precautions," said Cosimano.

"Good point. General?"

"Sir, Sky Ranger has the ability to drill his way through a wall of air at hypersonic speeds. To be blunt, if he wanted you dead, I think he could tear his way through to you at any time."

"Hmm. That's quite an image you create. I suppose you're right—in that case I don't see why I shouldn't go ahead and get to know the man, try to influence him. Remo, your suggestions seem a bit harsh, though well intended. For now, I direct you to cooperate with Glen on a low-profile investigation of the Rocky Mountain Park personnel, but there is to be no questioning or interfering with them at this time."

"Of course, sir."

"All right. We've discussed our plans; now let's get to the man himself. I guess the evidence is irrefutable—Sky Ranger does fly, and in fact he outflies everything that ever flew. I don't mind telling you gentlemen that I grew up thinking that kind of thing was limited to Peter Pan and Superman. Is there anyone in this room who can explain how he does it? Carl? Could he have a concealed device of some kind that allows him to fly?"

The President's science advisor gave his answer. "Sir, as you know, he has often been observed to fly in the nude, which would indicate against any large device on his person. Any such mechanism would have to be concealed within his body. However, it would have to be non-metallic, or Sky Ranger would have a much stronger radar signature. Also, it would have to be incredibly efficient to produce that kind of thrust while creating so little waste heat. Any amount of excess heat would certainly show up strongly to the Red Eye birds. Finally, such a device could not permit Sky Ranger, if human, to endure the enormous stresses of flying at such high speeds. Very few aerospace materials are capable of it, let alone flesh. I think it extremely unlikely that there is anything technological about Sky Ranger's powers."

"But where does that leave us, Carl?"

"It leaves us in the hands of a creature of the Devil," muttered Cosimano.

"Well sir, I'm not ready to appeal to magic just yet. His powers could be based on some unknown aspect of the natural world that is not yet accessible to machines, but which might be tapped by the mind directly."

"And that's not magic?" asked the President.

"It depends on how you care to define the term."

"You're implying that a team of research scientists wouldn't find a way to duplicate Sky Ranger's abilities."

"I'm stating it. There is no real theoretical or conjectural basis for them."

Hunter spoke up. "Mr. President, I'm inclined to take Sky Ranger at his word. He has an air of integrity about him which I believe would impress you. He implied that he learned to fly accidentally, as the result of some kind of study or meditation. I find no reason to suspect anything else."

"So you think he's some guru or yogi who can levitate while probing for Nirvana?" asked Cosimano sarcastically.

Hunter's eyes lit up, then he smothered a snort of laughter.

"We could all use a laugh, General," chided the President.

"Ah—sorry sir, an irrelevant thought just crossed my mind. A bad joke."

"Very well. General, continue your mission. Cozy up to Sky Ranger if you can. And let's leave things at that for now."

Chapter Eight

Remo Cosimano chose to interpret his instructions broadly. He located sandy-haired young agents bearing a vague resemblance to Sky Ranger and sent them into the park under various guises—as tourists, a repairman, a forester, and a visiting Ranger.

Early one morning, one of these men, walking through Park Headquarters in the guise of a copier repair man, noticed a blonde Ranger giving him a double take. He turned to her with an ingratiating grin.

"Why that funny look? Do I have spinach stuck in my teeth?"

Holly smiled uncertainly. "No. You just look like somebody."

"Oh yes? Maybe I am somebody. Who is it you think I am?"

Holly laughed. "Oh, I can see you're not John. He was just some guy who tried to bother my housemate recently."

"Oh. Well, give my regards to this handsome guy if you see him again."

"I will, but I won't." Holly went on down the corridor.

The agent continued in the opposite direction. He entered the park maintenance office, identified himself to the secretary, popped the cover off the copier and began to adjust it. In a few minutes the secretary walked out with a sheaf of papers. The agent went to a shelf and found a ringbinder labeled HOUSING ASSIGNMENTS. He'd noted Holly's name from her name bar and soon knew the names and divisions of her housemates. He walked out and happened to pause near an Interpretive Division office where the work schedule of the naturalist Rangers was posted.

Elise Boutin, he saw, was having a day off. He strolled out of the building to a pay phone on the front terrace and called the Park switchboard. A man answered.

"Rocky Mountain National Park."

"May I speak to Elise Boutin, please?"

"Let me check her schedule. Okay, today's her day off. I'll ring her house and see if she's there."

"Thanks."

"Hello?"

"Hello, Elise?"

"She's not here right now. Who's calling?"

"This is John."

"Oh, John. I'll, er, let her know she missed you."

"Well, I'm in the Park. Can you tell me where she is?"

"I don't think I should tell you."

"Look, I borrowed a bunch of money from her, and I just want to pay it back before I leave the state, okay?"

"Mail it."

"I'll just come by your house, okay? I'd like to meet you anyway."

"No!"

"Well then, how can I get it to her? I don't trust the mail for sending cash."

"Okay, look. She's off on a hike. I think she said she was heading up to Bighorn Flats from Bear Lake. Do you know where that is?"

"I have a map. Thanks."

"Yeah, sure. Don't forget that part about leaving the state. I don't know what you did to Elise, but she doesn't want to see you any more."

The agent contacted his fellows and met them at the Bear Lake parking area. They set off up the Flattop Mountain trail, looking like Nordic quintuplets.

The sun rose a bit later near Banff. It came up, filling John with a gift of matchless grace and freedom, and started him on the routine of vigilance he was still working to perfect. He flipped on the scanner and let it sweep through the frequencies in search of any trouble he could reach in time to avert. While he waited and listened he worked around the cabin, cleaning and clearing out the relics of its past use as a base for mindless slaughter.

The work was worthwhile, but he fretted over the time spent puttering around while he waited to learn of a suitable use for his unique talents. He'd have to find some long-term project, or at least devise a better way to keep up with world events. Waiting for news to trickle out of commercial radio stations sometimes left him too late to help, and reception of air and emergency frequencies was sporadic.

Just in case, he took a moment to tune the radio to the frequency he'd discussed with General Hunter. To his surprise, it was active.

"… repeat again, the President of the United States and the Prime Minister of Canada request that Sky Ranger meet them for lunch at the White House today at noon, Eastern daylight time. The President and Prime Minister would like to establish a mutually beneficial relationship with Sky Ranger, and discuss his mission and goals. This is an announcement from the Sky Ranger Information Project. We repeat… "

Well! Noon today! Let's see, the local daylight time was about 8 AM—that made it 10 in Washington, plenty of time. Rather short notice, but perhaps it was the President's way of not appearing to court him too eagerly. It was polite of him to include the PM—he was sure they knew by now that he'd set up housekeeping somewhere in Canada.

John smiled with satisfaction. Between the lack of recent harassment, the gift of the photovoltaic equipment, and now this invitation, he felt that his relationship with the governments of North America was going to be a good one. In fact, he felt such confidence that he thought it was time for a quick visit with Elise before heading to Washington. He hoped she'd be thrilled to hear the news—and it might make her feel safer about seeing him every once in a while. And yet it was not an easy decision for him to make. His fear of her scorn now greatly exceeded his fear of death.

He pulled on his third and last skating suit, still intact if a little scuffed—he'd have to deal with the clothing problem soon, too—stuffed normal clothes into a nylon backpack, and strapped it on. Outside, he scanned the pastel mountain sky with eyes of matchless sharpness, and joyously bounded up into the rays of the morning Sun.

A half hour later he dropped down in a pine grove near Elise's house, where he drew jeans and a flight jacket over the skating tights. It felt wonderful to once again be among the peaks of the mountain kingdom that would always be his real home.

With a jaunty step he marched up the flagstones to Elise's dorm, surprising another ranger as she walked out the door. She looked at him uncertainly for a second, as though she didn't quite recognize him.

"Who are you?" she said suspiciously.

"I'm John."

"John! Didn't I ask you not to come here? Didn't you find Elise?"

A sudden dart of apprehension nicked at him. "Find her?" he asked carefully. He glanced at the ranger's name bar.

"Yes. I thought you were going to look for her after you called."

The dart turned to ice, and his eyes sharpened with an eagle's intensity. "I never called."

"What do you mean? Okay, you do sound different, but what's going on? It was somebody else?"

"It was somebody else. Marysia, where is Elise?"

Marysia was getting scared. "Why, I told you she was going up to Bighorn Flats! Or I told someone, anyway. Do you know it?"

"I know it very well. I'll bring her back."

As Marysia stared, John flung off his outer clothing and let it fall to the ground. He stood poised for an instant, crouched like a figure of spring steel about to be un-pent, then flung himself straight up, arcing over to vanish over the nearest peaks with a bang and an echoing rumble.

Marysia stood staring after him for a good long time.

Like a thunderbolt Sky Ranger bore down on the tundra of Bighorn Flats. With an eagle's acuity he scanned the rocky slopes and snow-streaked tableland of the high alpine flats. No one was visible—Elise probably hadn't had time to get that far.

Stooping like a peregrine, he dropped down and rushed along the Flattop Mountain trail toward Bear Lake. The trail ran diagonally down the rugged slope until it fell below timberline, where it made switchbacks that carried it into the thickening forest. He recklessly followed the trail through the woods, just ten feet above the dirt, greatly slowed but still fast enough to blast through twigs and branches. Agile as a hummingbird, he hugged the curving trail, not being bound by the restrictions of aerodynamics.

A flash of color on his right sparked his reflexes into instant decision. He burst up through the canopy, did a tight loop, brought his feet toward the ground, and plunged down to make a hard landing. His legs absorbed a massive impact—vegetation spattered out like green soup, and a drumming thud shook the trees for twenty feet around. A group of figures stared at him from the Dream Lake overlook.

Before him were five men, dressed dissimilarly, but resembling him in general size, build, and coloring. They stood over Elise, who was seated on a log bench, looking dazed and wan. She looked at him at first with dread only, as though he might be another of these tormentors, but then she peered through her confusion to realize that no one but he could make such an entrance. Her face took on an look of intense hope and pleading.

One of the men, who was dressed as a park ranger, drew the holstered revolver at his waist. Before he could level it, Sky Ranger was moving; a wake of forest litter was still hanging in the air when he closed his hand on the barrel. He yanked at the repellent thing and threw it good and hard. It tumbled in the sunlight and landed across Chaos Canyon, somewhere in the rubble of Otis Peak. The mockranger stared at his palm, raw and bleeding from the friction.

John felt a killing rage. He took a few seconds to grip it in a steel hand, and summoned images of peace from his transforming pilgrimage. When he trusted himself to speak, he caught one of the men with a raptor's glare and said in a low, steady voice, "Which one of you is going to tell me what's going on here?"

The man he'd chosen, dressed as a repairman of some sort, pulled himself together and said, "Hey, we're just out hiking. This girl looked sick and we stopped to help her."

"That's the wrong answer."

John sprang forward, spun the repairman, then grabbed him under the arms and took off. He was rewarded by a shriek of terror as they ripped through the forest canopy and up into the sunlight. He sped up to about a hundred knots and shouted in his victim's ear, "You want to find out my secrets? You want to find out how high I can fly?"

"All RIGHT, put me DOWN!"

"Don't make me take you up again."

John dropped down through the hole in the foliage and none too gently tossed his passenger to the ground. That man got to his feet and staggered off to join his four cronies. The five of them stood there looking white-faced and grim. They'd stepped aside to leave Elise in conspicuous isolation on the bench.

Sky Ranger looked from face to face. "Now, one of you will tell me why you've chosen to harass and terrorize this innocent girl."

Another of the five, the one dressed like a college boy, thrust out his lip pugnaciously and said, "We're Federal agents, questioning this woman on matters of national security. Don't interfere."

John's gaze remained steady and unblinking as a falcon's. "Right now your own security is your chief concern."

The man reached unsteadily into his jacket—if he'd had any thought of bringing out whatever weapon might be hidden there, he'd thought better of it. Instead he removed a case containing a brass badge.

John raised his hand. "Put that away. It means nothing to me. I want to hear the truth from your own lips."

"We are not at liberty to say any more."

John bit his lip, turned aside and strove to master himself. After a long minute he turned back and said in a voice of deadly quiet, "I want you to listen to me carefully. I am not a violent man. It would be grossly unfair for me to raise a hand against you. But you have done something very serious in threatening this girl. I want to hear two things from you—the name of your organization and the name of your superior. Then I will allow you to leave, and to get out of this park as fast as you can. If you don't tell me... " he shook his head sadly "... something bad, something very tragic, is going to happen to you, and to me as well."

"FBI," piped up one of the men.

"I'm temporarily assigned to FBI," said another.

"The FBI director is Glen Horton," added a third.

"But it was Remo—" This remark was cut off by a glare from one of the other men.

"Remo who?" demanded John.

The group's apparent leader shrugged. "Remo Cosimano. The President's security advisor. He arranged this mission personally."

John nodded. "All right. Get out. You can tell this Cosimano that this park is now Sky Ranger territory. If I get a hint that you or any of your kind have returned, I'll come back and root you out like a nest of cockroaches. And tell him that this woman is under my protection. Any more interference with her, or with anyone else I know, will bring about some very harsh consequences."

Without hesitation they turned and started down the trail. The college boy looked back and said, "You can't fight the whole U.S. government, Mister Avril."

"I won't have to, if there are any decent men left in it."

As they vanished into the trees, John sat beside Elise, took her hand, and looked at her with concern.

"I'm so sorry, Elise. I'd never have come to you if I'd known it would lead to this kind of trouble."

Elise looked up with a dull expression. "They... they made me tell them... your name."

"I know, I know they did, don't worry about it."

"And then they gave me a s-shot... and made me tell them more about you."

John dropped her hand for fear of hurting her, turned and sent his gaze lancing through the trees toward the fleeing men. His fervent wish was to see the five of them lying broken on the floor of Chaos Canyon. He forced the image from his mind and turned back to Elise, who sat staring blankly into the distance.

"Come on, Elise. We've got to get you home." He helped her to her feet and guided her toward the trail, but she was so unsteady and disoriented that he knew she couldn't make it without help. "I'll carry you."

She showed a short-lived flash of animation. "Don't FLY!"

"I won't, I won't."

He lifted her gently and began striding down the trail with a tireless gait. He deliberately walked at a sedate pace, both for Elise's comfort and to avoid overtaking the agents, whom he did not want to see again. The walk gave him time to agonize over the trouble he'd brought to Elise, and to fret about his lapse into thoughts of violence and anger. The knowledge and the balance he'd gained among the peaks couldn't long survive the hot turmoil of emotions like those. They had no place in one with his enormous capacity for destruction. Evidently, even now the work of self-purification wasn't over.

In an hour he brought Elise to the Bear Lake parking lot. By then she was asleep in his arms. John looked around and selected a solid-looking middle-aged couple who were picnicking near a big station wagon. He walked up to them; they stood up at the approach of the oddly-dressed young man carrying an unconscious girl.

"Excuse me, but we need your help. This is Elise Boutin, one of the park rangers. She was assaulted and drugged by five men up on the trail and she needs attention. Could you drive her to the park headquarters and make sure she's taken care of?"

"Oh, of course!" said the woman. "Herman, help him get her in the back of the wagon."

Herman eyed John as he effortlessly carried Elise toward the tailgate. "Don't look like he needs any help, Helen."

John arranged her on blankets while Herman got behind the wheel and Helen hovered anxiously. Satisfied, John gave Elise's cheek a caress and straightened up to look Helen in the eye.

"I'm really grateful to you for helping her. Do you know the way?"

"Yes, but aren't you coming with us?"

"No ma'am. I've got an appointment in Washington that can't wait. But I'll be back to see her this afternoon."

Helen's look of uncertainty bloomed into amazement. Her mouth dropped open and her eyes grew wide. "You're that Sky Ranger, aren't you?"

"Yes Ma'am, that's right."

And to prove it, he ran a few paces, bounded into the air, and dwindled to a hurtling speck that was soon lost to view.

Oblivious to detection, or perhaps courting it, John flung himself into the stratosphere and higher still, stopping his ascent only when the atmosphere appeared as a band of violet-blue around the horizon. Only then, with the hard fierce blackness of space around him, could he pour on speed without blasting his last suit of tights into a spray of glowing droplets. And he did pour on the speed—he pushed until he went beyond orbital velocity and reached a speed that would sweep him out of the Solar System altogether if he relaxed his efforts. Let NORAD make of that what they would! He crossed the continent in about four minutes, then worked just as strenuously to kill his speed so he wouldn't reenter like a meteor. He dropped down on Washington, certain he was causing many sweaty palms in air defense bases all over the area, and wondering how much liberty the President's invitation conferred on him. He decided to test it and make a point at the same time—he made a low supersonic pass down the length of the Mall, yawed around over the Capitol dome, and thundered back the way he'd come, angling off at the last second to land in the Rose Garden on the White House grounds.

A troop of Marine guards in their dress blues approached at a run, their very non-ceremonial weapons in hand. They thudded to a halt, facing him in a nervous and extremely alert phalanx.

Their lieutenant said, "Sir, I request that you identify yourself and state your business."

John looked at him askance. "I'm Sky Ranger. I'm here to meet with the President at his invitation. Will you take me to him?"

"No sir, I will not."

John waited a beat. "Why not? Weren't you told I'd been invited?" he asked impatiently.

"Yes sir, we have. But my job is to protect the President. And I will not conduct into his presence anyone who has an expression like yours on his face."

"I'm sure I can find my way in without your help."

"Maybe so. But it'll have to be through us, as long as you've got that attitude."

John looked at his feet. The man was right—he was being obnoxious. These were no enemies of his, but only men doing a necessary job, and brave enough to face down something unknown and powerful to do it.

Well, it wasn't every man whose bad manners and self-righteous temper could survive a transit through death itself. He took a deep breath and tried to relax.

Feeling a bit sheepish, he looked up again.

"I'm sorry. I promise you I will not threaten the President or any other person. I never intended to do so."

The Marine officer considered him for a moment. "Very well, sir, if you'll follow me."

Plain-clothed Secret Service men emerged from nowhere and joined the procession as they entered the White House. The President's Chief of Staff met them, dismissed the guard, and led John into the inner regions of the office area. He said little, but kept an eye on John's face, which was firmly set but no longer visibly angry. In a moment they entered the Oval Office, where he introduced John to the President and the Canadian Prime Minister, who were sitting around a low table set with a silver tea service. The two men stood up as they entered. The President nodded his chief of staff out of the room.

The President offered his hand. "Well, uh, Sky Ranger, it was good of you to accept our hasty invitation. When the Prime Minister decided to visit Washington we thought it would be nice if we could all get together, since you seem to enjoy Canada as much as the United States."

John shook hands with both men, but his look remained guarded, and he said nothing. Suddenly he didn't trust himself to speak.

Awkwardly, the President ventured, "Uh, I don't mean to pry, but is there something we could call you that would be a little less, uh, impersonal than Sky Ranger?"

John regarded him steadily and spoke with a voice of tight control. "If your goons haven't already told you, they soon will, so I might as well do it first. My name is John Jacob Avril."

The PM's eyebrows shot up, and the President grunted in surprise. "Well. That was welcome, but not really necessary. You do have a certain right to privacy."

John's gaze narrowed. "Are you serious?"

"I consider this a serious matter, yes. Do you have reason to doubt me?"

"Do you know a man called Remo Cosimano?"

The President's expression clouded noticeably. "Yes, I'm afraid I do. Son, why don't you tell me how it is that you know about him."

The PM coughed politely. "Gentlemen, this is sounding like some private laundry about to be aired. If you'll excuse me for a moment..."

John's eyes locked onto his. "Mr. Prime Minister, please stay if you can. It might be to your benefit to learn the kind of—of—perfidy your neighbor and ally is capable of."

The President's face colored, but he managed a chuckle. "You might as well stay, Pierre. Our young guest's moral outrage makes it almost mandatory."

But he wasn't smiling by the time John finished telling of Elise's drugging and interrogation.

"John, I assure you I knew nothing of this. In fact, I specifically instructed Cosimano to do nothing to interfere with the staff of that park."

John felt cautious relief—he'd come here prepared to take on the entire country in Elise's defense if need be. "Mr. President, I'm happy to hear that. If you knew Elise you'd never want anything like that to happen to her."

"I'm sure that's true." The President sat drumming his fingers on the arm of his chair for a moment. Then he picked up a phone. "Esther, get me the Attorney General." His look took in both John and the PM. "I want to prove to both of you that American perfidy isn't universal. Hello? Yes, I'm fine. Listen, a serious matter has just been brought to my attention. I want charges brought against Cosimano and I want him detained. Acting above the scope of his orders, or something like that. I'll talk to my counsel and get back to you with the specifics, but I want him to spend some time in jail. Yes, that's right. Expect to hear from my office this afternoon. Goodbye."

He pressed a button on his intercom console. The Chief of Staff immediately entered.

"Dave, get in touch with the Secretary of Defense. Tell him I want a list of possible replacements for Cosimano by tomorrow morning. He'll be resigning very soon."

"Yes, Mr. President." The Chief of Staff, clearly startled, lingered a moment as if his boss might change his mind, then departed.

John sat feeling slightly stunned by this quick turn of events. "Sir, I appreciate that. I'm sure Elise will sleep more easily. So will I."

The President nodded. "I appreciate your making me aware of the, uh, perfidy of my subordinate."

John blushed slightly. "Sir, I have a tendency to let my passions fly away with me from time to time."

The politicians laughed at John's choice of phrase.

"Um... can you tell me what you intend to do, now that you know my name?" asked John.

"Actually, if it were possible, I'd keep the knowledge confined to those of us in this room. But there's no way I can wipe it out of the minds of Cosimano and whoever else he's told. I can leak a story that the name he got was a false one, but he'll know better, and a lot of other people won't believe it either."

"But he'll be in jail, won't he?"

"Well, John, that's my intention, but we can't just throw him there—this kind of proceeding can take months or years to resolve. Even once he is in jail, he'll still be free to talk."

"You know, sir, I've been kind of out of touch for the past year or so. I'm not quite sure just what did happen to your predecessor. Did he wind up in prison?"

"The President may prefer not to discuss that," said the PM diplomatically. "Perhaps I can help you catch up with current events after we've discussed your status in my country."

"Oh—all right. You understand, Mr. President, that I'm only trying to protect my family and friends."

"Of course. But there's just not that much I can do. Even if I declared your name a top state secret it would probably leak out sooner or later. You know, I'd feel a lot easier about trying to keep this under wraps if you would explain your intentions and assure me that you won't be making problems for either of our two countries."

John eyed the President speculatively for a moment. He said carefully, "Sir, I'm not a very political person, now even less so than a year ago. I'm not planning to make trouble or break laws. I'm only concerned with the well-being of people—I want to be helpful, to bring a spark of hope to those who might be in impossible situations. I want to show that even a very imperfect person can overcome his limitations. I'm not an alien, I don't have a magic word or a propeller beanie. I can do what I do only because in the end, I had faith that the universe has meaning and beauty, despite my own flaws and weaknesses that sometimes made them hard to see. When I gave myself up to that truth I found the way to miracles."

Both politicians sat blinking at this for a moment. The President finally stirred and spoke. "I see. That—goes far to removing any apprehensions I might have had about you. I'm sure that your actions will continue to reflect that standard, as they have in the short time you've been with us already. Er—you've also effectively answered another question. Apparently your flight is the result of a—mental technique or attitude of some kind—you couldn't teach it to others?"

John smiled. "In a book, or in a classroom, no. By example, over time, perhaps."

"And would you consider joining the United States Government as an extraordinary agent?"

John sat up straight with his eyes wide. He produced a startled laugh. "No sir, absolutely not. I am first a human being, and a free one. I'll work for the good of everyone equally, or my example will be meaningless and distorted. I will not act in favor of one nation over another."

The President laughed in some embarrassment. "I'm not surprised. But I had to ask that question, or the DOD and others would never forgive me."

The PM, looking rather more serious, spoke up. "Mr. Avril, if this country or its NATO allies were to become involved in a war, how would you react?"

"Hmm." John looked down at the table, taken by surprise. "I hadn't really considered that. I suppose I would try to act to minimize bloodshed. I wouldn't act on behalf of either side unless it had a clear moral superiority. I wouldn't kill for anyone. I'd have to act on my conscience."

The President tried to brush the matter aside. "That's all hypothetical. "

The PM seemed not to hear. "What if minimizing bloodshed involved interfering with the war effort of the NATO countries? By blocking a preemptive nuclear strike, for example?"

The President turned to the PM with some gravity. "Pierre, let's not involve John here in our nuclear strategy."

John's return gaze was cool and steady, but inwardly he felt uncomfortable. He spoke directly to the Prime Minister. "Sir, I can't imagine how any clear-thinking person with the power to interfere with a nuclear attack could refrain from doing so. I must stand with what I said before. I would be guided by my conscience."

The PM said nothing more, but continued to regard John with an appearance of suppressed satisfaction.

The President, on the other hand, suddenly seemed less affable. "Well… since it is, of course, not our intention to make first use of nuclear weapons, we can assume this discussion to have been, uh, philosophical in intent." He made an obvious attempt to lighten the atmosphere. "John, we did invite you here with the pretense of feeding you lunch. Let me pour you some tea, then I'll send for the food."

Though not in the least bit hungry, and inwardly ruing the waste of time, John spent the next hour eating and chatting with the two men.

When they walked him out to the Rose Garden to witness his departure, he went with several useful concessions: dual U.S.-Canadian citizenship, assurance of non-interference (though not of non-surveillance) in his activities, and hands-off his friends and family, with a promise to try to keep his name out of the papers. In return he offered a formal pledge to limit his actions to avoid interference with law, commerce, or the military. They advised extreme caution in trying to operate in certain nations, which were unlikely to be so liberal in granting him freedom of action. If they caught or killed him, the West could take no action in his favor. He soared away feeling he'd gotten a good deal.

The Prime Minister left for home at once. Alone in the Oval Office, the President touched a button and called in CINC-SRIP, the secretaries of Defense and State, the directors of CIA and FBI, and others. They arrived quickly, as they'd been listening to the meeting over a speaker in a nearby room.

The Chief of Staff questioned the decision to arrest and charge Cosimano.

"There are plenty of men like Remo Cosimano in the world," said the President. "He can easily be replaced. As far as I know, there's only one Sky Ranger."

Elated, filled with optimism, John made a leisurely return flight to Colorado. At the edge of space, he savored the silence and peace as a setting uniquely suited to clear thought and mental perspective. Poised between the green-gold Earth and the blue-black infinity above, he felt that every option was open to him, and nothing beyond his reach.

He felt a thrill of homecoming as the grey and white peaks of the Front Range poked up from the cloud cover far below. He dived below the cloud deck and found his way to the Park, where he set down in front of the Headquarters building, a massive log structure built on a foundation of grey rock. He strode in proudly, went to the secretary, and introduced himself as Sky Ranger. Flustered, but showing no tendency to disbelieve him, she called the Park Superintendent, who looked him up and down, gave him a cautious handshake, and informed him that Elise had been taken to the clinic in Estes Park to sleep off the drug.

John took off, and a few minutes later touched down in front of the small clinic, the only medical facility in the little tourist town. At the entrance he encountered three sober-looking men wearing sunglasses and nondescript dark suits. They stood up straight and watched him very intently as they witnessed his unconventional arrival.

"Ah—Mr. Sky Ranger?"

"That's right. Who are you guys?"

"I'm Special Agent Ramirez of the Denver FBI office, and these are agents Walsh and Schering. We have orders to keep an eye on one of the patients inside."

"Elise Boutin?"

"That's the name, sir."

"You don't plan to keep me out, do you?"

Ramirez laughed and raised his palms. "No sir, we have special orders to admit any flying men who show up. We're instructed to watch out for other Feds—mostly not FBI, I'm happy to say. I think the orders came from the very top."

"Hmmm." John eyed the men carefully. "Well, that's nice. I guess she does need the protection. I'll see you later."

"Sure thing."

John walked past the agents and entered the lobby. As usual, he had trouble seeing at first, as his daytime vision was specialized for detail in bright light and was poor in relative darkness. He blinked a few times, saw a nurse approaching, and was led to a ward where Elise occupied the only bed in use. Two more FBI men were stationed at her door. John walked in and shut the door behind him.

Elise, dressed in a hospital gown, lay asleep, covered by a sheet. John quietly pulled a chair over to sit beside her. He debated whether to wake her, but decided against it. He kept a vigil, grateful for the peaceful stillness on her face and the steady rise and fall of her breast. He sat there quite content to watch over her and to appreciate her fresh, innocent beauty.

After about twenty minutes her eyes slid half-open, wandered about, then settled on him with a fleeting frown.

John gave her a hopeful smile. "Hi. How are you feeling?"

"Sleepy. Woozy. Sick."

"Have you been asleep since I brought you down from the mountain?"

"Only on and off. I got the police to call my mom. She's flying out. In an airplane."

"Do you know there are FBI men here to watch you?"

"Yes, and it makes me feel so special to know they're here."

"Don't worry, the man who ordered your questioning has been removed."

"Nice to know."

"Have they bothered you? Tried to ask you any questions?"

"Not like you're doing."

"Then you're all right?"

"Yes. I've always wanted to be drugged and questioned by five spies who look like the stupidest friend I ever had."

"Oh, god. Um—I know who they were, in case you're interested."

"Speak, oh lord of the air."

John described his meeting with the President, finishing with news of his new status of quasi-acceptance and even cooperation from the government, hoping to brighten her up.

"So now you're a Republican too. My hero," said she in a monotone.

John gamely kept trying. "Um—once that Cosimano guy gets the boom dropped on him, I don't think anyone else will bother you. The President even said he'd try to keep my name under wraps."

"Right. Until you go astray, then they'll be all over me."

"I won't go astray. I told them I'd be good."

"Ha!"

"All right, I give up. I'm very sorry I got you into this. When I came back to life I only thought I was going to be a simple flying boy. I'm very stupid. I never thought I'd cause this much trouble."

"I don't know what I'm going to do," said Elise in a small shaky voice. "I'll never know when some creepy government men are going to jump me. I know they'll watch me. And if it gets out that I actually know the great Sky Ranger, I'll never have any privacy."

"I'm not planning to go to the networks to tell."

"You flying DOPE, everybody in the Park, and now this clinic, knows it."

"What are you going to do? What do you want me to do?" asked John miserably.

"I don't know what I'll do. I'll try to ride it out and hope it all dies down. As for you, I just want you to leave me alone. You can't help, except to rescue me, and if you stay away, I hope I won't need any more rescuing. Just go away, and don't come see me any more. I mean it this time. I never want to see you again."

John stood up to do something that would have been quite difficult for him in his previous life—make a graceful exit from Elise's life.

"But first, I want you to hand me that pan so I can throw up again," said Elise in a thick voice.

John held Elise's hand while she made a futile and wrenching attempt to empty an already vacant stomach. She did not withdraw the hand. He waited until her hard breathing calmed down, let go her hand and stood up again. "Well, I guess I'd better go. I don't want to tangle with your mother when she finds out what I've gotten you into. Good bye, Elise," he said quietly. "Take care. Be good. I'll —think of you—whenever I see the first sunlight touching the mountains."

Elise's composure dissolved. "Oh, will you stop that?" she said through tears. "Why do you always have to be so corny? Go save somebody's puppy or something."

He glanced back at her and stepped out the door, closing it again. He caught the FBI men with a look they'd never forget.

"You take good care of her. Take the best care of her."

A minute later he found that his own tears were taken from him, whipped away and dispersed by the cold dry blast of stratospheric winds. Would he ever learn?

Part Two
A Guardian from the Clouds

Chapter Nine

The door slammed open, jarring John awake. Ellipses of yellow light wavered over the walls and furnishings of the cabin; one settled on him.

"Christ, there's somebody here!" hissed an angry voice.

"Let's get out of here, eh?"

"No way, this is our cabin. Hey, you in there! Wake up!"

John rolled over slowly, sat up, and stared into the dazzling lenses of five flashlights all aimed at him.

"I'm awake."

"Well, boy, what the hell are you doing in our cabin?"

"I thought it was abandoned," said John gravely.

"Well, it ain't no more. Come on, men, let's see what this asshole's got going on in here."

The five tramped into the cabin. They lit no lamp, but John got fitful looks at them as they caught reflections from each other's flashlight beams. They were rough looking, dressed in shabby woolen jackets, and all carried rifles. John sat still and watched them as calmly as he could.

"What the hell kind of a union suit is this?" asked one, picking up a blue bodysuit from where John had flung it over a table. It was one of his new flight suits, far more durable than the old skating outfits, custom (and expensively) made from a fireproof fabric used for race driver coveralls.

Another man put his light a few inches from John's face. "Boy, you're trespassing. Why don't you haul your ass the hell out of here."

Without a word, John moved to stand up, but another voice stopped him. "Shit, look at these pictures on the wall. And here's a plaque from the Prime Minister. You know who this is? This is the goddamn Sky Ranger!"

That brought out snorts of derision. "Naww! What would Sky Ranger be doing in this old shack?"

"Sleeping, looks like. Look at this suit. Ain't you never seen pictures of it before? I've read in the papers that Sky Ranger's been sighted in this area a lot."

A rifle muzzle entered the beams crisscrossing near his face. John couldn't see the man who held it.

"Is that right? Is that who you are, Sky Ranger?"

John said nothing. An uneasy voice said, "I don't like the look he's giving you, Newt. If he's Sky Ranger, maybe we ought to get out of here as quick as we can."

"Man, we got five rifles pointed at him."

"I always heard bullets bounced right off this guy, eh?"

"Is that right?"

A flash ignited and a shattering concussion tore through the room. John felt a shock in his gut as if a knight with razor-toed steel boots had kicked him there. He looked down and saw blood start freely from a gaping wound in the side of his stomach. He also felt a warm flow from the exit wound in his back.

"Shit, he's no Sky Ranger, he's just some faggot who likes to dress up like him. Or maybe he's Sky Ranger's girl-friend. Is that who you are, blondie?"

John didn't even hear. He was intent only on trying to understand what had just happened, and to stop the horrid outflow of his life by pressing his hands over the slick, hot openings on his belly and back.

"Oh God, Newt, did you have to shoot him?"

"Quit whining. He knows what we're here for. If he'd turned us in for poaching, we'd have gotten some damn big fines and maybe jail time. It was him or us."

"Yeah, I guess that's right," the man subsided.

"You two boys pick him up and throw him out back in the boneyard. In the morning we'll bury him so deep even the wolverines won't find him."

Two men picked him up roughly, as though he were already dead. The movement brought John his first jolt of real pain as his nerves began to respond to the outrage that had been committed against them. It felt as though giant claws were tearing his guts apart.

The poachers carried him through the door and out into the night. Their light beams quested before them as they made their way to the back.

"There ain't no more boneyard here."

They dropped John in the tall grass where the remains of their previous slaughter had once been. The pain of the impact closed his throat and took his breath away.

"This boy's been cleaning up around here for a while now."

They shone their beams around; one of them alighted on the roof, throwing back a shower of purple glints.

"What the fuck's that on the roof?" asked one of them, more afraid of the alien sight than he was at the prospect of murder.

"It looks like one of those space solar panels."

The beams flitted back to John, where he lay quietly trying to staunch his bleeding.

"I'm not so sure this ain't really Sky Ranger."

"Then why didn't he fly away or anything?"

"I dunno. Maybe he has to take a magic pill first or something."

"Well, he's finished now, that's plain enough."

The two men considered him further. John made sense of their words with increasing difficulty.

"Y'know, whether he's Sky Ranger or not, how do we know the damn wildlife men don't know all about this place by now? This guy's been here for a while. He might even be a real ranger, for all we know."

One of them gave John a half-hearted kick in the thigh. "Well, Sky Ranger? What about it? Anybody else know about this place?"

John only gritted his teeth and sucked quick, shallow breaths through them.

"He ain't really got much reason to talk. The only thing we can offer him is a quick death."

"Well, he ain't getting that. Let's get back inside. This place is finished. We'll have to clear out of here in the morning."

"Damn. This was a great place."

The two passed beyond John's hearing.

The pain was like a cauldron of molten lead poured into his gut. It was beyond all endurance, yet John didn't scream, as he knew that might bring a fatal second shot to shut him up. Moving slowly, he grabbed dry grass and pulled out handfuls with his waning strength, then held them tightly against his wounds, feeling them flood with blood which gradually grew sticky and cold. He could move his toes. The bullet had missed his spine.

He had but a single thought—to survive until morning. He wasn't sure even the influence of the sun could save him from this kind of trauma, but it was surely his only chance. If he died again, he knew it would be permanent. He wasn't exactly in the right frame of mind to pull the same kind of trick he had the last time he'd faced death. It was too much to hope that he might ever achieve a state of such perfection again.

What time was it? It was late June, just over a year past his rebirth. He forced his attention away from the pain and looked at the sky. It was black, showing no trace of dawn, although wheels of red fire seemed to tumble across his field of view as the agony came up in swells and surges. He saw stars, real ones, and tried to piece together their fragmented patterns into something he could recognize. Overhead were Pegasus, Perseus, and Andromeda, with the mist of the Pleiades just clear of the mountains to the east. Thank God, it was late, and the sunrise was no more than two hours off.

He stared at the stars, begging them to hasten their slide to the west, but they seemed unmoving, each as rooted in place as Polaris itself. The blackness of the sky began to drain away to grey. But still the stars were unmoved—it was only the fading of his vision brought on by the loss of blood. The pain seemed to recede to a distant thundering echo as unconsciousness began to creep up on him. He clung to wakefulness with full desperation.

His urge to live wasn't brought on by fear of death. Death he'd faced and come to terms with long before. It held for him no terrors. The images that danced through his quaking mind were not of the grave but of life—the morning alpenglow on the snowfields of the Himalaya, the pristine keenness of light and silence at play among the high cirrus, the roaring fury of an ocean storm in the Screaming Sixties, with marching waves huge and terrible enough to daunt even him. He saw the faces of the many people he'd aided over the past year—faces reflecting the rebirth of hope where no hope was possible, and the reawakening of wonder where bitterness had long obscured it. What would happen to such people now? Would they lapse back into resignation, facing their deaths in terror or despair?

The bleeding had slowed. Masses of clotted blood matted the grass and chilled his hands. He dared not move— any shift would probably bring the blood flow back in full. Not that he had much strength left for movement. It was all he could do to force his diaphragm in and out for the tiny breaths that were all he could endure. He grieved at the mutilation of his body. It was as if he'd been entrusted with a wondrous temple which he'd permitted to be defiled.

He became aware of a light shining into his eyes from the side. He tilted his head a tiny amount and saw in the east the waning crescent moon. Its presence cheered him, but it was not a narrow crescent—the sun would not follow immediately. Still, its reflected light was a reminder that the sun was down there, somewhere, suspended in majesty while the Earth made its ponderous turning to bring it into his sight.

His hands and feet tingled as circulation shut down in his extremities. The pain in his gut receded further, except to flare up with stunning force each time the torn muscles of his abdomen twitched or spasmed. John lost all sense of time—his consciousness passed into an inchoate haze, an interminable, featureless stratum of thoughts, images, and fears, broken only by occasional shards of agony rising up like mountains in the fog. In moments of lucidity, John prepared to consign himself to the grand underlying principal which had made possible all such marvels as Earth, man, and himself.

He heard a far-off trumpet blowing.

Or thought he did. Whatever it was, it was enough to pry open his eyes again—he'd closed them at some point without realizing it. If he could believe his senses, the sky had taken on a soft shade of purple-grey. Over what seemed a period of years he turned his head; there shone Venus, casting its own parcel of borrowed sunlight on his face like a gentle kiss. He watched the brightening sky as if he were witnessing the first dawn of the world. The silence of the morning seemed broken to him—he was sure he could hear whispered words of encouragement from the massive life-source just below the horizon, words that offered strength and renewal if he could just hold on a few minutes more. His gratitude was absolute—even if he couldn't hold on, he'd die knowing that the universe that had spawned and nurtured him had not deserted him in his final distress.

Hazy fans of gold and scarlet bloomed in the east; they also suffused his mind and consciousness with a supernal light.

"Good God, he's still alive," whispered an awestruck voice.

"I'll let him have another."

A rifle popped with a puny crack; a wad of metal compressed John's ribcage and rebounded into the brush.

It was Sky Ranger whose eagle's gaze caught the five poachers one by one.

The five stood there paralyzed with fear and wonder as Sky Ranger surged to his feet. The matted grass, now caked with brown-black blood, fell away. His wounds remained, gaping wide as ever, but blood only seeped from their ragged edges. The poachers stared at the wounds with a fascinated dread. For them it was more terrible to see a man walking toward them while ignoring such mortal wounds than to see him lying dead because of them.

John stopped in front of the man holding the smoking rifle. He caught his eyes and held them as a hawk would hold a rabbit's petrified gaze. His hand flashed, and the rifle was gone, hissing through the air to clatter and bounce down the distant face of the mountain. In an instant the other guns were gone as well—all but one, which he kept aside for effect. He grabbed hold of opposite ends of the barrel and strained. Just as he'd seen George Reeves do on TV, the barrel bent like a length of black licorice. He held it out to one of the men, who grabbed it by the bend in the barrel and dropped it instantly, his palm seared by the hot metal.

Almost before they could react, John dashed into the cabin and emerged with a coil of wire. Without concern for their comfort he pushed three of the poachers down against trees, then used the wire to tie their wrists and ankles around the trunks.

"You men take it easy," he said. "Somebody'll be up to fetch you within twenty four hours."

John then turned to the two left standing: the one who'd shot him, and the vilest looking of the other four. They weren't equipped to understand the look they saw in his eyes. They interpreted it only as a mortal threat, but had they the sensibility to see it, they would have perceived not mere human wrath, but a force as impassive as the wind and as tranquil as a glassy lake.

"You two boys are coming with me," said John in a voice as low as a breeze and as quiet as wavelets on a pond.

He grabbed each man by the belt, gave them a shove, and marched them uphill, toward the tarn that was embedded in a rocky shelf just beyond the trees. The spell that held them quiet began to break down as they climbed through the belt of conifers. They stumbled and lurched under John's relentless urging, turning fearful glances toward his pale, implacable face. They expected no mercy—it was not a concept that entered into their philosophy of life. John's would-be assassin invoked every verbal foulness under his breath, while the other whimpered and tried to frame words that might result in his salvation.

They broke out of the trees and onto the shelf that contained the lake. John shoved them past it and brought them to a steep dropoff on a far edge of the shelf. Here was an almost vertical drop of more than a thousand feet. At the base was a slope of talus that had weathered down from the brink. The tall pines that held it back looked like green toothpicks at this distance.

John pushed his charges right up to the very brink. Their shoes scrambled away from the edge, knocking down pebbles which fell in excruciating silence until they finally hit with barely audible clicks.

John's voice was low and tremulous. "This is it, boys. You're going to visit the police."

"You're going to fly us there?"

John managed a grin. "That's right. You'll be crazy about it."

John pushed them off the cliff. He leaped after them, gripped their belts again, and held on. He didn't bother to apply power until the last instant; then their breaths were squeezed out and their belts almost snapped from the acceleration. While they continued to scream hoarsely, John flew them dangling from his hands like duffel bags. He skirted the treetops, soared high over valleys, and made long sweeping arcs over grand, snowy peaks while his passengers hung there face down, watching the woods and mountains rush madly by.

In a few minutes John dropped his limp, trembling burdens in front of the Royal Canadian Mounted Police outpost at Banff. He walked in the door and faced the astounded Mounties behind the desk. "Out front," he said, "are two men guilty of poaching and attempted murder. Their three comrades are tied up at a cabin about 30 kilometers northwest of here. These two will tell you how to find it. Oh, I almost forgot. I'm Sky Ranger."

He sank down onto a bench while three Mounties ran outside to round up the prisoners. A fourth stepped up to John with an expression compounded of amazement and horror. "Sir? You are terribly wounded. You need attention at once."

John stood up again. "Yes, I know. I'm on my way to Calgary right now."

"On your own, sir?" asked the Mountie in disbelief.

John nodded. "I'm stable for now. And I'm the quickest way I know to get there." He started out the door, stopped, and looked back with a look of sadness. "One more thing. That cabin I mentioned. It's my home. Please treat it with respect."

"I promise you that, sir. Godspeed. We'll call ahead to Calgary General so they'll be expecting you."

"Thanks."

John lifted off and made a quick flight east to Calgary. In a few minutes he touched down in front of the hospital's ER. He was met outside by a squad of doctors and nurses with a gurney. Although he could walk perfectly well, they insisted he lie down on the gurney. Several of them couldn't restrain gasps at the sight of him. To see a man still walking with those great bloodless wounds in his gut seemed to afflict them with an almost supernatural fear, as though they were dealing with a zombie rather than a man. The more self-possessed among them wrapped a blood-pressure cuff around his arm even as they wheeling him through the doors. Another probed with his stethoscope. John lay still and silent as they worked on him.

"His BP's too low to measure. This man's dead."

"No, he's not. Heartbeat is strong—at about six beats per minute."

"Get a blood type immediately."

Someone thrust a thermometer in his mouth. John accepted it stoically.

A nurse tried repeatedly to jab a needle into a vein inside his elbow. The needle depressed the skin like a rubber membrane, but it eventually would yield no farther and the point just skittered off. "Doctor—" she said desperately, "I —I can't get the needle to penetrate."

"Well, take some of the clotted blood from around the wound. That'll have to do."

John interrupted by raising his other hand. He pointed at his elbow and indicated she should try again. He stared at the area and concentrated, willing it to relax. His arm immediately felt cold and numb, but the nurse coaxed the needle into the skin at last. The doctor watched closely as the syringe slowly filled with a pale pinkish liquid.

"Good lord. I don't think he's got more than a pint of blood left in his entire body."

With the needle withdrawn, John instantly let his arm resume its normal daylight state. Without the grace of his flight impulse it was practically dead.

"Sky Ranger? Sky Ranger?"

John looked at the doctor hovering at the head of the gurney. It was about time someone asked him something.

"I'm Doctor Hogarth. Sky Ranger—why aren't you dead? What do you need from us?"

John looked cross-eyed at the thermometer projecting from his mouth. Hogarth belatedly realized the problem and yanked it out.

"Eighty degrees Fahrenheit. And yet there you lay, bright-eyed and alert. Can you tell us how to help you?"

"Doctor, you have until sunset to stabilize me. The moment the sun goes down I'll lose the influence that's keeping me going and will probably die instantly."

Hogarth frowned intensely. "That makes little sense."

"I assure you it's true. You have to get me into shape to live on my own by then."

Hogarth looked him in the eye, adjusted his headlight, then bent down to peer into the tattered mess of his entrails so clearly visible behind his ruptured abdominal wall. "You'll certainly need a lot of work here. I'll send for the best abdominal surgeon in the Province. Orderlies, I want this man prepared for surgery, stat."

They began to wheel him away. John sat halfway up. "Wait—" Everyone turned to him again. "Doctor, there's one small problem. I don't have much money... "

Hogarth stepped up to him with an incredulous grin and laid a strong hand on his shoulder. "What kind of nonsense is that? You're a Canadian, aren't you? That's enough by itself. My God, even if this were the States, I'd pay out of my own pocket to see you treated." He shook his head and turned back to the phone.

Six or eight people sent the gurney rattling down the corridor again. A nurse held his cold, pale hand and whispered encouragement. John found he didn't mind that at all. The sun would be below the horizon in about fourteen hours. He didn't want to face another such night by himself.

They wheeled him into the operating room. The natural inclination of the medical staff was to start replenishing his blood right away, but John said they might as well wait until they had him patched up again, as the bizarre fact was that the almost total lack of blood in his body wasn't actually a big problem for him just now. He also had to forbid the anesthesiologist's plan to give him a general anesthetic. He was sure that a loss of consciousness would result in his instant death. They flipped him on his stomach and prepared a spinal tap. When they were ready, John concentrated on the area of the wounds and the intended tap, willing them to relax, to revert to their more normal nighttime state. In a corner of his mind he briefly examined the idea that he might find some other use for this ability to consciously and even selectively turn off his flight powers, then turned back to the more urgent matters at hand.

He felt nothing as the surgeons began to operate, but he had them bring in a mirror so he could watch their progress and maintain his concentration. The small intestine was quite mangled. They were forced to remove and discard a section over a foot long, but they assured him anyone could easily sustain such a loss. The surgeons spent the next six hours carefully reconnecting the severed ends, and stitching up tears and damage to the rest of the intestine and to the blood vessels nearby. They worked with exquisite care, often peering through magnifying visors while using needles so fine that John needed his eagle's vision to see them. After a while they flipped him over and began to work from the front.

John watched all this with a curious sense of detachment. He felt no pain, and had no sense of imminent death. He noticed that he was barely breathing—making only two or three shallow breaths per minute. The line on the heart monitor was almost flat, and the alarm buzzer on the blood pressure monitor had to be turned off. He kept telling himself he was practically dead at this very moment, yet he knew that if he chose he could get up and fly into orbit—as long as the sun stayed in the sky. It was all rather eerie and dreamlike.

At last the surgeons expressed satisfaction with their work and with renewed energy sewed up the overlying muscle and skin. Despite his insouciance, John felt great relief that his body was no longer prone to leaks and open to the world. His heart rate gave a jump. Nurses plunged IV tubes into both arms, sending in blood that had been pre-warmed to bring up his core temperature. He sucked it up like an airplane flying on fumes, pint after pint. His heart rate and respiration moved back to normal, now that they had something to do again. The blood on the IV stand was replaced with glucose and massive doses of antibiotics. Only then did the whole medical team straighten up and take a deep breath. At last they felt they were dealing with a living patient instead of a weirdly animated corpse.

John allowed them to wheel him into the ICU, although he felt strong enough to wrestle a moose, which in fact he was. But the sutures holding him together had no such strength. He looked up at Dr. Hogarth as nurses helped him into bed.

"Was the surgery particularly difficult?"

"Why no, I'd say just the opposite. It's not often that we deal with such major trauma without any need for major life support during the procedure—hell, there was hardly even any bleeding. It was almost like—pardon my expression— operating on a cadaver."

"Well, I'm alive now by any standard, right?"

"You surely are. Far more so than any normal man who'd just undergone such a procedure."

"That's only temporary. The minute the sun sets I'll be just as much a basket case as anybody else in my position—maybe more so. I'll be totally helpless all night. Make sure the nurses don't have a shift change just at sunset—I might need some attention then."

"You will have it. Now, if you can do without me for a moment, I've been called upon to make some kind of a statement."

"Sure. And doctor... " He sat up in bed, moving smoothly against the resisting hands of the nurses as if they were columns of smoke. "... thank you, sir."

"It was the highpoint of my career."

He permitted the nurses to push him back down and lay there thinking rueful thoughts. All of a sudden his privacy and security were shattered. The site of his eyrie was known, he was trapped and convalescing in a public hospital, and worst of all, it would soon be common knowledge that at night the invincible Sky Ranger was no more formidable than any other slightly underweight, nonconformist daydreamer. That fact was now obvious, if it hadn't been before, and he saw no way to conceal it.

He looked around. The other beds in the ward were occupied by people who were not only critically ill, but acted it. Few of them were able to notice the commotion and activity that had heralded his arrival, and none now paid him any attention. They were approaching a mystery more profound and personal than any mere Sky Ranger could represent. He would live; many of them would not. It felt like an intrusion to occupy the same room as these men and women whose business here was so much more serious than his own. But it also did much to reduce his own problems to a manageable size. He studied those drawn, colorless faces in their nests of tubes and wires while half-remembered images of what they were about to face swam and wavered just below the surface of his conscious mind.

"Don't be afraid," he said to anyone who could hear. "It's all right. It all makes sense in the end."

At somebody's instruction he was soon wheeled into a private room. Six heavily armed Mounties took up stations at the door. He had to wince at the sight of their weapons—the sun was in decline, and the memory of the flash and the roar of gunfire was too recent.

For the first time he felt a trace of fear as the sun neared the horizon. He had an idea that his wounds might open up and start pouring out his lifeblood the moment that strengthening copper disk disappeared behind the distant mountains.

What actually happened was simpler and far more peaceful—he fell instantly into a deep sleep from which he could not be awakened.

When the voice of Aurora called him back to wakefulness, the first person he saw was a young nurse in a uniform that was noticeably and properly filled out. She had soft, sleepy hazel eyes under a neat cap of chocolate-brown hair. She beamed a gentle smile when she noticed his gaze.

"Good morning, my name is Bea. I'll be your day nurse. How are we feeling this morning?"

John opened his mouth. The words came out slowly and with effort. "I'm tired. And weak. And I feel—like someone shoved a lead pipe through my belly and left it there."

"Well, that's to be expected. Don't worry, I'll give you a shot and the pain will just float away."

"No—don't bother. I'll be all right in a few—minutes."

Bea studied her extraordinary new charge. She thought he looked very ordinary indeed—a lean, wasted-looking young man with purple under his eyes and unkempt sandy hair that could use a good washing. She knew as much as anyone about Sky Ranger's accomplishments, but looking at him now it was hard to imagine how he'd ever managed them.

"I'm serious. Sky Ranger—that name sounds ridiculous, but it's what's on your chart—I'm instructed to give you a sedative."

Just now the most compelling things about John Avril were his eyes. Though sleepy and hooded, they could still be piercing.

"Nurse Bea—give me three minutes. If you still think I need your shot at the end of that time, I'll take it."

"Three minutes? Okay. I'd like to see you recover in three minutes." She bustled about, checking his vital signs and drawing blood.

On the side of the hospital facing the plains, unseen by either Bea or John, the Sun was hovering beneath the horizon in preparation for its grand entrance. Its rays were already gilding the snowfields on the peaks to the west, but hadn't yet erased the shadows at their base or on the flats to the east.

Bea witnessed a most extraordinary thing as her patient appeared to straighten, to harden, to glow with vitality and strength.

She looked down from his face. "Um—it looks like you'll be wanting a bedpan next."

John followed her gaze, and his face, already flushed with renewed vigor, turned beet-red with embarrassment. He flung the sheets across his middle. "I can take care of it myself. And I won't need the shot, either."

Bea drew herself up. "Well, maybe not, but no way are you getting out of bed. You've got fresh sutures in you!"

John grinned shyly. "I know, but I can do things now that you wouldn't believe. I'm sure I can make it to the bathroom."

Bea gave a sigh of exasperation. "No, no, no. I'm not letting you up until Dr. Hogarth says so, and maybe not even then. If you fuss I'll have you catheterized." She produced the bedpan, stepped forward, and folded back his sheet. "Now let me help you. And don't be so self-conscious. I'm a nurse. I've—I've seen it all before." She folded back his hospital gown.

John studied the ceiling with all the acuity made possible by his eagle's vision.

Twenty minutes later, when Bea was satisfied that he was fit to face the morning, John ventured a request.

"Do you think I could have a radio brought in here?"

Bea looked over from adjusting the glucose bag on the IV pole. "What for? To listen to KSKY?"

"Well, yes."

"No, you may not. It would only upset you, and there's nothing you can do about any of it anyway. People will just have to watch out for themselves for a while. I think KSKY should go on vacation while you're here."

John didn't bother to protest. She was right; there was no point tantalizing himself with news of troubles and disasters he couldn't hope to avert. Although he felt fully capable of rocketing off for his normal day's efforts, he knew he was like a steam engine held together by scotch tape.

Bea eventually left him in peace, but it was soon broken by the arrival of Dr. Hogarth. He didn't bother to ask John how he felt—he could see who was eyeing him with such a bright-eyed gaze. He did gently peel back the bandages to examine the wounds.

"Hmm. Well, the healing's a little behind where I thought it would be, but it looks satisfactory. We'll have to work to keep infection from getting a foothold. Do you have any special properties in that regard?"

"I'm not sure. One night I felt like I was catching a cold, but the symptoms vanished in the morning and never returned."

"That sounds promising."

"Doctor, how long do you think the healing will take?"

"If you heal at a normal rate, I'd say about three weeks."

John rolled his head and winced.

"I know. You're thinking about the people who may get hurt during that time."

John nodded.

"The best thing you can do for them is stay quiet and get back in shape as quickly as you can. If you insist on heroics you might be years getting over this. I can see you flying out every day and coming back for major surgery every evening. Won't work."

"I know."

"We'll try to keep you from going off your nut with boredom, eh?"

"Okay, Doctor. Thanks again."

The hospital was besieged by a ring of vehicles from the world's media. The modern sculpture in the courtyard was the background for many televised reports, and all the American and Canadian networks had long lenses trained on the fifth-floor window they believed to be Sky Ranger's. Hogarth and the other doctors were called to give interviews and make statements at frequent intervals, and even Bea was bullied in front of a camera, to her intense discomfiture. But at the instruction of the governments of both Canada and the United States, no reporter was allowed above the first floor of the hospital. Even the relatives of the other patients had to be escorted while within the building. Plain-clothed agents and security men outnumbered the large contingent of Mounties who were on patrol.

John couldn't see any of this, but he heard it as plainly as he might have heard a force of Huns storming a Roman fort. With little to occupy him besides Bea's occasional chatter, his thoughts soon began to bear on things far beyond the masonry walls that hemmed him in.

At 11:16 local sun time (according to his internal clock) he heard footsteps echoing down the corridor outside. His guards made a request for ID, expressed satisfaction, and opened the door. John caught a glimpse of Air Force blue, and in walked Eric Hunter, CINC SRIP himself.

John grinned broadly, genuinely glad to see the master pilot, even if he was now in charge of spying him out.

The general carried a leather portfolio under one arm and a box under the other. He returned the grin, set down the packages and stepped up to shake John's hand.

"Good to see you, son."

"Yeah, same here. I'll bet it's nice to be able to find me without any help from those pesky infrared satellites for a change."

Hunter's face went carefully neutral. "Excuse me?"

"Oh, give it a rest. I've taken inventory of every major satellite type in orbit, and you know it. I've pretty much figured out which type does what. I haven't spotted any more of those Russian ASATs yet, but you'll know it if I do."

Hunter laughed and gave up the facade. "Yeah, our birds have gotten some pretty fair pictures of you poking around up there. We've also got some hand-held shots taken by the Apollo boys before they head out of orbit."

"That reminds me. Is today's liftoff of Apollo 24 still go?"

"Last I heard. Don't hear much about it, though. Your little scrape's knocked everything else off the front page—the moon shot, everything."

"That's too bad. It's the final lunar mission. People should be thinking about that, not me."

"You've got a lot of fans."

"I always liked to be at the Cape for the liftoffs—to watch, and maybe help if there was a problem during the ascent."

Hunter nodded. "NASA knows it. But don't worry about those boys. They haven't had a real problem in a long time."

"Not since *Columbia*. Well, I'll be thinking about them."

John's gaze refocused and returned to Hunter. "So. I guess your job will be easier now that you know where my hideout is. I'll have to find someplace else."

"Why bother?" We've known about your cabin for months now."

John looked crestfallen. "You have?"

"Why, sure. Actually it was one of our spy birds that first spotted it. We've got a few men up there right now, to keep an eye on the place until you're in shape to use it again. If fact, they sent this down for you." Hunter opened the box. Inside was one of his flight suits, neatly cleaned and folded. He tossed it down on the bed. "Of course, you won't be needing it right away, but when you're ready you might not want to make another one of your famous bare-assed public appearances."

John fingered the blue-and-white flight suit. He lay back and pondered the ceiling in silence.

"Uh... John? Do you mind if I call you that?"

John shrugged. "Don't see why I would."

"Do you mind if I ask you a question? Sort of a personal one?"

John leveled his eyes at Hunter. "Shoot."

"Those five dumb Canucks—the ones who tried to kill you. Why didn't you kill 'em back? Tell you the truth, I would have."

"I wasn't angry enough at them. I've... seen too much death to be that upset at someone who tries to kill me. The thought did cross my mind, but only because I was worried about what might happen—when people found out what they'd done. Besides, it would have been cowardly. Nobody would have known. There would have been no accounting for it. Someday I might run into somebody I feel I have no choice but to kill. But if so, I'll do it in full sight of the world, and then take the consequences."

Hunter looked at him with eyes twinkling in a neutral face. "So, what was the deal there? I guess they must have caught you off guard—woke you up? I figure you have to be wide awake and alert to fly and bounce bullets and such. I guess if they'd walked in while you were reading or catching up on KSKY or whatever, you would have just tossed their butts right back down the mountain, right? Maybe even risked a night flight to bring them down. You might bump into a mountain in the dark, but hey, so what, it's the Elmer Fudd boys that wind up with the headache, right? That's how I figure it."

John regarded him in careful silence for a few moments.

"You don't really believe all that crap, do you?" he asked.

"Shoot, what do you want me to believe? That your powers cut out like a light the second the sun goes down? Who'd buy anything as cockeyed as that? Makes no sense. No, I'm sticking with my first story. That's what's going into my official SRIP report."

John gave him another moment of silent consideration.

"General Hunter, you are one cool guy."

"You know it, John. I don't think it warms up around here until August."

John laughed. "Man, I haven't heard humor that lame since I quit talking to myself."

"Well, you might find something else in that category when you examine the contents of this folder." He handed it over.

John opened it up. The first sheet was a letter from the President wishing him a quick recovery. The other thirty or so sheets were similar notes from other prominent American politicians and officials.

"Gee, there's nothing here from Cosimano, is there?"

Hunter chuckled. "No, I don't think so. Maybe that country-club jail he's in hasn't delivered his engraved stationery yet. But to tell you the truth, if he had sent you one it'd be about as sincere as some of the ones in that folder now. I don't think I'm giving away any national secrets when I say you make a lot of folks pretty nervous."

John closed the portfolio and looked at Hunter ingenuously. "Why? I haven't done anything wrong, have I?"

"Doesn't matter. These boys are all in the power game, and they like to be on top. When they see you, they see a kind of power they can't match or control. And I don't just mean your ability to fly or bend heavy-gauge aluminum in your bare hands. I mean power over people. You're the best-known man on Earth, and loved by eighty percent of those who know about you at all, which is more than any politician can say. The fact that you've got that kind of influence without being under anybody's thumb makes 'em sweat. A lot of 'em are just hoping you blow it, make some dumb mistake that'll destroy the people's trust in you, just so they'll have an excuse to jump on you and take you down. That's why there are Senators pretending moral outrage every time you don't make it to some disaster, or when you don't manage to rescue every single victim of a flood covering a quarter-million square miles. That's why the FBI and SRIP have thick files on your family and everybody you ever met. That's why the President himself loses sleep trying to figure out how to buffalo you into becoming a living weapon in our arsenal. John, you've done a good job at staying out of it so far. But you want to be very careful."

Still holding the forgotten portfolio, John blinked in consternation. "You know, I'll bet you didn't come here with instructions to tell me all this."

"True enough. But I decided that the work of the Sky Ranger Information Project might extend both ways. Once in a while."

"Don't worry. I'll keep it to myself."

"That I know. But I don't want you to think that everyone in the Government sticks pins in Sky Ranger dolls every night. There's one agency that can't help being just a little bit fond of you, although they're afraid you might leave them and their Spam-cans in the dust."

John flipped through the letters until he came to a sheet with the NASA logo at the top.

To Our Brother in Flight,

We, the astronauts of Apollo 24, want you to know you have our thoughts and support as we prepare to make the final planned human exploration of the moon. We and all of NASA have been aware of the presence of your guardian eye as our crews are launched into deep space. We'll miss you this time. We intend to confer your name on some prominent feature of the lunar surface in the vicinity of Aristarchus, our destination. We find it fitting that your name adjoin the brightest landmark on the face of the moon.

(signed)

Jim McBride
Austin Guiles
James Horn

John found himself thrilled and touched by the letter. He grinned over it like a schoolboy.

"Calm down, John. I think there's more."

The next item was a large white envelope, also bearing the NASA vector logo. It felt heavy and a bit lumpy, as though it contained more than paper. John opened the clasp and upended the envelope. Out fell four glossy wonders, patches or badges made of some shiny, flexible material, each about six inches wide. Each consisted of a horizontal blue ellipse, with a smaller oval of brilliant gold contained within it. Superimposed over both was the spread-winged silhouette of an eagle, its wings spanning the whole width of the blue ellipse. It was an eagle soaring over the Sun, a graphic symbol of power and beauty.

The enclosed letter read:

Dear *Sky Ranger,*

Enclosed is the result of one of our smaller projects, initiated some months ago. I asked Bill Accardi, head of the NASA graphic arts department, to design a symbol which we hope you'll like and will wish to use. Bill has been responsible for many of the mission patches we've flown over the past few years. Since your durability requirements are rather severe, we put some thought into the materials used as well. The core substrate is a woven carbon-fiber reinforced fabric, while the colored outer coating consists of experimental ceramic glazes. We guarantee the emblems will survive conditions that would vaporize your flight suits. If you care to attach them to your suits, sew them with the enclosed spool of tungsten wire. Best regards to you from the staff of NASA.

(signed)

Nicholas Wilson
Administrator

John peered into the envelope. Stuck in the fold at the bottom was a roll of hair-like greyish-silver wire.

He set the envelope aside and arrayed the four emblems on his stomach. He picked one up and admired the play of light from the gold sun-disk and from the lapis depths of the vault of ceramic sky. He considered them perhaps the most beautiful man-made objects he'd ever seen.

"NASA sure knew the right buttons to push."

"I can see that," said Hunter.

The door swung open; in walked Bea. She faced General Hunter gamely, though she seemed more unnerved by his brass-and-beribboned uniform than she was by Sky Ranger himself. "General, you've gone over the time allowed for your visit by Dr. Hogarth. We don't want to tire our patient. I'm afraid I'll have to ask you to leave now."

Hunter stood and examined her over his long, narrow nose. "Young lady, I couldn't tire this boy if I dropped him into the Grand Canyon. But it's your hospital, so I'll be going. I think we were pretty much finished here anyway." He started for the door, turned and looked back at John. "You take care. And watch out for this one, she could give you more trouble than you can handle."

"She already has. Thanks for everything, General."

Hunter was out the door, and his footfalls receded into silence.

"Well, I hope that wasn't a typical American military man," said Bea, looking at the door.

"Nope, I don't think he is."

Bea turned back to him and noticed the glittering symbols still spread over John's body. "What are those?"

"They're emblems. NASA made them for my flight suits."

"Oh. I thought they were coasters."

"Um... Bea, how far do your services to me extend?"

She looked at him archly. "I can't comment on that until you get more specific."

"Well—do you know how to sew?"

"Well enough to fix a button, if that's what you want."

"I was wondering if you could sew one of these emblems onto my flight suit here."

She stepped over to where the folded blue garment lay on the bed. She picked it up and let it fall open, then held it up and looked it up and down. Her eyes widened beneath her dark bangs. The sight of that famous costume seemed to affect her as John himself hadn't.

"Yes...yes, I guess I could." She finished with a quiet smile. "Even though it's not really one of my duties."

"Sew it isn't. I can't do it myself, because I'm more appreciative than I seam."

"Ugh. If I heard that right, I'll be glad when you can fly again so nobody can hear your humor. Where do you want the patch?"

"On the shoulder, I guess."

"All right, that's for later. Right now, if you can relax your arm so I can get a needle in, I need to get some more blood"

"Oh, man. I don't know why you bothered to give me so much when you're just going to take it all back out again."

"Don't be such a crybaby."

Chapter Ten

Bea appeared early the next morning to draw still more blood and check his vitals before the sun could rise to harden him and mask his true condition with its freely-bestowed vitality. When she'd put him through his paces she went out and returned with his flight suit, now on a hanger. The emblem spread its wings over the chest rather than on the shoulder.

"I tried it on the shoulder, but it was too big and didn't look right. Is it okay?"

"It's fine. It was sweet of you to do it for me."

"You won't think so when you find out how much blood I'm supposed to get later."

Later that morning, Hogarth and some of the other hospital staff showed up with a wheelchair.

"John, there's something we'd like to show you down in the cafeteria. Care to hop aboard?"

"Do I really have to ride in that?"

"I'm afraid so. Hospital rules."

"All right," said John resignedly. He brushed them off as they tried to help him out of bed, slipped on the grey robe they'd provided for him, and sat in the chair. Hogarth pushed him out into the corridor, then let go while he talked to the Mounties on guard.

John found himself facing a long straight corridor. He was tempted to propel the chair along it with his flight impulse, but something about the solemn air of those around him prevented him. Instead he drummed his fingers on the armrest, hoping that whatever was about to happen wouldn't prove to be too tedious.

Surrounded by a cordon of doctors and police, John was wheeled into an elevator and taken to the cafeteria on the first floor. A wave of floral scent washed over them as they approached the door. They entered a large, sunny room whose walls were almost totally obscured by flowers, bouquets and arrangements of all kinds, some quite large and elaborate. Blue and white were the most popular colors, but there was no shortage of red and yellow roses and vivid greenery either. It was like being inside an inverted Rose Parade float.

John looked around in a slight daze. "These are all for me?" Though he didn't say so, this display of excess and adulation left him feeling uncomfortable and embarrassed.

"They are," said Hogarth. "They've been arriving in a constant stream since yesterday morning. Between the florists, the journalists, and the postmen delivering bags of letters, it's difficult for anyone else to get into this hospital. What do you want to do with the flowers?"

"A few for my room would be nice... preferably potted plants that won't die. Bea, will you pick some out? Would you like any for yourself and the other nurses? The rest you can give to the other patients. If there's any left after that, send them to other hospitals. Um... is there any way I can see who sent them, other than to look at every card?"

"We've been keeping track," said Hogarth. He handed John an alphabetized list.

John glanced over the names of dozens of individuals and organizations. He felt a little pang when he saw no Boutin was listed. Elise had vanished—he'd heard nothing from her, and didn't know where she was. There *were* a few Avrils—that was significant. He admitted it was about time to do something about his family—when he had the time and the freedom.

"I'll keep this list if you don't mind. One more thing. I'd like to make a statement before the press—let's say in two hours."

Hogarth raised his eyebrows. "Well. God knows they've been hounding us for that long enough. I don't see why we can't arrange it—if the security people can be convinced."

"Tell them I'll be here to protect them if they're worried."

"I'll talk to the hospital administrator and get it started. Shall we hold it right here?"

"Yes. I want them to see the flowers."

A few minutes later he and Bea were alone in his room.

"Bea, I want to wear the flight suit to the press conference."

"Do you have to? I'd have to get permission to undo your IVs and then plug you back in again afterward."

"Please do it. I don't want to go on camera looking like an invalid."

"All right, but I want to help you into it so your stitches won't get strained."

At the appointed time John permitted himself to be wheeled back to the cafeteria. A lectern had been set up at wheelchair height at the head of the room. Bea deposited him behind it and scurried out of the glare of the camera lights. The small corps of journalists who'd been allowed in were outnumbered by security people, both uniformed and otherwise. Three TV cameras were being fed to all networks. One 16mm movie camera was present, a few still photographers, and half a dozen reporters. They all stared at him with a predatory fascination.

As the clock marked noon, John stood up smoothly, with no sign of weakness, and stepped away from the lectern. He shot a glance at Hogarth and caught him rolling his eyes in exasperation. John studied the reporters while he waited for all disturbance to die down. The hot camera lights glittered splendidly on his new emblem as he surveyed his audience.

"First, I don't want to take too much time with this. The hospital staff is going to want to get their lunch without tripping over your cables and tripods.

"I want to talk to everyone who has sent these flowers, or is thinking about sending some. You can see that this room is practically wall-to-wall flowers." He made a gesture to encompass the cafeteria. "There are hundreds of arrangements, more than I can even appreciate individually, though the cumulative effect is impressive. I want to thank everyone who sent them for your kindness and concern. I feel bad that I can't give them all the attention they deserve.

"I'd like to tell you a little about how I came to be here. I was shot by a man who was in the mountains for only one reason—to make money by destroying wildlife. He and his four friends were there to kill magnificent wild animals, to take creatures who are masters of one of the most rigorous environments on Earth, and turn them into lifeless, glass-eyed objects to adorn people's walls. To me, the fact that they planned to poach the bighorn from a national park, where they are legally protected, is less important than the fact that they intended to take them at all, for the most senseless of reasons. The people who would have bought those heads would probably hesitate to go outside in the

Joe Bergeron

rain. They'd rather pay a criminal for a 'trophy' than venture into the wild to try to get one for themselves. They are people with such disregard for life that they think their homes are enhanced by hanging the severed head of an animal on their wall. And they are people with such a deadened regard for beauty that they don't realize the obscenity of displaying such a grisly relic. Meanwhile, we are deprived of the chance to enjoy the living animal in the wild. And far more importantly, the Bighorn themselves are deprived of their chance to live without the interference of a barbarian tribe that proves its dominance over nature by laying waste to it with indiscriminate death."

John looked around at the flowers again.

"My guess is that there's at least ten thousand dollars worth of flowers in this room. They're all beautiful, and I thank you again for sending them. But I have a request. Instead of sending more, give your money to organizations set up to preserve wild animals and the land they need to live on. Give to help put men like the ones who shot me out of business. That'll make me feel even better than these flowers. That's all, thanks for listening."

He turned and started to walk from the room, but a chorus of cries from the journalists brought him up short.

"Sky Ranger! Sky Ranger! Can we ask some questions?"

John hesitated, then returned to the glare of the TV lights. "I guess so," he said tentatively.

A well-known American TV anchorman stood up. "Sky Ranger, let me first state that we in the press have admired your good works for the past thirteen months, even as we have looked upon you with a certain sense of frustration.

You have a unique ability to avoid any questioning, simply by taking a running leap and disappearing over our heads."

There were a few rueful chuckles at this.

"Now that you're temporarily grounded, permit me to ask perhaps the most frequent question of all. Sky Ranger, what is your true name?"

John smiled and looked down at his feet. "I'm sorry, but I choose not to answer that. If you really don't know the answer by now, you haven't been doing your homework."

"We have reports linking you to… "

A more aggressive voice cut him off. "Sky Ranger, you've been observed to shrug off punishment that would have turned an ordinary man into soup. How is it that the rifle bullet fired by that poacher was able to injure you?"

"They woke me up. I was sleepy and I wasn't expecting the shot." That seemed to satisfy them, but John felt uncomfortable with the evasion.

"Sky Ranger, I'd say the most basic question hasn't yet been asked. How exactly are you able to fly?"

John smiled again, as here was something he didn't mind discussing. "Well, it's not something I can diagram for you, but I'll be happy to give you my guesses. I think I'm basically something like Maxwell's Demon. James Maxwell was a great physicist who studied thermodynamics. He invented his 'Demon' as a hypothetical being able to influence random events, and thus cause unlikely occurrences, like a bottle of gas separating into a hot half and a cold half, or a table rising into the air because all the air molecules vibrating beneath it happen to move up at the same time. To do that, the 'Demon' would have to be plugged into whatever underlying forces control these 'random' events. I think I'm like that Demon—I'm plugged in too. But I'm not consciously aware of any of this. When I fly, I just do it because I know I can. And it feels very good." He ended with a beaming smile.

"Sky Ranger, we've had reports that when you entered this hospital you were in a deathlike state, with little blood in your body, a corpselike temperature, and minimal cardiac activity, yet you were alert and even capable of flight. Are you in fact a normal, living human being, or have you achieved some form of animation apart from our form of life?"

John's buoyancy evaporated. Here they were skirting an issue far too personal to air in public.

"I'm not exactly normal, obviously," he said quietly, "but I'm alive. Really alive."

Hogarth stood up. "Gentleman, that's all the time we have. Thank you for coming." He stepped up and guided John to the wheelchair, pushing him into the seat before he could sidle away. He wheeled him out and into the elevator at a brisk pace.

John was quiet and thoughtful throughout the afternoon. Bea brought in sacks of mail—more than he could ever hope to deal with, even if reading it full time. He picked through it, reading a letter here and there, feeling guilt at ignoring so much of it, fully aware of how much pain, need, and yearning it likely contained.

He had mixed feelings about the press conference. The final question had brought back glimpses of feelings and realities that had been deeply buried by six months of cold and silence. He stared at the walls of his room and felt a growing sense of wrongness and oppression.

Around four o'clock, Doctor Hogarth walked in and tossed a stack of newspapers on John's bed table. Most gave responsible coverage of his statement and interview, but a few chose lurid headlines such as "Is Sky Ranger A DEMON?" and "Sky Ranger ADMITS DEMONIC TIES". John groaned and shook his head in disbelief. Any mentions of James Clerk Maxwell and his ideas were left to the end of the story.

One sidebar recounted the history of efforts to determine his identity. It contained a list of names that had been brought up as possibilities at one time or another—among them was John J. Avril. He found it astonishing that junk mail addressed to John Avril wasn't being delivered to his cabin by now.

An unrelated story was buried on page three or five. The men of Apollo 24, with their lunar spacecraft *Gandalf* and *Nightwalker*, were about to launch for the crater Aristarchus.

Late in the afternoon, as he lay there daydreaming, alone in his room for a change, he sat up to watch the alpenglow ripen on the peaks in the distance. He stared longingly at those remote, snow-streaked mountains. Visions of mountain solitude entered his mind: ice crystals dancing over a glacier's face in a stiff wind, lichen clinging to surfaces of rock known only to the sun and rain, clouds surging over a gap in a mountain wall and pouring into a valley like sea foam.

Daring the wrath of Bea, he stood up to go to the window for a better view, but the circus of activity below distracted his attention. Beyond the police line, picketers marched in circles beneath the watchful eyes of TV camera crews. Some displayed messages of support and encouragement, but the people getting the most attention waved placards with slogans like:

CAST OUT MAXWELL'S DEMON

and

HUNTERS, NEXT TIME TRY A SILVER BULLET

John watched sadly as an ambulance approached the hospital, but was slowed and stopped by the surging crowds that surrounded it, forced to inch its way forward while whatever poor soul within it suffered.

John's gaze was drawn irresistibly back to the rosy crenellations on the horizon. He looked dreamily at the mountains until someone below noticed him at the window, causing an uproar in the crowd and sparking a storm of flashes from handheld cameras. He stepped away from the window. A moment later the sun withdrew below the horizon. He barely made it back to bed before exhaustion pulled him down.

Dr. Hogarth appeared just after sunrise of the following morning to examine John. He lifted the dressings and examined John's wounds carefully. Covering the still raw-looking incisions, he looked at John with evident concern.

"Sky Ranger, the healing looks clean and normal, but it's definitely behind where it ought to be by now. I was hoping that your daytime stamina would promote rapid healing, but it seems just the opposite—I'd say you're healing at about half the normal rate. Do you have any idea why that should be so?"

"Maybe. My body possesses a quality of unusual stability when the sun is up—it resists any kind of physical change. Even my metabolic needs are reduced, not speeded up or increased. I suspect all my healing is going on at night, when my body functions normally. And maybe even that's not going as well as it should, because I'm always so tired after being Sky Ranger for fifteen hours."

"Even though you're not actually flying or exerting yourself."

"It doesn't seem to make much difference."

"Well, I advise you to take very good care of yourself after sunset from now on. If you ever suffered injuries more severe than what you have now, you might enter a kind of healing deficit from which you'd never recover."

"Pretty good advice. Doctor, when will you start me on liquid foods? I mean, besides what I get from the IV?"

"As soon as I'm sure you won't spring a leak. We sewed you up pretty well—I think today we can start you on some sterile water—only it'll be laced with an X-Ray dye so we can see if any gets loose in your abdomen."

"I guess you'll be glad to get rid of me, won't you? Given the way I'm disrupting the hospital's routine and everything."

Hogarth looked at him steadily. "I'll be glad when you're able to leave. Not before."

Later in the morning, John asked if he could meet some of the other patients, and Hogarth agreed gladly. Bea, however, wouldn't permit him to undo her IVs by putting on the flight suit again, so he was forced to go in his gown and robe, with IV bags suspended above his wheelchair.

His presence had a strong effect on the patients nevertheless. Children saw something familiar in his eyes, but it was those who were close to death, of whatever age, who paid him the closest heed. John insisted on being rolled up to the beds of patients so weak they were practically in comas, but each time, as he was brought near them, they showed a sudden surge of strength, lifting their heads with an alertness and clarity they might never know again. John had no profound message to impart. Some of them had never heard of him and had no idea who he was, yet they always smiled in his presence, and listened closely to his casual banter, as though some message hidden in his words did much to silence their fear of the imminent unknown before them. They lapsed back into twilight as John was rolled away, but always with a look of peace they hadn't worn before.

Bea, seeing this over and over, found herself deeply moved, so deeply that tears were forgotten as an inadequate response. And she found herself loving her patient with an intensity that was quite terrifying.

Afterwards, he was brought to a radiology lab where they conducted the leak test. As the dyed water made its way into his small intestine, the fluoroscope picture showed no sign of a problem. To celebrate, the doctors relieved John of his IV tubes and started him on a low-residue liquid diet.

Back in his room, Bea treated him to a comprehensive sponge-bath. She dabbed delicately at his wounds, and John of course felt no pain. In fact, the sutures looked and felt as solid as his body itself. A subconscious train of thought suddenly emerged from the tunnel and made itself clear with headlight shining.

"Bea, do you have scissors?"

"Yes, a little pair."

"Will you do me a favor? Snip one of these stitches."

She looked at him with dismay. "They're not nearly ready to come out. Doctor would kill me if I fooled with them."

"Please, if you trust me, do it. Just one. You won't do any harm, I promise."

Unable to refuse, Bea produced tiny bandage scissors. She slipped the tip of one blade beneath a suture and closed them.

The thread merely slipped between the blades. Try as she might, Bea was unable to cut it. "The scissors just slide off," she said.

John nodded. "You see? I said you wouldn't hurt anything."

He spent the rest of the afternoon lying quietly, relaxing the area of his abdomen to allow the healing to proceed. The concentration required probably took more effort than just letting his unusual nature take its course, but he wanted to give his injuries every last chance to repair themselves. The sutures, he now knew, were just as durable as he was.

The answer had come to him in a flash. Every time he flew to high altitudes, he had other pressure differentials to think about than those in his ears. He always did a certain amount of belching as the air in his stomach escaped to the outside. However, even at a hundred thousand feet, where the boiling point of water was well below his body temperature, the liquid contents of his stomach stayed put—they did not boil away, any more than his blood did, despite the almost total lack of pressure. That must mean that his body and *whatever was in it,* or intimately a part of it, shared in the stability that produced his durability—and that certainly included his sutures, but unfortunately not his clothing.

Bea returned just before sunset to feed him and to square him away for the night. She had, he realized, been working double shifts, just to be near him.

The sun went down and John's strength left him, yet he forced himself to stay awake a few minutes longer. Bea tucked him in tenderly. As she was about to leave, John reached out to touch her with a shaky hand.

"Bea... ? Why don't you... sleep in... tomorrow... come in... a little late."

Tears sprang from her eyes, and she nodded, a little too vigorously.

"I guess—you'll be leaving, right?"

"Yes. Thanks for being... so sweet," said John.

"You're welcome. Now close your eyes and get some sleep." she said in a husky voice.

"I will. But first... will you please give me... a good night kiss... ?"

She did.

The sun itself woke him in the morning, calling him forth with a quiet sense of urgency and purpose. Without hesitation he rolled out of bed, pulled on his flight suit, and quickly jotted down a note, which he left on his pillow. Then he swung open the door and stepped out into the hall.

The three Mounties on duty looked up in surprise at this interruption in their rather dull vigil. "Sir?" said one of them politely, "Is there something we can do for you?"

"No thanks, sergeant. I just thought I'd take a little stroll this morning."

"Well, sir, we have been instructed to discourage you from leaving your room," said the man doubtfully.

"Then I go forth in discouragement. You've done your duty."

"Yes, sir, but I'm afraid I'll have to report this."

"By all means. Thanks for keeping an eye on me for the past few days." John extended his hand.

The Mountie accepted the hand tentatively. "You will be coming back?"

"No."

"Sir…"

"Don't start."

John strolled to the nearest stairwell and climbed to the very top. The door to the roof was locked, but he twisted the knob and felt its mechanism shear away. He heard frantic footsteps pounding up from below, but of course there was nothing they could do. John pushed the door open. His first reward was a blast of cold, clean, outdoor air, fresh and sweet as a waterfall's mist after the closed-in chemical odor of the hospital. With a feeling of rebirth he stepped out onto the roof. The beauty of the open sky threatened to stop his heart, as the ivory-gold rays of the Sun of dawn brushed the edges of a few low clouds, leaving their shadows a soft lavender-grey. Beyond was a clear, boundless expanse of light and freedom, a serene, peaceful realm, apart from the trials and squabbles of the men who kept their eyes on the ground.

Ahead was the tarred expanse of the hospital roof, broken by sheet-metal ducts, vents, and fans. He started to run; immediately he felt the sweet rush of wind through his hair and past his cheeks. Around him he felt the play of ineffable forces, forces available to anyone, but which only he, as far as he knew, had yet learned to wield. He leaped, and the air took him gladly, bore him up and passed him along.

With the ecstasy of a falcon untethered, he soared off the roof and away, raising an uproar beneath as fingers pointed and heads swiveled to watch as Sky Ranger, unexpected as Hermes, rushed by overhead and swiftly vanished into the vast, unregarded kingdom of the air.

Chapter Eleven

The most popular radio station in the world was KSKY. Operated by the United Nations, its new main transmitter, the tallest structure on Earth, occupied a plot of land straddling the border between North Dakota and Manitoba. By special permission of the FCC and its Canadian equivalent, the station operated on an AM frequency forbidden to any other station on the continent. Scattered throughout the world were lesser transmitters broadcasting on other clear channels. It was the mission of KSKY to enfold the planet with its message.

The station's operation also permitted a small but politically valuable foreign exchange program. The announcers were graduate students from around the world who gave part of their time to KSKY in exchange for a year of study at the University of Winnipeg—not quite as prestigious as Cal Tech or Cornell, but neither of those were located near the geographic center of North America.

One such student announcer was Lobengula Masunda, who, since coming to North America, had received the nickname Lobo. Today Lobo piloted his battered VW Squareback to the station after five days of classwork in Winnipeg. He'd spend the next three days behind the microphone, studying during his time off—there wasn't much else to do, out on this enormous wheat field that must occupy half the continent. He was still five miles from the transmitter, but already it was the dominant feature of the landscape, a tapering, concrete-sheathed shaft rising almost two thousand feet above the prairie. Just now its tip was invisible, immersed in a river of dark cloud that rolled by

162

overhead, revealed only by the diffused aircraft-warning strobes that blinked at its summit.

Lobo pulled into the parking lot and extracted his lanky frame from the Squareback. The rain was holding off, but the day was raw and blustery, despite the season. Lobo pulled up the collar of his jacket. He'd never encountered weather like this in his native Zimbabwe. He checked in at the dorm and dropped off his bag, then headed for the broadcast studio, glancing up at the tower. As usual the odd perspective made it appear on the verge of toppling. Lobo was happy he wasn't one of the engineers who tended the transmitter at the apex.

A magnetic key admitted him to the main office. Although his shift was about to begin, one of the secretaries stopped him.

"Lobo, Mr. Johannsen would like to speak with you. Danielle will stay on the air until you're through."

"Oh yes?" Lobo raised his eyebrows. So—the Director was finally taking the time to meet him, when he'd already worked here for a month. He knocked on Johannsen's door and entered. Keir Johannsen stood up to greet him. He was a small, wiry Swede with lank blond hair combed to the side. Johannsen wore a smile as he came out from behind the desk to offer his hand. The smile vanished as soon as his grip was released.

"Well, Mr. Masunda. We meet at last. Please have a seat."

"Thank you, sir."

"You're an agronomy student, aren't you?"

"That's right. It seems to be what's most needed back in Zimbabwe."

Johannsen indicated the speaker on the wall. The volume was turned low, but they could still hear Danielle's smooth contralto. "I monitor the broadcast often, so I feel as though I know you. You do good work— you are calm and clear, with a no-nonsense delivery. To be frank, I'm not sure our work has been meaningful during the past few days—you know we've heard nothing from Sky Ranger since he disappeared from the hospital several days ago. No one knows his condition. He has failed to respond to any of our announcements."

"Yes sir, I have kept up with the news."

Johannsen nodded. "Of course you know your work by now. You don't need a lecture on the operation of the station. But I do like to meet our young people who go on the air. As far as I'm concerned, we're here only to meet Sky Ranger's need for information. I think it's particularly important to keep our mission in mind during this crisis of Sky Ranger's apparent absence. If he is ever to respond again, it may be that what we tell him over the next few days will make a difference."

"I am interested in hearing your views, sir."

"You may not know that I personally perform the final edit of most material that comes in from our bureaus. The people in the field do a good job of weeding out trivia, but still, more comes in than either we or Sky Ranger could hope to accommodate. Although we have the best communications system in the world, many crises are already resolved, for good or for ill, by the time the news reaches us, and I exclude those as well. I tell you this because I've been warned to expect an announcement of unusual significance, probably to be made during your shift. It is a crisis in which only Sky Ranger can possibly intervene. Wherever he is, whatever his condition, I hope to stimulate him to act in this matter. Our announcers must be careful to give it proper emphasis. You will recognize this announcement, if and when it comes to you. You'd best start your shift now."

Johannsen stood up again and Lobo did the same. They shook hands again, and Lobo departed. He felt no particular apprehension—after all, it wasn't he who was expected to deal with the crisis, whatever it was—but he did feel the same responsibility he felt every time he sat down before a KSKY microphone. He glimpsed Danielle in Studio A, went on to Studio B, and closed the door behind him. He glanced at the first few lines on the monitor, adjusted the mike, and began reading when the engineer cued him from the control room.

"This is KSKY continuing on the air. Lobengula Masunda reporting. Hello, Sky Ranger, I hope you are well, and that you're listening.

"In the town of Llanelly, Wales, a man is trapped and buried in a coal bin. Rescue efforts are underway, but the victim is estimated to have only thirty minutes of air remaining. Llanelly is located on the north coast of the Bristol Channel, west of Swansea.

"A storm in the Adriatic Sea has put two small freighters in danger of capsizing. Several small fishing boats may also be in danger in the area. No known fatalities as yet.

"The same storm is flooding parts of Venice, endangering many pieces of Renaissance art and sculpture. A power failure is hampering efforts to move the artwork to safety."

Lobo tapped the NEXT SCREEN key, bringing another page of text into view. He read it calmly enough—nothing unusual here yet. As usual he detected a distinct bias towards reporting problems occurring in white or Western nations, but he hoped that was attributable mainly to poor communications in areas such as his own.

There wasn't much going on in the world...the text began to repeat after only three screens. As he read, he tried to guess at the nature of the special announcement, but he didn't have to wait long for his curiosity to be satisfied. He tapped the NEXT SCREEN key again, calling forth a page he'd not yet seen.

"On the Moon—" He paused and raced ahead to be sure he'd read that first phrase correctly. There was no mistake. He cleared his throat and continued. "On the Moon, the astronauts exploring the crater Aristarchus are unable to lift off to rejoin the Apollo command module for the trip back to Earth. The mishap occurred when the Lunar Lander *Nightwalker* suffered damage shortly after landing about two days ago. Announcement of the accident was withheld by NASA until all repair options had been evaluated and found useless. The Command Module will soon be forced to leave for Earth to insure the safety of the orbiting astronaut. The two lunar astronauts have sufficient supplies to survive for another two days with careful rationing. There is no hope of rescue—other than intervention from you, Sky Ranger. To repeat... "

"Nightwalker, this is Houston.
"Nightwalker, this is Houston, come in."
"Houston, McBride here."
"Jim, Austin, we just made a public announcement about your situation. As of now, you've got everybody in the world pulling for you."
A moment of silence from the Moon.

"Roger, Houston, we copy that. Thanks for giving us a chance to talk to our families before the news went out."

"Ah—no problem, Jim. We've been watching on the Lunar Rover camera as you set up the experiments and we're getting good telemetry."

"We're glad to hear it, aren't we, Austin?"

"That's right, Jim, we sure are. Houston, we should be able to get some good shots with the all-sky IR camera once the Sun goes down, but, ah, we..."

"We might not be able to deliver the film," said McBride quietly.

"But at least you can get the data from the mass spectrometer," said Guiles optimistically. "I guess we'll be able to operate the spectrometer longer than we expected. We'll know if there's any outgassing from Aristarchus at sunset."

"Roger, *Nightwalker*. There's a lot of scientists on the ground who want to see that data."

"*Nightwalker*, this is *Gandalf*. I've got loss of signal in two minutes. You boys are going to have a real pretty night. You'll be the first to see the Moon by Earthlight."

"Right, Horn," said McBride. "See you when you come back over the hill."

"Roger."

In truth, the two men on the surface were preoccupied with neither the experiments nor the romance of the on-coming Lunar night. Lunar Module pilot Austin Guiles stood next to the crippled vehicle, peering into the descent stage through a hole blown in a thin metal panel. It looked like a bursting balloon frozen in time. The only light on the twisted mess inside was reflected from a map which Jim McBride held up to the sun. His helmet's gold sun shield was locked down to deflect the dazzle of the incandescent disk that floated low over the horizon.

"If I could work my way in there, and remove the damaged cowling around the ascent engine bell, and if I had a ball peen hammer, we might be able to pound out the damage to the bell enough for us to risk the ascent," said Guiles.

"But we can't do any of those things. Maybe we can disconnect the ascent stage, set it down on the ground on its side, fix the bell, then carry the stage back up to the descent stage."

"We could try it," said Guiles hopefully.

McBride laughed. "I'll tell you what, Austin old buddy. Another day or so, maybe I'll be ready to give it a shot."

Guiles straightened up. McBride folded his improvised reflector. They both turned with the ponderous grace peculiar to men on the Moon, their boots kicking up short-lived puffs of dust. Their feet sank an inch into the charcoal-grey powder as they came to a halt facing that glowing oasis of life, the sapphirinne Earth, half a billion footsteps away in space.

"Houston, this is McBride. Austin and I know as well as you do that we're not going to leave the Moon for a long, long time. We can't say we're thrilled about it, but we knew that the end result of a mission like this might not be parades in our home towns. In a way it'll be quite a distinction to be the first men to die on another world. But to tell the truth, it's an honor we could both, ah, live without. I don't want to get too weepy on you here, but Austin and I do have a few requests. First, be careful with the Horn. He's the kind of guy who might refuse to leave us here to die. We want him to get home. Second, we know there's a bunch of surplus Apollo hardware laying around, including a couple more Saturn Vs. If there's any way, we'd like to see you turn that stuff into one or two more Moon flights. The Apollo program has been a grand success up till now — we'd truly hate to see it end on a note like this."

The radio signals flickered Earthward. Their reply arrived a few seconds later.

"Roger, *Nightwalker*, we copy and we'll do everything possible to honor your requests."

Austin Guiles went back to studying the scrambled plumbing in the lander descent stage, wrecked by the mysterious explosion of the near-empty descent engine fuel tank just after shutdown. He'd been futilely examining it for the past two days, but the sheer, morbid wonderment of something so outrageous and so inevitably fatal brought him back over and over again.

Jim McBride, commander of Apollo 24, settled down in the left seat of the Lunar Rover. He glanced down at the readouts for his backpack — he had about two hours of oxygen left, or about an hour before they'd have to hole up in the lander for a recharge.

"Austin."

"Yes, Jim?"

"I'm going for a spin. See you in an hour."

"Sure thing."

Going for a solo joyride in the Lunar Rover was strictly against the mission safety rules, but somehow that didn't seem to matter anymore. McBride tugged at the control stick and the four electric motors began to turn the flexible wire wheels. The Rover moved out sluggishly. A glance at a tiny gauge showed the batteries were running low, but they had juice enough for another short trip or two.

McBride roved right up to the rim of Aristarchus and turned left to run slowly southward. He drove until the lander glittered like a tropical insect on the horizon behind him, then stopped to face the crater and admire the view. The same view was available a few yards from the landing site, but he felt betrayed by the LM, which he and Austin had babied all the way to the lunar surface. He wanted it out of sight for a while, but his training was too strong to allow him to venture away from it completely.

Although the sun was behind him, he kept his helmet's sun shield down to cut the glare from the crater's central peak, some fifteen miles away. Aristarchus was coated with a deposit far whiter and more reflective than the yellowish-grey of the surrounding plateau. It was the brightest feature on the Moon. That and the fact that color shifts and possible gas emissions had been reported by visual observers of the crater had been the main reason for targeting the area for Apollo 24. Now the rock boxes would remain on the surface, but at least the science instruments could relay information on whatever feeble wisps of gas the old Moon was still able to breathe forth.

The crater fell away steeply in front of him, and this near side was already draped in shadow. The far wall must still be sunlit, but it was below his horizon—only from the summit of the central peak itself might the whole crater be seen. From McBride's vantage, the peak looked like a dazzling iceberg afloat on a vast lake of blackness. The shadow would continue to creep up its flank until it was entirely enveloped, at about the same time the sun finally vanished below their own horizon. Then he could raise his gold visor to behold a light that was drowned out now, but would soon illuminate the Moon—the light of the sapphirinne Earth, nearly full, hanging above the crater's far rim, beautiful as only memory could make it, untouchable as a dream.

Lobengula Masunda stared in disbelief at his screen. His mouth worked as he searched for words, then they poured out of him copiously.

"Sky Ranger—I can't believe you haven't done anything about those stranded astronauts. This is my third shift since I first made the announcement, and you haven't made a move. I've often wondered how you choose which problems to handle and which to ignore. Granted, you were injured. Granted, you can't be everywhere at once. Yet sometimes you'll stop to get a cat out of a tree, and then later you won't be seen at some great disaster. Last month you did nothing for the victims of that midnight airliner crash in the Pyrenees, to say nothing of the many problems in Africa that have escaped you. I know your tendency to ignore the pain of black Africans, but these astronauts are no different than you. They even sent you their best wishes before they left for the Moon."

Anger began to dominate Masunda'a voice. "I just don't understand. You are injured, but not too badly hurt to fly from the hospital. If you are too weak to go to the Moon, why not tell us? Who do you think you are? Do you play God? Are you the judge of life and death? Where are you, Sky Ranger?"

The soundproof door of Studio B slammed open. In marched a furious Keir Johannsen. He wrenched the microphone away from Lobo and slammed his palm on the cutoff button on the board. Somewhere he found the strength to haul Lobo to his feet, even though the student outweighed him by at least fifty pounds. He took Lobo by the elbow and led him down the corridor to his office, snapping "Get someone else on the broadcast. Anyone at all," to his assistant in passing.

Lobo dared venture no comment as Johannsen directed him to a seat. The director himself declined to sit, preferring to stand, vibrating with wrath.

"Well, Mr. Masunda, that was quite a performance. In one breath you managed to accuse Sky Ranger of bigotry toward your race, not to mention calling him a malingerer, perhaps a coward. Mr. Masunda, at this station we do not editorialize. We do not scold Sky Ranger, insult him or shout at him. He is no agent of the United Nations, but a free man who does his work without compensation or obligation. If he is even still alive, and still paying attention, we have no right to ask him to do anything at all, let alone to *order* him."

Johannsen stared intently at the young Zimbabwean. "You accused Sky Ranger of being a judge to man. Then what are you to him? I suggest you examine the archives of this station to learn of the lives Sky Ranger *has* saved, including many in Africa, and including, by the way, my own daughter. And then you may depart. Your appointment to KSKY is cancelled. You may finish your semester at Winnipeg and then return home."

Lobo found himself behind the wheel of his VW with the engine running before he even realized what had happened.

Where was Sky Ranger?

The afternoon before Lobo's tirade saw him daydreaming on the summit of Illampu, a great peak of the Bolivian Andes overlooking Lake Titicaca to the west. Naked, he sat on the windswept snowfield of the summit and watched the glitter path on the waters far below. The sun began to decline over the Altiplano. The thin, clean wind caressed him like a lover's hand. He stretched out luxuriously over icy cobbles to stare up at the sky. As he often did, he also glanced at the C-shaped scar on his stomach. The external wounds were showing real healing at last. Now they were sealed well enough that he had little fear of reopening them during the day, but he was still obliged to be circumspect when the sun was down.

And in recognition of that, it was time to think about getting back "home".

John Avril picked himself up lazily and lofted from the east side of the mountain. The range fell away beneath him quickly, the greys of mountain rock and ice giving way to the mottled greens and tans of mixed forest and pampas. After a leisurely two hundred mile flight, he dropped down to the Rio Paray and skimmed along just over the surface. Spotting a few big catfish, he dived on them, scooped some out of the water, and killed them with sharp blows to the head. A stick from the river bank rammed through their jaws served to hold them together for the remainder of his flight. His benefactors, the *mbía*, were more tractable if he made some contribution to their scanty food supply. He disliked killing the fish, but it was better than slaughtering the legions of monkeys, tapirs, and peccaries they would have preferred. Once more aloft, he turned inland in search of their camp, hoping they hadn't decided to pull up stakes and wander off while he'd been absent.

He found the *mbía* where he'd left them. The men looked up with scant interest as he landed in their glade, but several women ran up to divest him of his catch. As usual they wasted little effort in preparing the food—they merely threw the fish in the fire, uncleaned, to roast. John walked around the camp looking for food he could tolerate—boiled manioc, papaya, a little soup bubbling in a crude clay pot. He would get his share—the *mbía* had learned not to contest his right to food, and in truth he ate little enough compared to the opportunistic gluttony of the tribesmen.

John had toured this area a few months ago during the height of the rainy season, and had spotted a tiny band marooned on an islet as floodwaters rose around them. They probably could have swum to safety, and they had very few possessions to lose, but crocodiles might have gotten some, and some of the infants might have been lost. So John had ferried them to higher ground one by one. This had terrified them, but when they realized they were suddenly safe and so far unharmed, they'd shown John a cautious gratitude.

Thus it had occurred to him that they might offer a secret refuge during his recovery. They were primitive, uncontacted, and frankly not the best company, but at least no one would think to look for him here. Another advantage—he was finally in an environment where nudity was appropriate—the *mbía* wore no clothing at all. They were small, but were basically not a bad-looking people. He was fully aware that to them he looked like a weirdly elongated oaf with sickly light-colored hair and ghastly blue eyes.

Some of the men offered wary grins as he passed among them, and the chief spoke to him, though he'd picked up only a few words of their language. One he'd come to know was *ngída*, or hawk, which was his name among the *mbía*.

The women regarded him with less reserve than did the men, even the *yukwáki*, young girls who were considered the most desirable. In fact, their scrutiny was sometimes so direct, and their chatter so animated, that he sometimes wished G-strings were in fashion among the *mbía*. Since hunting had been good lately, food wasn't quite the obsession it usually was among the *mbía*. With their foremost need fulfilled, sex had risen up to occupy much time and energy.

When John finished selecting and eating his few morsels, the day still had an hour or so to go. He lifted off and lazily explored the golden ramparts of the gigantic cumuli that sailed grandly through these heavy tropical skies. The rainy season was about over, but that didn't preclude an afternoon shower. He spotted a cloud that trailed streamers of rain and dove into it. Raindrops and ice crystals scrubbed him clean and left him feeling refreshed and strong. He let himself free fall and soon landed in his private haven—a platform he'd built high in the tallest tree overlooking the *mbía* village. This served two purposes—it spared his few possessions from the attentions of his hosts, and it spared him some of the attentions of the incredible hordes of mosquitoes, ticks, biting flies, ants, bees, snakes, spiders, and scorpions which avidly sought to torment or feed upon any mammal within their reach. Unfortunately, his perch did nothing to protect him from vampire bats.

He eyed his radio, powered by a fragment of the Skylab solar array, and toyed with the idea of tuning into KSKY to see what was going on in the world. But he decided against it. The world of man had gotten along before his coming; it would just have to go a little longer.

The sun set. As always he felt greatly weakened, though not nearly as much as he had right after he'd been shot. At least he could now stay awake for a short time. Despite the primitive conditions, his stay here had been good for him. South of the equator, the nights were longer than they were in Canada at this time of year, and long nights were what he needed for rest and healing. He pulled on his flight suit, although it was sweaty and uncomfortable in the heat and humidity. The protection it offered against bats and insects was worth it. Then he lay back on his pallet and listened to the activity in the camp below—an oddly comforting chorus of laughter, chiding arguments between the sexes, pleas for food, and the cries of children at play. He looked down between the poles of his platform. Beneath his tree ran naked children, leaping and bounding and shouting *ngída*, *ngída* as they sought to imitate him. John was fast asleep well before the village quieted fully. They all passed a peaceful night.

For the first time in days, John was awakened by the urging of Aurora rather than by the Sun itself. He rubbed his face to see if any unwelcome creatures were attached to it, and found nothing. Silence was absolute—even the hoots of the howler monkeys had not yet begun.

The Moon, a waning crescent, floated serenely in a rapidly brightening sky of cornflower blue, reminding him of the adventurers of Apollo 24. He couldn't make out Aristarchus as anything more than a white spot, but he knew where it was. Envisioning the astronauts bounding along the rim of the icy-white crater, he fell back into a half-sleep. His imaginings became a disturbing mixture of dream and reality, until he couldn't tell for sure where he really was—dozing in a tree, or standing beside the distant LM, with one panel blown out like golden foil...

The Sun made its return, greeted by the howls, cries, and songs of birds and monkeys. Instantly alert, John focused his newly-crystallized vision on the lunar crescent. He could plainly see the yin-yang spot of Aristarchus. As he stared intently he remembered a vestige of his dream-vision: the lunar module, its guts scrambled, standing crippled and useless.

With great apprehension he oriented his radio toward the Sun and flipped it on. Reception was poor now that the ionosphere was under the solar influence, but plainly enough he heard the final KSKY broadcast of Lobengula Masunda.

He kept the radio on when Masunda was abruptly replaced by another announcer, but he scarcely heard the repeated details of the lunar emergency. He kept staring at the Moon, wondering at the sublime stupidity of Masunda and KSKY as a whole. They expected him to fly to the *Moon* —?

Sometimes they'd alerted him to emergencies far beyond the scope of his abilities—earthquakes, for example, as though he could influence the movement of Earth's tectonic plates. But this seemed more ludicrous than most. Had they no notion of his limitations? True, he'd spent time in low Earth orbits, but a round trip to the Moon would be at least twenty times farther than he'd ever travelled in space. KSKY must not appreciate his need to breathe. They must believe his endurance to be limitless as well. Yes, his powers of flight were marvelous, but still he was a flying man, not a spaceship or an angel. It was absurd! He lowered his eyes from the Moon and stared sulking at the patch on his flight suit which hid his stomach wound. Right now he didn't feel like flying the length of his nose.

Right now, he realized suddenly, he didn't feel like he *could* fly the length of his nose.

Heart pounding, he pulled himself to his feet and leaned weakly against the railing of his platform. The Moon had gone soft again; his eagle's vision had departed. He squinted in despair at the Sun, but there was no comfort there. He'd lost it! He was standing in the Sun's full rays as a normal man. A crushing weight of remembrance fell on him—remembrance of his life before his rebirth, with all its fears and failures, anxieties and surrenders. Had they all returned? Had the past thirteen months been only a waking dream, now snuffed out by an unavoidable reality? He looked up again; now he saw multiple blurred Moons through tears. He'd worked so hard to purge himself of all this, to attain that unequaled state of harmony he'd lost but minutes ago, yet which already seemed as unrecoverable as the astronauts themselves. He couldn't fly to the Moon! A quarter of a million miles! To exile himself from Earth, to plunge into emptiness, into total silence! The astronauts rode in a ship, a familiar bubble of light, air, and warmth, and a link with home. But by himself, naked to the void, to the stars, to the infinity—to fling himself into an abyss of no return? The thought filled him with a dread beyond the fear of death—a dread of his smallness and of the enormity of the universe itself. He drew in upon himself, sat back down, shivering, with his arms wrapped around his knees.

The *mbía* seemed to sense something was wrong. A number of them clustered around the base of his tree, calling *Ngída? Ngída?* John gave out bitter, choking laughter. Their "hawk" was unfledged. Once he'd set out to banish despair from the world. Known to billions, he'd become the paragon of human aspiration. In the condition he was in now, he couldn't even get down from this tree.

At last his thoughts turned to the astronauts, the men who'd remembered him when his life was endangered, and who now would die on a distant world. They and their organization had bestowed on him the proud symbol he wore on his chest. He gripped the edge of the emblem and tried to rip it free, but his strength was less than that of the wire that held it on.

"Ngída! Ngída! Ténda cûi!"

John looked up. High in a nearby tree was Yikína, one of the friendliest and most active of the village boys. Somehow he'd managed to wriggle up the tree carrying one of the enormous longbows which were the *mbía's* only weapon. Chattering encouragingly, he clung to the trunk while fitting his single three-foot arrow to the string, drew, and let fly into the blue. The shaft sped upwards, then dropped down to vanish into the forest, a considerable sacrifice for a lad of the *mbía*. Yikína pointed upward, smiling at John and obviously urging him on.

John stared across the gap between the trees, his heart awash with shame. Now it had become the job of a fragile boy, child of a last remnant of stone-age man, to urge him to bravery and faith.

Wearily John hauled himself to his feet again. One way or another, this situation had to end. He started picking at the cords that secured the railing on the east side of the platform. When he'd gotten it loose he tossed the stick to the ground. He looked at Yikína, pointed at the Moon, and said *"Yási. Yási."*

The boy's eyes grew round at this—he had surmised John's intention to visit Yási, the Moon, the closest thing to a god in the rudimentary philosophy of the *mbía*.

John faced the Sun, closed his eyes, and spread his arms to drink in as much of the solar warmth as possible. He sought to reach out with his perceptions, to remember how to grab the sky, how to invert gravity and fall into the air. He'd only have one chance. He had no time for this perversity. The astronauts had no time.

He opened his eyes, looked into the space before the platform, and backed up to give himself all the takeoff space possible. His vision had not sharpened. He still felt weakness and pain. Yet he also felt a calm resolve.

Let me now be healed, or die. Better to die now than to languish here, and know that the men of Apollo 24 died for my fear.

He trotted forward and jumped off the platform. He fell; the ground rushed up at him in a blur. An inner voice yelled at him, *You fool, this is how*—but it was too late. He crashed face-first into the foliage. All around him the *mbía* cried out in horror.

To his intense astonishment and gratification, John found he wasn't hurt—to the contrary. He lifted his face from the dirt and saw the tableau around him etched with a raptor's clarity. He pushed himself upright, and felt the strength and vitality of Sky Ranger surging through him, as fresh as if he'd never known it before.

That was it. The last of the perversity that dragged me down before. From this moment on, whatever happens, as long as I'm John Avril, I am Sky Ranger too.

He beamed a radiant smile at his friends the *mbía*, not forgetting Yikína still up in his tree, then ran forward and surged into the air. He vanished at once, and for the first time, the *mbía* heard a rope of thunder falling from a cloudless sky.

John sought the ionosphere and bore north-northwest, his destination Cape Canaveral. He'd get some kind of portable air supply from NASA and then strike out for the Moon.

But an urgent alarm, something related to his mental sun clock, was hollering in the back of his mind. A sinking feeling struck him as he looked aside at the stark lunar crescent. One of the innovations of Apollo 24 was to have the men on the surface after Lunar sunset, the first humans ever to stand on the night side of the Moon. *The terminator was now hard against Aristarchus.* His isolation and hesitation had cost him dearly. He estimated he had only three hours to reach the astronauts before the sun sank below their horizon. Were he late, he'd be powerless to reach them before the passing of the 14-day lunar night. Then he could only go to honor their bodies, frozen like monuments to themselves.

Chapter Twelve

Eric Hunter, prowling through the new SRIP headquarters at Cheyenne Mountain after a near-sleepless night, was electrified by the bonging of an alarm that did not indicate approaching bombers or missiles coming over the Pole. He dashed to the bank of monitors manned by young airmen wearing the brand-new SRIP insignia—a modification of NASA's Sky Ranger emblem.

"What have you got, Sergeant?"

"Sir, small object just emerging into the coverage of our early-warning radars from south of the equator. Coming up from South America. Going up like a bat, accelerating at 15 Gs, altitude about three thousand miles. Has to be Sky Ranger."

"Three thousand! And he's heading away from the Earth?"

"No question, sir. He's now over northern Europe, heading straight out from there. Looks like he's making a smoking beeline for the Moon, sir."

The men and women of SRIP released a wild whoop of exultation. Hunter startled his command by joining right in. He stopped to stare at the figures crawling across the screen, cracked his fist into his palm, and danced again.

"That's my boy!" he said to the ceiling. "Go get that Spam back in the can."

And so Sky Ranger set out on his longest mission. He flew with his body held straight as an arrow, arms at his sides, eyes locked on the silver crescent as it crept inexorably sunward. He aimed himself at a spot about three Moon widths ahead of it—the distance the Moon would cover in its orbit in the time he had to reach it. Just now he had no thought to spare for further contemplation. He concentrated only on pushing himself outward—pushing relentlessly, pushing harder than he ever had before. After an interminable period he ceased his effort—his head swimming, the edges of his vision greying and blurred. He had no idea what speed he'd attained. Squinting at the Moon, it looked no larger for his puny efforts so far. And yet, from this vantage above the atmosphere, the remote disk looked infinitely clear and detailed. The craters along the terminator were etched with the precise definition of a silverpoint drawing. The chiaroscuro of Aristarchus itself looked particularly noble, but he would gladly have foregone the pleasure of seeing it in return for moving it a little away from the sunset line.

He looked down, or back, and almost lost the precious breath he'd hoarded before diving out of the atmosphere. There beyond his feet was the entire Earth, his first view of the planet as a whole. To see it spread out there as a luminous blue-white platter gave him his first real appreciation of the magnitude of his undertaking. It was tremendous, and awful too, to see his home planet visibly receding before his eyes. The sight also inspired a transcendent thrill at the realization that he made this awesome journey by his own effort. He couldn't help it—he gave in to a spasm of pride, soon dissolved in a hot rush of love—love of life, and love of the universe that was the true source of his adventures. He looked ahead and refocused his attention on the Moon, his destination. A passion for challenge and exploration fanned a hot flame in his mind.

He'd been aloft for half an hour. The Moon still hadn't swelled appreciably. Fast he might be, but apparently not fast enough. He resumed acceleration, but at a more moderate, sustainable rate. He estimated that a steady 1.3 Gs would get him there in the required time, but the more time he had to act when he arrived, the better.

It wasn't much longer before the strain of his effort began to take its toll. For the first time he felt daytime fatigue, surely exacerbated by the lack of oxygen. While not yet serious, he could feel the first twinges of an urge to breathe. He cut power and resumed a coast. Whatever his speed was now, it would have to do. He must arrive at the Moon with the strength to haul those astronauts into lunar orbit. With this in mind he made an effort to relax, concentrating on his heartbeat and willing it to slow down. He could hear it plainly as a rhythmic rushing sound—that and the random buzzings produced in his brain were the only sounds available in this emptiness.

Presently he was gratified to see that the Moon at last looked distinctly larger. He glanced down at the Earth and was startled again to see how small it looked. He guessed he was near the geosynchronous orbits, abode of the ring of weather and communications satellites that encircled the planet almost a tenth of the way to the Moon. Shielding his eyes from both Sun and Earth, John searched among the stars. He picked out a scattering of sparks of light, but they were hard to make out with his daylight-enhanced vision. They peered impassively out of the immense darkness. Here was a sky of perfect blackness, uncompromised by the airglow and light pollution of Earth's veil of air. Here was the very environment of the stars themselves, with nothing between him and them but distance.

He spotted one of the satellites, a mere point of light, but close enough to outshine any star. It fell behind, like the last buoy marking a forsaken harbor.

On he sped, the most solitary of men, and also, as it happened, the fastest thing in the Solar System.

The Moon swelled before him with hypnotic steadiness. As his lungs began to assert their needs more strongly, John sank into a deep reverie, half asleep, to keep his metabolism at its lowest ebb. The words of an old song, slightly mixed up, looped through his mind:

Fly, me, to the Moon, and let me walk among the stars. Tell me how to get the hell to Jupiter and Mars...

This went on quite a bit longer than was good for him.

With a violent start he returned to full consciousness. The sight before him froze his eyes wide open.

The Moon was an awesome disk spanning a third of his field of view. As in a perfect engraving, innumerable craters and rilles were etched with supreme clarity along the terminator. The great grey Oceanus Procellarum faded through deep brown to black as it entered the shadow which was steadily encroaching on the Earthward face of the Moon. And yet the night side was not entirely invisible—it glowed with an eerie blue-grey elf-light as it caught and gave back the bright glow of the Earth.

As for the region of Aristarchus itself, the pit was engulfed in darkness—only its raised rim still picked off any sunlight, drawn like a white-hot loop of wire on a background rapidly fading. Its shallow western neighbor Herodotus stood out in exaggerated relief under the low lighting, while the nearby rille Schröter's Valley looked as deep as a crack to the Moon's core.

The great disk expanded as he watched, its center bulging out to meet him. His speed was undiminished; in fact the Moon's gravity was speeding him up even more. Without further thought he twisted around and tried his very best to fly away from the Moon as fast as he could. There was no way to demolish his vast speed so quickly, but he must pour it on to slow his mad, deadly plunge. He had to warp his course toward the Moon's western limb as well. His aim had been almost too good—if he did nothing he'd hit near the center of the disk.

As hard as he'd worked to attain his present speed, he now strained three times as hard to get rid of it. The sight of the enormous, blasted slag heap that seemed anxious to swallow him up gave him the incentive. He knew full well he had only minutes to reach the astronauts before local sunset, and he hated to kill the speed that was carrying him to them so quickly. But he couldn't do them any good if he hit the ground hard enough to explode into a cloud of incandescent vapor.

Three hours without a breath were starting to get to him. The strain of concentration, not to mention fear, increased his heart rate and exacerbated the worsening starvation in his lungs. He needed to trade the stagnant, moist CO_2 in his lungs for a whiff of oxygen, but there was precious little of the pure stuff within a quarter of a million miles. He must find what there was, and the men who had it, soon, for his sake and theirs.

Like a boy zooming headlong on a sled beyond control, John felt a certain giddy, exhilarating fear as he plunged Moonward. The deeply shadowed landscape swelled into three dimensions as he watched, and suddenly instead of hurtling toward an astronomical body he was plunging down to a barren landscape. Near panic, he poured on the coals, obtaining enormous energy from some convenient aspect of the workings of space, more than enough to melt him down many times over if he'd actually generated it within his body.

Still Aristarchus surprised him, rushing up to meet him before he half realized it. He had time for a single thought as the horizon zoomed up around him: hold your breath! Then he stopped very suddenly indeed, blasting out a crater about twelve feet across.

He lay there in a heap, his vision swimming, heart pounding, lungs afire, and every bone still vibrating. He permitted himself a moment's rest before attempting to rise. Sometimes, he thought to himself, it seemed he spent as much time smacking into the ground as Wile E. Coyote.

When he felt it was within his capacity, he painfully hauled himself to his feet. Miraculously, he retained the lungful of tainted gas that was all that was keeping him alive. But he almost lost it in an involuntary cry of dismay as he looked around at the dim, silver-blue Moonscape around him. *The Sun was down.* Lost in confusion, he peered around desperately, automatically locking his gaze on the Earth. He sought out South America and stared hard at the bright light falling on its tapering cloud-smeared shape.

The sun is still up over there, he told himself fiercely, *and that's what counts. This isn't night—you're just in the shadow of this big rock. As far as you're concerned, it's daytime until sunset in Bolivia.*

It seemed to work—at any rate, his power did not desert him.

Elated, he took a moment to drink in the sight of the Moon by Earthlight. He could see well despite his daylight-optimized vision—the Earth was big, highly reflective, and almost full, delivering more light than sixty full Moons. He'd landed in the crater itself. The rim cut off his view of the plateau beyond it. The dust coating the crater floor looked as luminous as snow in the blue rays of the brilliant Earth. The light had an eerie, hazy quality—the long shadows cast by the rocks were soft and ill-defined. The crater's central peak, whose summit poked up over the horizon, looked cold and smooth as a snowdrift in the soft backlighting. He turned to behold his own shadow; it was ghostlike, and had a nimbus of cold blue light around the head.

He bent down and ran his fingers through the dust. Fine as powder, it tended to stick to his hands as it had already stuck to the ruins of his flight suit. It felt soft except for bits of embedded grit, and also cold, its warmth already fled into space with the passing of the Sun.

Pulling himself together, he ran toward the shadow, each stride a long, awkward bound in the low gravity, then gave his magic push and forced himself into shaky, tentative flight. He gathered a little speed and lofted himself over the crater rim in search of the landing site of Apollo 24.

It took only a moment for his eagle's vision to pick out the glitter of the stricken *Nightwalker* nestled among the gentle hills of the rim. Following the tracks of the Lunar Rover, he closed in on the lander. He discerned the two astronauts, out and about and apparently puttering with their science instrument package.

The sight of the two men working in this eerie nightscape struck John forcefully. Of course he'd come in search of them, but somehow, to actually find living men prowling this remote corner of creation seemed wildly unexpected. Their isolation and fragility awed him. Their courage, to brave such total removal from all the old haunts of Man, with nothing but thin metal and fabric to keep the vacuum at bay, moved him, filling him with admiration for the worth of Man, a thing not always easy for him to maintain.

He dropped to the ground well short of them and approached their tiny camp with the reverence he might accord some ancient sacred site, as this might well become after thousands of years of man's expansion to the stars.

The astronauts didn't notice him immediately. As he got closer, one of them glimpsed him out of the corner of his faceplate, gave a start which was not disguised by his spacesuit, and spun in his direction, a forgotten tool dropping from his hand. John could plainly see the stunned amazement on the square, solid face behind the visor. McBride, wasn't it? His blank-faced stupefaction was so comical that John had to grin. The commander's lips moved; radio waves crackled though the void. In response, astronaut Guiles turned towards him too. His lean, angular face showed animation and joy, without surprise, as though he'd expected this all along. Like a small boy he jumped up and down in his bulky pressure suit, throwing up puffs of Moondust which fell as quickly as they rose.

John stepped forward and gripped McBride's gloved hand briefly. The commander continued to regard him as he might some Moon genie called up by the mystical lunar night. Was it possible he didn't know who he was looking at? John glanced down at his chest. The front of his flight suit was severely abraded, covered with dust from his ungentle landing. He brushed it clear, revealing the gleam of the sun-and-eagle emblem he'd worn for so short a time. The sight of it evaporated McBride's bewilderment—his eyes blazed up with sudden hope and purpose. Seeing that, John gave him a thumbs-up sign.

Guiles bobbed over and joined them. John bent down and scratched the outline of the Apollo Command and Service modules in the dust, then looked up questioningly. The astronauts conferred briefly, then McBride grabbed a rock-collecting tool, wrote 17 MIN at his feet, then pointed at the zenith.

John nodded. How should he go about this? Each suited astronaut weighed perhaps sixty pounds, and still possessed his full mass. John knew he was in bad shape—should he try to ferry both men aloft at once, or take them one at a time? He decided he'd have to try both at once. With only seventeen minutes before arrival of the Command Module, he might only have one chance to find and rendezvous with it during this orbit, and he was in no condition to wait for it to come around again. Worse, if he took only one man up and left him in orbit, he might have a terrible time finding him again when he returned with the second.

That decided, John wondered how to carry them both at once. They were so bulky in their suits that he couldn't get an arm around them. Could he carry one man and let him hold onto the other? No—he couldn't assume that either man was strong enough to hold onto his companion during their flight.

As he thought this over, Guiles and McBride used their cameras to photograph the unprecedented sight of a man standing naked to space on the surface of the Moon.

Time was getting short. John looked around the area in search of an answer. His eyes fell on the Lunar Rover. It was a ready-made carrier for two space-suited figures, and he'd just have to take his chances with the extra weight. He pointed to it and the men got the idea right away. Guiles hustled to take his seat, but McBride bounded away and returned with an aluminum rock box and a smaller film container. John winced at the idea of still more weight, but he understood the commander's desire to salvage the scientific results of his mission. In a moment both men were strapped into their webwork seats. McBride hunched over the rock box, while Guiles clutched the film container.

John stepped to the front of the Rover, grabbed the frame, and tilted it up slowly until the astronauts were resting on their backs. Then he turned around and backed into it like it was a big packframe, wrapped his arms around the chassis, and lifted the whole assembly on his back, crouching so the astronauts sat fairly level. That was the easy part. Now he'd have to make the transition to flight. He was weak; there'd be no dramatic spring into space.

He started to trot. Between his crouched posture, his ungainly burden, and the unaccustomed lunar gravity, he wasn't at his most graceful. Nor was his gait a smooth one. The hapless astronauts were jounced and jostled far worse than they had been during their ride on the Saturn V booster.

Nevertheless, John kept building speed, throwing up a wake of dust and gravel, all the while marshaling the mental power of his flight impulse. When he thought he had a good grip on it, he gave a leap and set his mind on keeping them off the ground. It wasn't enough—despite his best efforts, they made a lazy arc that sent them back to the surface. John bent almost double in absorbing the impact to keep it from injuring his fragile charges.

Shaken, John sank to his knees to think. He didn't dare set the Rover down for fear of seeing the expressions on the faces of the astronauts. He had to get them aloft on his next try—each effort would only become more difficult. One thing was certain, he'd rather die with them here than be forced to abandon them by his weakness.

Standing again, John turned to face the crater rim. He'd have to take a terrible chance to get them off the ground. He started to run again, forcing more speed despite the stress on his passengers. He felt them stiffen as they approached the rim and its dropoff, which was substantial at this point. He made a desperate leap from the brink, sending his legs down like pistons to buy as much speed and height as possible. The ground dropped away beneath them. They were committed—the astronauts couldn't survive a fall from this height. Now he would either save them or kill them. He sought to tear aside the haze of exhaustion and anoxia to find the focus that had made him master of flight for these past months.

It wasn't enough—they were dropping, though not as fast as they would in free fall. His flight impulse was alive, but weak. The Moon's gravity was not cooperating with him the way Earth's did. He was fully subject to the Moon's gravitational influence. Earth was too far away to assist him.

It felt like many of the dreams of flight he'd had in his former life, in which he would start out strongly but tire quickly, his energy waning and his flight faltering, no matter how hard he tried. Even in dreams, flight wasn't something he could turn on like an afterburner—it was a real effort of the mind and will.

His concentration turned to panic as the pebbles on the crater floor began to loom large in his sight. He *must* stay aloft—this was no dream, where a failed flight meant only disappointment as he awoke in the darkness. He now had responsibility for the lives of two men. He closed his eyes, shutting himself off from the approach of the rugged ground beneath them, purging himself of all thoughts but the drive to take what the universe had to offer, propelling himself and his burden up and away. He could feel the flow of space—he seized on the sensation and urged it to flow by ever faster. He refused to look—he would know failure only by the sensation of making another crash-landing on his belly.

A flood of radiant warmth struck his face, warmth from a source he knew very well. Eyes snapping open, he beheld one of the most charged and beautiful sights of his life—the Sun, brought back into view by their great altitude, casting narrow arcs of dazzling brilliance on the distant craters of the Moon. Aristarchus was a ghostly glow far below. His jubilation almost made him forget the pain in his chest, which felt like a Joshua tree growing in each lung. With an eagle's gaze he began to scan the sky in all directions. Some providence showed him what he most wanted to see—a bright sunlit object, perhaps fifty miles away, approaching at high speed and growing ever brighter. John warped his course to parallel its track and gained speed to effect a rendezvous at zero relative velocity. It was a tricky maneuver which demanded concentration, but the reward of seeing the brilliant dot resolve into the cone-tipped cylinder of the CSM made it worth the effort. A few minutes later they drifted alongside *Gandalf*, a gorgeous sight, sheathed in white, gold, and silver, with light beckoning from the windows. The astronauts had called ahead. Command Module pilot Horn was waiting for them. The module was depressurized, and the hatch blessedly open to permit their entry.

John released the Rover and moved around to assist the men into their spacecraft. Horn stood in the hatch to receive them as John first guided Guiles with his film bag and then McBride with his rock box into his arms. John turned to give the Rover a shove that would carry it away from *Gandalf*. When he looked back, Horn gave him a wave and moved to shut the hatch, to John's shock and terror. He dove past him into the crowded cabin before Horn could so much as blink. John allowed his cheeks to puff out as he looked at the three puzzled men with wide, frantic eyes. They closed and dogged the hatch and began a quick repressurization. Cool, pure oxygen began to flow into the cabin. As soon as it caressed his cheek John violently expelled a rather fetid cloud and sucked in the clean, sweet gas with a feeling of ecstasy. It was several minutes more before the pressure built to the point where the astronauts could open their helmets.

Horn looked from one face to another. "Boys", he drawled, "your faces reminded me of the Carolina colors when I first saw you all."

McBride looked at him in puzzlement. "Why's that, Horn?"

"Because you two looked as white as the polar icecap, while this here hitchhiker looked about as blue as the Gulf of Mexico."

McBride turned to John, who was still gratefully venti-lating his long-deprived lungs.

"Ah, Sky Ranger, it's going to take us all a while to fig-ure out what to say, except thanks. And to apologize for almost shutting you out. We, ah, didn't know you needed to breathe." He looked uncomfortable, so ridiculous did this assumption sound when put into words.

John managed a cockeyed grin despite his panting. "It is... nice... every now... and then."

"You know, Houston told us you were heading our way, but I never really believed you'd make it."

"I believed it," offered Guiles brightly.

McBride laughed. "I know you did, Austin old pal. I'll try to share your faith next time."

John's grin stayed fixed. He saw no reason to tell them how many times he'd come close to failing them.

CM pilot Horn turned to him. "Sky Ranger, buddy, I'm wondering if you're planning to ride all the way back with us. It'll be a little cramped, but we've got the expendables and we'd be proud to have you."

"Thanks, Mr. Horn, I'd like that, but I don't think I can. I'm really tired—I need rest, and I can't get it riding back in this spacecraft. I have to get back to Earth and let... the natural rhythms of the planet take over again. I'll have to fly ahead."

"Some kind of a Catch 22 situation?"

"Yeah. I'll just take it easy until I've recharged a little, then be on my way."

Guiles brightened. "Hey, why don't I give him one of my backpack oxygen bottles? That way he won't have to hold his breath all the way back to Earth."

McBride said, "That's great, Austin. You can hook up to the ship's air system when we let him out. Good idea."

"I sure appreciate it," said John.

Guiles set to work squirming out of his spacesuit. The Command Module was so crowded that it was difficult for anyone to move, since the Moonwalkers had never intended to return wearing their bulky moon suits.

A radio speaker crackled from the communications console.

"*Gandalf*, Houston, come in, please."

McBride replied. "Houston, *Gandalf* here."

"Jim, we're awfully pleased to hear your voice coming over this link. Please update us. We haven't heard anything since the Horn bellowed he saw you guys approaching the CM in the Rover."

McBride maintained his most impassive command expression.

"Yes, Houston, I can confirm that. Austin and I did achieve lunar orbit and rendezvous in the Rover, using an alternative propulsion system."

"We read you. Would that system be the Sky Ranger?"

"That's affirmative."

"Lord almighty. And we thought he'd chickened out."

McBride spoke quickly. "Houston, Sky Ranger is with us now, visiting a little before he heads back home."

A moment's silence from the ground.

"Roger, Jim, I copy that. My apologies to the man in blue. Ah, stand by, I'm being relieved for a moment. Hold for NASA administrator Wilson."

"Standing by."

"Apollo 24, this is Nicholas Wilson. Do I understand that Sky Ranger is in your vehicle at this time?"

Response

The three crew members looked expectantly at the man in question. Horn handed him a headset.

"That's right, I'm on board."

"Well son, I'm going to save the speeches until you're back on the ground. You'll hear plenty then. But I just want to talk to you while I can get you on the private link. Switch him over, will you, Horn?"

Horn clicked a dial. "It's just you and him."

"Ready."

"Good. Sky Ranger, I've got a proposition for you. How would you like to work for NASA?"

John blinked in surprise. He'd been resisting conscription by the United States Government for over a year, but he'd never considered aligning himself with a civilian agency like NASA.

"In what capacity, sir?"

"As a—special consultant. A safety man. A rescue specialist. An inspector—of spacecraft in orbit. There must be a million things someone with your abilities can do for us."

"If I were to agree, it would have to be with the understanding that I'd remain a free agent, with no obligation to NASA or the government. The work I've been doing must remain my top priority. My work for NASA would have to be strictly as other duties allow."

"Agreed, we can do business on that basis. We don't want to limit your humanitarian work anyway, or the space-or-butter people will light up their torches again."

John's mind worked rapidly. "Now let's discuss what I get out of this arrangement."

"What do you want?"

"Flight suits. I lose a lot of them on my missions. The one I've got on now is a shambles. They're not easy to come by. I want NASA to design a superior flight suit and keep me supplied with them."

"Agreed. We'll be happy to do that. What else?"

"Hideouts," said John decisively. "My cabin is useless now that everyone knows where it is. I need a series of simple, concealed hideouts scattered in remote places all over the world. I need them to be secret, so I'll build them myself. But you can supply the materials and equipment. Maybe you can design them as little prefabricated cabins or something."

"Mmm. That sounds a little more complicated, but I'm sure we can manage something. Anything more?"

"One thing. An official acknowledgment from the government. Recognition of my right to function at my own discretion."

There was a silence somewhat in excess of the three-second lag imposed by the speed of light.

"To a certain extent that's implicit in our offer, but the President may be prepared to extend additional recognition."

"Excellent. Contingent on those conditions, I accept your offer."

"I'm happy to hear it. When you get back to Earth, please stop by my office at your leisure. Wilson out."

Horn flipped back to the normal open radio link and turned to John. "Well, partner, looks like you're going to be joining our team. Glad to have you aboard." He offered his hand.

John took it with a foolish grin on his face, then shook hands with the other two. "Can I ask a favor? I need to talk to someone on the ground."

"Shoot, yes. If they can set up phone links for the President, I reckon they can do it for somebody important. Who do you want to talk to?"

"KSKY."

A few minutes later, Capcom announced that the phone link was ready. John adjusted his headset and immediately heard a voice with a Swedish accent, thin but distinct.

"Hello, this is Kier Johannsen speaking."

"Mr. Johannsen, this is Sky Ranger calling from lunar orbit."

"That is what NASA has given me to understand. I find this a most extraordinary honor. Here at KSKY we are overjoyed that you were able to intervene successfully in the lunar emergency."

"Thank you. I really called to speak to your announcer, the African, the man who put a match to my tail this morning. If it hadn't been for him, I'd still be on the ground looking up."

"Ah—you're referring to Lobengula Masunda. I'm sorry, but he's not available just this moment. But I'll see to it that he's on hand if you wish to speak to him a little later."

"Would you? When you see him, thank him for that kick in the pants."

"Certainly."

"Your whole station could take a lesson from him. I'm only human. I make mistakes, I get scared. I can blow it, like I almost did this time. When that happens, let me know. Prod me. I may have a good reason for any inaction, but if not, I want to hear from you about it. Okay?"

"Of course. Thank you very much. I infer from this that you do listen to our station."

"Oh, yes."

Johannsen gave a small laugh. "We were never quite certain of that. I'm glad to hear it, and our funders at the UN will be too. Goodbye, Sky Ranger, I hope to meet you in person someday."

The transmission ended. John slipped off the headset.

Austin Guiles looked at McBride. "Do you think they'll make Sky Ranger an astronaut, Jim?"

McBride gave a shrug. "They're just as likely to call him a launch vehicle."

John laughed a little harder than was called for. The tension of this singular mission and the startling new prospect of working for NASA combined with his exhaustion to produce a certain shaky giddiness. He was probably hyperventilating as well.

And there was still the matter of getting home again.

He gave a big sigh, looked from one face to another, and despite his reservations, announced, "Guys, this has been fun, but I think I'd better head on out. You'd better start thinking about decompressing the cabin."

"You're sure you don't want to stay?" asked McBride. "At least until we've done our trans-Earth injection burn?"

John shook his head. "Can't."

"All right then, we'll see you on the ground. Buy you a beer or something."

"Jim, I might as well go EVA while we're at it, to get the film from the SM cameras. That way we won't have to dump our air twice," said Horn.

"Good idea. We might have to go around a few extra times while we set up the burn numbers, but we can afford it. I'll call the ground and see if this checks with them."

Horn and Guiles prepared to evacuate the cabin while McBride showed John how to use the O2 bottle Guiles had scavenged. In twenty minutes the astronauts were snug in their suits while the air bled into space with an evil-sounding hiss. John felt the pressure in his eyeballs as he was again immersed in vacuum. He felt a moment's fear. This was very much like going for a swim right after making a narrow escape from drowning.

Horn cracked the side hatch and swung it open. Clutching that precious bottle, John wriggled over the three astronauts, paused in the hatch, and gave them a wave. Then he was gone. Horn cautiously followed him out, hauling himself along the handholds on the skin of the CSM, but by then Sky Ranger was only a star which swiftly dwindled into invisibility.

Only when Horn was back inside with the film, the cabin repressurized and the astronauts out of their suits, did they abruptly cease their activities to eyeball each other with varying degrees of relief, amazement, and belated disbelief. None of them knew what to say. Horn looked quizzically at his two colleagues; McBride stared blankly into space, while Guiles just grinned quietly.

McBride, at least, was embarrassed at needing to be rescued, especially by some tousle-headed hippie, and he rued the dawning realization that his mission would be known primarily for that, forevermore. But it would be a long time before he'd admit any of that to anyone.

Eyes stinging, face tense, Lobengula Masunda hunched over the wheel of his battered VW as he numbly guided it over the same road he'd driven just hours before. Now the car's cramped cabin was packed with his possessions, all that he had kept in the dorm at KSKY during his brief tenure.

He rolled down the lonely highway in a state of seething resentment and grief, paying his surroundings only slight heed as his mind replayed recent events over and over again.

He had no idea how he was going to explain this disgrace to his parents. First child in their village to attain any significant schooling, his greatest achievement—his appointment to KSKY—had come to a bitter end. He saw no justice in it. What had he done, other than to upbraid that flying slacker for his negligence? If KSKY thought Sky Ranger was beyond criticism, he wanted no part of the organization. Africa had seen too many self-styled demigods who refused to submit themselves to any accountability.

He glimpsed a blue blur in his rear view mirror. An instant later it shot by him with a rush of air. The blue Volvo station wagon kept on going until it was about a half mile ahead, then braked to a stop and swerved to block both lanes. A small blond-haired figure got out and faced him.

Lobo Masunda coasted to a stop. In total bemusement he got out of his car and looked at his erstwhile superior. "Mr. Johannsen? Have you thought of further ways in which I have failed your station and endangered the world?"

Johannsen looked simultaneously grim and contrite.

"Mr. Masunda, I stand before you a humbled and chastened man. Please return to the station with me. You have received an endorsement—" he glanced up at the leaden sky—"from a high source."

John Avril hated to leave the tiny island of air and warmth that was *Gandalf*, yet he knew he had no choice. Even as he sped off toward the distant, sapphirinne Earth he felt himself weakening. His very consciousness was flickering like a home movie in a cheap projector. His muscles were quivering. Odd hazes superimposed themselves over his vision, like sandpaper to eyes that had been dried, baked, and frozen in vacuum for too many hours. He had overextended himself. He needed rest beneath the cloak of Earth's gentle night.

He made no effort to reach the extreme speed that had brought him here. With the air bottle, the urgency wasn't as great, and he didn't want to find himself nearing home at some vast speed he might not be able to reduce in time to avoid a meteoric crash. He accelerated gently until he passed the "equigravisphere"—the point at which the Moon's gravity gave up dominion to the Earth's. Then he ceased his painful effort, filled his lungs from the bottle, and limply allowed the Earth to accelerate him further. For the first time he felt an urge to sleep while he still carried the power, but that was a luxury he dared not risk.

For hours he drifted toward his goal, semi-conscious at times, stirring only to take an occasional pull from the bottle or to glance at the beckoning planet before him. When he looked back at the crescent body he'd just left, he wondered dimly if the astronauts were on their way home at the much slower yet more comfortable pace of *Gandalf*.

He emptied his lungs, put his lips to the nozzle of the O2 bottle, and opened the valve. He got a partial breath, then nothing. The bottle was empty.

That realization jolted his adrenal glands and restored him to a brief wakefulness. The Earth was a cream-spattered disk of sapphire blue dominating most of the heavens ahead of him. It was time to slow down. The bottle was useless, so he threw it at the Earth with all his strength, letting it slow him a bit through purely Newtonian means. Then he once more called upon the resources of his mind to give up the kinetic energy he'd accumulated by so much effort. The strain was almost unbearable, like trying to arrest a fall by grabbing a strand of barbed wire. It was beyond his strength. His view of the world fragmented into blue-white shards that spun crazily, then darkened to gray. His only regret was that he'd had so little time to appreciate the mystic beauty of the lunar night.

Another twisted fragment of song filtered through his mind before he surrendered to the void:

Lord I'm five, Lord I'm four, Lord I'm three, Lord I'm two, Lord I'm one thousand miles from my home...

At John's speed, hitting the atmosphere was like colliding with a solid object. He knocked the first few ions he encountered out of his way with such force that they lost every electron they had. As he penetrated to denser layers his inert form was surrounded by a sheath of multicolored plasma that trailed behind him for a hundred miles, the train of a living meteor. The last shreds of his flight suit flashed into glowing vapor and added trace contaminants to his path. The NASA emblem was the last to go, finally losing its integrity in a burst of rainbow fire. The air shrieked as the tunnel of vacuum he blasted out collapsed behind him. Like Lucifer cast out of heaven he fell.

Every degree of heat and decibel of sound took its toll on his insane plunge. The air which was his true element seemed willing to take on his pain in order to cushion him and ease his descent. In minutes his speed had decreased from the meteoric to merely that of a ballistic missile. When he finally hit the ground it was with little more than the terminal velocity of a falling man.

John Avril awoke with the newly risen Sun poised on the horizon. Naked again, he sat up to examine his surroundings. He'd slept through part of a day and an entire night—or perhaps several days, for all he knew. And now he felt very good indeed—healed in body, strong again in spirit.

He had no idea where on Earth he was, but it scarcely mattered. He was home. The country around him was dry and severely beautiful, mountainous, all sere tans and golds, already whispering with a promise of noontime heat to come. The sky was lucent, with a few feathery clouds catching the golden light of morning. To meet them, John sprang into flight with effortless grace.

Chapter Thirteen

And so began the heyday of Sky Ranger. With his reputation at its peak, and public sympathy strongly on his side, he was more than ever a citizen of the world, able to freely go almost anywhere his work took him. Even the Russians dared make no protest over his precipitous visit to its Kyzyl-Kum desert—they explained their massive effort to locate him as a mere attempt to render him aid.

John worked to perfect his routine and improve his efficiency in the far-ranging tasks he'd set himself. While waiting for NASA to provide the promised shelters, he hid simple camps in hard-to-reach areas all over North America—in the Sierra del Carmen of northern Mexico, and on a deserted islet in the Bahamas, for example. The camps would provide a refuge should his main eyrie be found out. He used them at random to keep from being too predictable by always making a beeline for the same spot as the sun declined.

He visited his Alberta cabin several times, sad to be forced to abandon it. Each time he found new evidence that it was being visited, and once he even arrived in time to scare off a party of hikers who were brazenly about to break in. He suspected only the cabin's difficult access kept it from being carried away bit by bit. Someday, he vowed, he'd have another home in a setting to equal or surpass the beauty around him here.

To his great surprise, his identity remained unrevealed. Pictures of his face were common, but he had not been notorious in his previous life, and his appearance had changed quite a bit since then.

The United States Congress declined to extend the Apollo Moon program, in the face of "demonstrated and narrowly-avoided risks to human life." NASA, however, was delighted with the PR boost provided by the renown of its new part-time worker, and managed to find something for him to do as often as he could find the time. They built and John tested a winged "trailer"—a glider he could tow to make it easier to lift small payloads into orbit. Editorial pundits popularized a new meaning for the NASA acronym—the National Agency for Sky Ranger Activities.

In July, John stopped by JPL to watch the first pictures transmitted by the latest Mars lander. He visited the offices of the imaging team to watch in wonder as the images built themselves up line by line. Here was a landscape he expected never to tread. He didn't stay long; his presence distracted the scientists, and he couldn't go near the auditorium without the journalists making him the story instead of the milestone of exploration being accomplished around him. Before leaving he took a phone call from Nick Wilson, who invited him to the Johnson Space Center in Houston for the fulfillment of the first part of NASA's bargain.

Two weeks later, John found a gap in his schedule and shot down to Houston. He arrived to find the JSC campus in a bustle—evidently, something more was planned than merely giving him a new suit. He touched down to be greeted by Wilson himself, who had just arrived from Washington in a T-38 piloted by an astronaut.

As a matter of fact, the greater part of the astronaut corps was present. Most were people he'd never heard of. The majority of the famous names of Mercury, Gemini, and Apollo had left the program at the conclusion of the Moon program. Those who remained would go flightless until the trouble-prone Space Shuttles could be trusted to fly.

Three exceptions to that rule were astronauts McBride, Guiles, and Horn, but even they were at the tag ends of their NASA careers. McBride and Horn had announced their resignations, effective as soon as they were past the aftermath of Apollo 24, while Guiles, the bachelor, would stay in, hoping to command an early Shuttle mission. John was happy to visit with the "Three Dark Knights of the Moon", as some comic book fan in the press had dubbed them.

The three of them and Wilson accompanied him to the workshop of the Sky Ranger Unlimited Integrity Textile (SUIT) project. Dr. Edwin Hike, the Coordinating Engineer, began his presentation.

"I'm about to show you a prototype SUIT, but we expect no major changes in the production model, if this test article meets with your approval," he said casually. With a dramatic gesture he swept aside the drapery concealing his masterpiece. "As you can see, Sky Ranger, we've continued your basic blue-and-white color scheme, and also carried forward the shoulder yoke design of your previous flight suit, which actually turned out to be quite an advantage. The construction is similar to the emblems we made for you earlier—an underlayer of a reinforced carbon-carbon fabric, with overcoatings of refractory ceramic glazes over a microcylinder fiber structure permitting flexibility, yet running parallel to your normal flight orientation to minimize turbulence. Overall, the fabric can withstand temperatures in excess of three thousand degrees Fahrenheit, and is also highly resistant to mechanical damage and chemical attack. Ah—another feature, which I suggested, is an additional underlayer of tungsten foil in the groin area. I don't know if you are totally resistant to high-energy radiation, and I thought you might appreciate the added protection someday."

John smiled and reached out. "Well, it sure can't hurt. Let me try this on."

"If you would, please allow me to explain its other features first."

John withdrew his hand and resumed his polite attention.

"We've done extensive modeling of the stresses you encounter in flight using wind tunnel and computer simulation. To cut down on your wind resistance, the general contour of the SUIT is skintight, yet there are some areas of padding to smooth out body contours which would otherwise give rise to turbulence. Our analysis of frictional heating patterns shows, as you'd expect, that you encounter the highest temperatures along your leading surfaces, normally your head, hands, and shoulders. We could safely leave your hands uncovered, and also your head, since the most refractory substance in the world appears to be your hair. For your shoulders, however, we reinforced the white yoke with additional carbon-carbon, ceramic, and tungsten layers. You see that we've incorporated your emblem into the point of the yoke. Note the boots, also made of the higher-temperature white laminate, though mainly for aesthetic reasons. They come up to the calf, permitting the bulge of the calf itself to act as a fairing, deflecting high-speed air flow and preventing it from forcing its way into the boot and blowing it off."

John waited a beat, then said, "I'm impressed with the careful thought you've put into this. Now I'll just... "

"And now for the electronics." Hike produced a wide white belt with a heavy buckle that looked like a rounded, gold-plated bar of soap. "You don't need a belt to hold up your pants since this is a one-piece SUIT, but the buckle may prove useful. It contains a radar transponder designed to emit a signal which will identify you on all airborne and traffic control radars. In a case where you wish to maintain surprise, the corners of the casing have contact switches— merely touch any two opposing corners to turn it on or off." He displayed the back of the belt, which had a rectangle of dark purplish-blue material. "The unit is powered by this photovoltaic panel. The casing also contains a battery, for operation during cloudy periods or at night."

John kept his face carefully neutral. He remained silent in the expectation that more was to be revealed.

"And now for the headset." Hike brought forth a handful of narrow white straps supporting two pearly hemispheres. "This provides several useful functions. First, the earpieces should enormously improve your sense of hearing while in flight by smoothing the turbulent air flow over your ears. They also contain radio circuitry. The receiver picks up the commercial AM band so you can monitor KSKY at all times. It also receives aircraft and air traffic frequencies. The transmitter is limited to a few aircraft channels, and it necessarily has a very small range, about five hundred feet. But that's enough to let you talk to the pilot of a plane if you're nearby. The neck strap contains a tiny throat microphone. The radio system is powered by these photovoltaic cells on the back of the neck. Control is through the earpieces—rotate the left dome for on/off and volume; rotate the right for band selection and tuning."

John and the others stood blinking, awaiting the continuation of the lecture.

Hike held out the headset. "Well?" he asked in apparent perplexity. "Aren't you going to try it on?"

John started. "Oh yes, of course. Thanks for the very thorough presentation, Dr. Hike."

"Certainly."

John collected the elements of the SUIT and stepped behind a screen. The fabric of the SUIT felt thick and solid, with a glassy outer coating that was a delight to touch. It closed up the back with a zipper that looked as if every tooth had been individually machined. It took him a minute or two to untangle the headset and figure out how it went on, but when he did it was comfortable and unobtrusive. He stepped out, feeling for the first time that he was dressed in clothing truly suited to the business of a Sky Ranger.

Hike beamed at the sight of him. With a self-conscious grin, John turned to him and shook his hand. "It looks to me like you've done a superb job on pretty short notice, Doctor. Thanks to you and your team."

"We're all proud to have been involved in it. Wear it in good health. It was perhaps the best eight million dollars NASA ever spent."

John's eyes widened. He turned aside to look at Wilson. "I'd say you've definitely kept your end of the bargain so far. I think I'll step outside and take this outfit for a spin."

"Of course, you'll need to test it thoroughly before we go into production with them. But first, I wonder if you'd mind joining us in the auditorium. We've invited a few journalists to share in the unveiling of the SUIT."

John glanced at the Apollo 24 trio. They offered shrugs and looks of embarrassment. "Well, I guess I don't see any problem with that."

"A few journalists" turned out to be closer to two hundred, with a dozen TV cameras and a hundred flashing still cameras trained on the stage. The room was also packed with NASA personnel, including much of the astronaut corps.

John shared the stage with Wilson and his old Apollo "crewmates." The lights gleamed splendidly on his new flight suit. He stood in the eye of a storm of winking strobes and whirring motor drives.

When the photo-orgy died down, Wilson stepped to the microphone and made a few remarks. John paid little attention until the mike was turned over to McBride.

"Thanks, Nick, and hello, everyone out there. We've got a surprise for Sky Ranger today. We invited him down here to give him the SUIT, but the timing also allows us to make another announcement. You remember the shock we all felt when Sky Ranger was shot and injured just about two months ago. Well, my crewmates and I made him a promise back then, and the International Astronomical Union has permitted us to keep that promise. May we have the lights down and the projector on please?"

The auditorium grew dark; a beam of light flared from the projection booth, widened, and was blocked by the large screen behind the stage. Projected there was a photograph of the Aristarchus area taken from the *Gandalf* Command Module.

McBride continued. "We promised our buddy to name a lunar feature in his honor. To be honest, we were a little too busy during the actual mission to think about it. But now we've made our choice." He picked up a projection pointer; a green arrow flicked over the image. "Note these peaks just east of the crater. They're called the Harbinger Mountains. We've selected the highest among them and given it the name Sky Ranger Hill. I don't know, maybe Sky Ranger himself is a harbinger of something, I'm not sure what. Anyway, we offer this to him along with our enduring thanks for making a rescue that otherwise would have been impossible."

John smiled and nodded absently as most of those before him broke into applause. He appreciated the honor, but he would've liked it better if they hadn't dumped it into his lap quite so heavy-handedly. As the applause died down he turned to leave the stage, but Wilson's hand on his elbow arrested him.

"Sky Ranger, would you mind taking a few questions from the press?"

John shrugged and turned back to the mike. He answered a few predictable questions about his Lunar flight, then took a couple that proved to be more memorable.

"Sky Ranger, you've demonstrated an ability to lift payloads into orbit and fly at least as far as the Moon. Will you now help the United States to conserve scarce financial resources by taking the place of our launch vehicles, performing missions which otherwise would have to be performed by expensive rockets?"

John frowned. "I certainly will not. It would be fatal to the space program for me to take on any such responsibility. Ignoring your overestimation of my abilities, I might not be available forever—and when I'm gone, the USA would suddenly find itself without any access to space if you don't develop and build rocket boosters. Let me say right now that I will perform no mission for NASA which could be performed by technology which now exists or could reasonably be developed. I'm here to help with emergencies and research. You'll have to do the main work yourselves."

He glimpsed a perturbed-looking Nick Wilson out of the corner of his eye, then was distracted by the next question.

"Sky Ranger, for more than a year you have refused to reveal your true identity to the world. Why are you hiding behind that mask, and what is it that you feel obliged to hide?"

John's irritation intensified. He peeled off the narrow straps of the headset, looked at them closely, then held them up. "You call this a mask? It's a radio headset, and I've never worn it before today. You know, I've been watching as you people tried to puzzle out my real name. I can't say I'm impressed with your detective work. I've seen fifty names sent up as possibilities, including the right one, though nobody seemed to realize it. I sometimes think you've deliberately avoided solving the puzzle because you get better ratings and more readers with a mystery man than you would with some known guy who happens to fly. Well, I'm going to prevent one of you from eventually figuring it out and making a big name for himself. My name is John J. Avril, and all I've ever tried to hide are my friends and family from your pointed pencils and clattering cameras."

"How do you spell that name?" someone shouted.

"A-V-R-I-L." He turned abruptly and stalked off the stage, bringing Wilson and the astronauts along in his wake.

"Ah, Sky Ranger," said Wilson tentatively, "we were actually hoping that you could take over launching some of our smaller payloads—Scout and Delta class—that's why we developed the towing glider."

John halted and looked down at Wilson in disbelief. "Did you really? You'd rather I start taking over NASA's mission, rather than assisting with it? Look, if America's going anywhere in space, it'll have to be through your efforts, not mine. In the long run you'd lose far more by giving up your responsibilities to me than you'd save by canceling a few small boosters. I'm here to help you learn the way into space. If that's not what you really want, tell me right now, and I'll end our bargain, peel off this shiny outfit and get out of here."

Wilson blinked, unable to summon a forceful reply in the face of a man more durable than any material known on Earth.

"No, no, please. I appreciate your point," he said mildly. "Of course we will continue to value whatever aid you're willing to give us."

A few minutes later John was free and clear of Houston, soaring through the stratosphere at Mach Five. The new flight suit stood up to it without so much as a ripple. Even more luxurious was the relative silence granted by the smooth domes covering his ears. Feeling a need for action, he clicked on the radio and tuned in KSKY, determined to handle any emergency he could reach, and to keep on until darkness intervened.

Danielle's sultry voice kept him hopping—to Europe, Africa, and the Middle East, then back across the Atlantic when the sunset line came too close.

And all the while he thought about something he could no longer ignore or avoid: the matter of his family. If they hadn't known it before, surely now his parents and siblings realized that not only was he still alive, he was Sky Ranger. It was time and past time that he gave them the attention and explanations they deserved. No longer could he excuse his avoidance of them by telling himself he was protecting their privacy—he'd devastated that with his impetuous announcement this morning. He shook his head in exasperation—enlightened as he supposedly was, he could still be terribly perverse. He'd always hoped that aspect of his personality was something he could outgrow or purge through wisdom, but now he saw it was something fundamental that he couldn't wholly lose without losing himself.

As the terminator approached the East Coast, John took note of a slack spell in accessible troubles. Despite his misgivings, he arrowed down to a small city in western Massachusetts. The magical hills of his boyhood wanderings cradled it in greenery, the unstinting foliage of summer in the Northeast. The town itself and its neighboring cities brought up memories more mixed. He shoved them aside as with his eagle's vision he sought and found the familiar house in its modest neighborhood.

There, he could plainly see, the consequences of his announcement were already being felt. The street was packed up and down with vans and TV trucks. The yard was a milling herd of journalists and cameramen, laying siege to the little house, churning the grass into mud. Policemen stationed at the periphery took no action.

John landed good and hard on the roof of one of the network vans. A great cry arose from the mob; in a frenzy they turned their cameras on him as he stood glaring down at them.

"Listen to me! I want you people out of here right now, away from this house and out of this neighborhood!"

He might as well not have spoken. Out of the hubbub he heard only fragments of shouted questions and demands. "How do you feel about your impending reunion with your family?" "Will you start going by your true name, or will you continue to call yourself Sky Ranger?" "Why have you gone back on your agreement to launch satellites for NASA?"

Most of the questions were similarly irrelevant or inane. Very few of these people had anything worth asking. It seemed that most of them just shouted something to try to justify their presence.

The demands and offers ran along the lines of: "Sky Ranger! My magazine will pay $150,000 for exclusive pictures of your meeting with your family."

John glimpsed motion at the house's front window as someone peeked out. He jumped from the van, scattering camera crews as he landed in the midst of the throng. He raised his voice to a level that was a little higher than humanly possible.

"This is your last chance to clear out of here."

Those nearest him quailed back, but a perfectly-coiffed young man in the braver ranks of the more distant called out indignantly, "Excuse me, but we're the press. The people have a right to know!"

John's eyes blazed. "This is my parent's house. No one on Earth has a right to know what goes on behind its walls." He seized a minicam that was thrust into his face and gave it a good solid fling. It arced away, all but exploding on impact in a nearby park. He reached out, grabbed hold of a zoom lens, and squeezed, shattering glass and deforming aluminum.

"That's valuable equipment you're destroying! You can't treat us like this!"

"Think for just a minute! I'm not a politician, or an entertainer, or protester, or advertiser. I'm not accountable to you. You need me far more than I need you. I say again: leave now. If I, or anyone in that house, wishes to make public whatever happens between us, we'll let you know. Now, will you do as I say, or must I do more damage?"

With much grumbling, and many surly over-the-shoulder looks, the guardians of public information shut down their cameras and unplugged the key lights that cast flattering highlights on the hair of the TV reporters. John stood there with his jaw stuck out pugnaciously until every last car and van had pulled away to take up new stations as close as they dared remain.

Then, with every last possible excuse evaporated, John strode up to the door. He heard it unlock just as he touched the knob, opened it, and stepped into the interior dimness.

The smell of the house struck him powerfully as he waited for his eyes to adapt. It was the same smell he'd absorbed and forgotten during his boyhood and adolescence, and it revived, with unexpected strength, memories and images of a previous life he'd thought all but lost.

His mother was standing before him, looking up at him with bright eyes and a full if fragile smile. "Well, look at you. You've gained a little weight since you left."

He smiled shyly. "I guess I have."

She looked up and down at his gleaming new flight suit with its proud emblem of black spread-winged eagle.

"That's quite an outfit. I was watching on TV when NASA gave it to you. We were all happy to hear you use your real name."

"I was happy to use it, Mother. Did you know it was me even before I gave it away?"

She laughed. "Are you kidding? I'm your mother! I knew it was you the first time I saw a blurry picture of Sky Ranger. The only kid in the world who could possibly become Sky Ranger was you. Don't you think I'd know that?"

John's doubts about coming home suddenly dissolved. He gave his mother a gentle hug. She was in tears, and his were not far behind. "Well, I'm back. And you see, I was eventually able to straighten myself out."

"I always knew you would."

They released each other. John looked around the living room. Standing there smiling broadly were his brother and sister, but someone was missing. With foreboding in his heart, he asked a question whose answer he felt he already knew. "Mom, why isn't Dad here?"

She looked up at him steadily. "John, your father died last fall. It was complicated, but we can talk about it later."

Somehow it had never occurred to John that the lives of his family would progress while he was off experiencing his metamorphosis. He'd envisioned a homecoming where everyone would be just as they had been on that remote day when he'd last walked out the door to head back West after a Christmas visit. It was during an aimless stay in Arizona that he'd decided to drop out of society and flee to the Rockies for a last-ditch effort to salvage peace and wisdom from a life that was rapidly waning.

Instead he found that mortality had not been in abeyance—and it hadn't been overturned by the intervention of some loving but inscrutable force. His father was dead—a troubled man, a man who had never come to terms with life, much as John himself had not before his pilgrimage. His relationship with his father hadn't been close, yet John knew him as a man who had tried to do the best he could with the resources life had allotted. If he hadn't succeeded, well... John's knowledge of the effort prevented the failure from dominating his memories of the man.

He had returned too late to share the wisdom of the world, which might have eased his father's passage, or even deferred it, and that he would always profoundly regret.

"Did Dad know? About me?"

"No, and we didn't tell him. I'm not sure what it would have meant to him—he began to drift away from us around then. We weren't sure we could trust him to keep your secret. He may have figured it out for himself, like we did. He always thought you were liable to get up to something strange."

"So Sky Ranger, don't you have anything to say to us non-flying mortals?" It was his younger brother Mike, his boyish face lit by a broad smile. He held out his hand. "Geez, watch that grip there, sun god. I wish I had a tan like yours, but I guess you have to lay out in the stratosphere to get it."

John laughed. "Without a tan like this, you'd need a number five hundred sunblock to survive where I go. How's it going, Mike? Figure out what you're going to do for a living yet?"

"Well, yes, I thought I'd ask for a million dollars to write the story of what it's like to grow up with a know-it-all brother who becomes a freak of nature. Either that or I'll stay in school until I get my teaching certificate."

Somewhat flabbergasted, John stood blinking. Teaching was about the last career he would've envisioned for his brother, who in his youth had been something of a wastrel. What other surprises would this visit offer?

He turned to the youngest of them, his sister Irena, tall and lissome, blond and blue-eyed. John's smile for her was particularly warm, as she had been a source of warmth and light for him since early childhood, a fellow dreamer, with whom he had shared many adventures, both real and imagined. She gave back a smile of equal quality, if a little strained. They embraced.

John looked closely into her eyes, normally so clear and untroubled. "What's wrong, Renie? Did you miss me that much?"

"Well, of course I did, you big dumb jerk—first we thought you were dead, and then I thought you must have amnesia or something, flying around without ever contacting us. But now you're finally back, and that's not what's bothering me."

John retained a gentle hold on her shoulders. "What else, Renie? You know you can tell me."

"I do know that. I always knew you were smart, and I always felt I could tell you anything. But looking at you now, I can see you've learned more in the past two years than you could ever tell me. There's a light in your eyes that I could almost photograph. Johnny, do you notice anything different about me?"

John studied her carefully. "You look like you've put on a few pounds too."

"That's right, I have, and there'll be more. I'm pregnant."

"Um—are you married?"

"You know I'm not."

"Well." John looked around for someone to resolve his confusion, but he found no comfort in his mother or his brother. Their faces made it unmistakably clear that this was their first news of Irena's pregnancy as well.

The family reunion suddenly became a good bit more complicated.

When things had gotten a preliminary sorting out, Mom and Irena went into the kitchen to fix dinner, while John and Mike blithely resumed their teenage roles of sitting around and doing nothing. The dinner was strained. Mike seemed quietly amused, but Mom couldn't keep her eyes from constantly shifting between her extraordinary son and her wayward daughter.

Afterwards, Mike and Irena left the house to run the press gauntlet and attend to their own business. John and his mother stayed in the kitchen, talking things over as the sunlight entering the bow window aged into late-afternoon gold.

"So John, have you met any girls?"

He chuckled ruefully. "Well, I've rescued quite a few, but they're usually either injured or too hysterical for me to ask them for a date. I spent some time with a girl named Elise early on—you probably read about that in the paper—but she's vanished—I haven't heard a peep out of her, and that's the way she wants it. My day nurse in Calgary was sweet, but I ran away from there and I haven't been back since. I don't know. To tell you the truth, being the way I am has kind of taken the, uh, urgency out of being with women. Thank God for that." He laughed in self-deprecation.

His mother looked at him closely but not ungently. "Can you tell me why you stayed away all this time? Without even a word?"

John sat back and let loose a big sigh. "I've been thinking about that for a long time. The answer didn't occur to me until I actually set foot in this valley once again." He paused, staring out the window, gathering his thoughts, not entirely comfortable with the subject. "I have very mixed feelings about this house, this town, this whole area. I made so many mistakes here—threw so much away, lost so many opportunities. I was so afraid to try to live, so adrift, so without any motivation or purpose. I feel I wasted those years, and they won't be back for me to try again. I suppose they weren't really wasted—they led to my eventually learning the things I know now. But when it came time to learn those things, I needed to start out clean, to live in the present, and hope for the future. I didn't want to be reminded of failure. Even afterward, I had this feeling deep inside that I might be diminished by returning, by facing that very weak, flawed side of me that led to my rather desperate effort to purge myself of it. Do you understand that?" Full of contrition, he looked at her for forgiveness.

"Yes, I understand that very well. But what changed your mind?"

John set his mouth more firmly. "I went through a tough episode—the whole stretch between my getting shot and going to the Moon. Despite having advantages literally beyond the limits of reason, I came close to blowing it all a few times. More than once I almost died… " he almost said "again", but that was still a matter he wasn't ready to discuss. "It was all very scary, but I learned from it too. You see, I *didn't* die, and I *didn't* fail. When it was all over, I was still Sky Ranger. Although I wasn't quite as bubbly as I was the first time I took to the air, I was still able to do it, and still ready for the work I'm fitted for. I figured that if I could go through all that and still hold myself together… it was just dumb to think I couldn't show up here and still be the person I've become."

Tears had returned to her eyes. "I was sure you were dead. It felt like a resurrection when I first saw you were back. I didn't know if it was you, or a ghost, or an angel, or what."

John smiled gently. "Well, I'm not bird nor plane nor even frog. Just little old me."

"Oh, more than that. I read an editorial in the paper that said you'd banished despair. It said that no matter what kind of danger people are in, no matter how hopeless it seems, they never really lose hope, because they know there's almost nowhere you can't go to save them. They know there's a real chance you'll get there in time, even if death is just seconds away. Of course you can't always make it, but even when you don't, they don't die in despair—they die waiting to see that blue and white suit flashing to the rescue. And then sometimes they *do* see it—you *do* appear, like a thunderbolt, and you snatch them from danger that would overwhelm any other man. And they know that you *are* a man, like them, and if you can work such miracles, what can't they accomplish themselves if they can only see the way? Ending despair, reawakening wonder—those are even more important than saving lives. Everybody is going to die sooner or later. You help people to know that when they do face death, the universe is not indifferent. That's all anyone can ask."

Although he was seated, John Avril, Sky Ranger, suddenly felt ten feet tall. He'd had praise heaped on him by presidents and kings, philosophers and Nobel laureates, yet none had ever meant as much to him as what he'd just heard. If cynicism had begun to encrust his spirit like arterial plaque, it was washed cleanly away by these words of his mother.

They sat and talked until the sun was about to sag below the horizon. John, promising to return when he could, led his mother into the back yard, and took to the air while she watched in amazement, scarcely able to credit the sight of such a marvel, despite herself.

Afterwards, however, it fell to her to fret about what to do about the revelation from her only daughter.

Chapter Fourteen

The news media petulantly tried to put the worst face on Sky Ranger's rough treatment of their representatives, but unfortunately for them, the entire incident had gone out live on the networks. Far from condemning John, most people admired his defense of his family's privacy. Of course, they were also avid for that privacy to be violated so they could learn everything about him. In the months that followed, the initial flurry of newspaper and magazine articles was followed by a mushroom patch of unauthorized biographies, most of them hasty and flawed. John scrupulously avoided all of them, fearing that the more accurate among them might prove the most embarrassing. The public was bemused to discover that he had never been a brilliant research scientist or millionaire playboy. Some of the more acute among them, aware of his rather muddled and misdirected past, wondered whether they too might someday walk a similar road.

NASA quietly began to provide him with equipment for setting up his bases. John was satisfied with what they gave him, but not extremely impressed—they seemed to have devoted their best efforts to the superb flight suits, which was fine with him. John soon had hideouts scattered in lonely places all over the world: in the Bolivian Andes overlooking the forests of the *mbía*; in the arid Atlas Mountains of Morocco, within easy reach of western Europe; in Australia; and in northern Greenland, from which he could span the entire northern hemisphere. He alternated between them as his duties and the Earth's inexorable turning demanded, and was careful to avoid any pattern, lest he become too predictable and easy for enemies to locate.

John still missed his cabin, and was ever alert for an opportunity to establish a new home of similar charm, a more elaborate base in his beloved Rockies, to serve as his main headquarters.

He found it quite unexpectedly one chilly autumn morning as he was soaring through a splendid mountain gorge in the Selkirks of southern British Columbia, not far from Mount Revelstoke. He'd lingered here many a time, and this day, with no news coming to him through his radio earpieces, he perched on the near-vertical face of a great flatiron-shaped crag to meditate and enjoy the view. He occupied a shelf beneath an overhanging brow, with shadows thick behind him. A turbulent mass of dark cloud, muttering and striking out with an occasional fang of lightning, rolled down the valley as he sat there. He was tempted to fly off into the midst of it, but he was distracted by a curious phenomenon—each peal of thunder was followed by an echo from directly behind him, an echo too long delayed to be a reflection off the rock wall a few feet from his back. As he cocked his ears in that direction he also made out a faint bubbling sound. He turned to peer into the shadows, but his daylight vision revealed little, especially with the sun blocked out by the storm. It was only when lightning flashed in the valley that he could glimpse an opening in the rock that was deeper than immediately apparent.

He stood up as rain and sleet began to coat the mountain outside the protection of the shelf. He walked to the opening, a mere slot between massive slabs of rock, and squeezed his way in. Inside, he was totally blind. The slit of light from outside served only to dazzle, rather than illuminate. He carefully paced off the interior, measuring an irregular area about twenty feet across. A cold spring issued from the wall and flowed over the floor. The flow didn't make it to the entrance, so it must be draining somewhere in here, perhaps to reemerge farther down the cliff face.

He groped his way back into the open, flung himself into the storm, and alighted on the valley wall opposite the shelf and ledge. Even from here, with his eagle's vision, there was no sign that the brow hid anything more than a rough rock face. It was indeed a fine and private place.

During the next month this grotto became John's new eyrie. It needed power first of all. He situated solar panels so they could be seen from neither above nor below, hidden as they were in the slot in the rock. Only someone clinging to the sheer walls on the other side of the valley would be likely to spot them. Yet they received decent sun exposure when the sun was at mid altitudes. Satisfied with the arrangement, he set up lights to survey the possibilities of the interior. He liked the view and the privacy, but he had no desire to live in a dank and gloomy cave. As time allowed he cleared out rubble, enlarged the entrance a bit, and smoothed out the walls. Then he brought in tools and materials supplied by NASA. By the time he was done, the chamber was quite homey, with a level wooden floor, a few rugs, and paneled walls. The spring was an unfailing source of water filtered by a thousand feet of sandstone. He channeled it into a little cistern which always rippled with gentle music.

The eyrie was about as luxurious as a camping trailer, but that seemed quite plush after his simple bivouacs in remote ranges. He set up a bed, a kitchen, and a radio. He hung a few pictures—of his family, Elise, and a view of Long's Peak. He spent almost half his nights here, sometimes staving off sleep for a few post-sunset minutes for reading by a small electric light, its glow hidden from the outside by a black curtain hung at the entrance.

An American election came and went. John found himself dealing with another president. Invited to visit Camp David, John found this man intelligent, earnest, and well-informed, as well as relaxed and casual. He left feeling fairly confident about his relationship with the new administration, though he never forgot what Hunter had told him in the hospital.

Shortly thereafter, John became an uncle. Irena had her baby, a son whom she named John Michael Avril. She elected to remain an unwed mother, continuing to work as a freelance writer while caring for the child. The Avril family allowed their privacy to be briefly violated: a national news magazine published a cover photo of the entire family, prominently featuring a smiling Sky Ranger, in full flight regalia, dangling a model airplane over the infant's face.

In August, John attended the launch of the Galileo probe to Jupiter. A few hours later he was in pursuit of it, wearing a modified space-rated flight suit recently developed at JPL, which incorporated an air supply, a transparent face mask, and an S-band radio receiver.

Telemetry from the probe indicated that its main antenna had failed to deploy properly. With some difficulty he located the glittering metallic mayfly and worked the antenna open like a cheap umbrella. That done, he drifted in formation with it for awhile, ostensibly to be sure there were no further problems, but mostly to marvel at the spacecraft and its mission. He'd had to attain a fearful speed to catch the probe. He was now on a trajectory which, if he did nothing, would carry him to Jupiter in a few years time, still in company with the probe (and no doubt seriously interfering with its instruments). It was a journey he could not survive, but it wasn't beyond the competence of this delicate mechanism, with its big ears and eyes, and its semiconductor brain roughly as complex as that of a grasshopper.

After a while he began to warp his course back toward Earth, keeping spacecraft in view until it vanished as a fading golden star. He looked after it for a long time, for he would never see it again, nor would any man. He could not have been more moved had he seen the sail of Odysseus's raft sink below the horizon.

He entered a long period of success during which he became a virtual world institution, his prestige mounting with each lifesaving deed. A few incidents stuck out like boulders in a plowed field:

One day KSKY brought him word of a man clinging to a huge trestle bridge over the Rhine. John charged to the rescue, arriving just as the man lost his grip and began his long plunge. John met him, fell with him, and only gradually slowed the man's fall to avoid breaking his bones. As he set him down on the bank, another man, carrying a video camera, ran up chattering excitedly. John became suspicious and enlisted an English-speaking bystander to question the two. Under Sky Ranger's severe glare they finally admitted they'd staged the event so they could profit from the videotape of the rescue.

At this news John grew coldly angry. He grabbed the camera and handed it to the interpreter, telling him what he was about to do and why. While the interpreter recorded all, John grabbed the two pranksters, took to the air with a heavy leap, and flew back up to the bridge, where he left them both in precisely the same precarious place where the one had started out. He then took possession of the camera and flew it to the main German TV studio, where he urged them to distribute it worldwide to prevent some other clever soul from trying anything similar. His tactics drew some protest, but appeared to do the job.

Not long after, a group of radical students invaded the U.S. Embassy in Teheran, taking hostage about a hundred Americans. At the President's request, Sky Ranger sat tight as the government tried to secure their release through diplomacy. It soon became apparent that the students were acting on behalf of the Iranian government. At this point the President asked Sky Ranger to take part in a U.S. military rescue effort involving a helicopter-borne commando raid. John refused to participate, believing that to align himself with the U.S. military would destroy the trust he'd painstakingly built up in the rest of the world.

The raid eventually took place and was an utter fiasco. The President privately invited Sky Ranger to take whatever action he thought feasible. John considered the matter carefully for several days. Eventually he decided on a relatively tentative first step. He made several low supersonic passes over Teheran, dodging missiles, shattering windows, and generally frightening the populace. The Iranian government responded by ordering the hostages slaughtered at the next sign of Sky Ranger's presence within its borders.

His options were these: he could invade the embassy compound, but despite his speed, hostages were sure to be lost. He could attack the Iranian military to render it vulnerable to the forces of Iraq, Iran's mortal foe, but that too would surely result in reprisals. Or, he could burst into the seat of Iranian power and threaten the Ayatollah himself, rendering him counter-hostage. This seemed to offer the best hope for securing the release of the hostages. But the thought of bullying a sick old man left him ill at ease, and he couldn't predict what the reaction of the rest of the Islamic world might be to such an act.

In the end he admitted to the President that he saw no course of action that wouldn't probably worsen the situation. The President agreed. Sky Ranger was to remain aloof until such time as the hostages appeared to be in imminent danger, in which case he would go charging in regardless of the consequences. In the meantime the U.S. Government would continue its negotiations.

To top it all off, the Soviet Union began a brutal invasion of Afghanistan. John immediately thundered into action, knocking out a dozen MIG-25 Foxbats by putting his fist through their canopies and ejecting the pilots willy-nilly. He thought he might be able to turn the Soviets back single-handedly, but the harried President warned him that the Soviets considered him an American agent, despite his protests to the contrary, and that his intervention was interpreted as a major provocation, even an act of war. He eventually persuaded the chafing Sky Ranger to desist, but it wasn't easy, for in Sky Ranger's eyes was a hawklike predatory light few people had yet seen. His casual handling of some of the world's most advanced weapons brought a nervous furrow to the brows of military leaders all over the world.

All in all, it was a frustrating year for Sky Ranger.

The American people, interpreting the waywardness of foreign peoples and their own flaccid economy as signs of the President's personal weakness, declined to elect him for another term. John was ultimately sorry he'd refused to offer his endorsement when asked. He soon met with the successor, a man who John considered an amiable simpleton, surrounded and propped up by an array of avaricious, gimlet-eyed ideologues and plutocrats. They received him with grand hospitality, but despite their hearty greetings and sweaty handshakes, John had no problem detecting their fear of him, as well as a rather ingenuous belief that he could be dazzled by displays of power and ostentation. He had this impression of almost everyone except the President himself, who seemed to regard him with a kind of glowing hero-worship more suited to a teenager. John found it impossible to take the man seriously, but John remained polite. He excused himself from the meeting as quickly as possible, with his misgivings on the rise.

In 1981 NASA finally assembled the disparate elements of their Space Transportation System into an ungainly pile of rockets which they prepared to test-launch with two astronauts in the cockpit. The Shuttle program had been troubled, delayed, and endlessly scaled back. The vehicle which now existed was very much a compromise foisted upon NASA by Congressional politics and Presidential apathy. With his inside knowledge, John harbored no illusions that the system would ever be as capable and economical as NASA had always claimed. The Space Agency was anxious to conceal this truth for as long as possible. In addition, the Shuttle as yet had no clear-cut mission. It would be used mainly to launch satellites, an activity which could be carried out more simply and safely using unmanned boosters. John found himself longing for the glory days of Apollo, when NASA had known where it was going, and how to get there.

On launch morning John perched on a grey platform about a mile from the launch complex. The Shuttle stack glowed white in the sunlight, like some Art Deco cathedral. It was beautiful in its way, yet John still found it hard to believe that in a few minutes NASA intended to light a fire under that bizarre pile of rockets and blow two men into orbit. He admired the nerve of the men in the cockpit, and even the daring, verging on hubris, of the men who'd designed and built this machine under such severe restrictions.

Though delayed, the launch went as planned. The main engines ignited with a transparent flame, their sound like that of a mighty wind; then the two solid rocket boosters lit up, hammering the sound-suppression water with solid pillars of sun-gold fire, sending shock waves of concussive sound rolling over the land. *Columbia* leaped up, and so did John, following as the vehicle hurled itself toward orbit, snapping pictures as it discarded sections of itself along the way. He followed it all the way into orbit, where he did a flyaround to look for damage. A few tiles were missing, but they weren't in critical locations. He slid forward to *Columbia's* nose, tapped on the cockpit window, and photographed the two astronauts as they grinned out at him. John left them to their work, returning to Canaveral exhilarated and relieved.

Later that year John learned of a French open-air nuclear weapons test to be conducted in the South Pacific. Mainly out of curiosity, he decided to observe the blast. He neglected to inform the French of his intention, as that would undoubtably result in loud objections and increased vigilance on their part. Shutting down the radar transponder in his belt, he approached the test area at an inconspicuous subsonic speed. He was careful to maintain a very respectful distance from the site—Moruroa, an atoll which had already known the sterilizing fires of other French blasts. In fact, most of the island looked like a moonscape incongruously surrounded by tropical Pacific waters of gorgeous royal blue. This was the last place on Earth where above ground nuclear testing was still taking place. There was heavy pressure on the French to conduct the tests underground, but protests from Australia and New Zealand and a drawn-out legal action in the World Court had so far failed to penetrate the thick-hided Gallic disdain for world opinion.

French naval planes and warships patrolled a perimeter far from the site. John circled the area at an altitude well above the ceiling of the patrol planes, turboprop antisubmarine planes by the look of them. As the time of detonation approached he felt tension even more acute than that surrounding the Shuttle liftoff. The bomb hung from a tethered balloon that bobbed over the coral island. Nervously he withdrew until the balloon and the test structures on the atoll were indistinct even to his eagle's vision. After that he ceased to look directly at the site. He didn't wish to be surprised by a sudden exposure to a blinding fireball. Durable as he was, he had no illusions that he could prevail in any contest with a nuclear weapon.

Scanning the surface of the sea, he was surprised to spot a small civilian ship within the perimeter of the patrolling French vessels. Worse, the ship was steaming slowly toward the blast site. John frowned in puzzlement and concern. Although the small white ship had obviously passed through the French naval picket and was probably still in sight of it, none of the fast grey frigates and destroyers were making any attempt to intercept it.

He hesitated a few indecisive moments, then stooped down on the wayward vessel, falling upon it like a falcon. As he lost altitude he made out a rainbow painted on the bow, and recognized her for what she was: *Emerald Dolphin*, flagship of the small fleet of the Earthwarden environmental group. Earthwarden had a history of clashing with the French nuclear test program, giving John an unpleasant inkling of what was going on.

John dropped down on the wing of *Emerald Dolphin's* bridge. The clang of his feet meeting the deck plates did not escape those within the wheelhouse, whence he received a collection of slack-jawed stares. He stepped into the wheelhouse.

"Sky Ranger!" cried the captain. He was a thin, middle-aged, bearded Brit who either had long experience of the sea or at least the inclination to dress properly for the role. Like the others on the bridge he wore heavily tinted goggles slung around his neck. "This is unexpected! I'm Brian Howard, captain of the Earthwarden Motor Vessel *Emerald Dolphin.*"

"Captain, you must turn your ship around and put on some speed," said John urgently. "You're heading right into a nuclear explosion."

The captain cocked an eyebrow at him. "Well, we're actually aware of that, wouldn't you guess?"

"Then turn around. What are you trying to do?"

"Make our point. Document this test and demonstrate that it's both unnecessary and very destructive."

"And the French Navy has no objection?"

"Huh! They hope we'll get too close and be par-broiled. They can then tell the world how they tried to stop us, but we went charging in heedlessly anyway. Get them clear of a bloody great nuisance."

John blinked at him in dismay. "You're endangering all your lives."

"We don't think so. We're ready for the blast, and we expect to catch only enough radiation to observe on our instruments. If the winds hold as they are." But even as he said this, the captain's eyes jerked aside toward the blast point with evident apprehension.

A woman who sat nearby monitoring a clock and a radio spoke up. "Captain, we have twenty minutes to detonation. I suggest we get our goggles on in case they surprise us with a premature blast."

Howard nodded and picked up a microphone. "Attention all hands. Twenty minutes until the French pop their soufflé. Don your goggles now. Repeat, don your goggles now, and don't remove them until you hear my order. By the way, we have a guest observer aboard—Mister John Avril. That is all—remember our mission, and keep to your duties." He turned back to John. "We're going to be a bit busy for the next little while, but I'll offer you a set of goggles, and you're welcome to observe the blast with us. Afterward we're going in as close as we dare to monitor radioactivity in the seawater and its effect on marine life."

John tightened his lips and looked at the captain steadily. "Sir, I hate to throw my weight around, because I respect you and agree with your cause. But you know you're endangering this ship. Please turn back now, or I'll be forced to turn you back myself."

"My dear boy, your concern is noted, but this isn't your responsibility. We're adults who've voluntarily placed ourselves in this position. Don't interfere with our mission."

"My mission is to defend life."

Howard waved his hand beyond the bow. "That abomination out there is ultimately a greater threat to all life than anything that could happen to us."

John shook his head. "Find some other way to fight it. Don't martyr yourselves. Get yourselves out of here now, or I'll have to."

"Lad, you couldn't do it. If you take over the helm, I'll order the engines shut down. If you go below to try to start them, I'll put us back on course. You can't push us out of here by yourself, can you?"

"No. Not in time."

"Then just relax." He turned away to check his course and speed.

Increasingly frantic, John paced up and down. He made a wild gesture. "There must be some way I can stop this!" he cried in frustration.

"You could stop the test," said a new voice. "That would be best for everyone."

John swiveled toward the hatch. There stood a woman, of average height, with black hair fluffed about her tanned shoulders, and a fresh, youthful face made mysterious by the dark goggles that covered her eyes but could not disguise her.

"Elise!"

"Hello, John. Why don't you go stop the test? Then we'd be safe, and so would the ocean. And it would teach the French a thing or two."

John stared at her in dumbfounded wonder. The years had not altered her. Indeed, if anything she was enhanced, somehow perfected. She looked more like Elise than she ever had before, if that made any sense.

Until this moment he had not fully realized the depth of his longing for her. Now he could think of nothing else.

"Young lady, who the devil are you?" said Captain Howard in confusion.

"Oh, I'm sorry, Captain. I'm Elise Boutin, a biologist. I joined the ship back in Bali, and I really should have introduced myself earlier. But I'm usually busy in the lab."

"Hmm, is that so?"

"Elise, what are you doing here?" said John.

"Didn't I just answer that? We'll have time for goofy questions later. Go on! Do something!"

Nonplussed, his heart pounding, John looked around in confusion. He *could* stop the test—destroy the bomb's control mechanism, cut the tether, or boost the whole thing into space. But he shook his head. "That bomb could be set off sooner than you expect. I'm not going near it. Besides, this is a political matter. None of my business."

Elise stepped closer and looked at him in disbelief. "Political matter? What's political when a group of foolish people decides to destroy life and contaminate the world with radioactivity for no reason?"

"They think they have reasons."

Captain Howard laughed with some irony. "Their main reason is to demonstrate their manhood after having been publicly buggered by the Nazis."

Elise punched John in the chest to regain his attention. "We don't have time to debate this. You can either stop the bomb, or just mind your own business and leave us alone."

John looked at her in agony. The thought of leaving Elise, of all the people in the world, in jeopardy was torture. Yet he knew with inner certainty that to stop this test would be the first long step down a road that could quickly become impassible. "I won't stop the test. Do what you must. But won't you please wait on the stern, in the shade of the superstructure? If things get too rough I'll fly you out of here."

"Fifteen minutes to detonation," came the calm announcement.

Elise yanked her goggles up onto her forehead. She studied John with something like disdain. "Are you kidding? I'll take my chances along with my friends. What's wrong with you, John? I haven't heard anything but dumb excuses out of you so far. When I knew you before, you were always loud and clear in your opposition to issues like this. Now you've got the power to do something about nuclear testing, and you can't even move!"

John took a moment to reevaluate the situation. This was a new Elise, lecturing him on the courage of his convictions, a major reversal in roles.

"Elise, you're right. But I've worked a long time to gain the confidence of governments so I can work within their borders with minimum hassle. If I start kicking them around it'll compromise my ability to get in and help people when they need it. Isn't there some other way to convince you to leave?"

"Yes," she said instantly. "You're the most famous and trusted person on Earth. Come out publicly and take a stand against nuclear testing. Put that sun-god face on television and we'll have it stopped in a year." She looked at him expectantly, showing every sign of having thought this through a long time ago.

John demurred further. "If I take a stand like that…"

"Oh my God, don't be so damned aloof! Don't tell me you're not even entitled to express your opinions!"

John emitted a strangled sound of indecision and rolled his eyes. In the end, the thing that made up his mind was the fact that the person standing in front of him was Elise.

"All right. You've got me buffaloed. I'll do it."

Elise's face, previously quite stern, instantly lit with excitement. She turned toward the helm. "Is that all right with you, Captain?"

Indecision was not John's problem alone. Captain Howard stared down at the deck. "It's not really a decision for me to make. But with time pressing, I think I'll take matters into my own hands and consult with our esteemed expedition leader afterwards. We can debate it then." He became suddenly animated. "Helm, come right, full rudder, reverse course. All engines ahead full. Colleen, contact the French command ship. Tell them we're on our way out of here at top speed. Maybe they'll see fit to delay the test until we're clear." Only then did sweat break out on his face, as he sank down in his chair with obvious relief. "I think I'm beginning to remember you, Miss Boutin."

Emerald Dolphin slewed around rapidly and settled on its new course, churning out of the area with considerably more enthusiasm than it had showed in entering.

His decision made, John relaxed and allowed himself to savor the presence of Elise. As he caught her in his arms he realized again that he'd missed her far more than he'd permitted himself to know.

They watched the explosion from a distance sufficient to put the fireball below the horizon. But the cloud rose up in plain sight, an ominous pillar of grey-white streaked with veins of orange fire. It melted away a layer of high clouds as it climbed, then spread out into a stormy canopy that rained down clouds of dying atoms. The shockwave rushed toward them at the speed of sound, giving the ship a hard slap and pulling behind it a blanket of sound like a thunderclap that refused to die. Elise squeezed John's arm with all her strength. They watched, awestruck, John no less than any. He felt insignificant. Suddenly he doubted his stature as a major force in the world. What was his ability to fly in the face of this?

And yet such explosions did not arise of their own accord, but must be arranged by men. And to men he was a power to be reckoned with.

They rode rough seas for the better part of an hour.

John tarried on the ship, sitting with Elise on the fantail while *Emerald Dolphin* steamed back toward New Zealand. The day was fine, the tattered remains of the nuclear cloud comfortably below the horizon. John and Elise sat on canvas chairs, facing each other, smiling shyly.

"You look just the same," said John. "No, better. You're not a girl any more."

"I'm not?" she cried in a pretense of dismay. "What am I, a mackerel?"

John laughed. "I meant you look like a woman now. Beautiful. And wise. Not a silly schoolgirl."

Elise batted her eyes ostentatiously. "Didn't you like me when I was a schoolgirl?" she asked with a sweet, if vapid, smile.

"I—of course I did. But I'm anxious to find out what kind of a person you've turned into. Besides a manipulative arm-twister, that is."

"Oh, don't complain to me. If I hadn't pushed you, you'd still be standing around wondering what to do."

John looked sheepish. "Maybe so."

"As for you, you don't look the same at all. You've gained weight—you don't look so much like a broom handle anymore. And your hair is so light I can hardly stand the glare."

"That's what happens when your head spends time above the ozone layer."

"And what a sharp outfit! I have pajamas with that design. But the emblem fell off in the wash."

"I'll send you one of my ceramic NASA emblems. You can clean those with a blowtorch."

For a while they sat there watching the foamy water churned up by the screw, glancing at each other often, breaking out in big smiles whenever one caught the other's eye.

"So, Elise. What happened to you? Where did you go after I left you?"

"Well, you should know, Mr. Avril, that my life was impossible after you got done making a celebrity out of me. I went back to school, but I had no peace at all. Government goons in big cars followed me around all day, and publishers and TV people called me all the time. I think there was a tap on my phone. I couldn't walk down the street without people stopping me and asking if I'd been out with you lately, and what it was like to fly with you in the moonlight. Even my housemates kept looking at me funny. I couldn't get a date—everybody called me 'Sky Ranger's Girlfriend, Elise Boutin'. I guess guys thought you'd come and throw them into a volcano if I went out with them. I started to get really mad. Not at you; by then I realized you really hadn't done anything wrong. I was mad at the whole dumb country. It made me look up from my schoolbooks and notice all the insanity about life in the United States, and how most people ignore all the things that are falling apart.

"As soon as I got my degree I moved to Bali. I figured that would get me out of the limelight, and it did. I goofed around there for a few months teaching school, and then I got involved with Earthwarden when *Emerald Dolphin* visited the island. I've worked with them as a biologist ever since, and it's the best thing I ever did. I've been all over the Pacific, and learned ten times more about the environment than I ever did at school."

John's eyes gazed into the past. "Wow. That's a much more exotic story than anything I'd imagined. Bali, huh? I always thought that place was perfect for you. I always knew you were special, that you'd find a path that anyone could be proud of. How I used to wonder where you were."

He felt a gentle hand on his arm. "John, I can almost hear what you're thinking. I was on another Earthwarden ship, trailing a whaling fleet, when you were shot. By the time I even heard about it, you'd already been to the Moon and back. Otherwise I would've been there. Afterward, well, I don't think you have a phone or anything. How could I contact you? But I knew we'd eventually meet again, when the time was right."

John smiled at her. "And the right time is now?"

"It's right as it can be."

John unaccountably found himself blushing. "Um—by the way—I do have a post office box. Perry Falconer, Box 406, Nakusp, British Columbia. I check it once a week or so. In case my mom or somebody wants to get in touch with me."

"And I still live in Bali. The way you get around, I guess we're practically neighbors."

John made a tape in a New Zealand TV studio rented by Earthwarden. The spot wasn't fancy—Earthwarden decided that the mere sight of Sky Ranger standing forthrightly before the camera would be more riveting than any expensive graphics or effects. Then they set out to place the spot around the world. To their gratification, that turned out to require almost no effort. So rarely was Sky Ranger captured on the tube that almost everyone was eager to run the tape. The American networks ran it as a news item. In other markets, Earthwarden was asked to make only a token payment for airtime. Even the Soviet Union gleefully picked it up as an embarrassment to France's troublesome "Force du Frappe".

The French themselves erred in broadcasting the tape while pompously denouncing it as "a threat to French independence coming from the American agent, John Avril". They neglected two factors: the average Frenchman's high regard for Sky Ranger, and his increasing suspicion and impatience with the nuclear test program itself.

The pressure of world opinion instantly bore down on the French. Greatly encouraged, Australia, New Zealand, and the World Court pressed hard with their legal challenge. The French suddenly faced the possibility of having their testing program declared wholly illegal, or even shut down by internal opposition. Scrambling to keep it alive, they hastily agreed to move the tests underground, and to allow greater access to the test area by independent observers. Their foes were inclined to ride their momentum and press for full shutdown, but finally they desisted, largely due to the quiet urging of the United States, which saw in that goal a threat to its own underground testing program.

Earthwarden declared a 65% victory, and vowed to continue the fight to end all nuclear testing in Mururoa and around the world. In private, they celebrated unreservedly—being more accustomed to heroic futility than to even partial victory.

John found a ready excuse to join the celebration by visiting Elise in her small house in the forested hills of Bali. Finding it was not easy. She'd told him about where it was, but rural Bali's dirt roads were short on street signs and route numbers. He zigzagged over the forest, and then suddenly there it was, a tidy, airy little cottage, leaving John to wonder how he could have missed it.

They sat on her screened-in veranda, sipping a cool mixture of tropical fruit juices which Elise had squeezed from local produce. As evening came on they watched and laughed as clouds of insects bumped into the screens in their zeal to get at them and their warm mammalian blood.

Elise cast a look of inquiry at John as the sun hovered low over the mountains. She understood full well that if it set while John were still here, here he must remain until dawn.

Tweaked by duty, John picked up his headset and tuned it in search of KSKY. He picked up the signal from the Philippines. The world seemed quiet; there was nothing to tear him away.

The Sun left him to his own devices. He remained alert; he'd had a short day as Sky Ranger, traveling eastward to Bali from his camp in Morocco this morning. He grinned at Elise and stretched in his rattan chair.

"So you've rejoined us lowly mortals, stuck on the ground for the night," said Elise teasingly. "Don't you find that humiliating?"

"Not at all. Even Zeus and Odin liked to disguise themselves as mortals and walk among them."

She launched a golden laugh. "As I recall, Zeus liked to do more than walk among them."

John's eyebrows lifted. Here was a remark of un-Elisian innuendo, but she quickly brushed it aside.

"John, what's it like on the Moon?"

He sat back and released his breath. "It depends on the time of day. While the Sun is up, it's surrealistic, like a disturbing dream—a barren landscape of rock and dust, white in the sunlight, not much different than parts of Nevada or the Namib, but made strange by the nearness of the horizon, an unfamiliar perspective. It's like the whole thing is a diorama that ends in a painted backdrop just a few feet away. The sky is the strangest part—that jet-black curtain, a drapery surrounding the diorama, with a round hole in it to admit a blinding light that casts long sharp shadows. I found it hard to accept a sky that black while the landscape was so brilliantly lit. It's like the Sun is a spotlight on a nearby stand, lighting just the patch of ground I'm on, like lights at a construction site at night. While all around is real night.

"When the Sun goes down, the Moon is transformed. Instead of the harsh light of the Sun, the soft blue light of the Earth remakes the landscape. It's like elvish magic seeping up from the core of the Moon. The horizon seems to fall away. Stars are visible, and suddenly I know I'm standing on a planet rolling through space, not some plaster stage set. The Earthlight washes over me, rich and mystical as moonlight reflecting from a field of new fallen snow."

Elise looked at him with glowing eyes.

John smiled and stretched out again. "These flight suits are like armor—they're not very comfortable for an Earthbound mortal. But I didn't bring anything else. I didn't know I was going to stay."

"Stay? That's very presumptuous of you, John. What would my neighbors think?"

He glanced up to assure himself she was kidding, then looked up and down the dirt road and the uninterrupted wall of trees that lined it. "Your neighbors? They'll probably think something like: 'Sun down. Woods dark. Find food. Don't get eaten.' That's probably what monkeys and beetles think."

She giggled. "I guess so. Okay, you can stay. I've got a spare robe in my closet if you want to try it on."

"Okay."

When he returned, wearing the robe, he found a candle lantern fluttering on the table, warming the purple light of dusk. Elise reclined in her chair, nude. The lines of her body were clean and supple, her nipples provocatively erect. Her tan was all-encompassing. John stood gazing down at her, shocked and entranced. She was even more beautiful than he had expected.

"Even us uptight Westerners get pretty casual about clothes when we come to an island like this," she said softly. "You don't really need the robe. It's not like I haven't seen you naked before."

"Maybe we'd better go inside," he whispered. "Your neighbors…"

"Monkeys and beetles?"

He was breathless and could not reply. She took mercy on him, stood up, and stepped into his arms. To John she was a living mist of warmth, fragrance, and enchantment.

"I love you, Elise."

"You'd better, you silly dope."

Part Three
A Warrior from the Heavens

Chapter Fifteen

After that, John established a new camp in Bali's remotest highlands. He contrived to visit Elise in her cottage at least once or twice a month, except when she was afield with Earthwarden. His hilltop camp went unused during those visits, but it remained as a refuge should their relationship attract the same sort of unwanted attention that had interrupted it six years before. They strove for discretion and secrecy, and to their knowledge, achieved it.

John had known many emotions in his time, and recently they'd been dominated by exultation, wonder, satisfaction, and even joy. Now that he had the love of Elise, he also knew the glow of something elusive yet also simpler...happiness. How had he failed to notice its absence for so long?

And yet sometimes John felt there was something wrong about Elise's house. One morning as they awoke in her bed," I had some strange dreams, and they seemed so real. I thought I heard voices."

"What kind of voices?"

"They sounded frightened. They spoke in a language I don't know."

"Huh, well, I haven't heard anything like that. Maybe it was monkeys? They tend to shriek and chatter a lot, but I rarely notice it."

"Maybe that was it." But John wasn't so sure.

Now at the zenith of his joy, heartened by the positive effect of his speaking out on the nuclear testing issue, Sky Ranger added a new facet to his activities. In conjunction with Earthwarden, he became a world spokesman for environmental causes. He decried the devastation of the Amazon rain forests, the frivolous slaughter of the great whales, the vast outpouring of waste into the oceans, and many other matters. Experimenting with a more active involvement, he notified KSKY of a new subject of interest to him: danger to wildlife populations through poaching or other illegal activities. Several times, the beleaguered staffs of wildlife parks in East Africa sent out the call when they were overwhelmed by elusive gangs of heavily-armed poachers. In reply came a spearhead of thunder, a decisive figure with the power to act where others could not.

As time went by John grew ever more adept at the work of Sky Ranger. He learned how and when to insert himself into situations for the greatest effect, developing an almost supernatural sense of where to position himself to intervene in situations that he foresaw.

Among common people his prestige was unequalled, except in those groups which saw in his apparent defiance of the laws of nature and the conventions of man a threat to their own beliefs.

Following its unprecedented succession crisis, the new president of Russia extended John an official invitation to visit him in Moscow, the first overture made to him by any country of the Eastern bloc. John accepted immediately and publicly, taking pains to assure that the full schedule and intent of his visit was known throughout the world. One summer morning he lifted off from the bivouac he'd hollowed out of a glacier in Greenland and set out towards the Norway coast. Following the protocol requested by the Russians, he crossed the Soviet border over Riga and proceeded toward Moscow at subsonic speed and fifty thousand feet. He acquired an escort of MiGs. The Russians hadn't forgotten that Sky Ranger could pick these planes out of the sky like butterflies, so to show their peaceful intentions they went unarmed.

In due course the planes peeled away, indicating he had reached his destination. Below was a solid overcast through which John allowed himself to fall. He broke through to behold a city like a crystallization of dull grey minerals. His final goal, the Kremlin, reared up colorfully like an outcrop of gemstones in a grey matrix. As agreed, he dropped down outside the wall, where he was greeted by a mob of officials. Beyond a police cordon was a vast crowd of Muscovites, a dun-colored carpet covering Red Square, permitted for the first time to witness a miraculous being who previously had been denounced as a secret weapon of the West, or even as an outright fraud or delusion.

The squad of dark-suited officials escorted him inside the Kremlin walls. He was received with courtesy by the President and his wife, who were people of ease and charm. He joined them and various Politburo members at a state dinner, an opulent affair of conspicuous consumption. John had little interest in food while the Sun was up, but he dutifully picked at overcooked vegetables and potatoes in endless variation. He even took a sip of vodka for a toast. But his hosts were puzzled by the fact that he ignored the masses of beef which they set so proudly before him.

Afterward he met with the President in his private office, with a female interpreter the only other person present. The President stated a wish to open his borders to Sky Ranger, joining the worldwide community of states which availed themselves of his services by means of the KSKY network. However, the idea of allowing a foreign national, however altruistic, free rein to overfly Soviet territory was anathema, despite the stated wish of the new regime to relax and normalize its relations with its rivals. With an embarrassment ill-concealed by his gloss of good humor, the President explained the conflict before him. First, would Sky Ranger be willing to add The USSR and its allies to the regions which benefited from his vigilance?

John sat back and blinked, finding himself in a position to negotiate with the leader of the Eastern Bloc. He said he would be so willing, if not for one large reservation: the Soviet assault on Afghanistan. The President leaned forward and candidly admitted that he too considered the invasion to have been a mistake. Still, there were limits to how quickly he could reverse the situation. Would he be willing to tolerate the situation while a face-saving means of withdrawal was sought?

John kept his face impassive while he considered. The hundreds of millions under this man's sway were not at fault for the policies of their government. They were just as subject to the kind of troubles which Sky Ranger helped to alleviate in the rest of the world. It seemed unfair to deprive them of his assistance.

And yet, the people of Afghanistan were just as innocent, and they were being slain in hundreds by the young sons of Soviet workers. He had already forsworn taking up that battle at the request of the previous American president. How could he reconcile going to the aid of the oppressors while ignoring the victims?

He phrased his response carefully. "Sir, I hesitate to involve myself in international politics, but to the villagers of Afghanistan there's nothing political about attack helicopters and tanks. For them, matters have gone from the ideological to the purely pragmatic. I have no wish to ignore the perils of the Russian people as they confront misfortune of all kinds. Nor do I wish to ignore the people of Afghanistan as they are slaughtered by Russian weapons. If you're not prepared to withdraw immediately, I can agree to your request only if I also enter the Afghanistan war with the intention of destroying your forces there. I would be happy to make myself useful to your people when I can. But I will not even appear to condone your policy in Afghanistan."

"I wonder if you would be so obdurate, if it were the United States doing the invading?"

John looked at him in surprise. "Oh yes, absolutely. Evil is evil, no matter what its origin."

The President regarded him stonily while he formulated his own thoughts. His formal response came through the interpreter. "I'm afraid I could not allow you to submit our military to such manhandling. It would damage Soviet prestige worldwide and crush the morale of our forces. In fact, we would be forced to try to destroy you, and to hamper you by representing you as an American agent. Are you in fact such an agent?"

"Not at all. I do not report to any branch of the United States Government. In fact, it maintains at least one organization whose sole purpose is to keep an eye on me."

The President nodded as if he were already aware of this. "Nevertheless, I'm sure you realize I cannot accede to your terms. It is a great shame. If we could have handled the security details, your occasional presence in our country would have helped bring us closer to the world community as a whole." He continued along these lines for several minutes, causing the interpreter to grope for various ways to express the same hopes and ideas.

John knitted his brows and interrupted. "May I ask a question? Why have you made this overture to me? I'm sure you anticipated my general response. Even if I had agreed, your military commanders and the KGB would have torn their hair out at the thought of an American over-flying your territory, wouldn't they?"

The President's look of opacity returned for a moment. "As I have indicated, I intend to end our presence in Afghanistan as soon as it is practical. Will you reconsider your answer when that is done?"

John waited an extra moment, expecting an answer to his own question. With none forthcoming, he said, "Yes. I will gladly reconsider at that time."

The President's affability blinked back on. "That is excellent. I have enjoyed meeting you and hope we may speak again soon. Would you care for a tour of the sights of Moscow while you're here?"

He would, but dusk was not far off, and something told him it was in his best interest to make a quick and graceful departure. "Some other time, sir."

"As you wish. I will accompany you to the courtyard. I would like the privilege of watching as you soar into the sky."

Together they ambled through the building. The President chatted volubly, showing a considerable knowledge of John and his exploits. They reached the courtyard. The overcast was breaking up, revealing patches of late afternoon sky. Intermittently visible was a formation of MiGs.

The President pointed them out casually. "There is your escort; they will guide you back to Riga."

"That won't be necessary. Good afternoon, sir." With no further delay John fell straight up, getting a last glimpse of the President's rather annoyed round face. He accelerated strongly, making about Mach 8 by the time he hurtled through the fighter group, which was rather larger than the one that had led him in. He kept right on going, not easing up until his inertia carried him through five hundred miles of altitude, a height from which the Soviet Union was indistinguishable from the tan-and-ochre stretch of the lands that surrounded it.

He headed due west; the sunset line was already crossing Moscow. He drove himself over the Atlantic and dived back into the atmosphere only when he recognized the crooked finger of Nova Scotia beneath him. He found work to occupy him in North America. A windstorm in Mississippi had blown down a decrepit frame house; John spent several hours helping to extract survivors from the debris. Eventually the sunset line caught up with him again, but for some reason he was averse to the idea of bedding down for the night in one of his North American hideouts. Instead he chased the Sun, making his way to Borneo, where he broadened his knowledge by visiting one of the primitive tribes of the interior.

Finally, after a long day, he knew he had to let the night overtake him. He flew to nearby Bali, where to his relief he found Elise still at home, her latest voyage delayed by mechanical problems in the Earthwarden *Vega*. He got there half an hour before sunset, and spent the time describing the day's adventures.

At the instant of sunset he fell into a fugue state, a confusion of mind whose chief quality seemed to be an overwhelming urge to tell all, say all, reveal all. For several hours he stared at her with fever-bright eyes and explained in great detail exactly how much he loved her, why he loved her, what he did and didn't like about her, and what a silly, bubble-headed flake she'd been to pass him up originally. She listened in bemused wonder, even through his long descriptions of other women he'd been involved with.

Kaleidoscopic fragments of a dozen emotions danced over Elise's face. Strained little sounds came from the back of her throat. Her toe busily tapped the floor. She said she wasn't sure if she wanted to put John to bed or slip a centipede in his pants. But beneath the pebbles of indignation and pique were strata of affection and wry amusement. Finally she dragged him into the bedroom, undressed him, pushed him into bed, and closed the mosquito net around him. She soon joined him, her skin gleaming with the sweat of the tropical night.

The President of the United States convened a meeting of select members of his administration. They gathered in a room near the office of National Security Advisor Charles Atkinson, a Navy admiral.

"Well, gentlemen," began the President, "you all know I've been saluting Sky Ranger's flag for a long time now, but I have to say, I am a little worried about some of his recent behavior. Chuck?"

"Mr. President, his recent visit to Russia is not only worrisome, but outrageous. Not only did he request no clearance from us, but he's made no effort to communicate the substance of his dealings with the Russians. We know he spent over an hour in private conference with the Russian president. Is he hiding something?"

The President chuckled and shook his head. "Well, if he is, he's pretty flagrant about it. He was publicly invited to visit, and he flew in and out just as bold as brass."

"Then why hasn't he come to us?"

The President shrugged. "Maybe nothing important happened. Wally? Do you have something to say?"

Walter Drake, a diffident, reedy-voiced man with a set of slightly spastic mannerisms, also happened to be Vice President. He spoke up hesitantly. "Uh, sir, I just wanted to point out that Mr. Avril has always shown a strong sense of, well, independence. It doesn't surprise me that he doesn't come running to us every time he does something interesting. He's under no obligation to do so."

Atkinson puffed out his florid cheeks and regarded the VP in surprise. "Mr. Vice President, that may be so, but regardless of his unusual status, Avril's still a citizen of this country. But not an ordinary one. Any time a man of his power confers privately with the Soviet leader, and then neglects to inform us of the results, I feel there are grounds for concern."

Drake shook his head in vague negation, muttered something, and turned away.

Atkinson's yellowed eyeballs swiveled back to the President. "Sir, the Russian affair is only the latest of Avril's questionable acts. I remind you of his involvement with the Earthwarden environmental radicals. His alignment with those anarchists has made waves all around the world. The people are inclined to believe any hogwash he may spout. He has publicly insulted our allies who operate whaling fleets, and challenged our approach to dealing with the matter. He has crippled the French H-bomb program and may have his eyes on ours. He's complained about our forestry and oil exploration policies. We're hearing loud moans from the heads of powerful corporations. We've started to wonder when the good he does will be out-weighed by the trouble he makes."

"Well now, let's remember, he saves an average of three hundred American lives per year," said the President sooth-ingly.

"Uh—that's actually five hundred, sir," said the VP.

"He may soon endanger corporate profits, military pre-paredness, and the jobs of thousands," said Atkinson firmly.

"Well, Chuck, it certainly hasn't gotten that bad yet."

"No sir. But I do believe we should prepare for the eventuality. That's why my group has recommended—"

"That we assemble an informal organization to take on a possible anti-Sky Ranger mission. Yes, I know. Remo, what can you tell me about your progress on that?"

Remo Cosimano adjusted his posture and favored the President with his most level gaze. "Mr. President, we pro-pose calling our team the Sky Ranger Multi-pronged Inter-vention and Termination Exigency—SMITE. It would be divided into three sections: a central planning group, led by myself if Chuck's nomination meets with your approval; a covert action squad, ready to round up those known to be close to Avril, except for our protected asset, of course; and a secret development project to define and build weapons capable of prevailing against Avril's unholy power."

"Sounds pretty expensive, Remo."

Cosimano gave a grim nod. "Yes, sir, especially the hardware group. We estimate a need for two billion dollars in the first year, coming, of course, from the black budget. Even if the weapons are never used against Avril, the new technology may have significant application in other arenas, particularly in missile defense systems."

The President's eyes brightened. "Now, I like the sound of that. The part that makes me nervous is that business about picking on Sky Ranger's family. Those people have been on the cover of every major magazine in America. I've spoken to them on the telephone myself. Things could start boiling up for us in a hurry if we were to lay a hand on them."

"I anticipated that, sir. We feel that the best and safest prospect for influencing Avril lies beyond our borders altogether. This ties in to some mysterious intel we've received. Our people in the Earthwarden cult inform me that Avril has been sighted with the Boutin woman. Rumor has it that Boutin was seen aboard the Earthwarden ship that was involved in the French nuclear testing affair."

Atkinson's eyebrows shot up. "Elise Boutin?"

"Yes, of course. The woman who, along with Avril, put me in prison, which I admit I'm still holding against her."

The President laughed. "Well, to be fair, Remo, that didn't happen because you were unlucky. You did accost her, drug her, and try to kidnap her. But tell me, how is this possible? We know her location, don't we?"

"Yes, we certainly do. That's why I don't give this information the utmost credence. Perhaps Avril has found some whore with a similar appearance to fornicate with."

Atkinson said, "We don't have any evidence that Avril and Boutin ever, er, fornicated."

Cosimano sniffed in dismissal. "Of course they did. Why else does any man bother to keep such a woman around? In any event, this contradictory intelligence further emphasizes the need for an agency like SMITE."

The President furrowed his brow. "I see. But don't we already have an organization designed to keep track of Sky Ranger?"

Atkinson answered this. "Yes sir, the SRIP. The information it collects will of course be of the utmost importance to SMITE. The SRIP commander, General Hunter, has reached the mandatory retirement age. He has several times demonstrated a lack of impartiality in dealing with Avril. I hope we may recommend a replacement whose views are more in line with the mission of SMITE."

"Yes, yes, of course." The President grinned genially. "It sounds like SMITE is practically a *fait accompli*. Well, run with it, gentlemen. But let's remember that this is just a contingency measure—we won't do a thing unless things get a lot worse with John. Oh, and of course this must all be kept totally secret. Despite your great qualifications, Remo, we can't let it be known that a convicted felon is running one of our agencies. You understand that, don't you, Remo?"

Cosimano's smile was cool. "Certainly, Mr. President."

"And an even better reason for secrecy—look at all the trouble I'm having with the Ethics Committee already. If the people of this country found out we were spending billions on a plan to knock down their great hero, well—I don't know how long we'd last around here, I really don't." The President's cheeks grew rosy as he laughed his smooth, affable laugh. His subordinates grinned weakly, although none of them were sure just what was so funny.

Chapter Sixteen

Each time the soft song of Aurora summoned John Avril to wakefulness, his first act was to flip a switch activating a KSKY radio. One morning, as the sky outside his Rocky Mountain eyrie brightened from mauve to peach, John heard a tale of disaster that chilled his blood. A fully loaded oil supertanker, the *Murex Torreon,* had run aground during the night in the Hecate Strait just east of Moresby Island on the Pacific coast. Tons of crude oil were draining into pristine waters which supported major fisheries and great concentrations of wildlife. John pulled on a flight suit while listening to the details. This morning the station gave word of nothing else.

He drank some water, and ate some fruit, bread, and nuts. He parted the curtain and stood on the porch of his eyrie, waiting for the fiery globe that would enable him to act. At the appointed moment it rose above the far end of the valley, awakening his potential, filling his mind with its abiding music.

He still had to wait for the sunrise to reach the Queen Charlottes and their hazardous straits.

At last he lifted off, flew his evasion routine, then thrust himself toward his target. Activating his radar transponder, his unique signature appeared on traffic control radars and on the smaller screens of half a dozen commercial transports in the area. By that means a few civilians guessed his intent and destination. The sensors of SRIP, of course, were vigilant as ever.

He arrived at the scene of the disaster just as the Sun was clearing its horizon. His throat contracted at what he saw: an enormous outpouring of filth into some of the cleanest and most nurturing waters in the world. The *Murex Torreon* lay at a slant, its port side deck awash in mild seas. Great gouts of blackness bloomed on the surface from some submerged wound in the hull. The Sun's first crimson rays made it look like a flow of dark, gritty blood, a semi-clotted hemorrhage that already streamed for miles down-current of the stricken ship. A Coast Guard helicopter hovered over the tilted deck, plucking off the crew. There was no other sign of other rescue or containment craft of any sort.

John circled, puzzled and angry. He was no seaman, but he couldn't see how the ship could have run aground here. The channel was at least ten miles wide, the weather was mild, and no ice was visible. Yet here the great vessel lay, not a mile from the craggy coast of Moresby Island itself. He shook his head. Here was a mystery to resolve later on. For now, what could he do to help? The obvious thing was to stop the outflow of oil. But the leak was below the water-line, in an environment quite alien to him. He looked at the undulating oily surface with misgivings, but saw no alter-native. He dived down, dropped through the oil slick into the new medium, cold and dense compared to air and space. His first impulse was to fly underwater, but the effort was painful, excruciatingly slow, even nightmarish, like a dream where some pursuing horror finds a victim trapped in molasses. He relaxed and decided to swim instead, which was almost as fast and much easier.

He saw nothing but a dim green translucence full of dancing motes and dark shapes lurking just within sight. A huge darkness materialized before him. He almost smacked into it before he recognized the hull plates of the super-tanker. He looked left and right. The great hull vanished in both directions like a cliff in the fog, with no sign of the location of the leak. He made his way to the bottom and began feeling his way along, almost blind in the cold murk. Suddenly he was completely blind as he entered the spout of crude petroleum gushing into the sea. He squeezed his eyes shut against the foul, opaque stream and felt around the edges of the tear in the hull, a gap some eight feet long and two feet tall. The hull plates around it were bent inward by the teeth of rock which had bitten into them.

John reached inside and gripped the ragged edge of one of the plates. Bracing his legs on the hull, he pulled with all the strength he could find. The edges of the plate dug into his fingers, but did not bend. Urging the power of his flight impulse into his arms, he heard creaking, and felt a quiver in the plate, but still it did not bend. His half-panicky impulse was to lapse into fury. Instead he called upon the balance which had made him Sky Ranger in the first place. He thought of the thousands of creatures who would die miserably if he did not succeed.

He was strong; he had to be to survive the rigors of hypersonic flight. In his time that strength had enabled him to tear through brick walls and put his fist through the doors of cars. But this task was beyond him—he was designed to fly, not to bend steel in his bare hands. His heart was pounding and his lungs ached. With all this physical exertion his breath wasn't lasting as long as it usually did.

The metal abruptly gave way, snapping off in his hands, fatigued beyond its limits. He flung the useless scrap away and stroked for the surface, swimming as hard as he could. He broke the surface in a dolphin-like leap, bent on his flight impulse and soared free.

Covered with oil, he choked on the stench and taste of it as it ran into his mouth. His eyes were clogged with a thick black paste; his hair lay matted atop his head in a heavy mass. For a moment he vividly knew the horror of a sea otter or bird surfacing into such foulness. He flew out to sea, pouring on speed, flashing through the Mach numbers, until friction heat cooked and vaporized the oil, blasted it away, and left him clean. He thanked God for the durability that let him do that, a durability far in excess of his strength. He turned and rushed back to the ship.

Was there nothing he could do? If he had an underwater torch he might be able to weld steel plates over the ship's wound and cut off the flow. But by the time he could locate such equipment and learn how to use it, the damage would be done. Indeed, it had already been done—millions of gallons were already in the water. One man could do nothing to contain it, whether he could fly or not. Here was yet another environmental catastrophe he could not materially abate.

Sick with grief, John circled impotently while *Murex Torreon* continued to extend its black tongue of death. He lingered while tugs, cutters, and aircraft entered the area, still hoping to make some contribution to their efforts. The radio told him that an empty tanker was en route to unload whatever oil remained aboard the *Torreon*.

He spotted tall black fins cutting the water—a pod of orcas heading for the slick. He shot down to water level and roared across their path, the force of his passage blowing a furrow in the waves. The orcas took alarm and turned aside. At least he could accomplish that much! He patrolled for hours, trying to steer seals, seabirds, and whales away from the area. But the afflicted area grew steadily, and was soon more extensive than even his raptor's eyesight could encompass. He began to encounter oiled birds. For them he could do nothing.

The Sun dropped down toward the west. John was forced to give up his efforts. He flew slowly back to his eyrie, wondering if Elise had heard of the disaster by now, wishing they could share their grief. But if he flew to Bali he'd be delayed in resuming his work in the morning.

That night his dreams were anguished, full of blinding jets of black opacity that battered him and held him under the water, and bedraggled, blackened sea birds that looked at him with uncomprehending eyes.

In the morning he returned to the scene as soon as possible and was appalled and angered again to see how little action had been taken so far. The empty tanker hadn't arrived. Oil still dribbled from the *Torreon*. Only small craft traversed the area. As yet no containment effort was underway. The slick was now at least ten miles long, lapping up against the beaches of Moresby Island with its colonies of sea lions and sea birds, and its solitary otters. He descended toward the soiled beach, where groups of local people patrolled up and down, capturing oiled creatures and taking them away for washing.

When John landed among them they looked at him with tired eyes suddenly bright with desperate hope, as if he could magically cause the black tide to flow off the rocks and recede back over the horizon. But this was a situation in which Sky Ranger could do little more than they, except to fly out to sea and pluck up oiled birds, bringing them to cleaning stations that were already overloaded. Nevertheless that was what he did. When the rescued birds and otters grew too many, he sat down with the other volunteers and washed them, with the sole advantage that their snapping bills and teeth couldn't harm him. His presence drew out the curious and brought into the workforce many who otherwise would have sat at home and monitored the disaster on the radio. The schools at Sandspit and other island villages were closed, and the older students also joined in, pleased to imitate their hero.

The press, getting word of Sky Ranger's presence, predictably decided to focus their coverage on his participation. Helicopters clattered to earth, disgorging newsmen whose lenses avidly drank in the sight of an oil-smeared Sky Ranger soaping down a wriggling sea otter. They clamored for comments, but at first John stayed silent, not trusting himself to restrain the wrath that roared through him like a gale. They tried a different tack—offering information of their own in the hope of drawing him out.

"Have you heard what caused the accident? There are allegations that the captain was drunk, that an unqualified subordinate was in command—the ship may even have been on autopilot."

Forcing himself to be calm, John looked up and caught the correspondents with a clear-eyed gaze. He had questions of his own.

"Who is the chief executive of Murex Energy Systems?"

"That would be Conrad Wandrei."

"And where is the corporate headquarters?"

"In Manhattan. The Murex Spire."

John nodded his thanks. He stood up and announced he'd try to come back in the morning to do what he could. Without another look he lifted off, heading southeast.

John considered leaving the oil stains on his flight suit and face, but decided that would be too theatrical a gesture — the masters of Murex were surely aware of the nature of the problem. He cleaned himself by air friction while speeding over the curve of the continent, slowing over Manhattan a few minutes later. New York City spread out below him, looking like grey, scabrous tissue from this altitude. He realized in surprise that this was his first visit to the city since his reawakening. Even when the UN voted him international status and inaugurated KSKY, he hadn't attended the ceremonies. The city had made few if any calls for his services.

He dropped down toward Manhattan, wary of the thick air traffic stacked up around the local airports. The skyline had changed substantially in the ten years or so since he'd last been here. One of the latest additions was the Murex Spire, sixty stories of pinkish granite and silvered glass, with a single setback that began at ground level and spiraled all the way to the pointed summit. It was a distinctive building, even melodramatic. Among its boxy neighbors it stood out like a fanciful wizard's hat.

Landing space was at a premium on the streets. He dropped down into a temporary opening in the swirling liquid of pedestrians, startling many and almost knocking down a few. The crowd, quick to realize who had materialized among them, surged forward with feverish expressions. John couldn't tell whether their intensity represented adulation, hatred, or was merely their normal way of conducting themselves. They clamored around him, suddenly a mob, driven by some quirk of group dynamics that might as easily have paralyzed them or sent them running. They plucked at him with ghostlike hands, thrust their glassy smiling faces into his, urging him on as if he were a football quarterback. Without comment he forced his way through the crowd to the entrance of the Murex Spire, looked over his shoulder, swept them with a look that stopped them in their tracks, and entered the building without pursuit.

He found himself in a soaring atrium more grand than any conception of the Pharaohs, a hanging garden clinging to inward-slanting walls of marble and gunmetal, lit by cool shafts of sunlight filtered and tamed by silvered glass. The beams shone through a palpable mist that nurtured the tropical greenery spilling freely from the walls, pools, and columns.

Half-distracted by splendor, John wandered among bemused groups of expensively-dressed men and women, eventually approaching a dais, behind which sat a woman as cool and refined as those select rays of the Sun which were admitted to this dazzling fortress. Just as he came under her supercilious gaze and was about to speak, he was interrupted by two uniformed security guards who came rushing up.

"What's your business here, sir?"

He looked at them. "I've come to speak to Mr. Wandrei." He turned his attention back to the receptionist. "Would you please call and tell him that John Avril would like to see him?"

Despite her refinement, the receptionist lacked the perception to see who she was dealing with, or at least it amused her to pretend so. She smiled with delicate cynicism and replied, "Sir, I'm sorry, but Mr. Wandrei sees no one without an appointment. Perhaps you'd care to call the office from another location and try to arrange one."

One of the guards put his hand on John's elbow. "Please come with us, sir."

"I have business with your employer. Please call him. If you don't, I'll get in to see him through the wall if I have to."

The receptionist simulated an airy laugh. "Oh, really. Look, you wear that suit well, but go somewhere else to get your publicity. Try climbing the Rockhurst Building; it has a narrow ledge on every floor."

The men tried to hustle their captive toward the door, but he was oddly difficult to move.

"Allow me to demonstrate my sincerity," said John in a subdued voice. Yet he allowed a glitter of mischief to show in his eyes. Flinging his captors aside, he took himself aloft, arcing gracefully along the walls, skirting the ceiling like a swallow in a barn. He circled, flying faster and faster, as fast as he could in the confined space, until to his spectators he was a blurry blue hoop hanging in the air with a loud whir. A wind filled the space. Plants bent into the clockwise vortex. Leaves and bits of mulch rushed swirling into the air. Fronds tore free, joining a growing storm of debris which sifted down on the stunned spectators on the floor. The wind rose to a howl. The light was dimmed by its passage through a spinning riot of leaves, sticks, bark, papers, hats, and folders. Someone screamed when a flash of electricity, generated by the spinning rush of moist air, cracked out and blackened a spot on a brass-bound pillar.

John slowed down and alighted, breathing heavily, a bit dizzy. He watched as the last of the debris settled down. The atrium looked like an Iowa cornfield in the wake of a tornado, its occupants like frightened scarecrows.

John returned to the dais. The receptionist, disheveled and dirty, with bits of leaves in her hair, made an inarticulate sound. When she could again control her trembling fingers, she picked up a telephone and shakily announced who had come to call. After a few moments her eyes widened. She replaced the handset, looked at him with haunted eyes, and said, "Mr. Wandrei will see you at once. Please take any elevator to the 55th floor. My apologies for the misunderstanding."

John nodded and set out for the elevators. Already his elation over his act of self-assertion was fading. Again his easily-aroused sense of self-righteousness had led him to an extreme. He had terrorized people who were guilty of nothing, just to make a very small point that served only his ego. His face reddened; he hoped he'd be able to make a better impression upstairs. He entered an elevator, feeling ridiculous to be gaining altitude in such a feeble manner. But it was the only way to reach his goal without causing further destruction.

The cage stopped; the doors slid open. Standing in a plush reception area was a man of medium size, in his early forties, with black hair a little too long to be in keeping with his expensive steel-grey suit. His tie, a rich, saturated violet, was another slightly jarring note. He had a pale face, with yellowish-grey eyes shaded by dramatic black brows. Eyes bright with excitement, he appeared animated even as he stood there, scarcely moving, as though wild and extravagant gestures were barely contained. He grinned broadly at John and stuck his hand into the cage.

"Sky Ranger! What a great honor it is to meet you. I've followed every detail of your career with intense interest. I'm Conrad Wandrei."

John eyed him curiously as they shook hands. This wasn't quite the man he'd imagined.

Wandrei went on enthusiastically. "Please come into my office! I have many questions I'd like to ask, if you have the time."

John walked beside him through the anteroom. "Mr. Wandrei, I have to begin by telling you that I made a mess out of your lobby. I put on a demonstration to establish my identity and I'm afraid I got carried away."

"Yes, I was watching on our security cameras. It was a great show! Magnificent what you can do! Don't worry about it; some of those plants needed to be cut back anyway."

Wandrei's secretary, who manned a station more complex than the consoles in the Firing Room at Cape Canaveral, studied John candidly as they went by. She resembled, he was surprised to note, the popular stereotype of a quiet librarian; he'd expected a bit more decadence.

They passed through a heavy oaken double door. The Murex Spire was considerably narrowed at the 55th floor, but it still had enough space to provide Wandrei with an imposing office. It was finished and decorated in black, silver, and Murex violet, the same shade as Wandrei's tie and the Murex logo itself. The main desk, whose top was a sharp-edged slab of black marble, commanded a view of the city through great panes of silvered glass.

Wandrei steered John to the other side of the room, down a few steps, and into a conversation pit furnished with chairs and couches upholstered in black leather. John took a seat before a low table of violet glass. Wandrei placed himself across from him and waited expectantly while John looked around.

The room was decorated with all manner of odd items that occupied tabletops and niches in the walls. There were Buddhist prayer wheels, a fine bronze statuette of the Hindu god Shiva, an amethyst geode flanked by large, perfect crystals of white quartz, several Medieval swords, an expensive purple-tubed amateur telescope, and other eclectic objects. There was nothing to remind one of the multiple interests of Murex: oil and coal, nuclear power, chemicals, shipping, even a well-known chain of fast-food restaurants.

"Can I get you anything? Coffee, some exotic teas, a sandwich?" asked Wandrei brightly.

John returned his attention to his host, who sat on the edge of his chair, leaning forward, regarding him with keen interest.

"No, thanks. I'm here to talk to you about the *Murex Torreon* spill."

Wandrei sat back. His gaze became more distracted. "Yes, I guessed as much. I'm aware of your efforts to help in that situation, and believe me, I appreciate it. I half expected you to come here—after all, you have become a primary spokesman for environmental concerns all over the world. If anyone has the right to question us, it's you." He shook his head and looked distressed. "The spill's a terrible thing. Terrible."

"That's an understatement. What are you planning to do about it?"

"Do? Clean it up, of course. Murex takes full responsibility for the disaster and its consequences."

"Mr. Wandrei... "

"Call me Conrad, please. May I call you John?"

"I'd prefer that you didn't. Mr. Wandrei, you know I've spent the last two days at the site of the spill, and I have to tell you that Murex's response has been inadequate. You had the chance to contain the spill when it covered only a few square miles, but nothing was done. Now it's beyond control. I consider that a terrible dereliction of responsibility."

Wandrei looked stricken. "Well, I certainly take your views very seriously. I'll look into this and make sure we stay on track from now on. But you realize that part of the problem was the time necessary to get the equipment into place."

John shook his head. "You had almost nothing available, even at the oil port the ship had nearly reached. How did you imagine you could ever deal with such a disaster with no equipment?"

"Of course, we have to spread our equipment over all our operating areas so we can get it into place wherever we might have a problem."

"I'm sorry, that doesn't work. Some of the heaviest supertanker traffic is along those routes, and they are also among the most environmentally sensitive areas. You can't do a responsible job of protecting them if you have to bring in equipment from the North Sea or the Persian Gulf."

Wandrei held out his hands. "Again, I'm sorry. It's a great tragedy which we will do our best to correct. But accidents like these are the price we pay for civilization."

John studied him coolly for a moment.

"You're confusing 'civilization' with profligacy, recklessness, and greed."

Wandrei smiled easily and waved his hand in dismissal. "Well, maybe you're right. Couldn't we talk about something else for a bit? I've just returned from several months in Tibet and Nepal—in fact, I flew back when I received word of the spill. I'm fascinated by aspects of Buddhist philosophy, and I'm wondering if they might be relevant to your spectacular flight ability."

Despite himself, John found himself intrigued. "You mean the levitation powers that some of the Hindu and Buddhist adepts are supposed to possess?"

"Basically. I must admit I never found any evidence of such an ability in practice—the one 'demonstration' I managed to arrange consisted of a man seated in the lotus position who hopped a few inches into the air by jerking his legs. But it seems to me that certain Asian philosophies might offer a path to the kind of self-control you obviously possess—if rigorously pursued to their extremes. Tell me, do you know the physical basis for your flight powers?"

John kept his face carefully neutral. He suspected Wandrei's approach to the question might be a good one, but he had no desire to share what he knew or suspected with this man.

"I didn't come here to answer questions. I came to ask them."

"Certainly. I have no wish to pry into your private affairs," said Wandrei agreeably.

"I've seen the spill. I'm no expert, but I can see that the cleanup will cost millions of dollars."

Wandrei shook his head. "Billions."

"And Murex is prepared to pay?"

"We absolutely are. Even if we didn't want to, the government would insist on it. We will be paying for this cleanup for some years," said Wandrei firmly.

"And what precautions will you take to ensure this never happens again?"

"We can't promise it'll never happen again. But the Coast Guard and the Canadians are already toughening their rules for the way our tankers operate in those waters. It'll mean inconvenience for us, but we don't mind. We don't want a repeat performance either."

John bit his lip, feeling uncertain. Wandrei seemed reasonable, if a bit callous. But there was something just too easy about his attitude—something was being slipped under the rug. He tried another question. "The cleanup money—that's really going to cut into your profits, isn't it?"

"Oh, only for the short term. Ultimately the expense will have to be borne by the consumer."

John said slowly, "You mean, your drunken captain runs a supertanker aground, you delay your response, botch the cleanup, and then expect the people who buy your products to pay for the mess?"

Wandrei's demeanor chilled slightly. "Let me give you a simple lesson in economics. If we paid for the cleanup out of profits, our dividends would fall, our shareholders would feel slighted and sell their stock, its value would plummet, and suddenly Murex would be broke, without capital, unable even to continue the cleanup. This is the only way we can remain healthy. A healthy Murex is important to the United States. The consumer ultimately pays for all our activities: exploration, extraction, refining, everything. The cleanup is just one of the costs of doing business."

John felt a flutter of revulsion for this attitude, this conviction that the abstractions of money and profits somehow had a reality apart from and above the physical well-being of the planet that sustained all life.

"This planet is too small to survive that philosophy," he said in a tight, quiet voice.

Wandrei grinned ingratiatingly.. "Oh, please. Your task should be easy, really. Instead of chiding me, simply convince the hundreds of millions of people we serve that they don't really need all that gas and—"

A melodious chime filled the room. "Yes?" said Wandrei, speaking to the air.

A clipped female voice said, "Sorry to interrupt your meeting. We've received a report of a rifleman firing down on the crowd from the building across the street to the north. I thought your guest would like to know."

John leaped up, gathered himself, ready to crash his way out into the open.

Wandrei looked at him and raised a finger. "Allow me." He touched two buttons on a console beside his chair. One of the big panes of silvered glass beside his desk slid open, admitting a flow of unrefined city air.

John ran, leaped, flew for the open window.

"Come back any time!" yelled Wandrei. "I'd love to continue our talk."

His guest was gone.

Wandrei closed the window, sauntered over to a wall of glossy black panels and slid one aside. Within was an alcove containing various instruments: high-speed cameras, radiation detectors, a gravitometer. The other panels concealed their own suites of instruments and sensors. He sent the video data to his secretary for immediate processing. He spent the next several hours viewing the video and assessing the data collected by the other sensors. Contacts and sensors in John's chair revealed his weight, EEG, EKG, respiration rate, and the chemistry of his exhaled breath. He studied Sky Ranger's liftoff and flight in 1,000-frames-per-second detail.

At length he stepped out into the anteroom, leaned against the wall, and looked at his secretary with thoughtful distraction. She held his gaze until he was ready to speak.

"It worked very well. We collected a lot of data. The oddest thing about it so far is how ordinary it all seems. It's as if the man flies without any external physical effects, except for the simple wind of his passage. Set up a meeting. Call Stanford, get Mannheim and his crowd in here. Get his whole physics department if he thinks it'll help. I also want a physiologist—you know my requirements. Meeting here at 9:00 AM tomorrow."

"Right away."

John shot out of the Spire and scanned the vertical glass face of the tower across the way. One of its windows was broken. A rifle barrel projected from the opening. As he watched it flicked out a tongue of flame; the report reached him a moment later. He dived, rushed down the face of the building, grabbed the rifle as he passed the window and snatched it away. He looped out over the street, making a 270° course change, slowed down, flew through the broken window, and dropped to the floor beside the gunman.

John confronted a man already thoroughly beaten. He was holding his left forearm, which he'd apparently broken against the windowsill when John snatched the rifle. He was young, with lank brown hair and hollow, pale cheeks. John eyed him with a raptor's merciless glare, unmoved by the agony which was just beginning to run riot along the gunman's nerves. He'd be relieved of his pain soon enough; his victims might not.

John neither trusted nor believed the coincidence of this crisis. Never before had such a problem arisen when he just happened to be in the area. He went to the window and scanned the crowd below. The street and sidewalks were packed with people. The crowd was so dense that only those on the outskirts had been able to flee the sound of shots from above. Each tiny figure was defined with minute clarity in John's sight. They all gaped up at him, their panic evaporating now that he had intervened. He saw no gunshot victims. A few people looked scuffed and battered, but they might have been trampled in the rush to escape. Several policemen were present, but they acted with no particular urgency. How could the gunman have missed, faced with a solid mass of targets?

John whirled, ejected the ammunition clip from the rifle, a semi-automatic assault weapon. He tore open the thin stamped metal of the clip to examine the remaining cartridges. Inside were brass shells crimped in the front— blanks. He cast the weapon aside and glared at the gunman, who gave back a ghastly grin of mixed pain and insolence.

John stepped up to him briskly; the gunman flinched and lost his look of mockery. But John merely frisked him and removed a battered wallet. He found several forms of identification, whether authentic he couldn't tell, but nothing illuminating.

Standing six inches from his quarry, John locked eyes for long seconds. The gunman stared into cold pools like arctic water, motionless and unblinking.

Without warning John snapped "Who hired you?"

The gunman started but did not speak. His eyes flicked out the window toward the Spire. His face was pasty-white. Sweat beaded his forehead.

"You're not feeling well?" said John. "Broken bones give a peculiar kind of pain, don't they? Like immersion in boiling oil, maybe. Don't worry, I'm sure help will get here soon. But here's the problem: if you don't tell me who you're working for, I'm going to disable every elevator in this building. It'll take the medics a long time to work their way up fifty flights of stairs. And then you'll have to go down the same way. Believe me, you'll feel every step. You'll get that morphine into you a lot sooner if you tell me what I want to know."

The gunman licked his lips with a dry tongue. "I don't know who they were. I was given a key to this room. I was told to wait here until the phone rang and I was given the signal. That's all I know." He looked anxious, certain his answer would be judged unsatisfactory. He sagged with relief when Sky Ranger merely nodded and turned away.

"All right. Be thankful there wasn't live ammunition in those clips. I feel a violent resentment toward idiots with rifles." He walked over and kicked down the door. In the corridor were wide-eyed workers from neighboring offices. "Please take charge of this person and call an ambulance. He won't give you any trouble."

The gunman shuffled out, glad enough to escape the wrath he had tempted. The others also vanished, deterred from asking questions by the grim cast of Sky Ranger's face.

John went back to the window and spent a few minutes staring across the gap to the mirrored windows of Murex. Then he looked down, satisfied himself that matters were under control, flung himself from the sill and soared away.

He returned on noon of the following day, his flight impeded by an unwieldy burden. He carried a steel pole across his shoulders. Dangling from either end was a bucket full of oil sludge he'd scooped up at the grave of the *Murex Torreon*. He touched down on one of the high ledges of the Murex Spire and set down the buckets. A wide broom was lashed to the yoke; he freed it and saturated its bristles with the brown-black petroleum "mousse". Armed with this he made a gentle takeoff, and at his lowest speed described a smooth double curve along the side of the building facing Central Park. He returned to reload his oversize brush when needed, and when the huge "S" was completed, he added a vertical stripe to form an enormous "$" which slowly sagged and dripped down the brilliant silvered windows.

The buckets still contained plenty of goo, so John also decorated the other three sides of the Spire. Two got dollar signs, but he decided to be more creative with the fourth—he sketched a huge skull in bold, simple strokes of black poison. He positioned it so that the windows lighting Conrad Wandrei's splendid office would be obscured.

As he worked, the window from which he'd exited the previous day again slid open, shedding clots of sludge as it did so. Within stood Conrad Wandrei himself, looking out at him with a small, benign smile.

John sailed up and arrested his flight a few feet in front of Wandrei. The strain of hovering was considerable—it felt like holding a heavy weight at arm's length. But he would not set foot in the building again, nor would he permit the strain to show as anything more than tension on his face. He knew the act of standing on air five hundred feet over the street did much to negate the prestige of Wandrei's exalted position at Murex. It put him on an even footing with Wandrei's profane power.

"So, did you come back to continue our discussion?" asked Wandrei with a mild air of patience.

"I think we've talked enough. I came back to draw my own conclusions, based on what you said."

Wandrei leaned out and looked down at the outward-sloping wall of the Spire. "You know, if you succeed in damaging the reputation of this company, a lot of people are going to get hurt."

"Your reputation was shot the moment that big obscene oil-pod ran up on the rocks."

"There are jobs at stake. Lives."

"Really. You mean the next nutcase you hire may use live ammunition? What was that about? A quick, colorful way to get me out of your office?"

"You are babbling. Murex is obligated to protect itself from your misguided interference. We will take whatever steps are needed."

John's expression didn't change. "Here's the first step you'll want to take, Wandrei." He hurled the oil-soaked broom at Wandrei's feet. The executive leaped nimbly out of the way. The broom left a swath of filth on the office's rich carpet of Murex violet. "Threaten me again, or anyone close to me, and that broom goes down your windpipe. Don't think any force on Earth could prevent me."

John peered past Wandrei, squinting into the shadowy depths of the office, where a black conference table was ringed by men with pale faces and troubled eyes. They stared out at him with a kind of dull horror, as though he were a demon or an angel—which one made no difference;

either represented a grave threat to their positions and their very conception of reality.

John paid them little heed. He caught Wandrei with a final hawklike glare, then turned his face toward the zenith, raised his arms, and shot straight up as though released from a bow.

Conrad Wandrei stared at the blank sky for a moment, turned and thumbed the switch to close the window. It closed only in jerky starts, its mechanism clogged by oil. He faced the massed scientific brilliance at his conference table, his face a careful mask to conceal the multitude of emotions he felt toward his departed foe—fascination, anger, fear...but primarily envy. "Well, gentlemen...and ladies. There is your first glimpse of the living anomaly who has troubled your dreams. Let's see if together we can't make some sense of him."

The scientists at the table looked dubious. Wandrei privately shared their doubts, but it was necessary to make the effort. He was convinced that the search for the power of Sky Ranger would take him through a door these men had not yet opened. But perhaps one of them carried the key, without knowing what it fit.

Chapter Seventeen

Sky Ranger flew, his mind also a seething welter of emotions: outrage, grief, apprehension, confusion. His inner mind was crying out for some kind of action, but the inhibitors of his conscious mind couldn't decide what that action should be. In his previous life he would've gone for a long walk, or simply paced back and forth, but now he had wider options. He flew, seeking out the loneliest places on Earth for his solitary thoughts.

He flew to Venezuela, where he perched atop Mount Roraima, one of the *tepuis*, great flat-topped mountains which reared above the rain forest like colossal battleships above an ocean of green. He spent the best part of a day bathing in the grey mists that cloaked it, bringing a moist silence to a place of sculpted sandstone and extravagant mosses. The place felt so far removed from the world that he could almost forget the swaths of rain forest being cut down or burned daily throughout the basins of the Amazon and Orinoco.

Following the sun, he made his way toward Nepal, first stopping to pick up some empty trash bags. The forests of the foothills, he saw, were also vanishing, destroyed by a growing population desperate for firewood. Many of the steep slopes were ravaged by erosion, their agricultural terraces washed away, since the soil was no longer anchored by the roots of trees. He passed over these stricken lands, ventured into the Himalaya, and reached his destination: the great peak *Chomolungma*, Mother of the World, otherwise known as Everest. He scampered up and down the most popular climbing route, filling the trash bags with cans, oxygen bottles, and other rubbish left behind by those who'd come to "conquer" the mountain. Afterward delivering them down below he spent an hour sitting on the summit, staring out at the daunting wilderness of savage ice-coated rock beneath him, and peering into the vast brown expanse of Tibet that lay to the north.

He looked down toward the obstacles that made this peak such a dangerous ascent: the Mallory Step, the Khumbu Icefall, the Lhotse Face. Deprived of two thirds of the oxygen their bodies were used to receiving, negotiating these dangers challenged even the strongest climbers, bringing them all within sight of death. And yet he, John Avril, could avoid them all. He could run up and down any of the climbing routes all day. He could fling himself off any cliff, fall to the bottom, brush himself off, and do it again.

A sudden storm pounced on the mountain like some grey beast. The blue sky was devoured. The wind grew stronger. John spied a climbing party on the ridge just a few hundred feet below the summit. John prepared to leave. He would not have them find him here, he who had attained this summit so easily. It would cheapen their great risk and effort in climbing so high. But he need not have worried. The climbers hesitated in the face of the storm, faltered, and turned back, just short of their goal. It was possible that all their great hopes for summiting the mountain had just been destroyed, all their efforts in vain, while their goal was in sight.

John could have ignored the storm and stayed longer, but somehow he felt uncomfortable. Although he'd reached the summit without effort, he had no sense that he had "conquered" the mountain—to the contrary, in this desolate place he felt like an invader too insignificant to merit a rebuff. He did not, somehow, deserve to be here. And the mountain knew it. He felt sleepy, something he'd never before experienced in the light of day. The mountain was trying to lull him, to tempt him to sleep. It wanted him to sleep until sundown, and then, very soon and very surely, he would die, and then they would see who had conquered whom.

John stood up and hurled himself into the abyss. He almost forgot how to fall upwards, but then he mastered himself. He was seized by a realization that seemed to come from outside of himself. Everest was a sacred place in some sense he did not understand. Not only did he not belong there, but neither did anyone else.

Thoughtful and chastened, John continued westward. He spent an uneasy night at his camp on the remote volcanic island of Tristan da Cunha. In the morning he flew to his Rocky Mountain eyrie, where he put on his NASA space-flight suit and set out for the Moon. Ever since his Apollo rescue he'd been meaning to return, and this seemed like the time. He took it relatively easy. The air supply in the suit freed him from much of the stress of extended space travel. Arriving after a passage of six hours, he perched on the central peak of the great solitary crater Copernicus. All around him was a hummocky landscape of brilliant, sunlit desolation. The terraced crater walls were barely visible above the horizon.

But the object which held his attention, set high in the starless black pouch of the sky, was a polished sphere of azurite, crescent-lit. He sat in the lunar dust contemplating that planet of cool water and gentle breezes. It looked perilously distant, so small he could almost blot it out with the tip of his thumb held at arm's length. To his eagle's vision it was a confection of exquisite detail and beauty, yet even he could barely discern the minute softening of the planet's limb that marked the film of air that sustained all life, and which constituted his true domain. The atmosphere seemed so vast and limitless when he played among its sunlit towers of cloud. Now it looked thinner than a hairline, a perspective that arrested him with a sudden awareness of life's tenuous hold on the great sphere of rock. For the biosphere, the layer of earth and water that contained virtually all life on Earth, was itself thinner even than the atmosphere. It was the merest stain on the surface of the planet, yet a stain that contained all the life, all the animal consciousness, in the known universe.

He looked around and saw nothing to comfort him. The lifeless rock of the Moon had lost any chance to support life when some chance collision had ripped its material free of the Earth and sent it into this sentinel orbit—it was too small, too dry to create by alchemy some unique lifeform of its own. The Sun, uncomfortably near the crescent Earth from this perspective, was necessary for life but could nurture none of its own. Its energy had quickened the Earth and still drove almost every process upon which life depended. Plant life had stored a fraction of that energy and locked it up by chemical means. Now Man was depleting the stored sunlight of millions of years in what was virtually an instantaneous spasm of profligacy.

A bright point ranged between Earth and Sun—Venus, Earth's "sister" world, but a barren one. Its surface was a poisonous furnace, baked by heat confined by a thick blanket of carbon dioxide. Plants and tiny marine organisms had helped steer the Earth away from a similar fate by fixing much of Earth's carbon in the forms of limestone, wood, and petroleum. Now man sought to return much of that dangerous gas to the atmosphere in a billion fires burning all over the planet.

In the blackness beyond the few local objects he could see were the stars, hidden by the Sun's domination of his eyes. But their invisibility was almost a blessing, for they were so remote that it was hard to see how anything or anyone they might illuminate could be of any assistance to Man and his battered planet during these troubled days.

He leaped up and pulled himself into flight, his heart filled with an ache of painful poignancy. He approached his home planet eagerly, yet with some apprehension, as if he were afraid to see what new outrages had been committed against it in the few hours he'd been away. He watched it swell before him, the place whose every corner he'd come to know, with no continent denied him, every island his home.

He aimed for an island for which he had a special love—Bali, soon to be covered by the advancing shadow of night. He flew in high enough so that no one in its teeming villages could see him, then over the forested highlands, to let himself drop down until he alighted in the garden behind Elise's cottage. He badly needed to talk to her, but one look at the garden, unkempt and weed-grown, released a pang of disappointment —she must be absent, probably on an Earthwarden mission.

He let himself into the cottage and moped his way over to the dinner table. A note from Elise, cryptically worded to confuse unintended readers, confirmed his fear. He heaved a great sigh, pulled off the flight suit (the dark stains of moon dust on the seat and legs were like souvenirs of a dream), and scrounged up something to eat.

Presently his power deserted him and he took shelter in the mosquito netting of Elise's bed. As always the bedding retained a hint of her scent, which brought him some comfort, but also reminded him of her absence.

For the first time he could remember, he had trouble getting to sleep. His mind refused to be quiet, continuing to spin and whirl, but uselessly, like a turbine disconnected from its generator. Fatigue cloaked his thoughts, and he was aware of the passing of every minute which brought the Sun closer to the eastern horizon, but still he tossed and turned while powerful, seething emotions fought to be free of the strata of inhibitions that sought to repress them.

Finally he gave up, fought his way clear of the netting, tossed on a robe, and went out onto the veranda. The air was surprisingly cool, and a fresh breeze played through the screening. Flickers of lightning pulsed along the horizon as thunderstorms worked their way over the sea like battleships spitting ghostly flame.

He stepped cautiously out of the veranda, aware of the possibility of snakes or spiders. He looked up and had his first clear view of the stars in a very long time.

Presently his mind grew calmer and he returned to the bed and slept.

He dreamed of Elise. In his dream she came clattering up the moonlit dirt road on her bicycle, looking harried and downcast. When she shook him awake he was momentarily unsure whether it was still a dream, but then he decided it was not.

"Elise!"

He saw her outlined in silvery moonlight before she lit a lamp, replacing silver light with gold. "John!" She bent and gave him a quick hug. "What are you doing here? Our ship just dropped me off this afternoon. I swear, this was the worst trip I've ever been on. We chased a ship that was dumping barrels of toxic waste into the ocean. We went out in the Zodiacs while they were doing the dumping—one of those creeps tossed a barrel right down on the Zodiac I was on. It just missed me, but broke somebody's arm. It was awful!" She took a look at herself in the mirror. "Ugh! I look like I've got a mop on my head. John, how do you stay so young?"

"I've been wondering the same thing about you."

"Sweet. But that was a serious question, sort of."

"Actually, I age at half the normal rate, since during the day... "

"Oh, shut up. Look, I'm glad to see you, but what are you doing here?"

"I came to talk."

Elise stopped her nervous bustling, brought up short by the tone in John's voice. She looked at him with a new intentness. "What have you been doing, Airboy?"

"I've been all over the world in the past couple of days. I just got back from moping and meditating on the Moon. Have you heard about the tanker spill?"

"Just what we picked up on the radio. It sounds horrible."

"Let me tell you about it." He did so, also describing his encounters with Conrad Wandrei. By the time he finished they were sitting together on the bed, in yellow lamp light diffused by the mosquito netting. "I looked at his face—and I knew there was no bridging the gap between us. He doesn't inhabit the same universe we do—I believe he has no real goal beyond fulfilling his own desires. No thought of the continuity of life beyond his own time. And I knew that he and those like him must be stopped. I flew off to try to figure out what to do. I pounded my head against the wall looking for a plan, but I didn't find anything practical. I'm the only man in the world who, sooner or later, sees every kind, and every site, of environmental destruction and social evil on this planet. I can't ignore it any more. But what can I do?"

Elise rolled her eyes and sighed in exasperation. She laid a hand on his arm and spoke to him softly. "John, instead of pounding your head against a wall, step around that wall."

John looked at her and blinked. "What do you mean?"

"Sweetheart, you've built a wall in your mind that's so thick even you can't knock it down. But it's only a few feet wide. If you'd only take a couple steps to the left or the right, you'd find your way around it. Or over it."

John maintained his plaintive stare.

"Oh, look at you. You don't have any idea what I'm talking about. What can you do to stop Wandrei and Murex and anybody else who doesn't know enough not to trade the life of this planet for Big Macs and forty-mile commutes? What can *you* do? God, what *can't* you do? If you see greedy people destroying things that can't belong to them and that we can't afford to lose, put a stop to it! Use your hands to do it! Don't let them get away with it!" Seriously worked up, Elise became inarticulate, waving her hands as she sought to voice her passions. "You're Sky Ranger, goddamnit!"

"But I mustn't involve myself in political matters. It's the only way I can function in the world."

"Political matters!" snapped Elise. "How is it political when thousands of species are wiped out so men can turn rain forest into grazing land for walking hamburgers? What's political about a few nations slaughtering whales for 'science' and then selling their 'specimens' in butcher shops? And when did politics become so freaking sacred? In fifty years today's politics will be forgotten, but the damage will be done. The people who ate the meat and raked in the profits will be dead and buried, but the forests and the whales and all the other animals will still be gone, and they won't be back ever! Wake up, John! Who's going to stop all that? In Earthwarden we do our best, but how do you expect normal people to put themselves on the line when the mighty Sky Ranger limits his contribution to whatever he can do in front of a TV camera? John, you're a walking, flying miracle. Don't tell me you're restrained by the miserable politics that protect greed and destruction. You were graced by a power far beyond that of the governments and corporations that are destroying us. Why aren't you using it? Governments, economies, money: they're all abstractions, they don't exist, we made them up! It's the world that's real. The world, and the life that makes it up. That's what we have to protect!"

John regarded her with amazement. Here was an Elise he had seldom seen, a creature fierce and passionate as a mother mink. Almost cautiously, he voiced his concern. "It would be wrong to use superior force to coerce people into doing right. They wouldn't learn anything from it except to hate me as a bully and a criminal."

Elise shook her head vigorously. "Then let them hate you! Be a bully and a criminal! What does it matter, compared to what's at stake? The people who will oppose you, they're all bullies and criminals. There's seldom been a major change in this world that wasn't enforced by a superior power. We try to deny it, but it's the accepted way of doing things. Right now, enormous power is tied up in a single human being, a person smart enough and free enough to use it wisely. Use it! You may be the only thing big enough to oppose the greedy men and pigheaded governments that are leading us to ruin. You're worried that people won't like you? Well, you didn't worry so much about being liked before you got this power. You've gotten to be too damn nice for your own good. And now I'm exhausted and my throat is dry from making this speech. I'm going to get something to drink, so you just stay here and think about what I've said. If you argue with it, first I'll clobber you and then I'll tell you why you're wrong." She bounced out of bed and skipped into the kitchen.

John Avril lay back in a daze, staring at distances far beyond the confines of the mosquito netting. His mind spun. Never had he foreseen such a role for himself as Elise had outlined. His goal upon entering into his mountain pilgrimage so many years ago had been simple: to seek salvation, to end a wasted life on a note of peace and wisdom. His success was manifest, but even upon his rebirth he hadn't imagined pursuing so grandiose a mission as he already had. Flight had been a natural extension of his communication with nature, a means of joining himself to it through his deep understanding of its voice and secrets. The fact that he was the only flier, and his desire to carry a message to the rest of mankind, had led to his becoming a "hero".

But the living planet which was the main incarnation of nature in this part of the universe was under attack by the very men and women he sought to aid. The drives and habits of the culture of materialism was causing terrible damage that would persist through the next several ice ages at least.

He felt the literal sensation of scales falling from his eyes, clearing his vision to a breathtaking panorama of possibility. It was dizzying to see at last the full extent of his freedom, his unique and unprecedented freedom, to arrest the destruction, to reverse the course of ruin and death. The human race would have to be dragged along kicking and screaming, but surely it must eventually see the wisdom of his actions.

His thoughts soared with a sense of joy and freedom like that he'd experienced on the morning of his first awakening on that distant mountain meadow.

When Elise returned she faced a different man. He caught her and held her with a probing gaze.

"If I become an eco-pirate I won't be able to continue my rescue work," he said quietly. "I'll become a pariah."

True to her word, Elise lashed out with a sharp punch to John's shoulder. "You think you'll go from hero to pariah overnight because you start doing what most people already know is right? You show me one person who'd rather die than let you save them because they don't agree with your policies."

"I might have to take on the military power of every nation on Earth."

"Do you deserve to be called a hero? Are you only willing to take on trouble that can't get past your durability? Okay, so they might get lucky and bring you down. What's that emblem on your flight suit, an eagle or a chicken? Maybe you'd rather trade places with me and have cursing sailors toss barrels of toxic waste at your round, pink, non-durable ass."

"Point taken. I find that you are right in all these matters. Astonishingly, searingly right, and I could kick myself for not seeing it myself."

"Let me, please."

John smiled at her, a smile intense, aflame, and full of life and joy unrestrained. He had never smiled such a smile before, neither in his old life or the new. He found himself wondering what Elise had awakened. "Elise, I think you might have tossed a stone down a mountainside and seen it trigger an avalanche."

They fell asleep in each other's arms. Elise often slept through John's morning empowerment and departure, but this time something brought her to consciousness at the first trace of dawn. She watched as he got up to stand at the window, the rising purple twilight leaking in and washing over his tall, straight form. She watched as he pulled on a flight suit, one of those he kept hidden at her cottage. It was a transformation he'd made many times, yet this morning he was also something new. He trembled with a premonition that this was the start of a new era for himself, and for the whole human race, and that nothing would ever be the same. The emblem on his chest was indeed an eagle, and the creature about to launch himself upon the world had much of the bearing of that great bird.

At the appointed moment the Sun cracked over the horizon and began to flood John with power, though its rays were yet blocked by intervening mountains.

He turned to Elise with that morning smile, as if the Sun were contained in his eyes. "I'll let you know how it goes," he said. He turned back and swung open a window, crouched, gathered himself, and leaped skyward with a rush of air and a billow of curtains.

Chapter 18

John tuned into KSKY, which revealed no ongoing emergencies to preempt his attention. He decided to start with the whaling fleets, a concentrated, isolated source of death that could be easily singled out. He felt a childlike excitement at the realization that he could stop them!

He soared high, heading south toward the Antarctic waters that were popular killing grounds for the whalers. He'd seen them there often enough. Their ships weren't hard to recognize, at least when resolved on a retina any eagle might envy.

Presently he made out a pattern of specks on the distant horizon and closed in to identify them. It was a Japanese whaling fleet—a factory ship surrounded by a squadron of fast harpoon-armed killer ships. With butterflies in his stomach, and a peculiar sense of self-consciousness as though he were about to step out on stage, he guided himself down toward the bridge of the factory ship. His nervousness was replaced with something colder as he crossed the ship's stern and saw the work going on there. The bloated carcass of some great baleen whale, pumped full of air to keep it afloat, was being drawn up a slip into the bowels of the whale-digesting vessel. There it would be rendered into oil for margarine, cosmetics... with the remainder going for pet food and fertilizer.

Action a couple of miles away distracted him just as he was about to set down on the flying bridge. The killer boats were swarming on a pod of whales who could be seen by the vapor plumes of their expelled breaths. John made a hard turn, added speed, and arrowed in toward the hunt. The lead boat was in hot pursuit of a large whale. Sky

Ranger wasn't naturalist enough to identify the species, but he thought it might be a fin whale, or even a blue. His vision was sometimes keener than he wanted it to be—now he clearly saw the man at the harpoon cannon taking aim at his lazily swimming prey. John urged himself to speed, setting a new personal record for breaking the sound barrier. The man fired the harpoon with John still a quarter mile astern. With his enhanced reflexes John watched it emerge from a gout of smoke and slide out into the air, trailing a cable which uncoiled from the deck in an unhurried manner. The whale seemed all but motionless; the harpoon moved toward it as inevitably as a train on a track. Sky Ranger shot over the boat at low altitude, heedless of the shattering effect of his sonic boom on those who manned it. He caught the harpoon, wrapped it in his arms and veered sharply upward. The jolt caused the harpoon's explosive head to detonate. John squeezed his eyes shut and endured a hail of steel shrapnel. It stung and left him with ringing ears. He released the shaft and watched it sail into the distance before splashing down. The explosion had been meant to occur in the gut of the awesome creature he'd just overflown. The thought did little to improve his disposition.

The pod had panicked at his sonic boom, and its members had scattered or sounded. Just to be sure of their safety, John went from boat to boat, indulging in a rare display of strength by ripping harpoon cannons up by the mounts and throwing them into the sea. Few things he'd done during his career as Sky Ranger had been as satisfying. The Japanese manning each boat scrambled out of his way as he alighted on their decks.

With the boats emasculated, John returned to the factory ship and entered the pilothouse in a fine state of con-

trolled wrath. The captain and the others on the bridge regarded him with wide, frightened eyes. The captain was in
an evident state of indecision— but nevertheless he stood
his ground gamely enough as Sky Ranger came forward to
tower over him. The captain spoke no English, and neither
did any of his mates. John had to go down to the common
sailors before he found anyone capable of interpreting his
demands. When all were assembled in the pilothouse, the
impromptu interpreter, a young man wearing jeans and a
filthy T-shirt, stood nervously waiting to see what insult the
flying Westerner might care to offer the authoritarian master of the fleet.

"Tell him his whaling days are over."

The young man chattered it out and added several small
bows to soften the words.

"I've decided to end whaling everywhere in the world."

Further translation and a look of disbelief from the captain.

"Here are your instructions: call in the pursuit boats.
Bring every man aboard this ship. Then empty your tanks
of all the whale remains you've collected. Flush it all into
the sea. You've seen your last profit from this butchery.
Then set a course for home. I will sink all the boats. When
you make port, this ship too must be dismantled or scuttled.
If you don't do it yourselves, I'll come and do it for you. Is
it clear?"

By the time he was finished, the interpreter was shaking, his face an anguished mask. The captain saw events
through a haze of disbelief and fury. He pointed and spat
out a peremptory command, evidently an order to his men
to throw this arrogant *gaijin* over the side. A few men took
a step forward, but John's warning look brought to mind

the fact that here was a man who had arrived with thunder and struck like lightning. They stood back shamefaced and hung their heads.

John said, "Captain, I regret this humiliation to you and your men. But you and they have made a living through evil, and it must stop. Go home and find yourselves a livelihood of greater honor."

The captain offered a bitter reply. "In our country, this is an honorable trade. It is not for you to deprive us of our way of life in the free ocean."

John did not waver. "It is not for you to deprive the world of these whales. It is not for you to deprive the whales of themselves."

The captain turned away, stuck out his lip, and scowled down at the deck as he weighed his options. Ultimately they appeared few enough, and with poor grace he ordered that Sky Ranger's demands be met. John bowed and offered formal thanks. He stepped outside and lifted off to orbit overhead while watching to be sure his orders were carried out. Sure enough, the pursuit boats worked their way toward their mother ship, which began to spew out columns of thin, clear oil to calm the waves. Also came a thick porridge of more solid material, a stinking mass which was all that remained of some of the greatest creatures ever to emerge from a universe rich in time and possibilities.

One by one the pursuit boats pulled up to the factory ship and bobbed beside it as their crews abandoned them to crawl up ladders thrown over the side. The boats, once empty, were allowed to drift away. The factory ship began to churn the water as it gained way and set a course for the north. It left behind a swarm of boats moving slowly under no conscious direction. John visited them one by one, going below decks to find and open the stopcocks, sending the boats to the bottom.

And so ended the threat of the Japanese whaling fleet once and for all.

John left the scene feeling a turmoil of emotions: first of all a burning exhilaration, a conviction that what he had done was right. Below that was a stinging regret, even an anguish, that only by forcing his will on the men involved could that good be brought about. It would be far too easy in the future to force his will on others for causes less supportable. Against that he must always be vigilant.

Most nations had already ceased whaling under the urging of the International Whaling Commission, but a few, notably Japan and Iceland, continued under the guise of "scientific" research. With Japan taken care of, the major remaining threat was Iceland. The next day, John stopped at the Earthwarden office in San Francisco to ask for the location of the Icelandic fleet. The Earthwarden staffers treated him with careful deference, as though a dinosaur had unexpectedly appeared in their building. They were thoroughly in awe of his deed of the previous day, and could scarcely believe that a threat they had battled for over a decade had now been eliminated. They looked at him with misty eyes and offered the information he sought as though it were holy writ and he a prophet of God.

Feeling self-conscious again, John took off and set out for the waters around Iceland itself, where its whaling fleet was preying on minke whales.

The Icelanders proved less cooperative than the Japanese. The captain of their fleet had received warning of Sky Ranger's likely intention, and on his own initiative had prepared to protect his vessels. John encountered the fleet in a formation obviously not intended for whaling. The factory ship was ringed by killer boats, with their harpoon cannons aimed skyward, as nearly as their mountings would allow. Other men stood on deck with rifles, scanning the skies for the flitting blue mote that would mark today's target.

As a defense it was more symbolic than effective. As John soared in, the few who spotted him let fly harpoons and bullets, but they had little chance of scoring a hit, and less chance of doing any harm if they did. Bullets whizzed by as John approached the factory ship's flying bridge. A few of the more zealous sailors even sent bullets zinging off the sides of the deckhouse as John set down.

He entered the pilothouse without further opposition and found himself facing a huge, red-faced, blond man in a crisp uniform of navy blue. His fists were balled and his eyes glared with volcanic intensity. John set his jaw and prepared for a tough confrontation.

The Icelandic captain spoke excellent English in a deep, commanding voice. "Mr. Avril, I demand that you leave my ship at once and depart from these waters."

John shook his head decisively. "Sorry, captain. I'm here to insist that you follow the lead of other civilized nations and abandon whaling." He stated the same demands and instructions that he had given the Japanese.

The captain stood unmoved. "Don't bother to offer us your reasons for this action. We will never submit to such piracy. We will not leave our ships. If you remove us bodily we will swarm back aboard as you attend to someone else. If you try to scuttle our ships we will close one valve while you open another. We will resist you at every turn. Only by killing us all will you stop the whale harvest of this fleet."

John exchanged pugnacious glares with the captain as he pondered his next move. Clearly he would have to escalate this conflict, and he must do it without killing or seriously injuring any of these men. His stomach gave an uncomfortable twist. He hated the necessity of opposing these brave men, but there was no other choice. Were he to back off, he might as well abandon his whole program right now. With such an example set, other groups would be much harder to intimidate.

"You must abandon your fleet." Without waiting for a reply, he turned, stepped out onto the wing, and lifted off. As he departed he noted that the sailors all wore survival suits, apparently half-expecting to find themselves in the frigid North Atlantic waters at some point today. They all jumped and cheered as he disappeared over the horizon, apparently defeated.

A moment later many of them were battered to their knees by an explosive concussion erupting from above. John turned and made another low pass at Mach 6. Panicked, the sailors began to claw their way below decks, anything to escape the shattering sound and impact of those meteoric passes.

Satisfied that all were below, John withdrew some fifty miles, then aimed himself at the fleet again and drove in under maximum acceleration, forcing himself through the Mach numbers as though they were floors in a high-speed elevator. He felt the thick marine air as a hot, solid wall against his face. He trailed fire; his shock wave blasted a deep furrow in the water below.

At this speed he passed ten feet over the deck of one of the killer boats. The heat ignited the deck house, but the fatal blow came from the shockwave, a hammer-blow that broke the back of the small vessel and left it adrift as two separate sections, rapidly sinking. John killed his speed and sped back to the stricken vessel. Sailors were frantically spilling into the water to avoid being dragged down. John wrenched life rafts into the water and helped the sailors into them. As the sections of the broken boat were about to go down, John took a breath and dived into them in search of any stragglers. He plowed his way through all the spaces, but found no one. With relief he returned to the rafts to check for injuries. The only serious one was a man who'd been scalded on the shoulder when a steam pipe burst. Another man spoke English; through him John asked the burned man if he wished to be ferried to the mother ship for treatment. He acceded readily, the pain being more than enough to overcome any fear of making such a flight. John picked him up carefully, made a strenuous takeoff from the tiny raft, and a moment later deposited the sailor on the deck of the factory ship, where other sailors awaited. Then John returned to the bridge, where he faced the captain with a grimness he'd seldom known.

"Captain, I detest having to abuse your men like that. But I am deadly serious. You must abandon the boats and head for port, or I will deal with each of them in exactly the same manner. Do you understand?"

The captain eyed him from a set, impassive face. "Yes, I understand, you vicious brute. I will issue the orders. You have gone mad. I am not surprised that the holder of such an unholy power should eventually lapse into tyranny."

John offered no reply. He left the ship and waited for the Icelanders to comply. In another hour their boats were on the bottom and John was heading away from the scene. The Icelandic whaling fleet was neutralized, but this time John felt little sense of triumph. He *felt* like a vicious brute, but a lucky one. If he'd been forced to crack open every boat, men might easily have been killed, and from that neither he nor his program would ever recover. He must devise ways of achieving his goals without endangering anyone else.

The day was still conveniently placed, so John returned to the San Francisco Earthwarden office to learn the disposition of the remaining whalers. Once again the young staffers regarded him with a certain awed ambivalence. This time, however, an older man came to meet him: a burly, wild-haired character in a frayed sport coat who looked him up and down warily. He held out his hand. "Sky Ranger? I'm George Spak, director of the U.S. Earthwarden HQ in Washington. I received a message from our world headquarters asking me to fly out here to meet you."

John took the proffered hand in a careful grip. "Well. What can I do for you, Mr. Spak?"

"Call me George. Shall we step in here?"

They walked into an office and took seats around a coffee table. Spak moved uncomfortably in his vinyl chair and cleared his throat. "So, Sky Ranger, we haven't heard. What was the result of your work in Iceland today?"

"It was successful. Their whaling fleet is finished. But I regret that I had to use more force than sufficed for the Japanese."

"Yes, that's very unfortunate. Sky Ranger, or John if I may call you that, let me be the first to tell you—confiden-

tially—that I'm all in favor of the direct action you're taking. It may be the only way to intervene in some of these problems before it's too late."

"Thanks. I admit that all this conflict and condemnation have got me a little rattled. I'm going to need all the support I can get."

Spak's discomfort level increased noticeably. "Yes. Well, that brings us to an awkward matter for Earthwarden. To be blunt, what you've done is piracy—a serious criminal act. We don't know what the eventual consequences for you might be, but they're likely to be severe, and frankly, Earthwarden can't afford to be involved in it. You've done superb work for us in your semiofficial affiliation with us, but we mustn't be associated with outright criminality. We'd be shut down *tout suite*. We've been very careful to observe this limitation over the years. Tell me, do you intend to continue this new policy of intervention?"

John gave a sharp nod. "I intend to escalate it."

"In that case, Earthwarden is forced to publicly repudiate your actions. We must condemn you, sever our relationship, and ask that you no longer visit any Earthwarden facility or ship. Please forgive us, but that's the reality imposed on us all." Spak released a shuddering breath and stared miserably at Sky Ranger.

John stared back for a prolonged moment. Then he quirked his mouth in a wry grimace. "George, sometimes my thought processes aren't as clear as I'd like them to be. I never even thought that my actions might endanger you, but of course you're right. I won't darken your door again."

Spak winced. "I don't see it like that. If anybody's going to turn this whole worldwide environmental mess around, it's going to be you. But we at Earthwarden would like to stay out of jail so we can do our small part too."

They stood up and shook hands again. "I've seen what you Earthwarden people do," said John. "You put your safety on the line in cold rubber boats while I flit around like Peter Pan. I salute you. And I'll be leaving—*tout suite*."

He was as good as his word. Spak and the rest crowded into the parking lot of their funky bayside building and watched Sky Ranger lift himself to soar out over the shipping entering the Golden Gate. George Spak choked down the lump that rose in his throat. Despite Sky Ranger's words of support, he couldn't help feeling like a traitor and a coward.

For his part, John suddenly felt very alone. His chief comfort was denied him, for at the moment night was heavy on the scented tropical isle of Bali.

The next days were among the busiest in John's career. They began with a matter of great relief as the Russians announced they were withdrawing the last remnant of their whaling fleet from service. Their stated reasons mentioned whale conservation and economic factors, but contained not a word about Sky Ranger. Thus was John spared from having to confront and destroy yet another fleet. In three days he had guaranteed the safety of the world's remaining whales—with the exception of those few taken by polar Inuit for their own survival. Even if he'd felt like interfering with their hunt, he could think of no practical way of doing so save to patrol the arctic shores in constant search of the Inuit and their walrus-skin kayaks.

His jubilation was shattered when he learned that the captain of the Japanese whaling fleet had committed *seppuku* during the voyage home, having failed to protect his command against the depredations of the lone *gaijin*. There was the first human life he must carry on his conscience. From then on he kept an especially close watch for KSKY stories originating in Japan, as a small effort towards atonement.

John worked harder than ever to keep up his rescue work as he pondered what the next step in his save-the-world program should be. He was almost happy when a volcanic eruption on a small island near Iceland cut off a village and threatened to immolate its inhabitants. By ferrying them to safety in Reykjavik he was able to mollify Iceland and its allies considerably. He wondered what it would take to jumpstart Mount Fuji so he could accomplish the same thing in Japan.

The face of Conrad Wandrei entered his mind. He thought of the huge chemical plants operated by Murex and its competitors—U.S. plants making deadly pesticides banned for use in the United States, yet still produced for sale in the Third World. The plants they operated in those "developing" countries spewed forth similar poisons—he hadn't forgotten Bhopal, which he hadn't reached in time to do anything but weep for the thousands of dead. He vowed to end the production of those chemicals, and any others he could be convinced were too toxic for any legitimate use.

Before commencing this new tactic, world events and the rotation of the Earth finally conspired to bring him the opportunity to visit Bali. As usual he arrived just before sunset, and as he dropped down in the garden he was pleased to see Elise's bike leaning against its usual tree.

Just as he put his hand on the doorknob he was arrested by a new alert coming over his KSKY headset. Would he be compelled to rocket off to combat some new disaster? No—the message was a request that he stop by the White House the following day to meet with the President and the NASA director. Well, it would have to be rather late in the day, he thought, as the Sun set and his power left him. With a shrug he let himself in the back door.

Elise stood over her little propane stove stir-frying vegetables. She grinned up at him happily as she noticed him standing there.

"Aren't you ever startled when I show up like this?" asked John.

"No, you always did show up at the darnedest times. I might as well jump every time a butterfly lights on a flower. My stir fry is only enough for me, but I'll stretch it out with some extra noodles, you whale-saver you." Her smile increased in intensity until he felt its light in his heart.

John stretched and took a seat at the table. "So what have you been up to?"

She jerked her head to clear the hair from her eyes. "Not much. You may be interested to know that I'm no longer in danger of getting barrels tossed at me. Take a look at that telegram on the table."

It was from Earthwarden, and it relieved her of any further affiliation with the organization.

"I'm afraid my unruly behavior is to blame for this," said John sheepishly.

"Yes, I expect it is," she agreed brightly. "But so what? The way you're going, we won't need Earthwarden in another year anyway. It just means that I'll be teaching full-time now. I will miss my friends there, though."

They shared a peaceful, cheerful dinner and then went to the veranda to watch the waning dusk. They sipped glasses of some exotic tea as John described his campaign and some of its more troubling consequences.

An hour or so after sunset, as wakefulness was becoming unendurable for John, a car rattled past on the rough dirt road out front. This was a rare event, as almost all of the meager traffic on this isolated road was by foot, bicycle, or oxcart. Seldom did an automobile venture by at night. They both fell silent as they waited for the engine noise to fade away. However, it did not—it muttered softly as if idling, and then, with the grinding sound of a decrepit transmission, it grew louder once again.

A sudden apprehension gripped John. He cast an urgent look at Elise. "Are you expecting anyone?"

She shook her head vigorously, tight-lipped.

"Elise," he said rapidly, "I want you to go out the back door right now and duck into the woods. Unless I call you back in five minutes I want you to get the hell out of here and hide out in the hills. All right?"

Elise nodded mutely and slipped away, white faced.

The noise of the backing vehicle increased. Tires crunched over gravel. John doused the light on the veranda and squinted out into the darkness as best he could, keenly aware of the hours that must pass before the Sun would return to restore his full competence. The car came back into sight—by the pattern of its lights John thought it was a jeep, not a comforting sign. Hordes of flying insects defined the beams of its headlights.

The car stopped, then moved forward to pull off the road. The lights went out and the motor died. Silence returned, absolute except for the ubiquitous whine of the bugs.

A shadowy figure swung out of the jeep and stood motionless beside it, evidently staring at the house. He began a quiet advance as John held his breath and wondered what to do. A flashlight beam flicked on and began to play over the path.

A tentative voice called out, "Hello? Anyone home here?" Light reflecting from the ground picked out a lean figure and a gleaming bald dome of head.

John's heart leaped. "Hunter!" he shouted. He jumped up, upsetting his chair; Eric Hunter jumped back two feet.

"Avril, is that you? Jesus, boy, you scared the piss out of me."

John laughed and fumbled to relight the lamp. "I scared you?" he called through the screen. "I was just trying to convince myself I was an Owlboy so I could fly the hell out of here. C'mon in." He held open the screen door so Hunter could enter.

In the lamplight John saw a face touched by time, but still keen and open. The general offered a grin and said, "Sorry. I wanted to get here before sundown so I wouldn't spook you, but these damn roads make more twists and turns than a pilot dodging a SAM. I just plain got lost."

"Understandable. So—just how did you manage to find me?"

Hunter chuckled. "Son, even a former SRIP commander remembers something about his target's habits. Tell you the truth, I expect even the Indonesian intelligence service knows about you and Bali, and they're amateurs. What is it that draws you here, anyway? Nice little cottage you've got here."

John laughed. "I'm surprised you don't know, what with your all-knowing intelligence apparatus and all. It's Elise, of course."

"Elise? Elise Boutin?"

"Who else?"

All at once John's apprehension returned, to be briefly superseded by something else. "Yikes! I almost forgot!" He stepped outside. "ELISE! Everything's okay! Come back in, we've got company!"

Presently Elise poked her head around the door frame and looked relieved to see John sitting and smiling, rather than at gunpoint. Her expression for Hunter remained cautious.

Hunter looked from one to the other. He appeared confused.

"Well, this is a big surprise." The retired general rose to his feet. "Good evening, Miss Boutin. I never expected to find you here, but I'm truly sorry to have disturbed you. Or is it Mrs. Avril by now?"

Elise relaxed and even laughed a little. "No, we're still kind of informal about that."

John stepped in. "Elise, this is Eric Hunter. You remember, the first commander of SRIP. I've told you about the favors he did for me."

"Sure, I remember. It's nice and slightly strange to have you here, General."

"Just Eric, please. I'm out of the generaling game."

They seated themselves around the table, and Elise brought a glass of tea for Hunter, who still appeared both bemused and distracted.

"So, Eric," began John, "I guess you're not here for old times sake."

"I wish I were, son. But the truth is, you've gotten yourself into a hell of a mess again, and since I take kind of a proprietary interest in you, I thought I'd better warn you."

John gave a comical look of concern. "Have I been a bad boy again?"

"You know it. Tell me, are you planning any more stunts like that whale business today?"

"That was only the beginning."

"Oh, shit and Shinola. What kind of a wild-eyed ecof-reak sideshow are you putting on next?"

John blinked. "I take it you don't approve?"

"Johnny, I hate to break this to you, but I voted for the winner in the last two elections."

Elise made a face at that, but John restrained himself. "That comes darn close to answering my question, but doesn't quite pop the target on the nose."

"Well, the full answer depends on what the hell you're going to do next."

"I've decided to regulate the chemical industry all by myself. End production of the worst toxins, pesticides, herbicides, all those poisons. I might clamp down on the oil business too, while I'm at it."

Hunter swore quietly but vehemently to himself. "Murex?"

"Among others."

"Well, John, that's just the kind of thing that'll get your butt nailed to the wall. Uncle Sam's tried his best to downplay the whale thing, since the U.S. doesn't have a whaling fleet and the whalers were technically in violation of international agreement. But if you start hitting American corporations, especially the muscle-bound ones like Murex, there'll be fiery hell to pay."

"Murex has already raised some fiery hell. Have you seen the results of the *Torreon* spill?" asked John with some asperity.

"No, I haven't. I can imagine it's a hell of a mess."

"That's quite an understatement. Y'know, I've been asked to stop by and visit the President tomorrow," said John thoughtfully.

"I'll bet you have. Tell me, have you ever heard of a little club called SMITE?"

"Is that related to SMERSH?"

"It stands for Sky Ranger Multi-pronged Intervention and Termination Exigency."

"You're kidding."

"They're not. It was set up by Presidential order a few weeks before I was retired out of the service. They have evil intentions toward you, and believe me, any quasi-military agency with a carefully worked-out mission plan is itching for a reason to use it. You're handing them one on a silver platter. And it gets worse. The director of SMITE is your old friend Remo Cosimano."

Elise gave a stricken squawk. "No! They let that *kidnapper* out of jail and gave him a job? How can that be?"

Hunter turned to her gravely. "Miss Boutin, to be blunt, the crimes he committed weren't considered that serious by the standards of his time and rank—certainly no more so than those of many other conspirators who are all on the loose. As for the job, the existence of SMITE isn't exactly a matter of public record, and neither is the identity of its director."

"But he hates John and me!"

"He hates John, certainly. I'm not sure he knows about you, or knows that you're here in Bali, anyway. I doubt he cares about you enough to hate you. But that wouldn't stop him from using you against John again, if it suits him. I'm sure it's part of his plan."

Elise suddenly looked very small and vulnerable.

Hunter continued. "John, the SRIP's practically a branch of SMITE by now. And SRIP can now track you under all but the worst conditions. If I can find you and Miss Boutin here in this hut, so can they. Have you ever heard of ORVRI?"

"ORVRI? Not another acronym. What's that one?"

"Orbiting Reconnaissance Vehicle—Radar Intelligence. It's a series of five satellites in high orbits. They use some kind of laser Doppler radar to detect erratic high-speed objects in the upper atmosphere—mainly you, sonny boy. Launched into polar orbits from Vandenburg."

John rolled his eyes and drummed his fingers. "All right—SRIP knows all, sees all, tells all. What can Remo do against me with his SMITE?"

"That I don't know. Ol' Remo never exactly took me into his confidence. But I think a big piece of the recent defense buildup has gone into his hardware programs."

"So SMITE might have some kind of weapon capable of swatting me down."

"Could be. I know the idea put stars in cousin Remo's eyes. And let's not forget, when the Sun is down, a lawn dart is an effective weapon against you."

That statement gave John's nerves a sudden jangle. "Do they know about that?"

"Can't say. I think I managed to hornswoggle everyone about that issue while I was still CINCSRIP, but they've had a while to think about it since then."

The three of them sat there glumly, each mulling over a separate set of possibilities.

Finally Elise piped up. "Well, I guess I've lived here long enough. It's time to try somewhere else."

John looked dismayed. Hunter said, "You're right, Miss Boutin. The best thing for you is to get yourself thoroughly lost."

"I'm sorry, Elise," said John miserably.

"Oh, it's nothing. Who needs a job, a home, or safety? Being a fugitive can be so broadening."

"You're not going to boot me out of your life again, are you?"

Elise looked as though she were considering it, then laughed. "No, I've learned my lesson. I can't get rid of you that way. I'll just slink away to Thailand."

Hunter frowned in disapproval. "Miss Boutin, I wish you hadn't said that. If I know where you are, you're not hidden well enough."

Elise studied the old test pilot. "Eric, what are you going to do, now that you've revealed all these national security secrets? I don't suppose Cosimano would treat you kindly if he found out."

"You're right about that. I'm heading for the Australian outback to take up life as a bush pilot. I want to get as far away from SRIP and SMITE and SMURF as I can."

"Well, you're welcome to spend the night here."

"That's kind, thank you," said Hunter with a crooked grin, "but there's a distinct chance that a commando unit could drop down on this house at any time. I'd rather be somewhere else when that happens. Make sure the two of you are too."

"I'll leave tomorrow," said Elise.

As he was leaving, Hunter turned to take a long look at Elise. He gave John a brief, thoughtful glance, shook his head, and drove away.

Chapter Nineteen

The next morning, John helped Elise pack a few possessions and close up her little bamboo house. He followed her as she took a last, sad look at the comfortable nest she'd made with the help of a hundred Balinese friends. Many of the walls were covered with native paintings—ornate, florid scenes seething with myths of the Hindu-Buddhist-Animist amalgam of the Balinese religion. Some were rare and valuable; these she rolled up and carried away, to put into the safekeeping of friends.

Looking relatively inconspicuous in khaki field clothing, John walked with her into the village, carrying her luggage and paintings down the quiet country road, past terraced hills with their paddies as green and unnatural as a setting from Disney World. In the village they passed the primary school where Elise had said she taught English and math.

John halted. "Elise, don't you think you should go in and let them know you're leaving?"

Elise looked troubled. "Yes, I suppose I should."

"I'll go with you."

"No, no, that would raise too many questions. You just wait here."

Elise entered the school. After twenty minutes John began to fear that something might have happened to her, but then she emerged, looking unhappy.

"There. I resigned, and I got a lot of sad hugs from my students."

John felt guilty and miserable.

That painful task accomplished, John and Elise rode a crowded, sweltering, and decrepit bus to Singaradja Airport, where she bought a ticket to Thailand under an assumed name. The plane wasn't to depart for six hours, so they made their way to the beach to spend a few quiet moments.

Shuffling along through the black volcanic sand, they saw ahead a group of perhaps a hundred Balinese seated in a semicircle, watching the antics of someone dressed as a colorful Hindu demon. They stood at the outskirts of the crowd and watched the show.

They were watched from a discreet distance by Eric Hunter, a cautious man who wished to be sure they would make good the escape of Elise Boutin, or whoever she was, without interference.

Presently the rather hapless demon was defeated by actors, only to be replaced by an entity far more dire — the Hindu "mistress of the graveyard", a grim and savage figure with long, knifelike nails.

The monster was attacked by near-nude temple guards who slashed at it with curved swords. The audience watched the drama with no sign of its former good humor. The attacks grew fiercer, but the blades did not damage the demon, although the weapons looked real.

Hunter abruptly realized that this was no mere play or pageant, but a mystical ceremony intended to maintain the balance between good and evil. The guards were real, and the person in the costume was supposed to be truly possessed by the graveyard demon.

Hunter watched as Elise trembled at the dancing demon with its great, flat eyes that seemed to glare out of a waxy, lifeless face. John placed his hand on her shoulder, and she looked up to see how he reacted to this spectacle. He regarded the demon with utter calm, looking upon it as he might a capering mouse or a monkey. Hunter was reminded that John was more than a flying man, he was one who had looked through the door of death itself and somehow closed it again. This demon was nothing he hadn't faced and come to terms with already. In his quiet way, his was a presence greater than that of the person dressed as the Mistress of the Graveyard.

Hunter departed, satisfied.

Back at the airport, John and Elise had their parting embrace, a separation which John hoped would be brief. John couldn't even accompany Elise's plane without the risk of giving her away.

He waited half an hour after the plane departed, then discarded his outer clothing behind a convenient baggage cart. He pulled on his headset and cast a grim eye at the broken clouds overhead. He took off, first hugging the roof-tops of the city, then skimming low over village, paddy, and forest until he was over open ocean. The radar transponder in his belt was turned off—he'd decided to leave it off until needed from now on, rather than habitually leaving it on.

He shot up though the wet murk of the troposphere, leveled off, and bore southeast at hypersonic speed, making an hour's stop in the harbor city of Wellington, New Zealand. Then he set a great circle course for the United States, heading for his Washington appointment like a good boy.

Minutes later he slowed as he approached Washington, not wishing to provide an excuse to test the city's air defenses against him. As requested he dropped down outside the White House fence and presented himself at the gate. He was escorted to the Oval Office, where the only occupants were the President and Gordon Rogers, the current administrator of NASA. John went along with the President's inevitable opening banter and permitted himself to be steered onto a brocade settee while the other men settled somewhat more heavily in matching wing chairs. John listened warily as the President finally got down to business.

"Well, John, heh, you've been a busy young man lately. I've had a talk with Con Wandrei—he's a fine young man too, make no mistake about that—and he's not too happy about what you did to his building a few days ago. I've also heard from a lot of congressmen who have Murex operations in their states or districts, and that's about half the Senate and a fifth of the House. Now, I realize that oil spill incident was upsetting, but I'm sure you know a country like ours can't survive without Murex and the personal freedom its products provide our people. Can I count on you not to repeat that kind of stunt?"

John eyed him levelly. "Sir, I'll admit that defacing the building was unnecessary and useless. I won't do anything like that again."

"Well, that's fine, I knew I could count on you—you won't forget that's an eagle on your emblem, not a bear? Or a loon?" The President laughed jovially.

"No, sir, it's an eagle—a nice, shiny, black eagle. I'm not likely to forget that."

"Oh, I almost forgot. The Secretary of State asked me to bring up another matter. His phone's been ringing off the hook about that business with the whaling ships. Now, I hope you've gotten the Captain Queeg out of your system too?"

John blinked. "Uh—you mean Captain Ahab, sir—I think."

"Oh, that's right, I can still see Greg Peck in that role. Anyway, the Icelanders are taking it easy on this, but the

Japanese are in an uproar, and frankly, with our economy we'd have a hard time getting by without their good will. I have to ask you again—you aren't planning a repeat there either, are you?"

John couldn't restrain a grin. "Absolutely not. There are no active whaling vessels left to sink." He grew more sober. "If there's any way you can express my regrets to the Japanese people for the death of Captain Ochiai, I would appreciate it."

"Yes, we can issue a statement like that for you, and I think it's a fine idea. Well, you've done a lot to ease my mind. Now I think Roger here has some good news for you about your fine contribution to our space program."

Gordon Rogers, who had been sitting back and watching the exchange closely, now shifted in his seat and said cheerfully, "John, I do have some good news for you and for everybody at NASA. The Space Transportation System office has declared the Shuttle mature and fully operational. After the past twenty four near-flawless missions, we feel confident that we've got all the kinks ironed out of the system. Basically, we feel there's no need to divert you from your valuable rescue work to watch over any future Shuttle launches or missions. You've been a magnificent help to us ever since your historic effort with Apollo 24, and we now free you from our service with gratitude."

John felt a coldness in his chest. "Are you sure this is the right time to do this? I mean, you've got a launch just next week, a special one with a civilian passenger... "

"Well, I think the presence of that passenger is an indication of the confidence we have in the system. Really, we won't be needing you any more."

"This is really about something else entirely, isn't it? I've become an embarrassment to you. You don't want me associated with any official activity of the United States."

The President broke in. "Those considerations did make it easier to reach this decision."

"I see. I'm not going to sit here and argue about it. If you don't want me anymore, I have no more right to the equipment you've provided me. I'll return the flight suits and the other items as soon as possible."

Rogers's eyes grew round, almost frantic. "Oh, no, that won't be necessary at all. We want you to keep the equipment. You earned that and far more the minute you plucked those Apollo men from the nighttime face of the Moon. In fact, we intend to abide by our agreement and continue to provide you with flight suits and the other equipment indefinitely."

"As long as you continue to conform to certain minimum standards of behavior," said the President offhandedly.

John cocked his head and eyed the two men as he might study a pair of oddly-behaving sandpipers.

After a few more minutes of Presidential banter and backslapping, John was escorted out.

For the next several days John kept an eye on his family's progress toward getting out of the country. Flights to New Zealand were booked. They had to wait a week to get seats. In the meantime John kept a constant ear on KSKY, busying himself by dashing all over the globe in the service of the helpless. His most satisfying moment came when he spent an hour convincing a 16-year-old Greek girl not to throw herself to her death from a promontory overlooking the Aegean. All it required was an hour of his time and a sympathetic ear.

Despite the admonition of the Administrator, John also kept a close watch on preparations for the Space Shuttle launch. On the morning of the launch he monitored NASA Select TV using a new satellite dish in his British Columbia eyrie.

With mixed amusement and dismay he looked over the shoulders of the technicians in the White Room as they struggled to remove a handle from the outside of the Orbiter's hatch. The screws holding the handle in place were stripped; the launch could not proceed with the handle still attached. The technicians called for a portable drill. To John's astonishment, the cordless unit was delivered with a dead battery, and there were no others to be had. The launch window closed, lost for the lack of a well-maintained hand tool. And this was the "mature" system whose reliability Rogers had touted!

The following morning John tuned in again. Cape Canaveral had experienced a night and morning of unprecedented cold. Even now the temperature was barely above freezing. Around the pad were pockets of bitter cold, intensified by the presence of cryogenic fuels. John watched in fascination as scanning cameras showed parts of the launch support structure encased in thick ice, with massive icicles hanging from beams, conduits, and pipes. And yet the countdown continued. The NASA commentator did not hint at a cancellation. John's amazement bloomed into horror. Why in the world would NASA insist on launching in conditions severe beyond anything ever expected or previously experienced?

He recalled that the President's State of the Union address was scheduled for tonight—could the White House be egging NASA on in order to invoke the peculiar PR value of this mission? Could anyone involved really be that venal, that irresponsible?

An incredulous John Avril sat mesmerized by the television, for once as passive as any normal man. The count reached zero. *Challenger's* engines erupted; the vehicle leaped up past the tower. John relaxed a little. All seemed normal so far.

It was just over a minute into the flight.

"Go at throttleup," said Mission Control.

"Roger, go at throttleup," replied one of the pilots.

Just then the climbing smoke trail of the solid rocket boosters expanded into a turbulent mass shot with fire.

John leaned forward, frowning. A premature SRB separation?

The boosters emerged from the cloud, arcing off on paths of their own, still firing, still trailing smoke.

John waited to see the orbiter emerge.

It did not.

He waited for some word from the crew.

None came.

"Clearly a major malfunction," said the emotionless voice of the NASA commentator.

John sagged back in his chair. For the next half hour he stared at the screen. The view was surreal: a calm Florida day, the camera panning over the quiet waters as pieces of debris splashed down. Very little was said. Occasionally the view switched to the dispersing column of smoke which ended so abruptly. The SRB trails curved out of the terminal cloud like horns. John had rarely seen anything more dreadful.

For several more hours he sat there, only half listening once it became clear there was no hope, that there was nothing to be done. Then, without realizing what he was doing, he got up, clicked off the set, and tore off his flight suit in a fit of unconscious violence. He stumbled out onto the stony porch of his hideaway and sat down in dappled sunlight.

Sky Ranger did not fare out into the world that day. He sat looking blankly out across the valley. Numb, he considered what he had just seen, and done, or not done, reliving every second of the deadly launch multiple times, confronting the harrowing *pastness* of it, the immutability of the event, the utter impossibility of undoing any of it. He thought of the seven, strapped into their seats full of hope and apprehension, bound into a machine that was shortly to kill them all.

When the sun went down he laid himself in his bed and slept.

The image on the television screen was alarming, incredible. Surely NASA didn't mean to fly, not with ice hanging from every surface of the shuttle? This could not be. NASA might be crazy, but he, Sky Ranger, was not.

John stood up from his chair. He erupted from the eyrie and made a record crossing of the continent, flying due east over the Canadian wilds, blasting out a tunnel of air at low altitude. Over New Brunswick he made a radical turn to the south, and soon was over the grey Atlantic, so low and fast that droplets of spray hissed into hot vapor as they touched the yoke of his flight suit. At last he made a turn southwest, and approached the Cape from the open ocean, going subsonic at the first glimpse of the pad and the VAB. He dropped quietly into the dense palmetto growth outside the pad's fence and peered through the fronds.

The Shuttle stack seethed and fumed on the huge battleship-grey mass of the Mobile Launch Platform. The hiss of vaporizing liquid hydrogen and oxygen filled the air, but John made out the words of the NASA spokesman as they emerged from speakers around the pad. The launch was still go; the count was just about to come out of its final hold with nine minutes remaining.

John's throat felt dry. He tried to swallow as he studied every detail of the assembled Shuttle with a raptor's vision. His heart was pounding, and he was afraid. He could feel the chill of the air. He still couldn't believe they intended to launch.

Never had he been this close to a launch while wearing only his normal headset. Hastily he wadded up dry grass to stuff into the ear domes.

The minutes ticked away into seconds. No one in charge came to their senses; the count continued. At T-Minus 15 seconds he clapped his hands over his ears. The three Main Engines ignited, enveloping him in a sound like the combined rush of a hurricane and Niagara. A few seconds later the twin Solid Rocket Boosters lit off, sending out an explosive, barbarous outpouring of palpable shock and violence. He eyed every detail of the firing with complete concentration. *Puffs of black smoke spat out from one of the field joints on the far SRB.*

Challenger leaped up, climbing on ravishing pillars of sun-gold flame.

Sky Ranger leaped up after.

He paced the accelerating Shuttle, forcing his way through the wall of sound that surrounded it. He kept his eyes locked on the leaking SRB joint. All too soon his vigilance was rewarded with another glimpse of the source of the shuttle's doom. A tongue of flame flared from the joint and grew by the second. It was striking the external tank!

Sky Ranger hesitated. Even at this distance, his skull was being rocked and vibrated by the din. That was no mere fire, but rocket exhaust...a stream of incandescent gas strong enough to propel a spacecraft weighing two thousand tons. He pictured himself interposing his body in that jet, and held back.

The jet ate out a larger opening, growing and intensifying by the second. Like a storm of white-hot sand it tore the thin wall of the tank. Still Sky Ranger held back. If only the shuttle could hold together for another minute, the solid boosters would fall away into the sea.

Challenger exploded into flame and smoke, tossing John back, blinding him, deafening him, stunning him. Chunks of debris struck him.

Too late! He had waited too long; the shuttle was destroyed.

He fell from the roiling cloud of burning fuel. The solids were off on their own, still thrusting, trailing curving plumes of smoke. Thousands of fragments arced out and down. Most of a wing fluttered by like a giant leaf.

A large bit of wreckage caught Sky Ranger's eye. Though tumbling, it seemed basically intact. It had windows—the crew compartment! John gathered himself, pushed over to it. Taking hold of the structure around the main hatch, he slowed and then arrested its spin. The thing weighed tons—he had no chance of halting its fall, but he could slow it down. Moving to the bottom, he grabbed hold of some torn plumbing, put his shoulders against the structural members, and did his utmost to keep the compartment and its occupants airborne. He had the incentive of seeing the ocean surface rushing up to meet them. He did slow it down—slowed it greatly, so that the impact drove them only ten feet underwater. The compartment surfaced. The hatch swung open. John held it steady long enough for the astronauts to fling rafts into the water and scramble into them.

John wept. "Thank God, thank God," he said. He floated with the astronauts, as stunned and dazed as they, sobbing with relief, as though he had been given a chance to undo a terrible mistake. And, he knew, he had.

And then he knew that he had not.

Still weeping, John awoke in his eyrie. His hands had crushed the posts of his bed. Now he was most desolate, the joy of his dream snatched away and made futile and desperate. The astronauts were dead. He, Sky Ranger, might have saved them, but instead he had watched them die on television, just like millions of people who could not have helped.

Never again.

Though he had known better, he had let politically-motivated bureaucrats keep him from his clear duty. He had accepted their counsel to remain at a distance, to do nothing.

No one would ever hold Sky Ranger back again, unless it were Sky Ranger himself.

John closed his eyes. He felt as though he were on fire. His mind remained a cacophony of thunder overlain by a cottony numbness.

He sat up in bed, noticing the torn and crumpled flight suit on the floor. He stood and pulled it into his hands, studying the proud emblem through tears.

He pulled on the flight suit. Somehow its shabbiness seemed to suit the moment.

Chapter Twenty

Stuffing a few items into a bag, John flew to Singapore, where he concealed himself in a park, stripped off his flight suit, and arrayed himself in nondescript clothing, going so far as to disguise himself with sunglasses and a dark wig. He took a public bus to the airport, where he left the telltale flight suit in a locker. An hour later he was aboard a commercial jetliner bound for Bangkok. He was uncommunicative as he sat and stared at the sky through the distorting plastic rectangle which afforded his only view. Seeing his domain as such a dim vignette was like seeing it in a dream— awakening memories of his first reveries among the silent, sunlit clouds of the high atmosphere, more than a decade gone. How joyous that life had been! He'd solved some of the fundamental riddles of existence, though those answers couldn't be communicated in words. But that wisdom wasn't enough to unravel the perversities of human behavior. Only the most ludicrous of circumstances could compel a Sky Ranger to ride this howling contraption through the sky.

The plane landed after an uneventful flight. John was grateful to disembark into the open air, close and steaming as it was. Yet his transportation ordeal wasn't over yet. He walked away from the airport, making his way through narrow streets so hopelessly clogged with traffic that his quick stride outpaced the vehicles.

At the main bus station he bought a ticket for an overnight trip to Chiangmai. As he stood in the boarding line, towering over the voluble, chattering locals, he got some suspicious looks from the police. So far he'd had no trouble with the false passport provided by the New Zealand covert operations people, which identified him as Johann Adler of Germany. His German was atrocious, but it was certainly good enough to fool most Thais.

Presently the police turned their attention elsewhere, and John climbed aboard the crowded orange bus, settling into his seat for a long ride. His seat mates were a young woman and her energetic little boy. John removed his sunglasses. The boy stared, smiling, into the alien blueness of his eyes.

The bus was late in departing, inching its way through teeming city streets, and then onto wider highways which were equally congested. It finally left the city on its way to Ayutthaya. John looked out at fields filled with the tumbled bricks of great cities destroyed long ago by invading Burmese.

Only when they left Ayutthaya behind did they enter the true Thai countryside, where the scenery along the road alternated between canals, rice paddies, and forested mountains.

John felt some apprehension as the Sun declined—it had been years since he'd spent a night at the mercy of strangers. Yet he'd done so all his life before his pilgrimage and rebirth, and he'd never come to harm from it. If these people were willing to trust their lives to his possible depredations, he'd do the same for them. He shrugged as the Sun touched the horizon. The woman glanced at him with some concern as he slumped, but her worry eased as he immediately fell into a profound and peaceful sleep.

When Aurora bid him awake he found the woman's head resting on his shoulder, while her son lay almost entirely in his lap. He smiled and felt a welcome sense of peace as they slumbered easily. They woke up as the Sun cracked the horizon, renewing his mastery of flight. They showed neither concern nor embarrassment at their closeness, but only smiled at him as they sat up. The mother pulled a basket from the overhead rack and brought out cold rice, fruit, and a bottle of tea. With a kind smile she offered some to John, who accepted gratefully. As he ate she kept giving him furtive glances, and her son openly stared, great glee and mirth twinkling in his eyes. A bit discomfited, John looked out the window and contrived to glimpse his reflection in the glass. His wig, he saw, was awry, revealing sandy blond hair under black. He straightened it and replaced his sunglasses to hide his embarrassment, but the flaming undertone that lit his tanned cheeks gave him away. Both his companions laughed merrily.

At last his odyssey neared its end as the bus rolled into the northern city of Chiangmai. As they disembarked into the hot, sticky sunshine, the boy turned to John and put his hands together with fingers outstretched to form wings. He flapped them and smiled broadly as his mother led him away. At a complete loss, John stood there staring after him, dumbstruck.

Shaking his head ruefully, John climbed onto another bus for the last leg of his journey. This was a rattling, particolored contraption carrying almost as many chickens as passengers. It rolled out of the city and onto rutted rural roads. John was the only foreigner on the bus, and as such attracted curious looks. He suspected that some of their chatter concerned him, and wished he knew more of the language. At least he didn't hear the words "Sky Ranger" or "Avril". Still, he was careful to keep his wig from sliding out of place, and looked forward to the moment when he could discard it.

After a couple of hours the bus entered a densely forested district of mountains, lakes, and scattered fruit ranches. This was territory John knew fairly well—he had seen it from the air, during a time when heavy rains and landslides had threatened the main local landmark. He disembarked in a tiny village and ambled up a narrow road that climbed a fragrant green mountain. As he ascended, the view around him opened up, offering glimpses of a U-shaped lake surrounded by cliffs, forests, and plantations. He flipped that silly wig into the brush. He shouldn't need it again.

An hour's walk brought him to a walled compound at the summit of the mountain. He stepped through the gate. Before him were the structures of a *wat*, or Buddhist monastery: elaborate pagodas, a small temple, and the more modest structures serving as living quarters for monks, nuns, and novitiates. All were set in a serene garden landscape of blossoms and pools.

John halted as a smiling, dignified young monk stepped up briskly to meet him. He wore saffron robes and steel-rimmed glasses and offered John a Western-style handshake. "So good to see you again, Mr. Avril. Especially under circumstances more pleasant than the last."

John shook his hand and looked around appreciatively. "Everything here looks shiny-new."

"Yes; we lost something of old traditions to the landslide, but I'm sure new traditions will grow up around what is new."

"And your Po trees?"

The chief monk's smile broadened. "They were saved. Much was saved, thanks to you. And now, what brings you here among us, if I may ask?"

"I'm here to see Elise, of course."

The monk looked blank. "Elise?"

John began to grow alarmed. "Yes, Elise Boutin. Are you telling me she isn't here?"

"I'm aware of no such arrival."

John looked around wildly. "She never made it? Why did I send her off on her own like that? I should have—"

But then John saw, seated on a bench in the shadow of a great teak tree that grew against the compound's far wall, a figure engrossed in a book.

"Wait, there she is! Elise!" he called.

She looked up, set her book aside and came running toward them. The monk watched her approach with an expression of bafflement that gradually resolved.

"Ah...Elise Boutin, of course. She introduced herself under a different name when she arrived. I'm sorry for the confusion."

Flooded with relief, John said, "Thank you so much for caring for her as you have."

"I'm sure it was our pleasure. I'll leave you alone now." The monk withdrew with a bow.

Elise ran into his arms and effectively silenced him by occupying his mouth with kisses for a minute and a half. Finally John was able to break away long enough to speak.

"I'm so glad to find you here safe. I felt like I was sending you into oblivion when I put you on that plane."

"Don't be silly! Flying's the safest way to travel, isn't it?"

John smiled down at her. "So I'm told."

"So what are you doing here? Is it safe for me to leave? Isn't it a little risky for you to be here?"

"No, it's not at all safe for you to leave. No, I don't think there's much risk in this visit. I took care not to leave any of the usual Sky Ranger trails that the SRIP relies on. But this will be my last visit for a while. I'm about to make a lot of people very angry. It's time to start my campaign in earnest, with no holding back." He described the events of the past few days, then outlined his plans for the future.

When he had finished, Elise sat subdued and thoughtful, glancing at him with anxious eyes.

John said, "Hey, don't look at me that way. You're the one who got me started on this. If not for you, I might still be only helpful, courteous, and innocuous."

"No, I don't think so. You were always working yourself up to this on your own. I only gave you a kick in the butt when you were stalled. But you're about to stir up a hornet's nest that you won't believe."

"Oh, I think I'll believe it, but I've got tactics to defer the full wrath of the powers-that-be. Keep your eyes open. You'll be hearing a lot about me in the next few weeks. That is, if there's any source of information here in Shangri-La."

Elise pointed to a paraboloidal antenna on a nearby rooftop. "What do you think that is? A mushroom?"

John looked. "Oh. Excuse my cultural chauvinism."

She looked at him with dark eyes that were suddenly swimming with tears. "I'm afraid I'll never see you again."

John attempted levity. "Are you kidding? What can anyone do to me that hasn't been done already? They're too late to kill me, after all."

Elise was not comforted. The look on her face made him feel as if someone were pulling at his heart with piano wires.

"John, let's go to my room."

"Won't that raise a few eyebrows around here?"

"Do I look like a monk? Come on, let's go."

John followed her into her room, a tiny chamber, but sunny and airy, with a simple palette for a bed. He was afraid she wanted to make love, which he refused to risk while the Sun was in the sky. But she only wanted to lie in his arms and talk, telling him a hundred little things about herself and her world that he'd never known.

By the time she was finished, John found himself reeling with the love he felt for this golden example of the human species. It was she who he thought of whenever he needed a reminder of the worth of the race to which he belonged. "Elise," he said in a low, choked voice, "when this is over, please marry me."

Elise responded with a tender kiss. "You goofy person. As far as I'm concerned, we're already married. But if you want to make it formal later on, I'll be waiting. Now you should go. But remember this. You're an eagle, John. Do what you know is right. And if you have to get a little blood on your feathers in the process, remember—time is still turning."

John departed, his heart so full he scarcely dared to meet the eyes of the people he encountered on the road.

He travelled overland to Rangoon, took a jet from there to Djakarta, where at last he returned to the air under his own power, stopping briefly in Singapore to retrieve his flight suit. From there he flew northeast across the broad Pacific to Hawaii. He touched down in Hilo just long enough to make a small purchase in a drug store.

From there he flew to Antarctica, or rather to an area of space some six hundred miles above that continent. The month was February, the southern summer, and the south polar area was agleam with perpetual sunlight. As a bonus, this was the one area on or near Earth that was scarcely touched by the probing beams of military radars.

Circling high above the frozen continent, John intercepted and examined every polar-orbiting satellite that came by. Only two types were placed in the energy-expensive polar orbits, and both looked straight down: a few Earth-resources satellites, and the much more numerous military reconnaissance platforms, most of which belonged to either the United States or Russia. The Russian hardware was easily distinguishable by its clunky appearance, and John ignored it. He likewise kept hands off most of the American spy birds, especially the classes he was familiar with, such as the big KH-11s which were the prototypes of the Hubble Space Telescope.

It was only when he encountered an example of an unfamiliar class of American satellite that John's antennae began to quiver. It was big, with solar arrays capable of providing a lot of power. The central bus bristled with radar and communications dishes directed at Earth. But his interest was most piqued by an elaborate optical system on an agile gimbaled mount. It was a sizable telescope, apparently some variety of Cassegrain, with its secondary mirror mounted on an optical window at the front of the tube.

Mounted piggyback on the telescope was a device of less obvious function, a collection of tubes, metal rings, gold insulation, and cables. It had a black maw about two inches in diameter aimed parallel to the telescope. John guessed it was a laser. He confirmed his guess by holding his hand in front of the aperture. He caught a flash of brilliant and distinctly warm red light on his palm.

A system like this, thought John, could easily qualify as an optical radar. He carefully examined the thin skin sheathing the bus. In an odd corner near some heat-control louvers he found a version of his own emblem, the sign of the SRIP.

John unwrapped his drugstore purchase. He reached past the telescope's sun shield and applied several broad, white strokes to the optical window, rendering it practically opaque.

After a quick dip into the stratosphere to recharge his lungs, John returned and awaited the passage of the other four ORVRI satellites. He dealt with them as he had the first.

Following the last of them in its orbit brought him over the continental United States. Below him he saw most of the Mississippi river, including its delta jutting into the Gulf of Mexico. The waters of the outflowing river were clearly visible, a brown stain swirling through the bluer Gulf waters, laden with sediments washed off the farm-lands along its vast drainage area.

The Mississippi. As good a place as any to start his new campaign. John detached himself from the blinded satellite and flew counter to its orbital motion to kill his 17,000 mile-per-hour speed. He'd already selected his first target. It waited beneath him, a few hundred miles upstream from New Orleans.

He dropped down on Memphis, home of a major chemical subsidiary of Murex. The plant, like all others of its kind, looked like a transplant from Mordor, a grim, grey wasteland of skeletal steel, storage tanks, fuming smoke-stacks, and a bewildering intricacy of plumbing, picked out day and night by the ghastly points of mercury vapor lamps.

John's advent at the scene was not low-key. He came screaming down at Mach 1, startling everyone at the plant with the roar of his arrival, bewildering them with his swift passage, which caused the plumes wafting from the stacks to swirl in his vortex. After circling a few times, he alighted in what looked like the only semi-habitable area in the plant, an office structure of grey sheet metal walls. Once inside he bulled his way past several secretaries and office workers to barge unannounced into the office of the plant manager, F. Harley Morse, according to the nameplate on his desk. Morse stared with a white, constricted face as Sky Ranger strode up to him.

John began without preamble. "I understand you make heptachlor and chlordane here, two pesticides so toxic they're banned in the United States."

"Yes—yes we do. For the export market. It's perfectly legal."

"Not to me. I'm here to tell you to shut down all production and shipment of those chemicals immediately. And to take whatever measures are necessary to render your remaining stockpiles harmless."

Morse was incredulous. "W-what?" he asked shakily.

"I made myself plain enough."

"I—I don't have the authority to order a shutdown like that."

"Oh, nonsense. You have more authority than I do, and I have enough to shut down your plant. Get on with it. Pick up the phone."

Morse obeyed, lifting the handset to his mouth and pressing a button. "Security... "

John reached out and crushed the phone's console. "Listen, Morse, you people are through. I'm doing what the government would've done years ago, if it was being run by people whose idea of the perfect environment wasn't Scrooge McDuck's money bin. I'm going to personally shut down the production of the most pernicious chemicals and waste products in the world. Here's your chance to be in on the beginning of an environmental revolution. Now give the orders, or I'll do the job for you. And I guarantee my shutdown will be a lot messier than yours would be."

John eyed Morse unblinkingly, aware that this was a critical bluff. He couldn't afford to go blundering about trying to destroy the plant's capacity for producing chlorinated pesticides; he didn't even know which areas of the plant were responsible. And he might easily set off a catastrophic leak of toxic chemicals that would be a far worse disaster than any he hoped to avert, an American version of the Bhopal horror. Would the look in his eye and the eagle on his chest be enough to sway Mr. Morse to his will?

Morse, for his part, was regaining his ability to analyze situations. He analyzed this one shrewdly enough. He knew enough about Sky Ranger to realize that no force at his command could stop him from doing whatever he pleased. But even in permitting Sky Ranger to have his way, he could still extract a cost. He stood up behind his desk. "Sky Ranger, maybe it's time we did get out of the business of producing those chemicals. But I can't order the shutdown without losing my job. Come over here if you would."

He led the way to a large schematic diagram on the wall and pointed to a complex occupying one corner of the plant. "This is the area responsible for the substances you mentioned. It's the northwest corner of the plant. Go there and do what you want. Just be careful not to breach any of the retorts or storage facilities, if you please. Some of the reagents are pretty nasty too. Elemental chlorine, for example... "

"I do know some basic chemistry," said John.

"Sorry, didn't mean to lecture you."

John glared at him a moment longer, then turned to the only window in the room that wasn't blocked by an air conditioner. He slid it open, stepped back, and made a dramatic exit, though the confidence he hoped he showed wasn't matched by what he actually felt.

When the papers on his desk settled down after the sudden breeze, Morse stepped out and spoke to his secretary. "Get on the phone. I want every TV news crew in town at Complex C as soon as possible. Call the main entrance. I want the gate wide open when they arrive."

"Shall I call the police?"

Morse reflected. "No. No point. But alert the spill teams and tell them to be ready to move."

John set down in front of the Complex C control building. Before entering he looked around in bewilderment at the maze of bins, ducts, valves, pipes, radiators, and evaporators that made up the complex. He was suddenly convinced he'd blundered badly in coming here without any clear knowledge of how to proceed. He'd permitted his righteous anger to set him off half-cocked. Yet now that he was here, now that he'd already made his melodramatic pronouncements, he had to go through with it or lose all credibility in the future. He fought down an attack of half-hysterical laughter, swallowed hard, squared his shoulders, and stalked into the control room.

The room was manned by six men, some wearing white shirts with narrow black ties, others in knit sport shirts and hard hats. They all gaped at him as he appeared in their midst, then they all broke into smiles. The smiles quickly fell into looks of concern. One of the white-shirted men spoke up. "Sky Ranger? Is something wrong? An emergency at the plant?"

John couldn't bring himself to be quite so stentorian as he had been with Morse. "No emergency. Is this the area responsible for producing the chlorinated pesticides?"

The man glanced around at his coworkers before answering. His answer didn't come easily. "Er—yes, that's correct."

"That's why I'm here. I'm stopping all production of those chemicals. I want you to shut down your process right now. When everything's buttoned up, I want you to tell me how to disable the plant so you won't be able to restart anytime soon."

Dumfounded, the six men stared at him with open mouths. At last their spokesman found his voice. "I don't think we care to do that, Mr. Avril."

John shrugged. "I'm not giving you a choice. If you don't do it yourselves, I'm afraid I'll have to do it all myself, and I might be a little heavy-handed about it."

With glazed eyes locked on John, the spokesman fumbled for a telephone. "Security—we have an intruder in Complex—"

A hand reached out and cut off the call. "Oh, don't bother, Chuck. The Security guys couldn't do anything except maybe get themselves hurt. This is the Sky Guy we're dealing with."

"I guess you're right, Pete," said Chuck, hanging up the phone.

Pete stood up and walked up to John. "Avril, you've done some questionable things lately, but I can't believe you've become a terrorist. What's this all about?"

John shook his head. "Look, I didn't come here for a debate. I'll explain myself thoroughly in some more appropriate forum. I don't want to do any more harm here than I have to, but I'm also very serious in my demands. Get to work or I'll shut you down the hard way."

Pete glanced over his shoulder at Chuck. "What do you say? I don't see how anyone could blame us. I don't see why we need to produce that shit anyway, to tell you the truth."

The phone rang. Pete answered it, spoke briefly, listened, and put it down.

"That was the boss. He says to go along with this guy."

Chuck said, "No kidding? What the hell. Start the shutdown." Then he leaned back in his chair and stared up at the ceiling.

Pete issued a few orders, made a few calls, and initiated the shutdown procedure. The control room began to bustle. John stood there with his arms folded sternly across his chest, trying to keep a careful watch on all the activity in case of any duplicity. Other workers came into the room and stared at John, but he ignored them. Twice the doors flew open to admit TV news camera crews who immediately set up glaring lights and began taping him and the activity he'd caused. John glanced at them in irritation, but otherwise ignored them as well. The control room was becoming a crowded place.

Presently John became aware that someone off to the side was yelling at him, trying to attract his attention. Impatiently, he snapped his head around, expecting to find some reporter bursting to ask an inane question. Instead he saw a hard-hatted plant worker dressed in smudged, dirty work clothes and a fully-loaded tool belt. He looked as hostile and combative as any man John had ever seen.

"What do you want?" asked John.

"What do I want? These are our goddamn jobs you're fucking around with!"

John turned on him. "Your jobs! Who do you think you are? You think you're entitled to a job that involves poisoning people, poisoning the land? You think your car payments and cable TV bill are worth that?"

"I've got kids!" raged his opponent bitterly.

"So make them proud of you! Get a respectable job! Go someplace else if you can't find one here! Don't tell me that the only way you can support your family is by attacking the planet that keeps you alive. Don't tell me things in this world are that insane!"

That wasn't what the man wanted to hear. He sprang forward, almost sobbing with rage, and tried to catch John with an extravagant roundhouse punch. John evaded it easily. The man almost went to the floor from the momentum of his own blow. He made no further attempt to attack, but stormed out of the room with a final withering look at John.

John scanned the faces of the other workers arrayed against him and saw a wide range of emotions: anger, uncertainty, wonder, and doubt. He decided to try to mollify them. "Look, you men, I know this seems like the end of the world to some of you, but it's really just a change, and a change for the better. I think a lot of you know you've been doing wrong by making these chemicals. Now you can rest a little easier."

One of the TV reporters, a carefully made-up young woman with a piercing black-eyed stare, finally got up the nerve to pose a question.

"Sky Ranger, Joy Cameron, WMPH Hotline News. Is this incident an extension of your reported vendetta against Murex Energy Systems?"

John gave a lopsided grin. "Nope. I'm planning to end the production of dangerous, unjustifiable chemicals all over the world. But I certainly don't intend to ignore those plants owned by Murex."

"How will you decide which chemicals are both dangerous and unjustifiable?"

"I'll heed the opinions of experts. Experts not employed by the chemical industry. I've got my eye on dioxin, PCBs, DDT, and furans. None of these substances have a place on a planet inhabited by creatures like us. Excuse me… "

Pete was standing at his side waiting for attention. "Sky Ranger, the process is cold. Since you've put yourself in charge here, it's up to you to decide what to do next."

"Can I wreck the plumbing around here without doing any harm?"

"Yep, I'm afraid you can, now."

"Then I guess I'll get started in here." Feeling very self-conscious John walked over to the main control console. He looked over his shoulder at his expectant audience. "Everybody step back. There could be some flying glass here." They all crowded back against the outside wall. The cameras kept rolling.

John put his fist through the console, grabbed a handful of wiring, and gave a pull. The console still had power, so he got quite a shock, though it seemed little enough to one who'd endured numerous lightning strikes over the years. He heard Joy Cameron narrating in case any of her viewers found John's actions too subtle to interpret for themselves.

"And now the Sky Ranger, John Avril, is destroying thousands of dollars worth of equipment belonging to Murex Energy Systems. He is now punching out the screens which monitored the production of several commercially valuable chemicals. After more than a decade of guarding the public welfare, this unique man has taken it upon himself to impose his will on those who cannot resist. We can only speculate where he might go from here, what drastic actions he might take."

After thoroughly destroying the controls and computers, John turned aside and started for the door. But first he halted long enough to catch Joy Cameron with a potent stare. "Better move your people outside, Ms. Cameron. I'm about to force my will on some helpless ductwork. God knows I'm depriving Murex of its inherent right to poison the Earth. He'll get me for it someday."

"God?"

"No. Conrad Wandrei."

One of the workmen shouted out, "Hey, asshole, I hope you still feel so smug when our kids're going hungry."

"Oh, cut me some slack. Nobody's going hungry. Maybe you'll have trouble paying your cable bill. Maybe you'll even sleep better from now on."

John pushed his way into the open. He'd half-expected to confront an army of police, or at least plant security guards, but he remained unopposed. He knew that must be a deliberate decision on Morse's part, and couldn't decide whether to be happy about it or not.

It was a lot more work than he'd expected. It was all he could do to rip out and break the smaller pipes, and uprooting the bigger ones proved impossible. However, the electrical system was vulnerable, and the sheet metal ducts and bins seemed like a few layers of tinfoil to him. Demolishing the place to his satisfaction took two hours. He could think of quicker ways to go about it, but none that would confine the destruction to this one area.

When he'd finished he dropped to the ground in the midst of torn and twisted metal. He was sweating and he was sure he'd be sore the next day. Maybe most of the force he exerted came from somewhere outside himself, but his own muscles contributed as much as they could.

The spectators grew convinced that the destruction was over and filtered back in to surround him. Pete and Chuck stood nearby surveying the damage. Chuck looked forlorn and dazed, but Pete merely studied the results with a critical eye. After a while he spoke up. "Well, Sky Ranger, congratulations. You've ended the world's capacity for producing heptachlor and chlordane."

As that fact sank in, John's doubt and embarrassment receded, replaced by a feeling of accomplishment. He grinned.

"Of course, it wasn't an exotic process," continued Pete. "We could easily configure any other area of the plant to do the same thing. Rebuilding here would take longer."

John's grin proved short-lived. "But you won't do any of that. I'd just shut you down again."

Pete shrugged. "Those are decisions for the execs. As another option, they could move the process to a plant somewhere else in the world. Sell it. Even disguise it.

You'd have to inspect every chemical plant in the world on a regular basis."

"I will, if necessary. But I don't think I'll need to. I don't believe you could keep an operation like that secret for very long. And I won't be the only guy watching."

Pete looked unconvinced, but offered no reply.

John went on. "I want the current stock of those chemicals destroyed."

"Not easy. They're pretty stable."

"I know."

"Can't burn 'em. Don't want all that chlorine going up in smoke."

"No."

"Gonna take some thinking. Stuff's kind of hard to get rid of."

"That was the problem with it all along, wasn't it?"

Chapter Twenty One

John flew off, knowing his action would set off an earthquake of fear and outrage in Washington and elsewhere. Before that reaction could become a threat, he decided to play his last few cards with the Federal Government. On his way East he made a stop in Gate City, Virginia, where he made a phone call from a convenience store. With some effort he managed to get through to NASA Administrator Rogers.

"Rogers? This is John Avril." He listened for a moment, then continued. "Yes, I know I've been a bad boy. No, you don't approve of what I've done." More listening. "Okay, you've gotten that on the record. I understand your need to say that. Here's why I called. I can offer you something pretty good. I want to come to Washington to talk it over. Can you assure me I can get into town without anyone taking a potshot at me?" He listened carefully to the reply. "All right, I'm on my way. I should be there in about twenty minutes."

A full ninety minutes later, John slowed as he reached the Chesapeake Bay, followed the Potomac upstream, and soon afterward dropped to the ground in front of the NASA headquarters building near the Air and Space Museum. He walked in and was escorted to Gordon Rogers's office.

Rogers, a beefy, sweaty man with close-cropped colorless hair, reminded John of a Polish dockworker. Now he glowered at John from behind his desk. "I'm taking a big chance meeting with you like this. It would be polite if you could at least be prompt," he chided.

"My apologies. I had to stop an airliner hijacking along the way."

"You're kidding."

"Check your radio."

"No, I believe you. But despite that, you know you committed a serious criminal act earlier today, and I don't think the government will be able to look the other way this time."

"That depends. I can do something useful for NASA, if you want it badly enough."

"And what is that?"

"I hear you're grounding the Shuttle fleet until you can fix the problems that blew up the last one."

"Yes, we estimate a downtime of several months."

"Let's be more realistic. Let's try several years."

Rogers's frown deepened. "All right, what of it?"

"That'll leave America with almost no access to space."

"We still have the Scout, Delta... "

"As I said, almost no access. And several very expensive spacecraft sitting on the ground with no way to get where they're going."

"Again, what of it?"

"Let's consider *Galileo*. That thing should have been on its way to Jupiter years ago. Now, I bet you'll cancel the Centaur liquid booster stage because of the *Challenger* disaster. If *Galileo* has to wait for NASA, it won't get to Jupiter for five years or more, if ever. But I think I can launch it. I'll use that tow-glider one of your predecessors developed for me. He tried to get me to launch half the NASA inventory with it. I turned him down, but I'm offering to do it now."

"Interesting. Could you handle other payloads? *Magellan*, for example? Or *Ulysses*?"

"No problem."

"The Hubble Space Telescope?"

"That's probably too big. Too heavy."

"What about military payloads? Or commercial comsats?"

"Not a chance. It's the science payloads or nothing. No more ORVRI satellites, for example."

Rogers reddened. "How did you disable them, by the way?"

"It was simple. I used a bar of ORVRI soap."

Rogers snorted, looked down, and drummed his fingers on his desk. "Well. It's an attractive offer, but I'm afraid I can't go for it. I assume the price you'd demand would be for the government to stay off your back during your eco-crusade. But then we'd practically have to sanction what you're doing. I don't think you're offering enough to offset the uproar you're causing."

"I figured that. That's why this is only the beginning. I want you to get on the phone and get me an appointment with the President. I've got some goodies to offer him too."

"What are they?"

"Sorry, you've got no need-to-know."

A mere forty five minutes later John was sprawled on a divan in the Oval Office. The President ambled in, accompanied by an impassive-looking pair of men whom he didn't bother to introduce. Today the President's usual affability seemed strained.

"Well, young man, it seems you've been a bad boy lately."

"I'm sure it seems that way to Conrad Wandrei and certain other outstanding campaign contributors."

"Now, John, let's not reduce this to personal pettiness. Businessmen like Con Wandrei make this country great."

"I have a different definition of greatness. And as far as I'm concerned, I haven't done anything that the government shouldn't have done years ago. But I didn't come here expecting to convince you I'm doing the right thing. Let me be blunt, Mr. President. I don't think you can stop me from doing whatever I think best. But to keep you off my back for a while longer, I have something to offer you."

"And what might that be, John?" asked the President coldly.

John sat up straight, leaned forward, and fixed his adversary with gleaming eyes and a roguish grin. "Let me use just one word," he said. "Evildoers."

After half an hour of wrangling, John had made what he felt was a decent deal. The intelligence apparatus of the United States would do its best to locate Western hostages held in Lebanon, and John would go in and extract them, keeping his involvement secret if possible. In return, the President promised not to interfere with military force in John's eco-crusade, although he couldn't prevent local authorities from trying to stop him, or foreign powers either. He also pledged to attempt no action against John's friends or family.

"But you understand, John, that there must be limits to this arrangement. If you cross the line, by endangering lives, or threatening the economic health or strategic interests of this country, the gloves will have to come off."

John nodded. "I understand. I accept those conditions. I trust that all appropriate members of your administration will be informed of this compact—Remo Cosimano, for example."

"Well, uh, yes, you can be assured, if Remo Cosimano is currently employed by the Government, we'll make sure he gets the word."

John did free several hostages. He invaded the hotel where three were imprisoned one morning just as the *muezzin* were calling the faithful of Beirut to prayer. He entered like a blue hurricane, scattering and overpowering the kidnappers before they realized they were under attack.

After that, the remaining hostages were separated and shuffled around the city and into the outlying valleys. Israeli intelligence managed to get a line on two of them, and John freed them both within minutes of each other.

The kidnappers panicked and murdered the remaining two men. Their headless bodies were dumped into the street before the American embassy. No longer hampered by concern for the safety of hostages, the President moved a naval battle group into the waters just off Beirut, and, using 18-inch shells from a World War II battleship, leveled several neighborhoods believed to be prime terrorist breeding grounds.

John launched *Galileo*. Berthed in the tow-glider, it was ferried up to 40,000 feet on the back of NASA's shuttle-carrier 747. John, hooked into the glider's towing harness, took over from there, giving the glider a gentle ride into Low Earth Orbit. Once there, he opened the glider's streamlined fuselage and freed *Galileo*, watching carefully as commands from the ground deployed its booms and antennae. Some of the ribs on the high gain antenna were snagged, John noted; he wriggled them free and the antenna unfolded like a golden parasol. Then, on radioed word from the ground, John got behind the big spacecraft and pushed it toward the stars, orienting himself by the stars themselves, guided by voices coming to him over NASA's Deep Space Network. Since John wasn't a rocket, and could accelerate moderately but indefinitely, *Galileo* got a gentle ride. At last the voices in his helmet told him that *Galileo* had a course and speed to take it to Jupiter. John pulled back a bit and watched as the spinning section of the probe spooled up to speed. Satisfied that all was well, John gave the Odyssean wanderer a final salute and turned back to Earth, already rather distant after the time he'd spent at interplanetary velocity. He returned to the glider, guided it back into the atmosphere, and deposited it on the lawn in front of the Press grandstand at Kennedy, in full view of the network cameras covering the unorthodox launch.

Then Sky Ranger began to push the outside of the envelope of tolerance he'd been granted in return for his services.

He attacked chemical operations all over the world. Sometimes he had to fight his way through a sleet of small-arms fire mounted by whatever authorities had jurisdiction in a particular place. Sometimes, especially in Third World or non-aligned countries, he even had to dodge a few SAMs or fighters before he could perform his mission. Sometimes the management of the plants decided to succumb to the inevitable and threw their gates open to him, maintaining an appearance of passive restraint and moral superiority. The Murex plants took no action against him whatsoever. In fact, Murex soon announced a voluntary curtailment of the production of the chemicals John had targeted. Other major manufacturers soon followed.

Needing money, John brought up some gold from Spanish treasure ships sunk off Cartagena. From Colombian arms merchants he bought a flame thrower. In high-altitude flights over Columbia and its neighbors, his eagle's vision spotted great coca plantations, which he attacked and set afire. The men set to guard these fields gritted their teeth in bitter frustration as their Uzis chattered uselessly at the swift, blue-clad dragon. The plants used to process and refine the cocaine weren't hard to spot either. John burned them as well. Despite his zeal, there was no way he could locate and eliminate the entirety of the South American drug apparatus, but he did put a mighty fear into the hearts of those whom he'd overlooked. These efforts, besides being immensely satisfying, gained him a little more slack from the generals of the futile, destructive American "War of Drugs."

On the insistence of a cabal of Latin and Middle Eastern countries, the United Nations issued a condemnation of Sky Ranger and ordered the closing and liquidation of the KSKY network and its facilities. KSKY went off the air.

In three days it was back, operating as usual, without fanfare. John resolved to determine how and why.

For the past several months, Conrad Wandrei had been steadily paring away the ranks of the "experts" he'd retained in his quest for knowledge of the Sky Ranger. One by one, as each person said or presented something that made it obvious they'd reached the limits of their discipline, and now had nothing more to offer than guesswork, bluff, or double-talk, Wandrei had terminated them. Now he was left with a corps of five or six, people with no information more solid than that of their former colleagues, but whose guesses were at least cogent and undisguised as anything more. Even so, Wandrei was convinced that before much longer, they too would reach the end of their ropes, leaving him to proceed alone.

Wandrei sighed and looked at his pale hands folded on the table before him, his left forefinger ornamented with a massive amethyst set in platinum. In progress was the now-habitual Sunday summary of all they had learned or determined about Sky Ranger in the previous week.

Just now Bryone was concluding her presentation. "I feel that this approach represents, if not a blind alley, then a crossroads with more branches than we could explore in our lifetimes. The facts of John Avril's life are widely known. If you halt his life story before the point where he emerges as Sky Ranger, it makes a quirky but uninspiring tale. He barely graduated from college, showed little personal drive or ambition, was socially maladroit, and never made more than $30,000 in a single year. This is scarcely the profile of a man who later takes on the task of rearranging the world."

Wandrei felt a pang of disappointment. Bryone was being facile and superficial in her analysis. It was foolish to assume that world-saving had never been on the mind of a confused man whose ambitions hadn't been defined by job, money, or career.

Yet she apparently realized some of this as she continued. "Somewhere in Avril's past is undoubtedly the seed which led to his eventual transformation into the physical anomaly called Sky Ranger. If we could read everything he ever read, see everything he ever saw, hear everything he ever heard, we might well eventually piece together the puzzle. However, to reconstruct his life in such detail is a project beyond our limitations. We can only hope to discover the relevant fragments though luck."

"Or by a process of analogy", amended Wandrei. "Permitting what we do know about Sky Ranger to guide us to specific, likely areas of Avril's previous interests. Dr. Barbee, your report."

"Precious little to add this week," said Barbee, sifting through a stack of papers thicker than a lifetime's published output for most scientists. "Just some observations. You'll recall we've agreed that Sky Ranger's powers are probably a variant of what we call telekinesis. However, this provides us with a convenient label, no more. No one knows the nature of the hypothetical telekinetic force. The source of the energy involved is deeply mysterious. Since Sky Ranger has already described himself as a manifestation of Maxwell's Demon, we thought he might derive the energy for flight by extracting heat from the air, in direct violation of the laws of thermodynamics. However, this has been disproved. In addition to the data collected by the instrument complex in Mr. Wandrei's office, we have obtained several observations of Sky Ranger in flight made with infrared radiometers, both ground-based and airborne. We find no sign of any cooling of the air in his vicinity, as would be caused by such an energy-drain. Therefore, we're still in the dark as to the source of the considerable energy at Sky Ranger's disposal." Barbee gave the pile of papers a push, tossed up his hands, and looked around in search of any challenges to his speculations.

"Of course, even had your hypothesis been substantiated, it wouldn't have explained where Sky Ranger gets his energy when he flies in space," said Dr. Krasnoff.

"I don't see that. Space isn't totally devoid of matter. Barbee's idea didn't put any limits on the volume of space subject to Sky Ranger's supposed Maxwell's Demon influence," said Wandrei impatiently.

"True," said Dr. Krasnoff, chastened. "If I may offer a few observations of my own. I believe the Sky Ranger actually has two separate modes of flight. He is usually observed to take off at exactly one gravity of acceleration, and to continue accelerating at that rate, until he reaches what we'd call terminal velocity at any given altitude. It's exactly as if he were falling upward, or sideways. Naturally, the higher he goes the greater the speed he can attain by such a method, given decreased air resistance. It's as if he can somehow direct his personal gravity vector in any direction he desires. He need not expend any energy in this case, as he's merely falling. I believe he uses this when he's in no great hurry to get somewhere. I call this his passive mode of flight."

"That's interesting," said Wandrei. "And the other?"

"I call this his active mode. He can, at need, accelerate much faster than one gravity, propelling himself by some means I cannot fathom. I wish I could say more about that."

Wandrei's interest in these speculations dwindled. "All right. I don't see that we're accomplishing very much. Let's adjourn."

Wandrei sat silently while the others gathered up their materials and filed out, muttering to one another in subdued voices. When they were gone, he stood up and rode his private elevator to his office. He paused at his assistant's desk before entering the office. "Consuelo, I'm dissolving the Sky Ranger Fact Team. Please notify the remaining members and take them off the payroll, as per our contract with them."

"Yes, sir."

Inside, Wandrei sank into a large black chair placed before a huge video screen. It showed a montage of views of Sky Ranger's flight from this very room, taken from various angles by hidden cameras. He watched it in an endless loop, dwelling on Sky Ranger's run, leap, and flight. By now he'd absorbed every detail, such as the lack of any sign of shock or stress on Avril's body, even though toward the end he was accelerating at close to 2 Gs. A man pulled by a wire or pushed by a rocket strapped to his back would be pulled or stretched or jerked by the outside force hauling his body behind it. But not Sky Ranger. The force acting on him came from inside, and what's more, it acted on every part of his body equally. He felt no more acceleration than does a man in free fall.

Wandrei knew he'd learn nothing more from his group of hired "experts". He already knew perfectly well how Sky Ranger had learned to fly. The information was all there, in the reports of the experts and in his own study. But no other member of the team had an inkling that the disparate facts they'd collected could be assembled into anything meaningful. Their discouragement was real, as each was convinced that the secret could only lie in his or her own field of research, with the others providing only corroboration, if that. As usual, it was left for Con Wandrei to see the pattern, to synthesize a confusing mass of knowledge into an illuminating whole.

Of course, knowing how Sky Ranger had done it was by no means the same as doing it himself. If he were to fling himself out the window right now in an attempt at flight, the only thing he'd achieve would a colorful headline recounting his suicide (brought on by grief over the *Torreon* disaster, perhaps?). No, Wandrei's goal was to follow the path taken by John Jacob Avril, as nearly as he was able, or as was necessary.

And then he would see what lay around bends in the path that even Avril hadn't taken.

He perched on his desk, touched a contact on the console.

"Consuelo."

"Yes, sir."

"Have a jet prepared for flight. I'll be going to Bali."

Sky Ranger flew over a sunlit deck of unbroken cloud. Ordinarily, he'd be obliged to bore his way through the rain and murk beneath those clouds to locate his destination, but this was a special case. For these clouds gave way to sun at 2,500 feet, while the structure he sought pushed up five hundred feet farther still.

And there it was, a steel and concrete needle piercing the cottony blanket, casting a long blue shadow in the sunlight of morning gold. John angled his flight to penetrate the clouds flowing by the great spire, knew a moment of blank, moist, greyness, then broke through to set down beside the main KSKY transmitter.

A cold rain flowed off the glassy surface of his flight suit as he strode toward the main office of the KSKY compound. Its glass doors were locked, requiring a magnetic key for entry. A video camera monitored the doorway. There was also an intercom grid, and John pushed the button beneath it.

A brisk female voice responded, "Visitor's Center to the right; all deliveries around back, please." The speaker clicked off.

John thumbed the button again.

"Please, all tourists must go—"

"Excuse me, I'm here on business. I'd like to see Mr. Johannsen, please."

"Do you have an appointment?"

"Nope."

"Then I'm afraid you'll have to phone for one."

"Miss, do you have a monitor for the camera that's pointed at me?"

"Yes..."

"Mind taking a look at it?"

A silence. Then, a small voice: "Is that outfit for real?"

"The rest of me is, too."

The door buzzed, and John gained entry. In the foyer, the receptionist he'd been dealing with looked contrite. After easing her mind, John was conducted to Johannsen's office.

The spare little Swede received him with some astonishment, as well as something close to servility. "Sky Ranger, Mr. Avril, it's such an honor to welcome you here at our facility. To meet you at last, it is truly a reward for all our efforts. Please sir, have a seat."

John creased his brow in discomfort as he sat; it always made him uneasy to be fawned over. "Take it easy, Mr. Johannsen. This visit is really long overdue. KSKY has performed a great service to the world, and to me as well. I should have come here to express my appreciation years ago."

"That's kind, very kind. It's especially gratifying considering the turmoil we've undergone in the past few days."

"Um—that's actually why I came just now. I heard about the UN shutting down KSKY, and when you went off the air I thought that was the end of it. But now you're back, and I'm wondering what's going on."

Johannsen's face lit up. "Well, sir, that's a matter of great triumph for us here at the station. Uh, you see, I anticipated some time ago that the United Nations might eventually shut us down due to some, uh, unpredictable action on your part. But I resolved to prevent that if possible. By no means could I live with the knowledge that hundreds must die because certain nations pretended outrage at your acts of so-called "environmental terrorism."

"But they did shut down the station," said John.

"Yes, so they did. But they made the mistake of putting the facilities on sale to the public. I was prepared for that. With the help of a corps of several hundred like-minded people, I raised the funds to purchase the KSKY facilities and equipment. We obtained licenses from the FCC and other relevant organizations. KSKY is now a private communications concern, with the same mission as its United Nations predecessor. We expect to fund the operation by means of private donations."

John smiled broadly. "Wow, that's great! I also figured the UN would eventually pull the plug on you, but I didn't think enough people would be on my side to take over KSKY themselves."

Johannsen looked puzzled. "Mr. Avril, do not let the shrill outcry of injured plutocrats deafen you to the cheers of the multitudes who support your work. And you should not forget, you have a cadre of thousands all over the world who owe you a great deal—I'm talking about those men and women whose lives you've saved over the years, not to mention the people who love them. It's difficult even for a thwarted and angry government to minimize the value of all those lives."

"Hmm. I never looked at it that way. Still, those angry governments may yet find a way to get at me. That's why I need to ask one more service of you and your organization."

"If it is at all feasible."

"I'm hoping you'll need to do nothing at all. From now on, I'm going to try to mail you a letter every day. Nothing fancy, just a note. Let's say you go, oh, three days without getting a letter from me. You may interpret that to mean I've been captured, or killed, probably by the United States Government or its proxies. Broadcast the news on your station. That kind of publicity might be the only thing that could save me in such a case. Of course, it would also pull a ton of bricks down on you."

Johannsen shrugged. "Without you, there would be no point to continuing KSKY at all. If things go as you suggest, we'll go to any length to try to secure your freedom. As long as your actions don't go so far as to outweigh the good you do, of course."

"Fair enough. Let's shake on it. And please, call me John. It makes me nervous when people take me too seriously."

Chapter Twenty Two

After that, Sky Ranger ran roughshod over the sensibilities of the merchants and money counters who saw no harm in degrading the Earth's capacity to support life, as long as it led to an increase in the holy numbers describing their incomes and their assets.

Soaring over the Amazon basin, he looked for dirt roads, fresh red scars in the greenery, conduits of infection into a massive organism beset by men and their destructive machines. Reaching the end of these roads, where the growling yellow dinosaurs of "construction" machinery tore yet deeper into the forest, opening the way to people whose technology had far outstripped their wisdom or prudence, John attacked. It was the machines that needed to be stopped; by themselves, the men were no more dangerous than any other like-sized primate. Therefore he yanked out the nervous wiring of the iron beasts the men controlled, stilling their roar. He flung engine parts into the forest, tore out controls, and poked steel rods into massive tires. Finally he left the machines as skeletons, a form the jungle could deal with, even if they were of iron—in twenty years they'd be little more than mounds of rust. The dirty, ill-clad men who served these machines, and who served above all the distant men with the wealth to command such destruction, reacted to John's deeds in every way possible, from cheering to wild cursing. But their attempts to stop him were limited to an occasional stinging rifle bullet.

On an Antarctic island, a French base whose purpose was "to study penguins" began construction of a huge runway directly through the island's main penguin rookery, dooming thousands of the birds. Hearing of this, John swooped down upon the base and left it a shambles, wrecking everything except what would be needed to evacuate the large crew, very few of whom seemed to be ornithologists. John grinned fiercely as he absorbed a blizzard of Gallic curses. He'd lost patience with French arrogance when they'd sunk the *Emerald Dolphin* in New Zealand, apparently to discourage Earthwarden from further interference in their nuclear test program.

With the horror of Chernobyl still fresh in his mind, John harried the construction sites of new nuclear power plants. He dared not attack functioning plants for fear of causing a worse disaster than he hoped to avert, but his action against plants under construction often pushed their already shaky economics over the brink and resulted in cancellations.

John longed to shut down all power generation, as virtually every form created its own unique blight on the planet. Oil-burning plants were tentacles of the entire oil industry, which poisoned and corrupted every part of the world it touched. Coal-fired plants spewed acids and other pollutants, and the extraction of the fuel they demanded destroyed great tracts of land. Even "clean" hydroelectric power required the damming and subversion of great rivers, ending the natural cycles of flood and flow and silt transport which had created the very landscapes through which they flowed.

But in the end, John knew that to plunge the industrial world into darkness would effectively end civilization and create massive hardship and death. He was sure that a profligate country like the United States could get along quite well on half the electricity it was presently consuming, by eliminating massive waste such as the uncontrolled outdoor lighting that set the night sky aglow around large cities for dozens of miles. Yet the U.S. power grid was far too complex for him to operate on it with the delicacy and control he'd need to prove his point. Random strikes against power generation would be mere vandalism, even in his own mind. Someday, he knew, the Sun itself would directly power civilization, but that time had not yet arrived.

Finally he decided to settle, at least for now, on making an example. Coming in from the Gulf of California, he flew low through the Colorado valley, hugging the water to avoid the radars of the many military bases in the area, popping up only to avoid the dams that drowned much of the river valley—the Imperial, the Parker, and the Davis. When he reached the biggest of them, Hoover Dam, he veered northwest for the short jog to what he considered the least justifiable settlement in the United States, Las Vegas.

Set in a wide depression of the most blasted desert country in America, Las Vegas reared up between sterile-looking mountain ranges like a mirage of banality and bad taste. John whistled low over the city at low speed, scowling at the dozens of gaudy hotels and the sprawl of dusty tract housing that sheltered those who operated them. Each hotel consumed as much electricity as a small city with their brilliant facades. These incredible cascades of light vied with each other to attract tourists, who fluttered through the streets like anxious moths. The mirrored-and-red-plush labyrinths of their casinos were like pitcher plants, luring their prey to drown with color and scent and sweetness.

John shot out a few miles and began to circumnavigate the city. At frequent intervals, ranks of huge electrical towers marched over the mountains, carrying the power needed to ignite a nightly festival of greed and debauchery. Even the megawatts already being consumed were evidently not enough, as John saw when he came upon the construction site of yet another line of high-tension towers. He swooped down on a stockpile of steel angles and, like an osprey snagging a fish, grabbed up a fifteen-foot length and soared high again. He came upon a functioning power line, added force to his flight impulse, and, holding his angle like a flagpole, used it to sever the lines. They draped gracefully down over the Mojave scrub and spat out angry tongues of blue fire, hissing and writhing until a circuit breaker somewhere up the line overloaded and broke. John yawed about and reversed course, slicing through the lines at half a dozen points, preferring places in rugged mountain passes which repair crews could not casually reach.

Circling the city, he knocked out most of its power, leaving only enough lines intact to power hospitals and homes, although he wasn't sure the Las Vegans wouldn't opt instead to keep the lights burning in a few of the casinos. If not, while they were still free to operate the vice-palaces, they'd be forced to skulk in the darkness to do so, until the lines were repaired. And then he'd just come back and knock them down again.

His work completed, he headed east, brazenly passing directly over Nellis AFB on the way, moving too fast to do more than tantalize them. Sitting on the flight line were a couple of very odd black planes, boxy and angular, like fighters from Star Wars. He might have scratched his head in puzzlement and curiosity, but the movement might have wrecked his stability and sent him spinning.

In minutes he was high, high over the slickrock country of Zion. He allowed himself a moment of sweet exultation, letting the thin, icy air dry his teeth as he bared them in a blissful grin. He'd done much to be proud of, and still he was only getting started.

Balbina was a dam under construction on one of the major tributaries of the Amazon. When completed, it would flood a huge area of rain forest, kill or displace untold animals, dispossess one of the few remaining primitive tribes, promote a quick burn of the forests surrounding the new lake, and produce a small amount of electricity to be used to "develop" the surrounding area. John flew to Brazil and found the dam virtually complete, a vast bleached rainbow of concrete, waiting for the spillways to be closed so it could begin to drown an area larger than some American states. He made a few supersonic passes to attract attention, then landed atop the dam, where he yelled out an announcement first in English, then in stilted phrasebook Portuguese: "Listen to me! You all know who I am and can guess why I'm here. This dam is a travesty and I won't permit it. I'm not here to argue with you, just to tell you that in exactly one week I will destroy the dam. Don't waste your time working on it anymore, and don't be too close when I come back." And off he flew, while behind him the construction crew shook their fists and shouted obscenities.

The Brazilian government, in conference with the international "development" banks whose loans had financed the project, as well as many of the other loans whose repayment threatened to crush the Brazilian economy, decided that Sky Ranger couldn't possibly make good his threat. He might fly fast, but they saw no way he could substantially damage such a massive structure, except possibly by hurling himself full into it, annihilating himself in the process. No, it must be only an attempt to intimidate them into stopping the project. Just the same, they decided to station some fighters and ground-to-air missiles nearby to try to fend him off if he should decide to harass the site again.

But Sky Ranger had some tricks he hadn't yet revealed. He spent much of the next week overseeing the construction of a weapon of his own. He had it made in a small machine shop in Switzerland whose proprietors were more impressed by sacks of Spanish treasure gold than by the environmental politics of South America. Since John's opponents were so enamored of acronyms, he decided to counter with one of his own. He called his invention SKREW—for Sky Ranger Kinetic Energy Weapon.

At the appointed time John donned SKREW and set out for Brazil, flying at an altitude of a hundred miles. SKREW consisted of a harness with two stubby winglets projecting from the sides. Beneath each winglet was mounted two shiny, finned projectiles, each with a lead core encased in nicely machined titanium. They were held in place by sturdy clamps; each controlled by a lanyard running to loops in John's belt.

John made a leisurely flight. He knew this attack was going to take something out of him. The vast grey-green basin of the Amazon drifted into view beneath him, the greatest single fortress of life on the planet, once unscarred, but now pocked and blighted by clear cuts, poisonous mining districts, and great plumes of smoke marking the pyres of forests being leveled for hamburger.

The sky over Balbina was clear. John could clearly see the dam even from this height. He narrowed his eyes as he studied the area and reviewed his plans. He hadn't practiced this maneuver, and if he fouled it up he might not only fail to wreck the dam, he might auger into the dirt at a very uncomfortable speed. Finally he stuck out his chin and decided to get on with it. He put his hands to his sides and put his fingers through the rings on the end of the lanyards. Then he pitched his face down toward the dam and began to put on speed.

By the time he reached the troposphere he was a meteor, squinting into a blast furnace of ionized air in front of his face, blasting his way by main force of will through a solid wall of air. He had no idea how fast he was going, but the ground was coming up awfully fast. He was also slowing as the air pressure continued to mount. Feeling out of control, he aimed straight at the dam, although his instincts cried out that was the last thing he should be doing. Seconds away from death, he pulled the first two lanyards, releasing one missile from each winglet. He strained to pull up as the missiles continued unstoppably on their original course. John paid them little heed, being concerned with saving his own life. He managed to warp his trajectory so he was heading up again. He never knew how close he came to hitting the dam, but he wouldn't have been surprised to find a smear of carbonized vegetation on his chest from blazing through the canopy. He relaxed and let his momentum carry him back up toward the ionosphere.

Each missile was a 300 pound metal-jacketed bullet, projected at a speed just within its ability to endure the stress. They hit the dam and exploded impressively, vaporized by the impact, their energy derived solely from John's speed.

He saw tiny figures running away, but they dwindled into invisibility as he sailed on up into the black sky region.

Then he did it again, launching his second salvo of missiles. He was up and away before a single man on the ground could aim a weapon in his direction.

Back in space, John removed and examined the harness, hoping it might be reused. It was seared and distorted, although it had been made of the finest high-temperature aerospace materials. John shrugged and cast it into a path that would eventually burn it up in the atmosphere. It had done its job.

The dam was far too massive to be destroyed outright by the four impacts, but the craters did necessitate close scrutiny of the structure, which revealed deep, unreachable fractures. The Balbina dam was finished.

A grim President presided over a meeting of his chief security advisors. At the focus of the meeting was SMITE director Remo Cosimano, who looked contained yet triumphant as he listened carefully to the President's words.

"Remo, it appears the time has come to act. Sky Ranger, I regret to say, has apparently gone insane, and his actions have become intolerable. Roy, let's have the lowdown on the damage he's done so far."

Roy McGiver, the moon-faced new FBI director, leafed through a substantial sheaf of papers, pursing his mouth in disapproval as he extracted the choicest tidbits of information.

"Several recent actions: Destroyed logging equipment and blocked roads being used to harvest old-growth timber in the Pacific Northwest.

"Performed high-speed overflights of several nuclear weapons plants both here and in Russia. Wrecked railroad tracks leading to those installations.

"Cut, weighted, and sank drift nets used by the fishing fleets of several nations, including our own.

"Dumped industrial wastes from pipelines leading into rivers and lakes into ornamental ponds fronting the head-quarters of the corporations involved in the dumping. The list goes on."

The President shook his head in dismay. "Thanks, Roy. Well, Remo, you predicted all along it would come to this, and it has. I'm turning you loose. Tell us about the goodies that the SMITE weapons program has produced."

Cosimano became momentarily nonplussed, but his composure quickly rebounded. "Sir, I'm sorry to report that the more exotic components of the SMITE weapons package are still under development. Usable hardware is still perhaps three years down the road. I'm referring primarily to the particle beam and laser energy weapons options."

The President looked disappointed. "You're not telling me we have no present capability to act against Sky Ranger, are you?"

Cosimano gave his wintry smile. "No sir, not at all. In fact, what I consider an excellent option is open to us. It is low-tech, low cost, and may be implemented at any time. It requires only that we take no hostile action against Avril for the time being, to lull his suspicions. We call it Project Deadfall." He handed over a bound report which the President flipped through in a desultory way.

"Yes, Remo, this looks fine. I'll study this more carefully later. What other approaches do you have? What about Elise Boutin?"

"Sir, I continue to believe that Avril's greatest weakness is his lingering attachment to that woman. Rumor has it that he has found himself a closely similar woman with whom to fornicate. She is of course available to us at any time. This gives us a potentially great deal of influence over Avril."

"Yes, yes. Well, I don't much like this idea, but I don't see what else we can do when we're dealing with a man who doesn't seem quite human."

"I do not consider him human in any way, Mr. President."

"Hmm. Well, I'm authorizing this Deadfall thing right now. I want Sky Ranger brought down."

"We are well prepared to obey your order."

Chapter Twenty Three

Sky Ranger gave himself a gift. Seizing a few hours from the constant effort of the past few weeks, he returned to the Southwest to enjoy his handiwork. With the Sun grandly poised near the western horizon, he cruised over the golden towers of the Grand Canyon. He'd shut down so many of the huge coal-fired power plants in the area that the hazes which had frequently despoiled the view had dissipated. The sunlight bathing the western sides of the canyon's convoluted pinnacles was clear and unsullied, while the purple shadows of the depths did not obscure the silver trail of the Colorado at the canyon's heart. Following the Sun, he made an unhurried tour from east to west, savoring each new vista as it rolled over the horizon to greet him.

A keen, delicate sense of incipient triumph vibrated within him. So radical, so dangerous, had been his recent actions that he had hardly dared acknowledge the possibility that they might result in permanent change. Yet all over the world, people were beginning to come over to his side. He had already changed much, and yet, they had found, the world was not ending. It was heady indeed—he felt as if he were in the vanguard of a bold exploration into new and more positive ways of thinking and living.

A gleam of reflected light not far from the Sun caught his attention. He squinted into the glare and made out a distant plane, obviously a big one, making slow progress only about three thousand feet over the canyon rim. Curious and faintly alarmed, John sped up and approached the plane. It was indeed a big one—an Air Force C-5A Galaxy, the biggest transport in the western world, obviously in distress. Spurts of black smoke erupted from both port-side engines.

The enormous plane skidded along with a drooping wing and too much rudder, right on the edge of stalling and spiraling down into the canyon.

John came up beside the cockpit and looked inside. In the seats were two pale, sweating Air Force captains, each gripping his control yoke with white-knuckle intensity, trying to wrestle them around by sheer muscle power.

John tuned his headset to a military frequency and keyed his throat mike. "Galaxy, Galaxy, this is Sky Ranger, do you read me?"

Both pilots started craning their necks around the sky, and both started when they spotted their caller pacing them just a few feet off their left window. "Roger Sky Ranger, this is Galaxy, we read you five by and we—uh, see you pretty well also. Can you lend us a hand?"

"I hope so. What's the situation?"

"Well, this is one unhappy airplane we got here. We've had some kind of an onboard explosion, and two port engines are out. The real problem is that we've also lost our hydraulic systems, and without them these yokes are about as easy to move as two fire hydrants. We have virtually no control over the airplane. Over."

"Understood. What's your cargo? Anything dangerous?"

"Uh, negative, we're flying practically empty."

"Okay. How can I help you?"

"Any chance you could take over the control surfaces? Grab on and steer the plane for us?"

John bit his lip and looked back over his shoulder at the colossal plane, with its broad wings and towering stabilizer.

"Sorry, guys, I don't think I can do that. She's just too big, and awfully unstable, especially with two engines out. That's a last resort only. Are your controls totally out?"

"No, theoretically we've got full control, but in a plane this size, without hydraulics you'd have to be King Kong to budge the yoke."

John looked down at the high plateau on the north side of the canyon. They were low enough now so that with his eagle's vision he could spot ground squirrels poking their heads out of their burrows. "All right, I'm not King Kong, but I might be able to help you there. If I can get inside, I might be able to manage the controls."

"That sounds good," said the pilot enthusiastically. "We can crack open the rear cargo loading hatch just enough to let you in."

John frowned. "Aren't the doors operated hydraulically too?"

"Uh, they are, but they're on a separate system."

John considered. He had a funny feeling about this. He suspected that this flight might represent the end of the tacit truce he'd enjoyed with the Feds. But even if a platoon of men armed with anti-tank weapons awaited him inside, he was confident he could escape any trap that could be contained in an airplane. Surely this wasn't a suicide mission—any force great enough to harm him would bring down the plane as well.

John keyed his mike. "All right, Captain, you got it. I'll drift back and you crack the door."

"Roger. Thanks, buddy."

John let the plane overtake him and kept station directly behind the monster's tail. The big cargo door, located on the underside of the Galaxy's rear fuselage, showed a widening line of blackness as it dropped down on hydraulic struts. It lowered only a few feet and stopped, the better to preserve the plane's shaky flyability. John approached the dark opening, grabbed the lip of the door and looked inside, but he could see nothing. He pulled himself inside and slid down into the plane. Instantly the door hummed shut behind him.

John stood up and waited for his daylight-adapted vision to adjust to the darkness. The plane's interior smelled of machine oil and canvas. The scream of the two remaining engines was scarcely muffled by the thin skin of the fuselage.

After a minute he could see some small green lights ahead. Gingerly he made his way forward. He called for the main interior lights to be turned on, but apparently his tiny transmitter lacked the necessary range. He half tripped over some kind of raised rim or lip on the deck. Some unseen barrier rose ahead of him to block his view of the green lights.

He spun, determined in an instant to fling himself right through the skin of the plane. Loud detonations surrounded him, and he felt a sudden increase in air pressure. He was jarred by the merciless clang of heavy metallic surfaces being rammed together.

Now lights came on, fluorescent fixtures which shed their sickly glare from behind heavy metal grates. John found himself inside an ovoid steel chamber, no more than fifteen feet in any dimension, formed of two halves joined like a walnut shell. Outrage roared up from inside him. The scream of the full-throttled starboard engines lessened to their normal cruising whine; simultaneously, the port engines awakened and spooled up to speed. He felt the Galaxy enter a normal bank, leveling off with a new course due east, full away from the rapidly setting globe of the Sun.

Shocked, almost paralyzed, John stood on the bottom of his curving prison, thick and strong as the armor of a battleship. His racing mind sought an escape, hampered by his subconscious, which cried insistently that his most precious asset, his freedom, was now gone.

"Deadfall to Shotgun. Deadfall calling Shotgun. Come in."

Remo Cosimano's thin voice crackled in the Galaxy's cockpit. "This is Shotgun. What's your situation?"

"Bird in the hand. I say again, we've got a bird in the hand. We're hightailing it east with the Sun in the rear view mirror."

"Excellent. That is superb. I congratulate you. Monitor him carefully, and report what happens when you lose sight of the Sun. Shotgun out."

"Yes sir. Deadfall out."

The Galaxy commander turned in his seat. "What's going on in the shell?"

A SMITE technician sat at a console in the rear of the flight deck. He watched his TV monitors with unblinking intensity. "Nothing yet. He's just standing there with his mouth hanging open."

The pilot laughed. "He probably can't believe how dumb he was to get caught like this."

His mouth twisted, the copilot said, "He probably can't believe we suckered him in like this."

Ignoring his copilot's uncertain tone, the commander said, "We accomplished our mission, no problem."

They all felt the plane shudder. The technician yelled "Whoa! Our man just woke up. Slammed himself against the side of the shell like a linebacker."

"Won't do him any good. The shell's too small to let him get up the speed to punch his way through that steel," said the pilot confidently. "What's he up to now?"

"He's picked himself up—doesn't look like he's hurt at all—all right, he's grabbed the lip and he's trying to pry the shell open." The technician studied the gauges on his panel. "He's—he's applying a force of almost three tons—"

"How much force in those jacks? Holding the shell together?" snapped the commander.

"Twenty tons."

"Either of you guys know anyone Sky Ranger has saved? I do," said the copilot.

"Shut up, Mitchell. It's way too late for second thoughts. Report!"

"Pressure climbing steadily," droned the technician, as if hypnotized. "Five tons. Seven tons. Sky Ranger looks like he's straining. Ten tons. Twelve. He looks very angry. Very angry. I wouldn't want him to get loose right now. Fourteen tons. Pressure increase leveling off—now at fifteen tons—still level—still holding—okay, meter coming down; he's given up. Thank God."

"He's a strong one," said the commander admiringly.

"I hope Shotgun can handle what we're bringing him," said Mitchell.

"A few minutes more and Mr. Avril won't be any tougher than he looks, according to Shotgun," said the commander.

"He's getting ready to—"

Another jolt rattled the ship.

"—launch himself into the side again. That time was stronger. There he goes—" Another jolt. "Stronger still. He's still at it—"

The three men felt another shock, then still another, each in faster succession, each stronger than the one before, until the whole plane shook with a rapid-fire drumbeat.

"Report! What in hell is he doing in there now?"

"He's—flying! Bouncing off one side and then the other, fast as a goddamn racquetball, hitting harder every time. He's knocked out some of the lights. He's just a blur. I can't believe any human being can take that much punishment."

"Mitchell! How long to sunset?"

"Three minutes."

"Let's try to cut that." The commander advanced the throttles to their limits and shoved his yoke forward an inch. The plane pitched down and sped up. The shaking from the caged fury in the cargo hold grew stronger.

"Strain gauges in the shell are nearing red lines. I don't think he'll get through the wall, but the impacts might be enough to break the shell free of the jacks. If that happens—"

"He'll be loose in a second," said Mitchell.

"We're at full throttle, flying five hundred feet above the real estate," said the commander. "We're flying into the shadow. The Sun's slipping down behind us."

"I'll be damned. I'll be damned. He just slid to the floor of the shell in a heap. He looks all done in."

The commander turned back with a confident smile. "He is that."

Even Mitchell looked relieved.

Part Four
The Passing of Sky Ranger

Chapter Twenty Four

The giant plane touched down at a strip at the White Sands Missile Range in New Mexico. It taxied up to a floodlit area where it was awaited by a squad of SMITE troopers armed with automatic weapons. At their head was Remo Cosimano, a lean, saturnine figure in a dark grey suit. The Galaxy came to a halt; the engine whine died out. The SMITE team hustled to the rear where the plane's tailgate was being lowered. They mounted the ramp, where they beheld the steel ovoid of the Deadfall trap, garishly lit by the Galaxy's yellow interior lights, its wall dimpled outward by the multiple impacts of its prisoner.

The SMITE squad surrounded the shell. At a sign from Cosimano, a technician triggered a series of controls. With a loud hiss, the jacks holding the halves of the shell together released. The top half was raised, while the bottom tilted toward the tailgate to reveal its contents. There stood John Avril, shaky on his feet, his flight suit torn and abraded. He faced them with a calm yet penetrating gaze. Cosimano fixed him with a small cold smile.

"Mr. Avril, we haven't met, but I expect you know who I am. We're certain to find a lot to talk about over the next few years."

John regarded him and the threat he represented with the eyes of one who had seen the planet dwindle behind him as he took his first small steps toward the stars.

At another sign from Cosimano, a man stepped forward quickly and plunged a hypodermic needle into a tear on John's sleeve. Immediately the keenness bled from John's eyes, and he stood there swaying—vacant, dull-eyed, and lost.

They half-led, half-dragged John into a masonry structure of the secret White Sands SMITE complex, and into an elevator. Five floors below ground level, they confined him in a vault eight feet cubed, with six-inch steel walls set into bedrock. The door was a foot thick, and equipped with a variety of locks and security devices. It had a small slot for inserting food, with heavy doors at both ends like an airlock, so that the operator need not supply John with even the smallest connection with the outside world. The cell walls had no substantial openings, only a water line, small grates to admit air and, if necessary, various other gases. An opening in the floor was a chemical pit toilet dug into the rock.

They seated John on the narrow cot, stripped off his flight suit, and withdrew, slamming the great door closed behind them. Cosimano and his men went to an adjacent room to monitor John via the cameras recessed into the cell wall. The cell had only the dimmest of lighting, but the image intensifiers in the cameras made the scene perfectly clear. By watching him, and by noting his vital signs by means of the sensors built into the cot, they saw that he fell into an immediate deep sleep. For now, they were content to permit that.

In the world above, dawn approached, but it made no visible signs in this dungeon—certainly the light in the cell never varied. Still, as Sunrise grew near, John's bio-monitors showed signs of increasing activity, warnings that he was about to wake up. Cosimano, now somewhat bleary-eyed himself, gave an order. Again accompanied by armed men, a medical technician entered the cell. John was awakened by their entrance, but he only looked up at them blearily. The technician knelt beside him and gave him another injection. They all stood back and watched tensely. A moment later, a signal audible only in the earpieces they wore announced that the Sun had returned to the living world above.

But John only smiled vacantly at them. The technician knelt again and gave him a saline injection, just to see if he could. John made no objection, and the needle slid right in.

The men left the cell. John spent the day in brief periods of wakefulness, sitting on the floor, smiling stupidly, and talking to himself incoherently. The rest of the time he slept, sometimes on the cot, sometimes not. Food was introduced through the airlock, but John ate nothing, only playing with the Jell-O and then ignoring it.

There was no injection for him that evening. After Sunset John grew gradually more alert, if no more energetic. The evening wore on. Just as John dropped into a natural sleep, banks of brilliant lights blasted on, startling him and paining his eyes. He frowned at them. They were recessed in the wall, protected by thick glass. Nothing more happened for a while. They left him to stew.

At midnight Cosimano entered, accompanied by two armed troopers. He was freshly dressed, shaved, and showered, trying to add to the corrosion of John's time sense.

One of the men threw John to the floor to allow Cosimano to prissily take a seat on the bunk. John sat up against the wall and stared at him, listless and impassive.

"Well, Mr. Avril, your wings have been clipped. They say the Devil takes care of his own, but he must have been looking elsewhere this time."

John's silent stare went unchanged. He thought of at least three possible replies, but he had neither the heart nor the energy to trade barbs with this obsessive creature.

Cosimano tried again. "Your ungodly rampage has ended. I will see to it that you never again interfere with God's plan for man's dominion over the world."

John tried to frame a response to that, but he only felt a strong impulse to parody Cosimano's pronouncement in a smug, pretentious voice. He overcame the impulse, but the absurdity of it got to him, and he laughed.

That angered Cosimano, who was even more prickly than usual due to excitement and lack of sleep. "In a few days you'll wonder why you laughed, Mr. Avril. I intend not only to confine you, not only to discipline you, but to extract from you all your secrets. I will hear from your own lips the source and method of your ability to fly."

"I'll tell you right now. Go take a flying leap."

This seemed absolutely riotous to John, and he chortled happily in a heap on the floor. Cosimano's gaze burned into him, then he shook his head and stood up to leave. As the three of them stepped out, John caught a tight, involuntary smile compromising the impassivity of one of the guards. The door whooshed shut with a wave of air pressure.

"Nobody really likes you, Remo," whispered John.

The cell lights began a random sequence of ons and offs. John also received injections at unpredictable intervals. Some were saline and some were not, as Cosimano didn't want to tip him off to the day-night cycle by drugging him just before each Sunrise. He did order the dose of the active drug cut down, to allow John a little more lucidity during daylight hours—enough at least to permit him to eat and attend to his bodily needs.

Cosimano's questioning remained persistent, as was his interpretation of John's honest answers as impertinent evasions.

"Why can you fly?"

"I fly because I know I can."

"Who gave you this power?"

"I get it from everything that is."

"How can we duplicate this power?"

"By being better, more honest, calmer people."

"That is all? There is nothing more?"

"Well... " John furrowed his brow in uncertainty. "I'm not sure. You might have to drop dead first."

A sharp backhanded blow marked Cosimano's first descent into violence against John.

Shortly after John's abduction, inexplicable, ominous things began to happen in the world.

In Bali, the sacred mountain of Agung erupted in full violence for the first time in memory. Fast rivers of lava raced down its jungled flanks, immolating everything in their path, barely missing large villages, then capriciously veering to destroy temples set on prominences which should have been spared. During the night, the volcanic crater cast weird purple lights on the clouds that swirled by overhead.

In the oceans, the small Earthwarden fleet came under attack by whales. Orcas leaped upon and devoured the crews of the Zodiacs harrying toxic waste dumpers in the North Pacific. Off the Carolina coast, sperm whales shattered the hull of the small sailing vessel *Deneb*, drowning her crew. Off the coast of Antarctica, a few of the pitifully small remnant of the mighty blue whales which man had deigned to spare sacrificed themselves by swimming headlong into the screws and rudder of the *Earthwarden* itself, flagship of the fleet. They could not breach its steel hull, but at the cost of mutilation and death they were able to disable the ship's propulsion and steering. Helplessly adrift, the distraught crew awaited rescue. Before it could reach them, a huge storm blew up out of nowhere, toppling the ship with hundred-foot waves. Earthwarden, paralyzed with shock and horror, suspended all operations.

In the Straits of Georgia, Murex's desultory effort of cleaning up after the mess left behind by the *Torreon* came to a halt as everyone involved studied a bizarre new phenomenon. To all appearances, the oiled beaches began to clean themselves. The thick brown pudding that coated every rock and grain of sand for miles grew noticeably less every day. Observations showed that things were eating the oil — birds and animals, but also bacteria and fungi. Otters and seals, eagles and bears, flies and crabs, all were treating the sludge like a vast free lunch. They began to die in appalling numbers. A great stench arose.

It occurred to someone to analyze the oil. The results were not immediately accepted since they were so obviously incorrect, but multiple tests gave the same result. The oil now seemed to be a substance closely resembling liver paté, albeit liberally dosed with the poison botulin. In a few weeks the entire area would be devoid of any wild creature willing to dine on meat. Murex, refusing to expose its workers to the dangers of botulism, ended the cleanup. It was continued by the bacteria and fungi which treated it as it would any rotting carcass.

Cosimano's methods of extracting information became more obtrusive. Exhausting his captive, disorienting him, drugging him, imprisoning him, produced only a stream of philosophical ramblings, quasi-mystical aphorisms, and senseless riddles relating mostly to trees, the sky, and small furry animals. The SMITE inquisitors swept all this mumbo-jumbo aside impatiently. Only one sort of answer would satisfy the SMITE "experts"—something relating to a technical breakthrough, a secret device, a new drug, or even a wire attached to a hypothetical high-flying Russian stealth plane.

The exception was Cosimano himself, who alone had access to the government's best information on Sky Ranger. He tolerated the others mainly as an additional harassment for Avril. He himself was sure that no scientific secret would be found to account for Avril's unnatural gift. Cosimano knew full well the source of Avril's power, and he would not relent until he'd extracted from Avril's mouth the name of the evil master he served.

Thus the inquisitors of SMITE were given considerable latitude in dealing with Sky Ranger, and they took advantage of it. They took satisfaction in producing pain in that formerly adamant body, to see it bleed and bruise. They'd never been comfortable knowing there was a man in the world who they could not intimidate with threat of harm or the authority of their office. Now that impertinent eagle was brought down, and they could reassume their proper place in the hierarchy of men.

The staff of KSKY took gloomy note of the fact that for three days many disasters had occurred without intervention from Sky Ranger. Keir Johannsen himself observed that today no note from Mr. Adler had arrived. The mail arrived three days after its date of posting—to fulfill Sky Ranger's condition, he'd have to wait two more days for the mail flow to resume.

Until then, he ordered a change in station policy. Whenever people died from a disaster in which Sky Ranger might normally have intervened, he ordered that Sky Ranger's absence be specifically stated before the story was dropped. Let the people of the world make of that what they would. It might prepare them for the announcement he felt sure he'd have to make in two day's time.

In the wetlands of the Louisiana coast, an unknown "purple tide" swept in from the sea, wiping out all life, turning a burgeoning spawning ground into a stinking, rotting morass. The wetland had been proposed as a Federal wildlife refuge , but now that some freak of nature had sterilized it, there was no reason not to offer it for offshore oil exploration.

War in the Middle East exploded beyond all reason. The leaders of all sides were inflamed by the religious miracles of a slender burning-eyed man who appeared to them dressed in violet and black. Like some malignant spirit, he appeared first on one side and then the other, goading both to total war while planting visions of paradise in their minds. The populations of several nations threw themselves at each other without thought or plan, killing at such a rate as to leave the region essentially depopulated within a year. In the Persian Gulf, oil tankers were free to ply the waters, free of the threat of missile or speedboat attack from either side, carrying crude pumped into their holds by Murex crews who went ashore to work the abandoned wells and transit terminals.

The catastrophic events of the past few days had only served to reinforce Cosimano's suspicions as to John's nature. He began to pipe KSKY into John's cell to gauge his reaction. John would obviously gain time references from the broadcasts, but by this time Cosimano had given up trying to avoid this. The rhythms in the biosensor data showed that somewhere in Avril's makeup was a solar clock that could not be confused. Cosimano was gratified by John's obvious anguish each time the announcer pointed out that people had needlessly died because the Sky Ranger had not acted. It never occurred to Cosimano to try to reconcile John's concern for human life with his theory about John's demonic nature.

The third day passed with no letter from "Mr. Adler". A grim Keir Johannsen squared his jaw, stood up from his desk, and went into Studio A, where he interrupted the announcer on duty and sat down in front of the live mike. His mind raced over the text he'd memorized days ago, and he began.

"People of the world, this is Keir Johannsen, director of KSKY. We have all taken note of the absence of Sky Ranger from the world stage for nearly the past week. The time has come to announce, on the authority of instructions given me by John Avril himself, that in all probability he has been either killed or abducted by an agency of the United States of America. I was asked by Sky Ranger to make this announcement in the event that no word came from him after the passage of a certain amount of time. That time has passed. I now call upon the American government to make public all information on the whereabouts of John Avril. I further urge the people of the world to demand this information from the American government. I repeat... "

Hearing this announcement, Remo Cosimano stormed down to John's cell, where its drugged occupant smiled knowingly at him as its words echoed off the steel walls. White-faced, Cosimano extracted an automatic pistol from his jacket. He aimed and fired three rounds into the speaker grid in the wall, silencing it. Eyes glittering with triumph, he stormed out again.

The FCC informed KSKY of the immediate revocation of its license to broadcast from American soil due to violation of the public trust. When the station failed to go off the air, U.S. Marshals swarmed over the property, shutting down everything, while a few Canadian Mounties watched sternly from their side of the joint complex. Johannsen and his staff were detained and questioned by a severe, sour-faced zealot who failed to identify himself or the organization he represented. He could find no excuse to hold the KSKY people, but warned them they would probably be indicted for violating FCC regulations. Then they were released. As they stepped blinking into the sunshine of a

North Dakota fall afternoon, they saw their inquisitor enter a big U.S. Air Force helicopter and be swept away.

Johannsen and most of his staff drove to Winnipeg, where they rented hotel rooms and sat around anxiously while Johannsen made some ticklish phone calls. Finally he seemed satisfied, if not overjoyed. They got back into their cars and drove to the airport. From there they flew to Mexico City, passing directly over their magnificent, but now mute, transmitter soon after takeoff. From Mexico City they flew to Havana. The Cuban leaders conducted them to a powerful AM radio station on the north coast of the island, which they turned over to the KSKY team without reservation. It went back on the air as the new American KSKY, less than twelve hours after the old one went off the air.

In Washington, the President and his men contemplated an unprecedented action—jamming a foreign radio broadcast entering the United States. But in the end, the President, who still retained a few tainted shreds of idealism, could not bring himself to don the mask of censorship he so excoriated when seen on the faces of the other side. Besides, the damage was already done. The announcement was out. The White House was besieged by reaction from around the world. It ran two to one in favor of Sky Ranger, and that the President could not comprehend. Didn't these people believe in economic development? In free enterprise? Didn't they want to keep their jobs, and drive their cars to get to them? Baffled, the President shook his head and read a selection of messages. They were all impassioned, but he thought the arguments of the anti-Sky Ranger side were far more compelling. Still, he had to admit, those same messages often had a cruel and ugly tone to them.

The KSKY affiliates of the rest of the world had lost no time in intercepting and broadcasting the message. It penetrated even to the Australian outback, where no man listened more intently than Lieutenant General Eric Hunter, USAF, retired. The company he flew for, Goanna Airflight, operated turboprop cargo planes between Adelaide and the various settlements of the interior, though plans were afoot to expand into chartered executive transport. When Hunter heard the message, he was sitting in the lounge of Goanna's dusty headquarters shack in Alice Springs, nursing a beer as he waited for his plane to be checked out, refueled, and loaded.

And as usual, especially recently, he listened to that rogue radio network, KSKY. What he heard now soured his stomach and tightened his mouth in old lines of concentration and resolve.

"This is Keir Johannsen, repeating this newest development. Representatives of the American administration have refused comment on the matter, just as they have consistently denied involvement in the disappearance of Sky Ranger. For the record, the government of New Zealand has taken the Avril family into protective custody to prevent any action from being taken against them."

Hunter snapped off the radio. Avril could take care of himself one way or another, but who could say what a cold-eyed bastard like Remo Cosimano wouldn't do to get his hooks into a little dove like Elise Boutin? It was time he flamed brother Cosimano's tail once and for all.

He pushed his airplane south to Adelaide as fast as he could, which wasn't nearly fast enough to suit him. As soon as his wheels were chocked he marched straight into the office of his boss.

"Harry? I need a word with you."

"Anytime, Eric. Have a seat."

"Thanks. You know that sparkling new Learjet of ours that's sitting out on the field? I think she needs a good, stiff, shakedown flight before we put her into service."

"That right, mate? And where you thinking of taking her?"

"Well, I've given it a lot of thought. I'm thinking Thailand, and then I think Cuba would be a good choice. Funny thing, I never got a chance to visit it while I was wearing Air Force blue."

Harry leaned back and looked at the ceiling contemplatively. "Hmm, Cuba. A good long run. I don't know if we'll ever get much call for Cuba as a destination, but it should increase our passenger's confidence that we can get 'em from here to Brisbane if we have to."

"No question about it."

Harry glanced over at the radio mounted on the wall. "Well, Eric, I say give it a go. Double flight pay—I daresay you won't be wanting a copilot."

"Might be most convenient for Goanna if I go alone."

"Agreed. She's yours when you want her."

Hunter stood up and extended his hand. "This means a lot to me, Harry."

"Means quite a bit to me too, Eric. Means something to any right-thinking cobber. Just bring our pretty bird back in one piece, will you?"

Hunter laughed. "Buddy, I used to be a professional test pilot. The only planes I'm willing to crash are the ones with ejection seats. Oh, and one more thing...the fuel? This is going to be a thirsty trip. "

Without a word, Harry produced Goanna's corporate credit card and handed it over.

It wasn't difficult for Hunter to deduce Elise's probable hiding place. John's most prominent deed in Thailand had been to assist a certain *wat* in a rural Thai backwater during a major flood. Hunter made his way there from Bangkok and asked to speak to the master, who sat beneath a great central teak tree and listened with a troubled expression to the news coming over a pocket radio. He stood up upon seeing Hunter, his grave face alert and questioning.

"And you are, sir?"

"My name's Eric Hunter, and we have a mutual friend. He wears blue and white."

The monk nodded. "I've heard of you. The news of our friend is not good?" he said quietly.

"No, it's terrible. John's in big trouble."

"And you must help him if you can."

"That's right. I think I know who's got John. I've got to get back home and raise the biggest stink about it that I can."

"Yes, I see the need to do that. But why have you come here?"

"I'm here to check on Miss Boutin and make sure she hasn't been dragged off too."

"Miss Boutin?"

Hunter felt a chill. "Yes, Elise Boutin. Are you telling me she's not here?"

The monk looked confused. "No. No such person has been here."

Hunter spun in frustration, looking around as though he might spy Elise in the shadows. "That's bad news. I don't know where else to look for her."

The monk looked at the ground, frowning in concentration. "Wait. It's a strange matter. John did visit us here, not so long ago. I remember a woman being with him. That was noteworthy, for normally we monks do not consort with women. Or rather I should say, we are not permitted to consort with them. John asked us to shelter her. But soon after he left, she was gone."

"She left?"

"I assume so. She was simply gone. It's all very—indefinite in my mind."

"She may have been abducted by the same men who have John. But John..."

The monk's expression turned still more serious. "There is one thing you should realize about John. In a very real sense, he is beyond any harm his captors may do him. When you act to set him free, do so with the welfare of the world in mind, not primarily John's. The world needs him more than he needs it."

Hunter stared at him intently. The monk continued. "John... is *Bodhisatva*—a man who has found Enlightenment, but refused to be released from life, preferring to remain, to help those of us who still suffer and struggle." He looked down at his hands. "I—have never referred to anyone as *Bodhisat* before," he said in a quiet but troubled tone. "I have never had occasion to do so. It is not a term we use lightly. But there has never been anyone like John Avril before. Not in my lifetime."

"I think I know what you mean," said Hunter. "My daddy was a Kentucky coal miner. I got out of there by joining the military, whose mission isn't exactly to promote cultural understanding. But talking to you, and knowing John, and other things, they've all opened my eyes to some things my people back home don't think about too much."

The monk looked troubled. "But John is not—perfect. In one way at least, I fear he is still attached to the world, or at least to one thing *in* the world. When he realizes this... when the truth is made plain to him...I fear we will lose him."

Chapter Twenty Five

Although KSKY continued to broadcast from its new communist base of operations, exhorting the people of the world to demand the release of Sky Ranger if he were still alive, so far little had come of it. The populace seemed unconvinced by KSKY's rantings—there was, after all, no evidence to support the station's claim, and it was just as easy to believe the rumors promulgated by, for example, Murex Energy Systems, that Sky Ranger had simply folded under the pressure of public outrage over his eco-piracy and was keeping a low profile. For Americans, the choice between keeping faith in their government or in their great, but errant, hero was a difficult one, and most preferred to sit on the fence until there was proof on one side or the other. The President had admitted no knowledge of Sky Ranger's whereabouts, but he gave Cosimano instructions to hold onto him at any cost.

His confidence restored, Cosimano instructed that KSKY be reintroduced to Avril's cell so he could be oppressed by the body count of people he might have saved were he free. Cosimano's gunshots had obliterated the sound system built into the cell, so now the word came in via a speaker bolted to the cell wall.

It happened that Cosimano and his team was questioning John in his cell when KSKY broke the news about the probable abduction of Elise. On a sweltering afternoon that warned of thunder to come that evening, Cosimano listened while the hated voice of Keir Johannsen again interrupted the apocalyptic parade of death and disaster that was the sole recent fare of KSKY—most notably just now, the monstrous, freakish hurricane that was bearing down on

North Carolina's Outer Banks, threatening to flatten every structure on the barrier islands and beyond.

"I'd like to introduce someone who has travelled from the far side of the world to reveal pivotal information on the whereabouts of Sky Ranger and Elise Boutin. The next voice you hear will be that of Eric Hunter, a retired general of the U.S. Air Force. General?"

Cosimano's face turned white. In a reflexive spasm he crushed the fountain pen he was holding, blackening his hand.

Hunter's drawl came over the speaker. "Uh—hello out there, everybody. I'm not exactly a trained radio announcer, but I've been asked to report to you in person, so I'll give it a shot. As Mr. Johannsen mentioned, I used to be in the Air Force—some of you might remember hearing about me as a test pilot. Well, my final assignment was as commander of a government agency very few of you have ever heard of, the Sky Ranger Information Project. Its sole mission is to keep track of Sky Ranger through various means and to compile all possible information about him to help in forming the President's policy regarding Mr. Avril. And that's all the SRIP did, until a few years ago, when a new organization called SMITE was put together. I won't bother to say what SMITE stands for—but its mission is simple, to find ways to control or destroy Sky Ranger and to implement those plans if so ordered.

"The first director of SMITE was a convicted felon named Remo Cosimano, who you might also remember. He was charged with the attempted kidnapping of Elise Boutin, and he served several years in a federal prison for his crime. I'm willing to bet he's still in charge of SMITE—he hates Sky Ranger too much to let a job like that get away.

He's hated Sky Ranger since day one. I never was sure just why. I'm out of the scene now, but I'm convinced that both Avril and Boutin are prisoners of Cosimano and SMITE. I'm not going to argue whether John's recent actions are right or not, but anyone with an interest in simple justice might like to know that, last I knew, the main SMITE installation is hidden on the White Sands Missile Range in New Mexico. That's all I have to say for now. I can tell you this, I never expected to have to come to Cuba to make a statement like this, accusing my own country of kidnapping and injustice. It's a black day for America when her leaders can do something like this and hope to get away with it. Goodbye."

The news brought on a disconcerting change in John. Up until now he'd been quite relaxed during his imprisonment, insouciant, even a bit goofy, through beatings, torture, and other privations—because of the drugs, Cosimano had supposed. Now John's gaze sharpened instantly, his eyes narrowed, and he caught Cosimano in a chilling, unblinking stare.

"Set her free, Remo," John whispered. "Set her free."

Cosimano kept his composure with an effort. "You are in no position to make demands of me, Mr. Avril. I owe you nothing. I owe you no explanations, no sympathy, no regard of any kind. But I will tell you this. I have never understood your obsession with the Boutin woman. She is unexceptional, hardly worthy of a lifetime's pursuit. But she is perfectly safe. She is free to come and go as she pleases, or at any rate, she is as free as any American truly is."

"Then why does Hunter say you've abducted her?"

"Abducted? Hardly that. I can only think—"

Cosimano stopped speaking suddenly. He stood staring at John for almost thirty seconds as he reached a conclusion so startling and outlandish that it left him momentarily mute.

"I think I see it now. I thought, we all thought, that you had simply found yourself some other woman. Another woman who resembled Miss Boutin. Younger. Prettier. We badly wanted to interview her, or bring her in, but she was elusive. But now—now I perceive that you actually believe this woman to be Elise Boutin. I had no idea that you were, in addition to being so obsessed, also so delusional. I am fascinated. I could almost laugh."

"Of course she's Elise! Who else could possibly fool me like that? Who would?"

"I don't know. But I do know this. Shortly after my initial attempt to gain information from Boutin, the government approached her a second time. It was a kinder, gentler approach than mine. She was offered a deal. She disliked the notoriety she had achieved by her involvement with you. She wished to lead a quiet life. In exchange for revealing everything she knew about you, the government agreed to relocate her. They gave her a new identity. She couldn't actually tell us much that we didn't already know, but she did her best, and we kept our end of the bargain. She has since married a pleasant if rather dull man who manages an organic produce market or something of the sort. They have two children, and a dog. She has left you behind."

"You are—you're—"

"Lying? You can't even bring yourself to speak the word. I see in your eyes that you know I speak the truth. If you have any doubts at all, I can send for some of our surveillance files on Boutin. But I won't reveal her current name or location. She specifically instructed us never to do so."

The pain he saw in John Avril's eyes caused a feeling of vast triumph to bloom within Cosimano's chest and expand to fill his every fingertip and toe. Almost by accident, he had found the key to demolishing Avril's insufferable tranquility and confidence. By this one revelation, he felt that Avril might have been neutralized forever, for surely no man so beaten and betrayed could ever rise to such heights again.

But he had little time to savor this triumph. His own situation was bad enough.

It was daylight topside—to be safe, he ordered that John be given a strong shot of sedative. John's intensity immediately faded, and he was left limp and dull-eyed, to Cosimano's relief.

He walked over to the KSKY speaker and tore it off the wall, vowing never to take the chance of allowing it in this cell again. A subordinate buzzed the intercom. "Priority call, Mr. Cosimano. It's the President."

Grim-faced and sweating, Cosimano stalked out and went to his office to take the call. His complexion went from pallid to livid as he listened to the words of his angry, half-panicked commander. He put down the phone just as three of his lieutenants burst into his office and looked at him with the faces of frightened boys. Cosimano ignored them as he sat drumming his fingers on his desk, his expression showing a sour abstraction.

"All right," he said at length, "we'll have the media and a dozen nut groups pounding at our gate within three hours, and three Congressional committees three days after. We'll have to let them in sooner or later. We'll transfer Avril to the North Dakota site tonight. Hunter can't have heard of it. Prepare an aircraft, and arrange to transfer all SMITE records at the same time. Before any civilian is allowed in these corridors, this installation must appear to be only a center for the study of the effects of isolation in long-term space flight."

"Yes sir, we know the drill."

The normal functioning of the SMITE base ended immediately, superseded by frantic preparation for its abandonment. Every phone line was tied up with incoming calls demanding explanations and verifications, and much of the SMITE staff was tied up making protests of ignorance and innocence. Records were packed or destroyed, hard drives were wiped, and in their place was put false data about experiments in sensory deprivation and its effect on man's internal timekeeping and emotional stability. Devices of outright torture were loaded onto a small transport waiting on the flight line. All the while the weather grew more oppressive, with ominous rumblings and towering cloud tops projecting over the Sacramento Mountains to the east. Everyone was anxious for nightfall to arrive so they could be rid of the silent but damning prisoner locked up five levels down.

After a long afternoon, the Sun at last disappeared behind the San Andres range. Just to be safe, Cosimano decided to wait for full darkness before moving Avril. That seemed to be the cue for the thunderstorms to pounce. They lashed the airfield with hard curtains of rain, while the nearby gypsum dunes glowed eerily from the frequent flashes of angry white lightning. But Cosimano would not be deterred—his prisoner would fly out tonight.

Down in the cell, Cosimano, wearing a drenched grey trench coat, presided over the preparations for transferring Sky Ranger.

"Shouldn't we give him something to wear?" asked a medical technician. "He's too weak to take into the storm in that hospital gown. If he gets soaked he could become hypothermic."

Cosimano frowned and considered. "Do we have anything for him?"

"Not really—not on the base. We could commandeer somebody's—"

"No, don't bother, I have the solution. Dress him in one of those ridiculous flight suits we took from his hideout. They're waterproof, and I'm sure he'll enjoy having a final opportunity to wear one."

His men complied, though they looked dubious at the prospect of arraying even this burnt-out shell of a man in the colors which had been a legend on their planet for more than a decade.

Getting John into the suit wasn't easy—he was limp and weak, and the suit was heavy and stiff. Their only advantage was that John had lost weight and didn't fill out the suit the way he used to. But there were some tight throats among them as they looked down at that black eagle silhouetted over a glittering sun. At Cosimano's instruction, they even fitted him with a headset.

"Shouldn't he be drugged?" asked a medical technician nervously.

"No need," said Cosimano. "It's fully established that Avril's power is Sun-related and is inactive after dark. However, we will manacle and hobble him to prevent him from bolting, should he summon the will and energy to attempt it. He is, I fear, a broken man."

As usual, John cooperated meekly and quietly with the preparations. Heavy steel chains were locked in place, binding his wrists and ankles, preventing him from moving at more than an awkward shuffle. At last Cosimano was satisfied that John was fully neutralized. Accompanied by a squad of men armed with light machine guns, he led John into an elevator which conveyed them to the base's top level.

Outside, they encountered a furious Nature, its wrath given form by wind-driven rain and sand. All was darkness except for the blurred aureoles of the arc lights shining on the plane, still a few hundred yards away. Beyond those few islands of artificial light was a roaring void. The billowing, menacing shapes of the storm clouds were picked out strobe-fashion by frequent lightning. Rippling tears of thunder often drowned the murmur of the jet's idling engines.

John turned his face toward the lightning, as though he were listening to someone speak.

The party pushed themselves through the rain towards the plane; dimly they saw a figure dash down its ramp and run in their direction. He pounded up to Cosimano and said, "Sir! The pilot says he absolutely cannot take off in this weather. The blowing sand would foul the engines. We must wait for the worst of the storm to pass."

"Blast!" spat Cosimano. "All right, we'll wait. But we'll sit right in the plane, and the minute this eases up we're gone. Tell him that."

"Yes, sir." The man dashed back to the plane.

Cosimano glanced at John to see how he was taking this, but as far as he could tell, his prisoner was ignoring the whole procedure. He stood there with his face tilted back, his hair slicked down with rain, and water running onto his shoulders. His eyes were closed, and his expression reflected rapture, even something resembling beatification.

This irritated Cosimano considerably. He gave John a sharp jab in the shoulder to get him moving again. John's eyes snapped open just in time to catch the reflected glare of a multiple lightning strike that hammered down nearby. The Sun-disk on his chest seemed to ignite in an instantaneous revelation.

When the bolts blinked out, John resumed shambling and clanking towards the waiting plane. Cosimano followed behind, his eyes locked on John's back. John kept his face turned skyward. Despite the chains, his stride grew steadier. He almost seemed to be growing inside that suit, or at least straightening up, though who could see anything reliably in this damnable rain and carnival spook-house lighting?

Another bolt crashed down; its light showed a tall figure which, although chained, was unbeaten, unbroken, and unbowed.

Something snapped in Cosimano at that moment. Rank fear surged into his mouth. "Shoot him!" he screamed wildly. "Kill him now!"

The six troopers fell back into a semicircle behind John, who ignored them, continuing toward the plane without looking back. The troopers shot back the bolts on their Uzis, and with a chain saw purr, six streams of bullets poured into John. He was slammed to the pavement and rolled over by the impact. A sharp metallic report rang counterpoint to the detonations of thunder, followed by another. Finally John lay there limp and motionless.

The clips in the weapons were emptied. The troopers and Cosimano remained motionless as they stared at their victim.

In the sudden weird silence, John rolled over and looked at the seven men with eyes like windows into a bright blue sky. He was on his feet, and the chains on his wrists and ankles were already broken.

Totally unnerved, the troopers turned and ran. Cosimano was left alone, trying to formulate some response to the impossibility before him. Finally he could do nothing more than shrilly deny the obvious. "This is impossible! You can't be doing this!"

John walked up to him with the graceful stride of a hunting tiger. "I owe it all to you, Remo," he said quietly. "The day-night cycle of my power never was intrinsic. It was just a device my unconscious came up with to insure that I wouldn't burn myself out by staying powered twenty-four hours a day. The Sun made a convenient time-piece—and it was also appropriate for me symbolically. But the power comes from in here—" he tapped his cranium—"and from everything else—" he made an all-inclusive gesture— "not from the Sun. Your drug therapy helped me bring the cycle under conscious control. And your revelation about Elise motivated me to take the final steps. I learned that if the power could be inhibited in the daytime, by drugs or by my own will, it could also be brought out at night. All I had to do was look at things the right way."

He stepped another pace forward, putting his face mere inches from Cosimano's stricken mask.

"So that's the favor you did me, Remo. Now, I don't have time to wallow in the misery you intended for me when you told me about Elise. Oh, I'm going to find her, or at least I'll find the person I thought was Elise, make no mistake about that. If you don't have her, I'm pretty sure I know who might. But in case you haven't noticed, strange and terrible things are going on in the world. I must stop them, if I can."

"The end times," muttered Cosimano. "And you are their harbinger."

John raised his eyebrows. "The end times? Yes, I suppose we must all rationalize these events according to our own experience of the world. Are you sure you have no idea where Elise—I mean, this other Elise—might be?"

Cosimano rolled his head from side to side, his eyes bulging, and he cried out in despair. "I don't know! That's the damnable thing! We didn't get her! Someone else got to her first! I've lost control. All decent people, we've lost control of the world. I can see it coming."

The unmistakable sincerity in Cosimano's words almost poleaxed John; he stood there stunned as Cosimano continued to whimper and babble. Finally John came back to his senses.

"Wandrei." John turned from his former tormentor and gathered himself.

"Wait!" cried Cosimano. "You aren't going to kill me?"

John relaxed and turned back to Cosimano. "No, and don't sound so disappointed. You told the truth. Remo, you've been picking on the wrong guy all along. I'm on the side of the angels. You trusted me to recognize the truth when you spoke it. I wish you'd do the same for me when I do as well."

And he turned away again, and hurled himself full into the face of the storm, which tried to strike him down with angry bolts of lightning, but to no avail.

John left Cosimano with a better impression of his state of mind than was really warranted. Discovering that he had been abandoned and betrayed by Elise—the real Elise—years ago was as crushing as anything he'd ever experienced. It left his heart feeling like a cold, dry well lined with stone. As for her replacement, this impostor...clearly, she must have been sent by someone to manipulate his emotions, and perhaps his very actions. But why? The only person he knew who had the resources and the perverse interest in him to do such a thing was Conrad Wandrei, but why would Wandrei goad John into attacking his own interests? And the woman herself? He had been far too close to her for too long to dismiss her as some sort of villainess. For all he knew, she was now in terrible danger. He would soon discover the truth.

From New Mexico on east, those few whose pleasure or necessity found them beneath the bare night sky, whether backpackers or burglars, amateur astronomers or the homeless, streetwalkers or poets, looked up startled at a sudden glass-rattling boom. It was somehow unlike the sonic booms caused by military aircraft—it had a certain presence, a portentous personality. It commanded attention and made people take notice. The most alert among them noticed a point of red light dwindling over the eastern horizon even as the shockwave rushed over them.

John Avril pushed himself through the stratosphere at hypersonic speed. The steel cuffs on his wrists and ankles glowed red from air friction, softened and brightened to yellow, until John was able to tear them like putty and cast them away.

He slowed to Mach 5 and looked around at an aerial beauty he'd all but forgotten in his years as a diurnal Sky Ranger. Around him was a realm of stars, a world entirely unlike the Sunlit heaven he knew so well. The Milky Way burned unnaturally bright, like a frozen pillar of glowing vapors cutting the sky. Below, a crescent moon cast a cold glow on cloud-ramparts that swept by like ocean waves. Even the land itself, where it was visible between banks of cloud, was picked out clearly enough by the light of Moon and stars. Apparently, if his vision could attain an eagle-like acuity to suit the brilliance of the day, so too could it expand to the light-grasp of an owl to suit the dimness of the night.

But this wasn't the time to revel in the newfound beauties of night flight. His course would carry him straight to Manhattan and the Murex Spire.

Almost by reflex he tuned his headset radio to KSKY. The news was dominated by the fearsome hurricane Violet. For several days the storm had crept north, paralleling the East Coast two hundred miles out to sea, but just as it seemed about to swerve east and end its threat it instead made an inexplicable 120° turn to the left. Now it was boring in towards the Outer Banks at sixty miles per hour, with winds exceeding two hundred miles per hour. According to the report, the storm's huge eye was just off the coast. There was no time to evacuate the thousands who inhabited the low-lying barrier islands. They seemed doomed to drown in the twenty-foot storm surge pushed ahead of the hurricane.

Now over Kentucky, John wrestled with his duty and his intentions. With an inarticulate cry he turned aside and headed for Hatteras. Whatever danger Elise was in, it must wait until he'd done whatever he could for the thousands who were in immediate peril. He climbed above the atmosphere and poured on awesome speed. In minutes the whole vast spiral of Violet lay spread out beneath him, luminous in the moonlight like a foreign galaxy, beautiful except for the ominous black hole at its center, the eye. John rolled on his side, yawed about to put his nose toward the eye, and cast himself into the center of that great fusion of the power of air and sea.

All around him, spinning cloud walls towered up until the stars were contained in a circular patch far overhead. It was like being in a well, except for the blistering forks of violet lightning that clawed out from the clouds. John plunged into the west side of the eye. Its screaming winds were nothing to him, but when he envisioned their effects on the lands that lay in their path he couldn't help but be awed. A storm like this wielded millions of times more energy than he himself controlled—for the first time he wondered what, if anything, he could do against it. And there was another odd thing about this storm, a disturbing thing. John loved storms as magnificent expressions of nature. In the past he'd sought them out, courted them, practically made love to them while carried about by their gales and updrafts. But this storm felt evil to him—evil, almost consciously malevolent, as though it knew what fragile beings lay in its path. He knew this conviction was more than just the influence of the storm's darkness and violence. For the second time that night the name of Conrad Wandrei crossed his mind.

He pushed onward, leaving the storm surge and the most devastating winds behind, though they'd catch up soon enough. Power was already out across the narrow islands of the Outer Banks. Cars were moving slowly over the two-lane bridges connecting Nag's Head with Okracoke and the mainland, though in places traffic was reduced to one lane by disabled cars blocking the road. John stooped on these, checked them for occupants, and then, as refugees watched with amazement, flipped them over the railing and into the water. He lifted off and continued south.

The people of Okracoke Island were most endangered; their only communication with the mainland was by ferry. Coming in over Okracoke village, John saw that one of the ferries had tried to leave a little too late. Heavily loaded with passengers, the winds had grabbed the vessel's tall, broad sides and pushed it against some dock pilings. There it stayed, with no manipulation of engines or rudder able to budge it. Half a mile away, monstrous waves were eating away the island on the Atlantic side, but if the ferry could escape into the more sheltered waters of Pamlico Sound, it should make its way to safety.

John dropped down and lit on the ship's railing, his back to the pilings. The hundreds of terrified faces on deck turned toward him, sending up a cry that cut through even the wailing of the wind. John looked to the bridge, where other faces looked down on him.

"Captain!" shouted John. "Full power to your engines! I'm getting you out of here!" He waited until a wave tilted the railing away from the pilings, then allowed himself to drop down between the hull and the pilings. The ship rolled back, knocking out his breath and pinning him with immense force. The people looking down at him sent up a moan. But when the ship rolled back again John braced his palms and his knees against the hull. The next roll could not flatten him again. Someday, when he had more time, he'd calculate how many tons of force the winds were exerting against the broad sides of this ship, but for now he only knew that he must overcome them, no matter how great they might be. It was a huge strain, and a frightening one, with the cold grey hull of the ferry always about to crush him into the dock.

Without the friction of contact with the pilings, the thrust of the ship's engines began to tell. It slowly gathered way while John fed it along. It pivoted against him, and the bow hit the pilings with a nasty thud, but the ship's momentum was in charge now, and it kept sliding along until it was finally free and clear. As the stern passed by, John half leaped and half flew back up to the railing, perching on it to catch his breath for a moment.

Instantly he was faced with a mob of sobbing, laughing, hysterical passengers, mostly women and children—the men of Okracoke evidently retained an old-fashioned maritime tradition. Even in the stormy darkness they could not mistake their rescuer. He seemed to carry a light of his own that was plain even in the fierce, warm rain.

"Sky Ranger, we thought you were dead!" cried a young boy.

John said, "I've thought that myself once or twice, but I'm all right."

"Were you captured? Imprisoned by the government, like the radio said?" asked a woman.

"No time to go into that now. But Washington hasn't seen the last of me—you can say so to anyone who asks. Now stand back!"

He sprang into the storm, a sight no one there would ever forget, and they sent cries of encouragement up after him.

Touring the islands at a low altitude, John grabbed at a wind-driven piece of plywood that slammed into him. It turned out to be a hand-painted protest sign. John read it in the garish lightning.

NO TORREON ON OUR SHORES: MUREX STAY HOME!

John flung the board away in disgust. It was becoming plain that he could do little here. If Wandrei was by some insane means behind this storm, his best chance of stopping it was to take the battle directly to its maker. Regretfully he climbed above the hurricane, leaving the keepers of the Graveyard of the Atlantic to make their way as best they could.

High above the influence of any storm, he forged his way north along the coast, all the while praying that Wandrei was in his lair. Soon he saw New York City, illuminating the cloud deck from below like a flashlight beneath a blanket. He dove beneath the clouds. Breaking through, the subtly changed aspect of Manhattan made him gasp.

The Murex Spire, previously notable mainly for its eccentric design, now dominated the island like a spike of evil. A weird glamour shimmered around it and over its surface, a quality of wrongness that made John's skin crawl. The buildings around it looked like slabs of charcoal in comparison to the shifting phosphorescence of the Spire.

Cautiously, John slowed to subsonic speed and approached the Spire. Wandrei, he was certain, was present, though he wondered if it was precisely the same Wandrei he had known.

Chapter Twenty Six

Somewhere in the redefined, indefinite spaces in the top of the Murex Spire, Conrad Wandrei sat thinking in a sprawling black armchair that rotated slowly in three axes in a purple void. He looked up from his meditations to behold a small figure glaring at him from the shadows across the room.

"Ah," he said. "Does your presence mean we can soon expect a visit from your lover?"

A boom rattled the windows before Elise could answer.

Wandrei made an easy gesture. "Of course. That would be John, arriving in town with his usual flair. I never thought for a moment that those government imbeciles could conquer him. Still, our friend is predictable. In a moment he'll come crashing dramatically through a window, here to snatch you away from my wicked clutches. I'd best prepare for his arrival."

A wall came into existence, and then others, until the space somewhat resembled the sybaritic office it had once been.

A chime sounded, announcing the arrival of an elevator car from below. Wandrei, slightly annoyed, turned his head to see who had arrived at this critical moment.

The door slid open. A blue projectile launched itself from the car, slamming into Wandrei with stunning force before he could think, sending him sailing end-over-end through the air. He fetched up hard against a huge outer window and shattered it. He was given no respite. The blue blur projected itself into his face and hauled him upright. Wandrei found himself looking into a fierce, Sun-bright gaze.

"Well, John, what's your business here tonight?" asked Wandrei lightly.

"Simple enough. I'm here for Elise."

"I won't insult your instincts by asking why you think I have her. What if I decide not to give her up?"

"Then I guess I'll just have to kill you."

"Oh, come now, I read the papers. You don't kill."

"What do you see on my hands?"

Wandrei looked down with difficulty at the fists which were so close to throttling him.

"Ah—could that be blood?"

"From those interesting creatures who wear your uniform down in the lobby. You'll get no chance to brew up more like them in whatever wizard's vat you've got hidden away. Killing and dying are unavoidable parts of life, Wandrei. See this bird on my chest? What do you think it does for a living, call out for pizza? When it has to, the eagle kills."

"Oh, I see. May I remind you that you're not actually an eagle? And you're vegan too, I believe. But before you crush my neck with your mighty talons, I'm to reveal the location of Miss Boutin."

"You can if you want to, but I'll find her anyway. Why not give yourself a break and tell me?"

Wandrei laughed dismissively. "All right, I'll play along with you. Have you tried simply looking around?"

John looked. He spied Elise huddled on a leather couch in the conversation pit, looking drawn but intact, wearing a filmy white dress. At the sight of her, all John's doubts dissipated. This *was* Elise. If he survived this encounter, he would find out later why Cosimano had conspired to lie about her.

"My compliments to you, John. She's not a bad-looking woman," said Wandrei. "I could hardly have done better myself."

John ignored this obvious attempt to infuriate him. His eyes met those of Elise, and a current of warmth and recognition flowed between them.

John said, "Elise. Are you all right?"

Elise sat up straighter. "I'm okay. Dr. Strange here has actually been fairly polite, except for dressing me up like this."

"Oh, please," said Wandrei. "I had nothing to do with the way she's dressed."

"What's going on here, Wandrei? You lured me here. What do you want?"

"Lured you? Actually I'd have preferred not to deal with you right now. Or ever, really. Your actions have been inconvenient to me now and then, but far more importantly, you've been my inspiration. I wouldn't be the man I am today if not for you."

"And what kind of a man is that?"

"That I will reveal in my own good time."

"You don't *have* good time," John growled.

"Actually, I do. Our chat has given me a moment to clear my head. You did surprise me, but now I'm ready to show you what I've learned from you, and how the student has surpassed the teacher."

An impalpable force grabbed John and flung him away, smashing him against the far wall. He didn't stay there long. Wandrei heard something like the chattering of an angry eagle; realized it was human speech, but spoken too fast for him to understand. John exploded from the wall toward him, once more a whistling blur. Some part of John struck Wandrei in the face. Wandrei saw a red film and felt disintegration, but in an instant he managed to pull himself back together again. John's blows kept coming, harder and faster, until they sounded like the demonic moan of an aircraft cannon, each landing with the force of a mortar shell. Wandrei's dismay gradually turned to glee. He was getting the hang of this quickly. John's motions seemed to slow as Wandrei attuned himself to this new level of speed. Each blow was less painful than the last as he learned to harden himself against physical damage, just as John did.

Wandrei laughed full into John's furious face. "Hang it up, Sky Ranger! I can do anything you can do! In fact, I can do anything you *can't* do!"

He vanished from John's grip, popping back into being on the far side of the room, still with the same manic grin on his face. "Didn't it ever occur to you that this would be a faster way to travel than flying? Of course, it doesn't quite have the same romance as the old up, up, and away, does it?" He vanished again even as John gathered himself to spring.

"Here I am!" Wandrei reappeared in a corner. "And here!" Another Wandrei popped up in another corner. "Here too!" A third materialized three feet in front of John. "Why is your thinking so linear, John? Is there any reason someone like you or me can't occupy a given time more than once?"

John launched a fist that nearly exceeded Mach One at the end of its swing, but its target had faded before it could land.

"Don't group me in with you, Wandrei!"

"Why not, John?"

John looked for the source of the voice. A huge version of Wandrei's face floated in one of the mirrored walls. "We're just the same, John, except, I think, for a few blind spots on your part."

"You're losing it, Conrad. You don't know what you're talking about. End this now while you still can."

Mocking laughter invaded the very spaces of John's ears. "Oh ho, what is it now, mighty hero? Can't stand the thought of not being the only person in the world with advanced awareness?"

John yelped out a laugh of his own. "'Advanced awareness!' Is that what you're calling it? Wandrei, you pathetic infant, I'm not aware of anything more than your need to have somebody change your diaper."

John's surroundings went fluid; the confines of the room melting into unreality like the scenery in an animated cartoon. He found himself adrift in a purple void in which images of normal places and objects flickered in his peripheral vision, vanishing when he tried to look directly at them.

Wandrei, nattily attired in a charcoal-grey business suit, appeared before him, apparently standing on some invisible surface. "You know, John, this is a very hostile environment I've dreamed up here. Poisonous atmosphere and hard radiation. If I can just yank away your power for a second, *pffft!* It's the demise of Sky Ranger."

John's gaze was steady and confident. "But you know you can't do that, don't you? If I didn't have my act together better than that, I would have been finished a long time ago."

"Yes, I suppose I must give the angel his due. Well, don't think I'm at a loss. Since I can do anything and you won't, I can afford to take my time with you."

Four huge, scaly hands, each massive enough to moor a battleship, reached out from some unseen hole in purple-space to grasp John by the wrists and ankles. John fought them, but they were immovable. He applied his flight impulse, but that only threatened to tear him apart. He sagged in their grip and glared at Wandrei, his eyes like two round skylights.

"I think I've come up with a fitting way of destroying you, if it comes to that, John." Wandrei raised his hand. Between thumb and forefinger he grasped a bead of impossible, searing radiance, a pea-shape so far beyond mere brilliance that John turned away and squeezed his eyelids shut.

"Do you know what this is? It's a bitty-bit of the inside of a neutron star, awfully hot and terribly heavy. If I release this I think I can dissolve you in it, as I doubt even a Sun-god like you could deny. See?"

Wandrei flicked the pellet at John. It entered his right upper arm and passed through with no more resistance than if John had been a hologram. John's grimace deepened to one of pain as he looked at his arm. Steam and a fog of blood jetted from the tunnel bored through bone and muscle, as the tissue expelled the heat absorbed during the passage of the neutronium pellet.

"You'll get that damage under control, won't you?" asked Wandrei. "You can do that much at least. That's just to illustrate what I can do to you whenever I'm ready. But really, I'd rather release you unharmed, if you'll permit me. I'd much rather we part on terms of a wary neutrality, if we can't be friends."

"Don't listen to him, John! I knew you'd come for me, but I was hoping you'd be in a better position to get me out of here," said Elise.

"Yes, I know what you mean. Looks like Conrad has me well in hands."

"Ugh. How can you joke about this? Those hands—they look like they're alive!"

John turned his head to study the massive, malformed claws that gripped him. "Yes, I suppose they are, after a fashion."

"Where do things like that come from, John?"

"From my imagination!" cried Wandrei triumphantly.

John shot him a look of irritation. "Oh, you pathetic dope. You think your mind is so vast that things like this just spring into being to serve your whims? Give us a break and shut up for a minute. Please restrain your gloating while we talk."

He turned back to Elise, who stared at him in wonder, hardly believing his audacity in the face of his helplessness. "Oh, John. None of this has turned out quite the way I hoped it would."

John laughed loudly and unconcernedly. "I suppose not."

Elise's perplexity took her over. "John, what's wrong with you? This is serious! I don't understand what's so funny."

John's mirth subsided, to be superseded by a bright-eyed glance that cut through the space between them. "Sweetheart, it's like this. I don't know what this black-and-violet bubblehead intends for me—I'm not sure just how far gone he is. But now that he's got me, I'm counting on him to let you go eventually." With that remark, John

shot Wandrei a warning look, as if promising dire consequences if Wandrei failed to fulfill this expectation. Then
John turned his attention back to Elise. His expression for
her grew even more intense, more reassuring.

"Whatever happens to me, I want you to remember, *I'm
all right*. I've already passed the test. Nothing Conrad can
do can try me the way I've been tried already. Nothing he
can do can destroy the part of me that really matters. He'd
have to destroy more than the universe to do that."

A disparaging snort from Wandrei ended their conversation. "Don't talk about me as if I were a child, Sky Ranger.
If you go, so does she. Don't you realize that?"

Elise screamed as a wall of blue-white flame washed
over John, dissolving his flight suit, annihilating the wall
behind him, blasting through the wall of the Spire itself,
and erupting into the night air as a fearsome, roaring plume
that froze the heart of every person in Manhattan.

And leaving John, seared and smoking, still in the grip
of those inhuman hands, which now terminated in some
unseeable direction beyond the perceptions of the human
mind. John opened his eyes and speared Wandrei with the
defiance of a trapped eagle.

"John, why do you look so outraged at what I've
done?" asked Wandrei ingenuously, his anger as transient
as a child's tantrum.

"Because you've insulted nature, you monster," interrupted Elise hotly. "Because you've made your madness
into reality!"

Wandrei glanced at her incredulously. "Don't make
your puppet answer for you, John. What do you think you
do each time you launch yourself skyward on one of your
righteous crusades? Somehow, somewhere, you learned

what I too have discovered—that reality is malleable, that it can be manipulated by a mind attuned to its ways. What a scowl! You know I'm right, and you can't stand it."

Elise sat back, looking dismayed and confused.

"And what will you do with all your grand power, Conrad? More hurricanes? More plagues and volcanoes?" demanded John.

"Oh, no, no, no. Those were only tests, only games and tricks meant to get back at people who've frustrated me in the past. An outburst of childish vindictiveness, I'll admit. No, I've got bigger plans. The time is ripe for a United Europe, a New Roman Empire, and I fancy myself as its founder, a new Napoleon, a stronger Alexander. After that, who knows? The fundamental nature of life on Earth is now open to reinvention. It's hardly ideal the way it is, is it? Yes, who knows what I might do?"

"Who indeed. Conrad, take a close look at yourself. You can't handle this power. It's too much for you. Give it up before it's too late. Before it drives you mad."

"Hypocrite!"

A new force lashed over Sky Ranger, a crimson light which was not fire or heat, but a physical blow, a light like a battering ram. Outside, those gaping up from the street fled for cover as debris rained down from the thunderbeam that flashed through the heavens.

"Sky Ranger, you sanctimonious loser. You know the nature of the power we share. If a psychic researcher were to put a name to it, he'd call it psychokinesis. Only, for some reason, you've chosen to internalize the power. You fling yourself through the air, impel your limbs to feats of strength, even hold the atoms of your body together to defy heat and other punishment. But I've gone beyond that. I see no limits to this mastery of reality, and I choose to impose none upon myself. Tell me, what property of John Avril makes him fit to control this power, while the miserable Conrad Wandrei must not? What undiscovered facet of your rather paltry biography makes you such a superior person? You know I'm only doing what any person could do, with the right way of thinking."

"No, that's not true." said John quietly.

Wandrei said nothing, waiting for John to continue.

"You're right about me, Conrad. I was a loser...a nasty, confused, misdirected mess. A big disappointment to myself and to most everybody who knew me. If I had somehow gained this power then, I would have messed up just as badly as you have, probably worse. Even now I've got all the power I can responsibly handle—maybe even a bit more than that. I'm just a man, not fit to play God. But to get to this stage, I had to pass through a trial you haven't even considered, despite your spectacularly successful study of metaphysics and philosophy."

Wandrei's hands came clawing up. His face assumed a look of torment, as if despite all he had done, some final secret was missing, the lack of which was destroying him. "What was this test?" he cried desperately.

"Never mind, Wandrei," said John sternly. "I doubt you'd be willing to submit to it anyway."

"I will. I must!"

"Very well. You have to die, Conrad. Or at least be willing to die. Place yourself in a situation in which you expect to die, but not out of despair. Maybe you die. Maybe you are born again. Die to the world, be reborn. See what happens from there."

Thunderstruck, Wandrei stared up at John with his mouth hanging open. The flow of thoughts through his fevered mind was almost palpable. Gradually his amazement faded, to be replaced by a crafty humor.

"Are you saying you have died and been resurrected?"

John shook his head wearily. "Not literally, maybe. I'm not sure. It was a spiritual rebirth which I cannot possibly explain or illuminate for you."

But Wandrei might as well not have heard. "My, and you thought *I* had delusions of grandeur! There you are, Sky Ranger, hung up to dry, and you try to convince me to kill myself as your only hope for salvation. If you weren't such a weakling we could have this confrontation on equal terms."

John shook his head sadly. "No, Conrad. Even now, I know my limitations. No human being is fit to wield the kind of power you have taken up. If I were to take on such godlike powers I'd soon degenerate, even as you have. If I must lose my life to save my soul, I will do so gladly."

"Ah, such nobility," said Wandrei in admiration. "Truly, any man could be proud to have such words as his epitaph. But maybe there's still hope for you. That cooperative creature who's holding you—its strength is limitless. It is infinitely stronger than you have ever shown yourself to be. It could tear this planet in half. It could tear you, even you, to pieces. And it will. It will, unless you are willing to step up your game, to assume power of the same magnitude as mine, if wielded a bit less imaginatively. It's your choice to make."

"Having a giant monster tear me apart isn't even slightly imaginative, Wandrei."

For a moment Wandrei was taken aback. "You're right, it isn't. All right then, let me try an experiment I've been thinking about for a while now. This will definitively be novel, though with the disadvantage that if it succeeds I'll never know it."

Wandrei raised his arms like a conductor about to launch into a symphony. John tensed, expecting flame or some crushing force. His captor stood before him, hands poised and trembling, a grin of anticipation on his pale, bright-eyed face. He held that pose for what seemed like minutes, tantalizing, tormenting.

Abruptly Wandrei flung down his hands, flipped a negligent gesture at John, and turned away. John watched in confusion as Wandrei ambled down into the conversation pit to sit beside Elise, giving her a charming smile.

John was taken by surprise, so much so that he didn't even hear what Wandrei said to Elise as he sat there beaming at her. In fact, he was unable to hear them. His surroundings seemed to go dim and grainy; even his thoughts felt distant and muffled. A cold chill settled over his mind. It took minutes of concentration simply to speak.

"What's happening to me?"

He was shocked at how small and remote his own voice sounded. The two shadows conversing on the couch appeared not to have heard him at all. He called out again and again, but it seemed a lifetime before he got any response, and when it came it was like listening to the last vibration of a bell struck an hour before.

"Oh, are you still hanging on? You should just relax and let it happen; it'll be easier that way. Or—stop me."

"What—what are you doing to me?"

"I'm going to blot you out of all reality. In a few minutes it will be as though you never existed. Elegant, don't you agree?"

John moaned as a terrible soul-deep fear overwhelmed him. His mind, his self, his very existence, all were crumbling. Images and dreams bubbled up through the broken structure of his consciousness—dreams of a world in which he had never been. His mother; what kind of a life would she have had without him? What about Elise, cast into the power of Wandrei with no valid memory or means of resistance? And what of the thousands—the many thousands—of lives he had saved as Sky Ranger... all lost? He felt tears trying to form in some far corner of infinity as he considered them all. He foresaw a universe in which Sky Ranger had never soared with the eagles. He would be lost, even to himself.

Another tiny voice broke through the turmoil: "No! John, don't go! If Wandrei is right, if anyone can do what he does, defend yourself! Fight him! Don't go!"

For some reason he could no longer see Elise, not even dimly. though Wandrei was still visible as a vague black form.

John shook his head, or thought he did; he cried out, though he had no way of knowing if any other being were still capable of hearing his words.

"I can't, I can't. I've fought too hard, tried too long, to give in to temptation now. If I save myself, I'll become as bad as Wandrei. No, I'll be worse, in time. I can't. I have to go."

Now grief was almost all he had left. Even now, he could sense the doors which Wandrei had opened. Unlike Wandrei, he knew how to open those doors instead of battering them down. But those doors must stay closed to him—on that he must not waver.

"Elise! Try to remember me... even if it's only as a flutter in your heart... when you see... the blue of the sky... "

There was a shock—a blinding light, as of rebirth—and a tingling of his whole being, as though body and mind had been asleep and were coming back with a vengeance. Full awareness flooded John's mind. He hung in the grip of the giant hands, as real and solid as he'd ever been.

But he had no inclination to celebrate, for the scene before him was so profound that he had no awareness of himself. He squinted into what seemed a focus of supernal light hovering in the pit, before which Wandrei cowered, his every shadow blasted away and laid bare.

In the dazzle John's vision began a swift re-adaptation to its daylight acuity. Presently he was able to peer into the heart of the gorgeous radiance which informed every atom in the room. There he was awed to discover Elise, standing tall and wrathful, a vision of Athena, or of Artemis at the hunt.

Her voice rang out like steel bells, lashing over Wandrei in waves of cold fury. "Conrad Wandrei! You monster! You think a person like me is too stupid to listen to what you say? You say anyone can do what you do. Well, I'm anyone! Maybe John is too pure to defend himself, but I love him, and how dare you threaten him! Here's what I have for you!"

John cried out and fell back. Something had passed from Elise to Wandrei—something non-physical; a force or a feeling of some sort, indefinable but awesomely powerful, more than John could easily tolerate, even at a distance. Wandrei shrieked and raised his hands to defend himself, looking as if he'd just seen a mirror into the horror of his own soul. In sheer terror for his life he rallied. The air around Elise became somehow a thing of dire menace, radiating a dread power that beat upon her being and pushed inward upon her light. Her radiance became yet more intense as it contracted around her. John lost all sense of what was happening. Elise somehow fought clear and counterattacked, but to John the universe became an interplay of meaningless forces acting in unknown ways. He was certain that the sensory manifestations he beheld were no more indicative of what was really happening than a blip on a radar screen resembled a flight of bombers. He was aware only of intertwined yet dissimilar lights, competing against each other with deadly strength. Only when he forced himself to see into the conflagration with a sense beyond sight did he behold Elise, and then his heart was almost stopped by awe and admiration, for Elise waged this battle as an apotheosis of love, her true self stripped bare.

And then there was Wandrei, a tangle of confused and conflicting forces, motivated mainly by greed, envy, and fear. John couldn't imagine how such a man could prevail against Elise's purity of purpose, but Wandrei had more experience with omnipotence, even if he couldn't match Elise's fury and passion. It seemed that this battle, waged on some metaphysical level, wasn't the preferred stage for Wandrei, whose mind was still rooted in the material, and obsessed with the wealth of the world.

And then it was over. Wandrei lay defeated, his body ravaged, hair burned away, skin smoking and blistered. Elise stood over him, shining, untouchable, immaculate.

"Well, John," said Wandrei in a pained, shaky voice, "I have to admit, that was a most impressive display."

"What are you raving about now, Wandrei?" demanded John. "That was Elise, every bit of it." Even as the Sun rose outside, John felt an overpowering indignation and wrath flame up within him. He saw a great eagle flying before the solar disk. He screamed, demanding something extraordinary from his body, and got it. With an explosive effort he brought his hands together before him. The alien claws which had gripped him exploded into fragments. From some dismal corner of existence he heard a wail, and the grip on his feet was released as the thing that owned them retreated to its own domain.

Wandrei sat up slowly. He stared at John for a long while, his mouth agape, until gradually some measure of clarity returned to his eyes.

"I think I'm beginning to understand now, John. I owe you an apology. All this time I thought you were a hypocrite, but I see now that I was wrong. You are not a hypocrite. You are simply delusional. I never imagined this, but you actually believe that this luminous creature of yours is Elise Boutin. The real Elise Boutin. Or a real person at all."

John glared at him, daring him to continue.

"Don't you see, John? You were so obsessed with that woman, so desperate for her love, that when she rejected and abandoned you, you created a new one, a projection, an image from your own mind. A perfected image, an ideal muse, always there when you most needed and expected her, always encouraging you, when it was really you, encouraging yourself with a different voice. A woman, a lover, far superior to the poor, real, ordinary Elise Boutin, who could never live up to your lofty expectations. You made a projection so perfect that others could see her too, speak with her, even touch her. And through her, you could exert the awesome power you needed to save yourself from me. It's really quite a wonderful feat, but to judge from the pain I see in your eyes, I'm sorry to have been the man to reveal all this to you. Truly I am. It must be a terrible thing to realize that the great beacon of love that shone from your heart for all those years was directed at someone who did not exist. Such a waste of all that light. The world is drenched in absurdity. Everyone is ridiculous in their own way, and even you are no exception. I don't know whether to laugh, or cry along with you."

Stricken, filled with a misery he had never imagined, John turned to Elise, whose fire had dimmed.

"I'm sorry, John! I tried to be real for you. I almost was. You almost made me real, body, mind, and soul. You almost created me."

"Stay with me, Elise. I don't care who or what you are. Please stay."

"I can't, John. Now that you know the truth, you can't hold on to me anymore. I have to go now. Goodbye."

And so she faded away, leaving a gap in the universe that would never again be filled. Her sudden, unrecoverable absence was the most terrible thing John had ever seen or felt.

"Elise. I loved her so much." John felt a cold void open within him, filled only with the knowledge that he was alone, had always been alone, and would always be alone. Failing to find a love in the real world, he had created one in his own mind, and tricked himself into believing in it. Was any man ever a bigger fool?

The whole, vast, towering structure of the ego of Sky Ranger crumbled within him.

Wandrei stood up and brushed himself off. Already he looked better. He would soon recover from John's assault. John could not bring himself to care very much.

"Who are you really mourning right now, John? The real woman, busy with painting her garage door and trying to get her pre-baby figure back? Or your loving, imaginary companion of many years?"

John did not reply.

"I can tell you where she lives, if you like. The real Elise, I mean."

"No." John could say no more. In a daze, he wandered over to a great gap where the building's wall had been blown out, exposing the chamber to the chill dawn air. The sky looked weirdly unnatural, seething with a dark purple energy.

Wandrei came over to stand beside him, looking out as well.

"I can no longer use this power," said John in a dull tone.

"Well, if I had known how easy it would be to neutralize you, I might have done it long ago. I for one will not stop using the power. It's too magnificent. My thoughts dissolve, and I find myself within the wheels of the world, manipulating them as suits my fancy, forcing them if they resist. I have mastered so many things."

"But you've never used the power to fly?"

"Fly? Like you? Like Superman? No, John, I've never flown. That's a comic book vision of power. A child's vision of power."

"I'm glad to hear that."

John placed his hand on Wandrei's back and pushed. Wandrei fell. John leaned out to watch his silent fall, idly wondering if he would recover from the shock in time to save himself. He felt a twinge of pity, but only a twinge.

An asymmetrical red flower bloomed on a sloping ledge three hundred feet below.

John watched for a long time, half expecting Wandrei to resurrect himself somehow, but nothing happened.

The sky, still flush with the pinks and golds of dawn, brightened and returned to normalcy. To John Avril it looked as remote and unattainable as some distant cluster of galaxies. Sunlight dazzled him and made it difficult for him to see, unless that was more the effect of his tears. He sagged down, weeping as he had not wept since he was a child, a grief of inconsolable, hopeless loss.

After another long while he sighed, returned to the elevator, and departed.

Chapter Twenty Seven

The wondering world heard nothing from Sky Ranger for three days. At the end of that time identical videocassettes appeared at the offices of all major TV networks, who lost no time broadcasting their message.

The poorly-lit video showed a grim and haggard-looking John Avril standing in some dusty shack. And it was indeed John Avril, not Sky Ranger, for the famous flight suit was nowhere to be seen.

"This is John Avril. Many of you are wondering what has happened to me lately. Many people swear I was trying to pull the world down around mankind's ears, but I know there are a few of you out there who believed in me. I'm inviting those few to assemble on the Washington Mall, one week from today, at noon. I'm specifically inviting those who don't believe that money is a fit thing to worship; those who know that we can get by without waste and greed and be at least as happy, and those who revere the life of this planet and want it to endure, even at the expense of 'progress' and 'development' and 'commerce'. Go to the Mall. This is supposed to be a free country; let's see if your government can tolerate your presence in that great public place. Meet in front of the Air and Space Museum. There will be an announcement. Goodbye for now."

Then John could be seen fumbling with the off-screen controls of his video camera, and the message was over.

The world buzzed and throbbed with speculation and guesswork for the next week. Some thought the Sky Ranger was likely to announce his retirement; others were certain he would proclaim himself king of the world.

The President declined to forbid anyone from assembling on the Mall on the appointed day. He approved only a token crowd-control and security force, as he dismissed the possibility that large numbers of people would turn out on short notice to hear the ravings of an infamous criminal and madman like John Avril. His aides were far less sanguine in their view of the situation.

And well that they were.

The Sun's first light flowed over the monuments of Washington like rose water on the appointed day, a sharp and blustery November morning with amber clouds tumbling low over the city.

The light shone on the faces of the hundreds of thousands who thronged the Mall, with still more pouring in, until by mid-morning there was a solid belt of people from the Lincoln Memorial to the steps of the Capitol. They'd come from all corners of the continent, and from every foreign land whose politics allowed quick passage to the United States. To be sure, not all were supporters of Sky Ranger, but those who weren't were silenced by the numbers and the emotional intensity of those who wore the Sun-and-Eagle emblem and scanned the skies, even though the Sun was still far from its apex.

The D.C. Police and various agencies of the government were dismayed and apprehensive. The only way they could hope to disperse such a crowd would be by sending in massive forces authorized to employ the most ruthless riot tactics—tear gas, armored vehicles, rubber bullets. They were prepared to do so if necessary, but only if they were also prepared to brave the implacable eyes of the thousands of cameras, both commercial and private, in the hands of that so far quiet and ruly mob. They could only pray that they stayed that way, and that Sky Ranger, if he had the nerve to appear, wouldn't incite his followers to a rampage.

Many thought that Sky Ranger would indeed need a lot of nerve to appear, for SMITE had not been idle. Under the command of a deputy (Remo Cosimano having inexplicably resigned from his job), SMITE had ringed Washington with the most powerful air defenses ever to defend a Western city. Radar trucks and orbiting AWACS planes supplemented the coverage of the powerful radars at the many military bases in the area, creating a curtain of microwaves over DC and a hundred miles beyond. These were supplemented by acoustic and infrared sensors designed to detect airborne objects in rapid motion. Radios were tuned to short wavelengths to pick up radio reflections from any ion trail Sky Ranger might leave behind if he were to approach at a meteoric speed.

To attack whatever might be detected by these sensors, SMITE had used emergency powers to order half the fighter squadrons in the United States relocated to the DC area. All were on maximum alert and ready to fly on three minutes notice. The city was also ringed with banks of radar-guided surface-to-air missiles. SMITE could lace the air with so many of these that Sky Ranger would hardly fly in any direction without bumping into one of them. To top it all off, several prototype beam weapons from SMITE and naval research programs had been brought into the area on a crash basis. These could project infrared lasers powerful enough to blast through six inches of steel in a tenth of a second, their beams nimbly aimed by gimbaled mirrors.

That was SMITE's land-based defense. At sea, three carrier battle groups swarmed in the waters east of the

Delmarva Peninsula, weapons tipped with nuclear war-heads. Orbiting radar planes searched the heavens for any hint of the elusive Sky Ranger. The commanders of this deadly fleet were tense and dry-mouthed, but several high officials in Washington dearly hoped that Sky Ranger would choose to approach by sea.

The morning advanced and warmed slightly, but the wind still had a raw edge to it. People were grateful for the radiant warmth that the occasional sunbeams provided.

Tension and anticipation soared as the Sun neared the meridian. For a while there was a swelling outcry every time someone caught the glint of a distant fighter. After a half-dozen such false alarms the murmuring of the crowd gained a note of doubt, as the sky failed to reveal the flashing blue-and-white form they craved to see. No bird, no aircraft, no bit of drifting fluff went unseen by the millions of eyes that scanned the heavens unceasingly.

As the Sun touched the highpoint of its daily course, ignoring the human conventions of time zones and the equation of time, a man emerged from the museum. He was not especially tall, but he stood straight and walked with confidence. His hair was white and sparse and his face was leathery. He wore a tan suit that, while new, was a little out of date. His eyes were keen but his expression was sad and troubled.

He approached and mounted the podium that had been erected by NASM near the tall sculpture in front of the museum, a narrow spire surmounted by radial objects like sparse dandelion heads. The murmur of the crowd diminished as it gradually realized that someone was seeking their attention.

The man tapped the microphone and spoke with a coal-country accent.

"Good afternoon, everyone. My name's Eric Hunter. I'm a former Air Force general and someone who a former President once put in charge of trying to spy on Sky Ranger. I know you're all hoping to see and hear from the man himself here today, but that's not going to happen, you'll have to settle for me. Sorry for your disappointment. But Sky Ranger—John Avril—gave me a message to read to you all. It's long, but I'm going to read every word, just as he wrote it, and hope that my voice holds out."

Hunter produced some papers and frowned at them.

"Here we go. John says, Greetings to the people of Earth. Thanks for coming out today, those few of you who see things my way."

The crowd affirmed that with a prolonged roar that helped shake the last few leaves off the trees.

When it subsided, Hunter continued. "You've wondered what happened to me recently, and especially what went on at the Murex building just a few nights ago. I'll make it short; you can ferret out the details yourselves. I was captured and held prisoner by a secret U.S. Government agency called SMITE. I escaped, and I believed that Conrad Wandrei, the late CEO of Murex Energy Systems, had kidnapped a friend of mine to use as a hostage against me. I confronted him at his headquarters and discovered I was very wrong about that. I choose not to go into detail about what happened after that, except to say that yes, I killed Wandrei, to spare this planet a fate I will not describe. If I hadn't, you would all by now be slaves and victims of a power more terrible than any of you can, or should, imagine. That's the blood I have on my hands. I spilled it willingly, and a great danger was averted. I do not intend to submit myself to the system of justice that prevails in this country, such as it is.

"But I don't expect to escape all consequences for my recent actions, however right or wrong they may have been. My place on this planet has become untenable. I know that many governments, as well as some private interests, will not rest until I am destroyed or permanently chained. There is no refuge on this planet that can shelter me for long. Therefore, I've chosen the only remaining alternative, a hard choice, but one that offers my only chance for survival. I must leave the Earth forever."

Hunter awaited a reaction. When none seemed forthcoming, he continued.

"No other planet in the Solar System can sustain me. I'll have to seek a new home in another star system altogether. And no, I don't have some kind of warp drive that can carry me to the stars in a few hours. I can't even survive in space for more than a day or so at a time. But that's a day or so of my personal, subjective time. I hope you're all familiar with the theory of relativity, or this next part's going to lose you. My only chance is to accelerate to close to the speed of light, which will dilate time and make it seem to me as if I'm going much faster than I really am, enabling me to reach a neighboring star in only hours of subjective time. But to anyone watching from the outside, I'll be crawling between the stars at less than the speed of light, and it will take me years to reach even the nearest. Five years from now, or maybe ten or fifteen, you might look at the night sky and wonder if I found some cosmic island to harbor me. And I'd better be smart and lucky in my choice of stars—if I don't find an Earth-like world at the one I select, I might as well hang it up, because I probably won't have the strength to try another."

Hunter felt doubt and disbelief radiating from the crowd—disbelief that Sky Ranger, their great hero, could flee the planet, ignominiously running away, just when they expected him to unify them and lead them as an army dedicated to a new way of life on Earth. Disillusionment hung over the vast crowd like a pall.

Sensing this, Hunter squared his jaw and continued on.

"This isn't a lecture on environmentalism or social justice. Most of you already know what's right; so do many of the greed-mongers who are benefiting from the plunder—they just enjoy their loot too much to care. It's now up to you to make the changes in society that I tried to impose. You can do it a lot more smoothly and painlessly than I could have, because you *are* the society, while I was just an outlier, a man marginally connected to the world, just one pushy guy who tried to drag the world kicking and screaming into a new ethic of responsibility. Here's the best advice I can give you: look for your life inside yourself. You don't need gasoline or plastics or weapons to live the most adventurous and wonderful kind of life possible—you only need what little it takes to hold body and soul together. Simplify your lives. The highest experiences in human life are available to anyone who makes the search. Material wealth is just a distraction to those who seek the truth that pervades the universe and everyone who is a part of it. Look for that, and your guilt and doubt will fade. Eventually the Earth will grow green and clean around you."

Hunter studied the crowd closely, wondering if John's words, which seemed so fuzzy and naive to him, had made any impact. But the mood of the crowd was opaque.

"Goodbye, people of Earth. By the time you hear this message, I will be gone. Goodbye."

Hunter folded his papers, cleared his throat, and looked around. "Thank you for listening. While I personally disagree with some of the things John did, especially lately, I respected him as the man with the highest integrity I ever witnessed, and also as a friend. To him I say, wherever he is, go with God, carry with you our prayers and our good will, and may the stars be kind to you. That's all I have to say."

Hunter turned and re-entered the museum, parts of which were like a museum of his own past. He sought out the director, who happened to be an old colleague who also happened to have ventured to the Moon long before, and had a long talk with him.

The crowd scarcely moved for long minutes. Many were thoughtful, some were stunned, others cried quietly at the knowledge that never again would they see a man hurl himself at the heavens like Hermes returning to Olympus. Suddenly much mystery and wonder had fled the world. Yet others saw farther, and knew that whatever his nature, Sky Ranger was a product of the world, so that whatever wonder had been in him must be inherent in the earth and sky and waters around them, and in themselves. They looked at each other with a new awareness.

The crowd dispersed quietly, diffusing back into every corner of the world, much to the relief of the civil authorities in Washington DC.

Yet to the rulers of the world's nations, this was an ambiguous day. True, the great gadfly had removed himself and would annoy them no more. But the more farsighted among them awaited with apprehension the rise of a new way of thinking, one which would oppose the way men had run the world's affairs for centuries, and which would lead to consequences unimagined.

This group of farsighted leaders did not include the President of the United States, who went about his business beaming with enhanced joviality, at least until he tried to launch the rebuilding of America's petrochemical industry with a program of billions in low-interest loans to the headless, foundering Murex, only to encounter massive public outrage and resistance.

A few days later, the President's mood was further blackened when Remo Cosimano turned up on television with graphic videos and blunt talk about his former work at SMITE.

KSKY went off the air. The world had suddenly become a more dangerous place for those whose path took them too soon to the brink of death.

Chapter Twenty Eight

2055

As usual, Christopher Lane found himself slightly at odds with his son Neil when he took the boy to visit a museum. As a space engineer, Chris Lane was primarily interested in the exhibits relating to pragmatic matters, especially the ongoing space projects in which he was personally involved. He also enjoyed making an occasional salute to the machines that had started it all—the Wright Flyer, the Apollo 11 command module, Skylab—and now NASM boasted a major new exhibit, its most spectacular yet—Space Shuttle *Discovery*, a survivor of the unlucky fleet of five, now displayed in a new wing cantilevered over Independence Avenue.

Yet Neil, having never visited NASM before, had other priorities, which his father was willing enough to accommodate. Chris clearly recalled his own excitement when another NASM addition had opened, back when his own boyhood infatuation with the legend of Sky Ranger had been at its peak. Thus, with good grace and patience, he subordinated his own desires to Neil's bright-eyed anticipation as they approached the portal to the John J. Avril Wing of the National Air and Space Museum.

The Avril Wing, opposite the *Discovery* Wing, was suspended from the Mall side of the original structure. Its most famous feature was a life-size statue in brilliant metal, a figure of Sky Ranger, poised looking skyward, as he might have before he was forever lost to the sight of anyone on Earth.

Neil ran to the railing around the statue and wormed his way through the crowd. His dad followed more sedately, standing back and studying the likeness before him with the sort of detached affection he felt for King Arthur or Dave Bowman.

The statue was lit by broad, sparkling daylight, for it was located at the far end of the wing, and the walls, ceiling, and even parts of the floor around it were transparent. The statue was cunningly made— parts of its surface were covered in gold, bronze, steel, and some bluish alloy, to suggest the natural coloration of Sky Ranger and his flight regalia. In a bit of sculptural realism seldom seen since the days of classical Greece, the eyes were formed from white moonstone and blue topaz, adding greatly to the impression that the gleaming figure might at any moment erupt and launch itself into the clouds. For the statue was not confined to the building—above it yawned an oculus, an aperture into the open air which was never closed, summer or winter, rain or shine. Often a stiff winter breeze found its way through, and those who chose to endure it wondered how the winds of the stratosphere must have felt to the man whose memory they'd come to honor.

At length Neil had his fill of gazing at the famous statue, and he and his father wandered off to examine the other Sky Ranger exhibits. There were artifacts from Sky Ranger's many exploits, including the Lunar Rover which had served as an astronaut carry-all during his rescue of the Apollo 24 crew, retrieved from its looping Earth-Moon orbit just twenty years ago. There were models and images detailing Sky Ranger's association, unfortunately cut off at its peak, with the old National Aeronautics and Space Administration. There was a huge world map, sprinkled with color-coded lights to show where Sky Ranger had saved lives over the years, with small holos showing reconstructions of particularly difficult or impressive rescues. It seemed that Antarctica was the only continent where he'd never found it possible to preserve a human life that would otherwise have been lost.

A black tank displayed the nearest stars in three dimensions, while a solemn-voiced recorded narrator discussed them and speculated on which of them Sky Ranger might have tried to reach. While the narrator didn't rule out Avril's chances of finding a suitable world, no listener came away with a sense of optimism. The basic properties of the planets circling all these nearest stars were now known. None offered much hope as an abode of men.

Most surprisingly, there were extensive exhibits about Sky Ranger's career as an outlaw, including the actual "walnut" trap in which he'd been captured, as well as the broken manacles from which he'd later escaped.

Having taken all this in, Chris and Neil entered a small theater where a continuous 3D loop discussed those aspects of Sky Ranger and his work which were still relevant to them and their times.

A soft-voiced female narrator said, "The long-term effects of John Avril's message of environmental awareness did not become fully apparent until a decade after his departure from Earth. In the immediate aftermath of his loss, commercial and government interests scrambled to resume all the wasteful, damaging economic activities that Sky Ranger had interrupted. However, Murex Energy Systems, with its leader killed and discredited and its corporate headquarters largely destroyed, was hard pressed to resume business as usual and was eventually broken up, its various divisions made independent, sold, or simply shut down for good."

Part of this was accompanied by views of the Murex executive suite as it had looked just after the battle.

"Many Murex employees, upon examining the wreckage, swore that in addition to the damage caused by heat and other physical effects, the offices themselves had changed—as though they'd been taken apart and then rebuilt by someone who didn't know, or remember, their precise former layout. We can only speculate on the exact nature of the combat that took place there between Sky Ranger and Conrad Wandrei.

"The major revelation following Sky Ranger's departure was that of the secret para-military organization which had been created to destroy him. When the old Republican party was voted out of the White House in the following election, the United States government came under the control of Democrat Sylvester Ryder, who ran on a platform promoting peace and environmental reform. Once in office, Ryder began an intense dialogue with the first President of the Soviet Union, at that time an empire spanning much of Eurasia, which would result in a ninety percent cutback in world armaments by the end of the Twentieth Century. Ryder also instituted a series of environmental reforms in his own country, including the outlawing and phaseout of nuclear fission reactors, stringent new controls on the emissions and fuel efficiency of internal combustion vehicles, and the establishment of vast new wilderness and watershed preservation areas throughout the country.

"In perhaps his most farsighted move, Ryder redefined the mission of the National Aeronautics and Space Administration. In view of NASA's lack of a clear mission and the poor utility and proven dangers of its fleet of Space Shuttles, Ryder ended most of NASA's ongoing missions and future projects, instructing it to pursue a vigorous research and development program to perfect new technologies which could open the Solar System to human exploration and use on a truly practical, economical basis. The results of that wise policy may be seen around us as the basis of the modern world's way of life."

Neil began to squirm in his seat. The scenes of the great geosynchronous solar power stations, with their fragile-looking tethers linking them to the power-reception points on the planet below, were fine, but otherwise this was too much like a classroom world citizenship lesson. He was sure he'd prefer the theater where old video of Sky Ranger in flight was displayed.

Nevertheless, the narrator continued in her hushed voice. "Unfortunately, Ryder's intervention in his country's economy was too radical for its time, and the world spiraled down into what was called the EcoDepression. With many occupations proscribed or severely limited, the American standard of living, which was then measured by the level of consumption of goods and energy per capita, fell dramatically.

"However, Ryder did not allow the country to plunge into chaos. With the wise use of resources freed by the shrinking military budget, he was able to provide basic services to the public to prevent major suffering. In fact, the lot of the previously disadvantaged, such as farm workers and recent immigrants, was actually improved by these programs. The general result was an economic leveling of the American people. Although many were nostalgic for the days when golf courses could flourish in Phoenix and it was practical for a worker to drive a thousand-pound petroleum-powered vehicle fifty miles to work and back every day, the majority of Americans found, to their surprise, that life was at least as pleasant now that it had been slowed down and simplified."

Neil found himself marveling at the sight of massive lines of heavy steel vehicles, each spewing a miasma of fumes, inching into a city, most carrying only a single passenger.

"Nevertheless, President Ryder was ousted in the 1992 election, perhaps the most dramatic in the history of the USA. For the first time, an upstart political party was victorious over the two entrenched parties that had dominated American politics since before the time of Lincoln. Alan Burns Kirk, a former folk singer and environmental activist, won the Presidency under the banner of the Land-Sea-Air Party, with its trappings of blue and white, the first party to invoke the memory of Sky Ranger in its campaign. Sky Ranger was officially rehabilitated, leading, among other things, to the construction of the museum wing in which you're now seated.

"After years of economic turmoil, a smaller-scale, more sustainable, world economy began to emerge. Although the path has been disguised by twists and turns, failures and unexpected triumphs, the world we inhabit today can largely be traced back to the unique person called the Sky Ranger. It was Sky Ranger, John Avril, who disenchanted our grandparents with greed, with short-sightedness, and with disregard for the health of our planet. Although many question his methods even now, it was Sky Ranger who banished despair from the hearts of our ancestors, and brought them to know that miracles had not vanished from their often bleak and crumbling world. We salute him, and pray that he is well, wherever his flight has taken him among the stars."

The film ended well, with a holo simulation of Sky Ranger bursting through the clouds, accompanied by the soaring notes of a famous old film score, played, it seemed, on authentic acoustic instruments.

Neil began to fidget when the loop began again with an overview of Sky Ranger's career, and he and his dad left the theatre. Chris eyed the exit hopefully, but Neil remorselessly steered him into the other theater, where he sat enthralled by a compilation of virtually all existing video of Sky Ranger in flight. Chris viewed the scenes with a curious sense of ambivalence. It was hard to believe, even disturbing, that someone who could do those things had once actually existed. He was just as glad that today's world was rational and predictable, with no citizen able to flout the laws of nature as Sky Ranger had done with such joyous abandon. But he could hardly express these sentiments to Neil without being called a "greyzone", current slang for a dull, unimaginative person.

At last Neil seemed to tire of the contemplation of his hero, and permitted himself to be led out into the main body of the museum. His father looked down at him and said ruefully, "Can we go see the asteroid mining exhibit now?"

At the end of the day, having familiarized themselves with this imminent wonder of space technology, Chris and Neil boarded a maglev train, to arrive home in Huntsville in time for a late supper.

Chapter Twenty Nine

2062

Somewhere beyond the orbit of Mars drifted 17373 Ling Ling, one of the most curious, and valuable, asteroids yet discovered. An irregular, elongated body, Ling Ling was divided into two sections of vastly different composition: a coal-black carbonaceous portion, rich in organic compounds and water, and a much brighter portion composed almost entirely of metals, mostly nickel and iron, with contaminants of cobalt, iridium, and other elements. Some planetary scientists speculated that Ling Ling was a fragment of a once much larger body whose materials had been differentiated by melting, with Ling Ling representing the interface between the core and mantle of the parent object. Others believed it was simply a contact binary asteroid.

Whatever its origin, Ling Ling was an object of immense potential value to Mankind. Although only about seven kilometers by four, it contained enough metals to supply all conceivable needs for thousands of years, plus a bonus of water, oxygen, and even nutrients invaluable to the growing human population orbiting Earth and living on the Moon. If it could be tamed and guided toward the Earth, the utilization of space would boom as never before, and the Earth itself would be relieved of much of its remaining burden of mining and other industrial activity.

These were precisely the intentions of the three hundred men and women now living on and near Ling Ling. At vast expense of energy and materials, they had come in great ships, equipped with massive tools and implements meant to reshape the path of a small world. They also brought several thousand relics of a previous age of madness—hydrogen bombs, equipped with fission triggers incorporating the plutonium which great nations had brewed by the ton as recently as forty years before. With a great sigh of relief, the people of Earth had watched the last of this pernicious substance being lofted into space, never to return. One hundred and twenty two years after its first synthesis, humanity had finally found a good use for the explosive potential of the deadliest element ever made.

After three months on route and a year and a half on site, the Orion Project had succeeded in modifying Ling Ling into a great rough-hewn spacecraft. Powerful lasers had sliced and welded slabs of natural nickel-iron into an immense concave disk. Huge springs and shock absorbers, hauled from Earth by the most brutish rocket boosters ever designed, attached the disk to the asteroid at a balance point near the junction between the metallic and carbonaceous components. Modular injector units and bomb storage bays were bolted into place. The final additions were command and habitation modules, installed on the side of Ling Ling opposite the disk, to shield their inhabitants from the fury soon to be unleashed on the other side.

All in all it was by far the most expensive and elaborate space mission ever mounted, and the greatest economic gamble ever taken by Mankind. If successful, it would begin a new age of expansion and prosperity; if it failed, the Earth's economy would long feel the void left by the vast outpouring of treasure necessary for the attempt.

The one guaranteed benefit of Orion was that the Earth need never again fear the deadly metal plutonium, a substance nature had never intended to exist.

With all preparations complete, the ships *Hephaestus* and *Demeter* withdrew to a respectful distance and radioed good luck to the crews on the asteroid. Opaque shields slid into place over all ports. Everyone who had leisure to do so stared at display screens, waiting to see if the crazy old idea behind Orion would actually work.

The surface of the asteroid suddenly burned with pinpoints of fearsome blue-white light, fierce enough to burn holes in the retinas of anyone foolish enough to look at them directly. The lights rapidly flared out and began to cool toward yellow-white, though as they expanded their overall light output actually increased. The bombs had been placed in cavities hollowed out all over the asteroid. As the glare subsided enough to allow human inspection, jets of incandescent material could be seen spurting from the pits.

After fifteen minutes of pyrotechnics, yelling, and hooting, silence descended as the people of Orion checked instruments and made observations. A renewed cheer went up a few minutes later as the results of Phase One were announced. Ling Ling's five-day rotation had been cancelled. In the process, they had demonstrated attitude control over the great rock, a capability to be needed again for later maneuvers.

A few days later, when Ling Ling and the planet that coveted it reached the proper orbital relationship, the asteroid's awesome Main Drive went into operation. Once every three seconds, a hydrogen bomb was ejected to trail just behind the asteroid, timed to detonate as it drifted over the focus of the great iron disk which dominated the yin-yang boundary between rock and metal. The bombs bloomed into fire, vaporizing a bit of the pusher plate with each explosion, but transferring some of their force to the asteroid in the form of kinetic energy as the rapidly expanding explosive spheres slammed into the plate.

The plate was aligned to face the direction of Ling Ling's orbital motion. Each bomb negated a bit of the velocity which had kept the asteroid steady in its orbit for many millions of years. Gradually the massive ellipsoid slowed down. After two hours, during which almost two thousand hydrogen bombs were expended, Ling Ling's ancient path had warped into a long fall which would eventually bring it close to the Sun, if not for the large rock-and-iron planet it would encounter along the way.

The Main Drive was shut off for now. After an interval designed to let the dangerous gasses of atomic holocaust disperse, *Hephaestus* and *Demeter* hove in close, maneuvering to accompany their great treasure during its fall toward Earth.

Several months later, with Ling Ling and the people of Orion now well within the orbit of Mars, it became apparent that a mid-course correction was necessary. Again space-suited figures scrambled over the pocked, primordial surface of the asteroid, placing small bombs in the pits that served as attitude control jets. When all were in place, the ships stood off, the first set of bombs went off, and Ling Ling began a nearly imperceptible turn on it axis. Hours later, a second set of bombs erupted, stabilizing the asteroid once more.

When satisfied that all was well, the commanders on the surface reactivated the Main Drive. Only twenty bombs would be required, spaced at five second intervals to allow finer control.

The first bomb was ejected, but failed to detonate. The sequence continued, and a second bomb was set adrift; it too failed to explode, following its predecessor as both floated across Ling Ling's face. Ten seconds had passed. A technician punched the control computer's Emergency Reset button just as the third bomb was launched. It exploded as intended; the other two bombs went off at the same instant.

Bomb Number One was drifting along Ling Ling's light-dark interface when it went off, vaporizing a pocket of volatile materials just beneath the black, foamy surface of the carbonaceous side. Bomb Number Two was still near the pusher plate, and its blast caught and twisted it with off-axis forces it was never meant to endure, melting the shock structures and fusing them into place. Bomb Three, of course, contributed its intended kick, transmitted directly into the ground as a hard shock by the locked supports.

Computerized sensors, detecting a wrack of forceful tremors ringing through the asteroid, shut down the drive just as Bomb Five exploded over the wreckage of the pusher plate. The people on the far side of the asteroid held their breaths as they stared at their readouts, waiting to see if they and their enterprise would survive such an inconceivable mishap.

They would, but their enterprise would not. They released sighs of relief as the tremors died down, until frantic, crazy-sounding calls from the two ships set their hearts to pounding again. They rushed to their windows to try to verify the mad claims being made by their colleagues who were safe on the ships, and saw something so vast and incomprehensible that most had difficulty relating the sight to their own mundane experience of life.

Orion's command structures had been attached to Ling Ling's metallic section, though not far from the carbonaceous boundary. Now as its crew looked in that direction, they saw a black cliff on the rise, a towering mass like a solid storm cloud, though veined and pocketed with lighter materials.

The ships insisted that Ling Ling's two sections had split apart, and those on the ground could deny it no longer. Not only that, but the two halves were rotating contrary to each other, and there seemed a distinct chance that the base would be crushed between them like a burr on a tooth of opposing gears.

Most of those in the control center remained paralyzed at the windows, but a few, fascinated by the spectacle, hurried into space suits and floated out into the open, where they gaped at the mighty wall of pitted stone rising up and tilting over in their direction. In a few minutes the black rock loomed overhead like a ceiling, with only a thin band of stars visible along the horizon. The monster slid by overhead, catching only a few sidewise gleams of sunlight, a presence more felt than seen. Someone turned on her helmet lamp; its beam could actually be seen skittering over the rough surface of the multi-billion ton mass. Anyone wishing to abandon ship and transfer his hopes to Ling Ling's carbonaceous half need only release his tether and make a gentle leap across a narrow void.

But then the sky began to open up on one side, even as it closed up on the other—the two halves had separated cleanly and were now on separate but very similar paths. Shaking with relief, everyone on Ling Ling's metallic half watched as the slowly-rotating black half both receded and sank beneath their horizon. Their last sight of it for this rotation was of the mangled remains of the Main Drive, or those portions of it not still clinging to the far side of their own fragment.

Those on *Hephaestus* and *Demeter*, although their lives hadn't yet been threatened, felt no relief. Their radar screens revealed a swarm of small metallic objects drifting between the separated halves of Ling Ling.

And the preliminary orbital analysis of the two "new" asteroids did not look good.

Three hours later, Lori Malinova, director of the Extraterrestrial Resources Agency and therefore the chief administrator in charge of Orion, found herself in urgent an holoconference with Isabel Lundine, the outgoing World Coordinator at her office on the far side of the world. They still had the luxury of time before they need make any potentially chaos-provoking announcements, since communications between Orion and Earth were by laser and theoretically immune to interception, and there had been no "live" coverage of the maneuver, which should have been only a pale imitation of the spectacular deorbit maneuver of a few months before. ERA had released a bland announcement of a malfunction aboard Orion, but so far there was no sign that anyone suspected just how horribly awry things had really gone.

"All right, Lori," said Lundine grimly. "Let me have the facts, as simply as you can."

"Yes, Madame Coordinator."

Lori glanced down at her screen, although there was really no need; she knew the basic situation better than she could remember the first ten years of her life. "Orion experienced a sequencing error in the computer which controlled bomb injection in the Main Drive—it may have been exacerbated by human error; we're not sure yet, and it scarcely matters. Ling Ling experienced a series of unmitigated bomb explosions—that is, either the pusher system was jammed and incapacitated, or the bombs missed it entirely. Ling Ling took quite a jolt. It—it split in half—"

Lori glanced up with an agonized expression at the impassive figure apparently seated a few feet in front of her, so outrageous and unforgivable did that statement sound. Though burning with mortification, she forced herself to continue.

"We can only conjecture about the cause at this time. I think Ling Ling never represented an example of a differentiated object, but was a contact binary, as many thought, the result of a low-speed collision between two dissimilar objects, held together only loosely, possibly with internal fractures we did not detect—"

Lundine made a dismissive gesture. "Yes, yes. And we were greedily trying to round up the most useful asteroid in the belt, even though we didn't fully understand it, and it seemed too good to be true. But tell me about the results."

"Yes. Well—I have good news and bad news. First the good: Ling Ling was, before the attempted course correction, on a trajectory which would have brought it rather close to the Earth. After the separation, the orbits of the two components have changed slightly. The carbonaceous half will miss us by a good six thousand kilometers. However, the metallic half is on a direct intersect with Earth."

"A collision course."

"That is correct, Madame."

"And this is the bad news."

Lori managed a strained smile. "No, Madame Coordinator, as a matter of fact, it is not. The Orion commanders believe they can round up some of the bombs, attach them to the metallic fragment and give it enough of a nudge so that it will miss Earth. They believe they can even arrange it so that the fragment will go into a stable but eccentric orbit around Earth, so we will still have access to it, though not as conveniently as we'd planned."

Lundine stared at her blankly across the few meters that apparently separated them. "Wait a minute. What did you mean, 'round up' the bombs?"

Lori's face fell again. "That's the problem. When the asteroid split, the main bomb magazine was ruptured. The bombs floated out into space and are now adrift between the two fragments."

"And their course?"

"Ah—I have a visual on this—"

Lundine raised her hand. "A simple sentence will do."

"Most will hit the Earth."

"With what result?"

"They can't explode. But entering the atmosphere at a meteoric velocity, they will vaporize, introducing an estimated five tons of finely dispersed plutonium into the biosphere."

Lundine felt herself freeze. It was as if Lori had announced that a horrid and legendary mass murderer would rise up from the grave to kill again. One of the reasons Orion had been funded had been to rid the world of the deadly man-made metal. Yet now that substance was hurtling back toward its makers as though its destiny were inextricably linked with that of its creators.

The Coordinator shook off these fantasies and said sharply, "Order the ships to collect *all* the bombs."

Lori shook her head helplessly. "We're talking about roughly one thousand bombs, a swarm which is steadily dispersing. The ships simply do not have the propellant to make the many velocity changes that would be necessary to reach all of them. They would exhaust themselves before a tenth of them were collected, and they would then be helpless to brake themselves into Earth orbit."

"Then the bombs must be detonated."

"I'm sorry. We cannot even do that. As a—safety feature, the bombs were designed to be armed only by passing through a special device in the ejector mechanism. Without that, the free-floating bombs are quite inert. We never imagined a contingency in which we would need to detonate so many escaped bombs. If a few, or even any reasonable number, had gotten away, we could have dealt with them individually."

"Then you are telling me there's nothing we can do."

"There is nothing anyone in the Solar System can do."

Some months later, SkyScan, the world agency responsible for monitoring orbital comings and goings in the Earth-Moon system, sent their strongest radars questing into translunar space for the first echoes of the swarm of death known to be approaching Earth. The two great asteroid fragments had been detected weeks before, and were now even visible in optical binoculars. As they prepared to cross the boundary into SkyScan's particular domain, it was inevitable that the first echoes of the bomb swarm would be detected soon after.

There weren't as many bombs as there had been at first. The crew of Orion, moving with a decisiveness that left their Earth-based superiors stammering, had acted almost at once. *Hephaestus* and *Demeter* had rendezvoused near the Ling Ling command base, where *Demeter* had taken aboard the command crew and also most of the crew of *Hephaestus*. That done, *Hephaestus* went off in search of bombs. Maneuvering by brilliant on-the-fly navigation, *Hephaestus* had steered a course through the swarm that enabled the ship to rendezvous with almost two hundred bombs, which were not taken aboard, but armed during EVA. When *Hephaestus's* propellant was finally exhausted, *Demeter* came in search of her, transferring her skeleton crew and leaving her derelict. *Demeter* then retreated to the shadow of Ling Ling and relayed a command to detonate the bombs. The explosions gave about a hundred other bombs enough of a kick so that they would miss Earth. Then the combined crews had settled down for a long, hard cruise home under survival conditions of severe overcrowding. Their morale, unbeatable just after the roundup, soon sank. For their feat, brave and noble a gesture as it was, still left some seven hundred bombs on a course for Earth.

Now *Demeter* trailed behind the incoming swarm, for it had thrust itself into an orbit which would bring it to a gentle rendezvous with the Land's End orbital complex in a few days time.

SkyScan Platform 5 was a feathery-looking contraption occupying one of the Lagrange libration points. It consisted of a small habitable nucleus festooned with great wand and dish antennae that looked like diatom skeletons or the antennae of moths.

Inside, SkyScan controllers Nestor Hafacile and Edmund Skoda sat in their darkened holographic environment, where Earth and Moon shone as perfect models surrounded by thousands of tiny colored lights, each with ID and orbital information text floating beside it. Occasionally a vector symbol would extend from an object under power, followed by a glowing thread depicting its new orbit when acceleration ceased. But usually these routine operations did not require the attention of the two operators.

Hafacile and Skoda were unusually alert, for Platform 5, on the anti-solar frontier of the Earth-Moon system, would surely be the first to detect the incoming swarm. A computer-devised schedule older than the Orion Disaster had led to their being on duty at this fateful time, rather than one of the platform's four other crews.

"Here it comes," said Hafacile quietly, somehow anticipating the computer announcement, as he often did. The two men stared into the darkness opposite the Sun-symbol in the display, and watched as a faint green nebulosity began to materialize there. Skoda ordered a viewpoint change, and they sped across their miniaturized simulated domain in the direction of the green glow and the two far more definite symbols that flanked it. As it came farther into the range of their radar, the cloud resolved into a swarm of many glowing points.

Skoda keyed a voice pickup. "Control 5. Control 5. Bomb swarm now in range. Base trajectory as expected, no surprises. Control 5 out."

Their duty done, Hafacile and Skoda stared in silence as new pinpoints continued to be depicted by the holosystem.

After a while, Hafacile whispered, "I hear there will be parties."

Skoda glanced at his partner in sharp amazement.

Hafacile reacted to the unvoiced question. "You know, viewing parties, for the bombs. Like for Halley."

Skoda remembered last year's apparition of the famous comet, and the inevitable predictions of world disaster that had accompanied it. Those mystics, fanatics, and religionists must be crowing now.

Hafacile continued in his soft voice. "Since the bombs will enter on the night side, they should be quite spectacular. Anyone with a clear sky should have a good chance of seeing at least one. Some will graze the atmosphere and draw long fiery lines into the sunset or dawn. Others will hit straight on, and maybe even make it to the ground partially intact. The school kids have been told what to do if they encounter a lump of burning plutonium on the ground."

"And what's that?" asked Skoda irritably.

"Expel the air in their lungs and run away. Throw off their clothes, take a shower and call for help."

Skoda shook his head in the darkness. The world had been in a very strange mood since the announcement of the Dusting, an uneasy dreamlike trance. There'd been little panic, for almost everyone knew that the Dusting wouldn't kill them right away. Indeed, after the man-made meteor storm and the close passage of the two asteroids, life could go on apparently as normal. For years, even decades, there would be no sign of the insidious damage being done to all advanced forms of life.

Yet in one way or another, consciously or not, everyone would be engaged in the business of concluding his or her life, perhaps even preparing for the end of Man's time on Earth.

And even if Mankind should not perish: if filters, drugs, replacement organs, and advanced surgeries could save most of humanity from the ravages of plutonium-induced cancers, there was no way to protect the birds and mammals, the lifeforms of many kinds, which would surely fall away. The Great Extinction of the twentieth and early twenty first centuries, halted through such effort and turmoil, would come again, filtering imperceptibly from the skies, to put all wild places wholly under the control of the insects. Man might survive, but he would inhabit a deadly, sterile world which might eventually smother his spirit with loneliness, if not with guilt and grief.

For another hour the two men called in periodic reports of the swarm's progress as it passed the Moon's orbit and swept inexorably Earthward, less than eight hours from impact. In all the Earth-Moon system there were only three spacecraft, the Earth-Moon shuttles, theoretically capable of matching velocities with the bombs and intercepting a few of them. But the effort would exhaust them, sacrificing the ships and their crews, and the attempt was not made. Plans had been hatched to net the bombs, or scatter minefields in their path, but the bombs were too fast, too widely dispersed, and there was just too little time.

Grimly, Skoda and Hafacile continued their watch. By now other SkyScan platforms had also picked up the swarm, so they were free to divert their attention to other traffic in the System. The two asteroid fragments continued their predicted courses. At about the same time as the bomb entry, Ling One, the metallic object, would experience a very close encounter with Earth which would slow it into a highly elliptical orbit. Ling Two would miss by a greater margin, about one Earth radius, still close enough to be easily visible to the naked eye in the night sky. It was a new Apollo-class Earth-crossing asteroid, and would be seen occasionally in Earth's neighborhood for the foreseeable future, at least as long as anyone remained alive to see it. There was reason for gratitude here, and admiration for the efforts of the Orion crew, for the impact of either fragment would have ended civilization instantly, and much of life as well.

Still, they could only imagine what emotions stirred the billion and a half men and women inhabiting the planet that lay Sunward from their lonely, and privileged, vantage point. One thing was certain—in the past few months, the space stations and Moon bases had acquired all the personnel they would need for a long time to come.

The computer announced a new contact. Skoda and Hafacile rotated their viewpoint to take in the night side of the Earth. Projecting from its shadowy continents was a glowing blue filament that stretched itself further even as they watched.

"A new launch," said Skoda in irked surprise. "Up from central Asia, it looks like. And already a thousand kilometers in altitude. How could the system have missed it for so long?"

Hafacile studied the flickering digits that accompanied the bright point at the end of its trajectory trace. The figures were changing so rapidly that the computer could not even assign the object a meaningful vector.

"It's only been off the ground for a few seconds," said Hafacile slowly.

"What? Are you kidding? Look, it's already pushing fifteen hundred kilometers."

"Have you noticed the acceleration figure?"

Skoda did notice, and his jaw dropped. He called for an acceleration plot. Both men viewed a steep curve that started out at twenty Gs and went up from there.

"It must be some kind of an interceptor," said Hafacile without confidence.

"Not a chance. No vehicle or missile was ever made that could accelerate at this rate for so long. Hell, it could reach the swarm in an hour. Look, it's not even flying a ballistic trajectory. In fact, there's only one thing in the world that ever flew like that—"

Skoda's words froze in the air. He and Hafacile exchanged wide-eyed looks of mingled wonder, doubt, hope, and awe.

Without knowing quite what he was going to say, Skoda keyed the voice pickup, but sat silently during a futile search for the right words. Hafacile gently touched Skoda's arm and took over the circuit.

Never before in history was the imagination of Mankind so inflamed as by the dry three-sentence message that Hafacile sent to Earth.

"This is SkyScan Platform 5. We have detected an unidentified flying object on a high-speed intercept course for the swarm. Based on its flight characteristics, we can say only this: Sky Ranger, or something very much like him, has returned."

Chapter Thirty

Neil Lane shouldered his pack, checked to make sure his campsite showed no sign of his brief occupancy, and set out into the soft mauve light of dawn, continuing his pilgrimage before the Sun even cracked the horizon. His mind was still swimming with the events of the past few days: Earth's peril, its miraculous reprieve, and the rumor that a new Sky Ranger had risen up, flitting from bomb to bomb, sending them on new paths far from Earth. Like everyone else, Neil now often looked toward the sky, but this hypothetical new Sky Ranger had done this one great task and then vanished again into mystery.

A worldwide Thanksgiving Holiday had been declared, and Neil had taken advantage of the unexpected break in his fall semester to venture into true Sky Ranger country. This was the heart of the Front Range Wilderness, the section formerly known as Rocky Mountain National Park, thought to be the origin place of John Avril himself, and a place close to his heart. By exploring its peaks and forests, Neil could honor the memory of the first flying hero, and contemplate with gratitude his continuing legacy, which apparently had inspired another to rescue Man from folly once again.

Neil hiked along a contour of a ridge, well below timberline, making his way though fading meadows and patches of aspen and pine. The dried grasses, their season at an end, crunched with frost at every step. The valley below was obscured by a luminous mat of fog, while beyond it rose a jagged ridge of bare rock, its crest rising and falling like the teeth of a broken saw. The Sun gathered its strength in the misty, hidden country beyond the ridge, preparing to mount the sky and proclaim its mastery over the planet once again.

Neil's breath smoked in the cold. Though his sleeping bag hadn't quite been up to the task of warding off the night's chill, he was still so bemused by the novelty of being free from the cloak of fear that such minor discomforts meant nothing to him. He ambled along, thumbs hooked under the straps of his pack, musing on fate, while once in a while stealing a glance at the brightening heavens.

He entered another meadow and was halfway across it before he happened to glance upslope. There he was startled to notice a man sitting with his back against an isolated pine. Neil was surprised to meet anyone in this remote place, the more so since this man didn't seem to have a pack, and there was no sign of a camp. All he had was a small bundle at his side.

Still, the man was obviously in no distress. His only reaction to Neil was an amiable nod. Neil returned a little wave and continued on his way, feeling a bit disoriented, though he couldn't imagine why.

A few steps later he again looked up at the seated man, and felt something like an electric jolt. The wisdom of his body brought him to a halt. He peered intently at the stranger, somehow convinced that here was something beyond his normal experience of the world.

Aware of his heartbeat and of a feeling of unreality, Neil started up the slope. The man offered no objection to his approach. He wore an ancient leather flight jacket, a relic of the last century if the leather was real, and old time cowboy pants—bluejeans, they were called—that were equally beaten up. His face had about the same color and texture as the jacket—still vigorous, but obviously rich with years and experience. Lean and planar, it was a face from which everything superfluous had been pared long ago. His hair and beard were bright, a mixture of gold and silver, a Sun-and-Moon head of hair like the mingled lights of heaven's great luminaries. And his eyes were twin disks cut from the daylight sky, blue and fathomless as sunlit air.

Neil came up beside him, so as not to block his view of the east, and looked at him with his mind spinning and his tongue disconnected.

The man looked up and said, "Isn't it a beautiful morning?"

"Yes." Neil's reply was little more than a whisper.

"It's the kind of morning that makes a man want to leap up and get around to doing something. A day of infinite promise."

Neil said, "You're him, aren't you. Sky Ranger."

"Hmm. Make that John, why don't you. I'm a little too old to go by a silly, vain name like Sky Ranger." He chuckled.

Neil's legs suddenly refused to support him. He flopped down onto the grass beside Sky—beside John Jacob Avril. For a few timeless moments he stared as Avril serenely and cheerfully awaited the dawn.

"May I ask you a question?" Neil blurted.

"Why not?"

"What are you doing here? I thought you went off to the stars."

John laughed and slapped his thigh. "No, no! I never went anywhere. That's just a story I cooked up to keep everyone off my back. Go to the stars? Ha! I always had trouble enough making it to the Moon. An earthworm might as well announce that he's going to Antarctica. I'm amazed anyone ever bought that story."

John paused and looked more thoughtful, almost embarrassed.

"I actually did try it, but I was lucky to make it back to Earth alive. I really wanted to get away, back then."

Neil had never been so shocked. "So you've been on Earth all this time!"

"Yeah."

Neil found himself making meaningless, excited gestures. "Oh, my God. Oh, my God. So you've been here among us all this time, and no one ever knew. I almost think I ought to be angry. But—that was so long ago!"

"Hmm, yes, I guess it was. I'm...one hundred and seven years old. But holding off old age was one of the first tricks I learned."

"What have you been doing all this time?"

"Oh, just wandering around. Meeting people, seeing things, thinking things over. I decided to try life as a regular human being for a while. I wanted to see if I could help anyone without flying, using only whatever brains and heart I possess. And I did all right with that, I think."

"Ahh!" Neil's eyes sparkled. "No flying! You must have missed that more than anything."

John gave Neil a gentle look of sadness that silenced him for a moment.

"No, son. That's not quite true."

Somehow chastened, Neil joined John in watching the warm colors of dawn march up the sky beyond the ridge. It was a while before he could bring himself to speak again.

"And then, after hiding for all that time, you still rose up and saved us all from those bombs."

John cocked an eyebrow at him. "Well, what else could I do? After working as hard as I did to try to save the world, and getting into so much trouble over it, I couldn't just let those damn bombs undo all my efforts."

"But you gave yourself away."

John shrugged. "It doesn't really matter anymore."

"That was some pretty amazing flying you did to get rid of all those bombs."

John made a dismissive gesture. "Oh, tricks like that get easier as you get older and get the hang of it."

At that John's attention seemed to leave Neil as he resumed his watch on the gathering dawn. Neil found it difficult to take his eyes off this incredible person he had discovered, but his staring didn't seem to trouble John at all.

"Oh yes. I did sneak away for a trip about fifty years ago. Went to Mars—wanted to be the first man to reach it. I wasn't, of course, but I don't suppose you know about that yet. Now there's a place, Mars. A man can really lose himself in that landscape. Grand, silent and peaceful. Also a cold, empty, and bitter place. It was awfully good to feel Earth's sweet air against my face again. This is the place for us, right here."

Neil assimilated that revelation before framing a remark of his own. "You know, uh, John, I've made a hobby of studying you since I was a kid. And the only thing about you that ever really bothered me was that message you left just before you supposedly left the Earth. The one about having to leave because everybody was mad at you and out to get you. That always seemed—unSky Ranger-like. It made you seem a little bit like a—well, like a—"

"Like a wimp?" broke in John. "Do you know what that means?"

Neil grinned. "I've seen some old videos. Well, yes, I guess that's what I had in mind."

"Then let me ease it for you. That story was a crock too. But I could hardly afford to tell the real reason I knew Sky Ranger's day was over."

Another silence ensued, with Neil waiting and hoping for John to continue. When that didn't seem to be forthcoming, he asked tentatively, "Can you tell me now?"

That brought Neil the most searching and intense look he'd yet received. He was reminded of the scrutiny of a golden eagle he'd once trapped and banded.

"You look like an honest, upright young man," said John. "Yes, I'll tell you. I had to vanish because I'd learned how dangerous it is for the world to be aware of a person with my kind of power. It's a power that anyone can find, either as an accidental consequence of the kind of life they lead, or by a deliberate search. The trouble is, if you search for power as an end in itself, it surely means you're not fit to have it. A person like that will make a hell of the world. Mankind as a whole isn't ready to do the kind of things I can do. When it is ready, if ever, the power will be there, waiting. But the people who attain it won't care much about it. It's what they'll discover inside themselves that's really interesting. That's just the way it is."

"But what if you're needed again? For some other disaster?"

"Then someone else will rise up to take my place. And you'd better hope he'll be a better man, or woman, than I ever was."

Neil snorted. "Who could be better than you?"

John laughed. "Son, I'm a very imperfect man. I came to my power through despair. Not through hope, or from anything more positive. I wanted to die, but I wanted to die on a good note, if I could. At the very end, I had one moment, one tiny, fleeting moment, of insight and clarity, and that made all the difference. Without that, I'd just be an old skeleton you discovered here on this mountainside."

"Who are you, Sky Ranger? Where did you come from?"

"I'm not sure I remember. Some kinds of knowledge are hard to hold onto, once you find yourself back on the playing field of time and events. I think I was ready to go somewhere else, but I was needed here for awhile. I was an arrow launched by an archer beyond my sight."

Quieted and awed, Neil asked, "Why are you telling me this? What if I go around telling everybody else?"

"It won't make any difference. If you tell your story, nobody will listen, because it isn't sensational enough. We're just two guys sitting here chatting peacefully. Who'll care about that?"

"So what will you do now?"

John's eyes were now locked on the horizon, where a glory of hot golden light revealed the imminence of the Sun.

"I think it's time to go back to wherever I came from."

"Are you talking about death?"

John nodded. "Death isn't the enemy. Everybody dies, sometimes more than once. If every death that's ever occurred were a tragedy, the universe itself would be groaning in agony...and it isn't. All those people I saved—I only delayed their deaths, I didn't prevent them. I gave them another chance to learn what's really important in life, or to appreciate it, if they already knew. Because the real enemy isn't death, it's despair. It's a lack of hope and wonder. And

I gave people hope and wonder. Even now, when many people believe I was only a legend, I give them that. Just the idea of me is enough for that."

He sighed. "Yes, I've kept her waiting long enough."

"Her? Do you mean…what was her name…"

"Elise. Elise Boutin."

"But—which one? I've read your biographies. I read that, well, the second one, she wasn't exactly…"

"Real?"

"Well, yes."

John laughed. "Yes, I suppose that's true. But she was real to me. And soon I won't be real either, whatever that means. I'll truly be nothing but a legend of the past. Then we'll see what's real and what isn't."

Do you really think that's how it's going to be? You'll die and see your imaginary girlfriend again?"

John gave the boy a look of exaggerated astonishment. "Well, of course! What kind of a world do you think we live in? Look there, in front of you. Have you never noticed the colors of the sunrise? Yes, there's a fine scientific explanation for them. But is it necessary for light of different wavelengths to be refracted at different angles? It isn't. The world tries to tell us things, if we'll just pay attention. In a world without hope, a sunrise would just be — grey."

"I see how it is now. You've based your entire life on believing in crazy, impossible things."

Neil was distracted by the warm shaft of radiance that struck his face. The Sun flamed yellow in the notch in the ridge across the way. Despite its warmth, an inexplicable chill ran up Neil's spine.

When he turned back, John was gone, or rather, he had been transformed. There sat a figure, dressed in the same clothes as before, though now they were faded, worn, and half crumbled away. John, on the other hand, now appeared scarcely older than Neil himself. He sat staring blissfully at the Sunrise with unblinking eyes. Unblinking, and unmoving. His face was pale, and when Neil dared put out his hand to touch it, the flesh was frozen hard and cold. The feather of an eagle lay in his lap.

After a while, Neil found himself on his feet again. He wandered down the mountain, head bowed with knowledge of the enormity and mystery of life.

THE END

www.ingramcontent.com/pod-product-compliance
Lightning Source LLC
Chambersburg PA
CBHW071631260626
47170CB00001B/59